HUNTER

Immortals of New Orleans, Book 10

Kym Grosso

Copyright © 2019 Kym Grosso

All rights reserved. No part of this publication may be reproduced, distributed, or transmitted in any form or by any means, including photocopying, recording, or other electronic or mechanical methods, without the prior written permission of the publisher, except in the case of brief quotations embodied in critical reviews and certain other noncommercial uses permitted by copyright law.

MT Carvin Publishing
Carlsbad, California

Editor: Julie Roberts
Cover Design: Clarise Tan, CT Cover Creations
Photographer: Wander Pedro Aguiar, WANDER AGUIAR :: PHOTOGRAPHY
Cover Model: Jonny James
Formatting: Jason Anderson, Polgarus Studio
Proofreading: Rose Holub, Read by Rose

DISCLAIMER
This book is a work of fiction. The names, characters, locations and events portrayed in this book are a work of fiction or are used fictitiously. Any similarity to actual events, locales, or real persons, living or dead, is coincidental and not intended by the author.

NOTICE
This is an adult erotic paranormal romance book with love scenes and mature situations. It is only intended for adult readers over the age of 18.

Acknowledgments

- My children, for encouraging me to write and supporting me in everything I do. I'm incredibly blessed to have you in my life. You are amazing, special people and I'm so proud of you both!

- My readers, for waiting patiently while I wrote Hunter! I'm so thankful to have each and every one of you, supporting me and my books. I hope you love my sexy werewolf as much as I do, and I look forward to writing more adventures in the series!

- Julie Roberts, my friend and editor, who spent hours reading, editing and proofreading Hunter. As always, there are not enough words to thank you for all you do to help me. I'm so happy you are finally living in that gorgeous log cabin and can't wait to come visit you in Scotland someday soon! You seriously are the best ever!!!

- Shannon Hunt, publicist and all-round assistant who gives me support! Thank you so much for everything you do to help me, your patience and friendship!

- My dedicated beta readers Carolyn, Denise, Karen, Kim, Leah, Maria, Rose, and Vicki for beta reading.

I really appreciate all the valuable feedback you provided. You guys rock!!!

~ CT Cover Creations, for designing Hunter's sexy cover.

~ Wander Aguiar Photography for the gorgeous cover image!

~ Jonny James, cover model. I'm so happy you're my Hunter!

~ Polgarus Studio, Jason, for formatting.

~ Rose Holub, Read by Rose, for proofreading. You are awesome!

~ My reader group, for helping spread the word about the Immortals of New Orleans series. I appreciate your support more than you could know!

Chapter One

The Alpha couldn't remember how many days he'd spent in Hell, but it was long enough to remind him to never go back. One week ago, Viktor Christianson had nearly been killed by a demon, and Hunter had deliberately opened the gate to Hades on a mission to save him. When he devised his plan, he never thought he'd find Ilsbeth, the High Priestess of New Orleans. The elusive witch, accused of murder by some, had been missing for over a month.

Hunter sucked a breath at the sight of her battered face. She blinked open her distant eyes and gazed toward Viktor's lifeless body.

"What happened?" It was more a question of who. Hell was filled with a hierarchy of demons all capable of assault and torture.

Although badly beaten Ilsbeth shook her head; determination shone in her eyes. A warning to be quiet.

Jesus Christ, Hunter inwardly swore, carefully avoiding speaking out loud again. *Demons. Sneaky little fuckers.* Last thing he needed was for any of the bigwigs to get wind that an Alpha was loose in the underworld. They'd spike a spit through his ass just for foreplay and roast him. He had to keep his fucking shit together and get the hell out before they knew he was missing. He closed his eyes, sending a relaxing energy through his mind, calming his nerves. *Viktor. The High Priestess. Get in. Get out.*

Hunter rushed to Viktor's side and scooped the ancient vampire into his arms. Barely alive, Viktor bore the marks of his torture. Hundreds of bloodletting lashes marred his skin. The Alpha released a hard sigh, aware he'd need to be fed.

Feeding was a tricky business. Viktor had been starved for so long, the scent of blood would drive him feral. Hunter glanced to the vampire's bloodied wrists. Bound in silver handcuffs, he'd been immobilized while they'd tortured him. As much as the Alpha wanted to remove the painful device, he reasoned it would keep him restrained sufficiently while he fed him.

Getting the blood into him, however, was an entirely different matter. Vampires either bit for pleasure, inciting arousal, or pain. Hunter gave a smirk as a flash of being bitten by a hot redheaded vampire flashed in his mind, but the memory served to remind him that while lost in ecstasy, he couldn't think clearly. Allowing Viktor to inflict pain wasn't an option as it would call attention to his escape.

With only one logical choice, Hunter extended a claw, sucking a breath as he pierced his wrist. *Goddammit.* Blood dripped down his arm and sizzled as it hit the scorched earth. He'd have to move quickly. The hellhounds would scent the open wound. With one hand he clasped Viktor's jaw, forcing it to open. *Drink*, Hunter silently urged as he held his wrist over the vampire's mouth. A thick sanguine drop hit Victor's tongue. Hunter's heart beat faster, anticipating the awakening.

Come on, man. Let's go. Let's go. No, you cannot die on me. Quintus is going to kick my ass if you die. Droplets flowed freely into the mouth of the ancient one. Hunter took a deep breath and coughed. The smoke-laced air coated his tongue and he spat onto the ground. His focus faltered as Ilsbeth shifted and blinked her sullen eyes, a sad smile on her face. Although beaten, the ethereal beauty and strong spirit of the High Priestess lingered beneath her battered skin.

Strong fingers clamped around Hunter's wrist, and he cursed as the slice of fangs stung his skin. "Fuck."

Through clenched teeth, the Alpha grunted, attempting to pry Viktor's grip loose. The vampire's eyes flew open as he desperately suctioned blood from his arm.

"Look Vik, I need you to ease the fuck up. Take only what you need. We've got to get outta here." The sound of a metal door creaking in the distance stopped him cold.

"Sixty seconds. I need you to get your shit together." Hunter breathed deeply, fighting off the aphrodisiac effects of his bite. Jesus Christ, could this night get any worse? Like fuck. He was getting a hard-on from a vampire deep in the ass of Hell. He considered himself open to new experiences as much as the next guy, but this was so not happening.

"Ten seconds." Hunter blinked away the sensations. He

glanced to Viktor who wore a small smile. "Fucking vampire." Hunter wrenched back his arm. "What the fuck is wrong with you?" He stared down at his wrist, which had begun to heal.

"About fucking time you saved my ass." Viktor shoved to his feet and stretched his arms above his head. "It's hotter than a demon's balls at Coachella. What? Too soon?"

Hunter glared at the naked vampire, his skin perfectly healed. "You think this is funny? Jesus, you're an asshole."

"Yeah well, I've been called worse. Wait…" Viktor's brow furrowed. "Where is she…"

"You get Ilsbeth." Although Hunter felt sympathy for the High Priestess, he didn't for one minute make the mistake that she was defenseless. Like a viper in the grass, Ilsbeth was more deadly than any creature on earth. Kill you now or kill you later, she'd strike without mercy.

"Ah, little witch." Viktor's voice softened as he knelt down next to Ilsbeth. "But where is the wolf?"

"Wolf? What wolf?" Hunter froze as a barely audible moan sounded from the far recesses of the cave. He brought his finger to his lips. "Shh."

Silence. The Alpha concentrated, searching for the lupine presence. A shallow breath. A barely audible heartbeat. The fleeting energy rippled through him. Hunter nodded at Viktor and stepped into the darkness. Deep within the belly of the cave, he spied a small woman curled into a ball lying in the corner. *What. The. Fuck?* Slowly he approached, cautious not to scare her. "Ah, sweetheart. What'd they do to you?"

Sensing her fear, he reached for her slowly and brushed

a lock of hair away from her face. His anger surged at the sight of her bruised cheek, but he shoved it away. He could sense her lupine nature but had no idea who she was or how she'd landed in Hell. Seconds ticked by and the urgency to leave mounted. He would seek answers later, but right now he didn't have time.

"Easy, little wolf." Without asking, Hunter gently scooped her limp body into his arms. "It's time to go."

"I'm sorry," Viktor whispered, shaking his head. "I never meant to…"

"Can you flash?" Hunter's fingers brushed over a scabbed bite mark and he immediately suspected what the vampire had done to her.

"I'm not sure yet. Let me get Ilsbeth." Viktor reached for her, and she flinched. "It's okay. I'm sorry…this wasn't in my control."

The witch silently nodded, but still refused to look at him as he lifted her into his arms.

"You go first," Hunter ordered. The stench of demons permeated the air. *Time's up.*

"No way. I'm not leaving you here," Viktor protested.

"We go together then. Hold on." With one hand, Hunter reached in his pocket, fingering the crystal. With only one chance to reopen the portal, he prayed it'd stay open long enough for him to get them all through. It sparked as he threw it onto the ground, a soft glow morphing into a swirling cloud. "It's time. Let's go."

"You go first," Viktor told him. "It might not stay open."

"Go! Now!" Hunter yelled as he caught sight of the hooved feet approaching. The forked-tongued beast screeched in anger.

As Viktor leapt into the portal, the demon spat at Hunter. The spray of acid burned through his skin, but he held tight to the she-wolf. As the vampire disappeared, the Alpha dove through the cloud, flames chasing him.

Hunter grunted as they dropped through the portal and rolled onto the grass. He cradled the fragile female to his chest and fought the nausea that rolled through him. The escape had been a clusterfuck, but they'd managed to find their way back to their realm.

The Alpha groaned in pain, the demonic acid burning his flesh. "Fucking hell. That asshole got me." He exhaled a deep calming breath. He'd have to shift to heal. Hunter embraced the stranger he'd brought with him. The moonlight revealed deep puncture wounds marring her body. "Jesus."

"I've got to get Ilsbeth to the coven," Viktor told him, urgency in his tone.

"No," Hunter snapped.

"I don't know about that, wolf. In Hell…" Viktor gently laid the witch onto the grass and knelt before her.

"I said no. I need to talk to that witch. I don't want her going anywhere just yet. She comes with us." Hunter shook his head, cradling the female protectively in his arms. "It's getting cold. We need to get shelter."

"I know she's been on everyone's shit list but…"

"It was my ass that just saved both of y'all. Now do this for me. Just get her inside. We're all going. Now. I don't want the pack getting wind of visitors just yet."

"She's not in good shape," Viktor commented as he lifted Ilsbeth.

"Neither is she." Hunter grunted and shoved to his feet, clutching the woman against his chest. He might be stupid as fuck for keeping a stranger he'd found in Hell, but he couldn't let her go.

"I'd flash but…" Viktor shrugged.

"This way. We gotta get them upstairs. Fast. Remus is going to be here any second." Hunter strode across the yard, his back raw from the licks of fire.

"Remus. What kind of name is that?"

"The kind that will kick your ass if you talk shit about him." Hunter approached the back entrance and clicked open the door.

"You always leave your house completely unlocked? You're going to end up with a bison in your living room."

"Who says I haven't? And for the record, animals are a lot better than humans." Hunter's skin tingled as the warm air brushed over him. A shower would help to ease his pain, but he needed to shift.

"You a country boy," Viktor said in his best southern accent.

"I'm a Louisiana boy. Through and through. One who happens to be livin' in Yellowstone. It's a natural fit. A little colder but us wolves love the cold."

"I'd starve to death out here. How would I ever work on my tan?" Viktor rolled his eyes and followed the Alpha up a grand staircase that led to the second floor. "Nice mansion. For a country boy, you're livin' the dream."

"I've invested well. As have you, I'm sure."

"I do okay." Viktor shrugged.

"Put her in here." Hunter nodded to a guest room on his right.

As Viktor set off with Ilsbeth, the Alpha strode toward his bedroom, and quickly settled the injured female onto the bed.

Relieved her breathing remained stable, Hunter knelt beside her and shook his head. Wearing only tattered bra and panties, the injured female's body had been brutalized. Multiple puncture wounds mottled her skin. She'd been tortured. *Who the fuck did this?*

"I bit her. As did others," Hunter heard the vampire confess.

He swiveled his head around, his blood pumping with anger.

"What are you doing in here? Where's Ilsbeth?"

"Exactly where you told me to put her. She's sleeping."

"Seriously?" Annoyance laced his voice.

"She's like fifteen feet away. I think I'd know if she woke up."

"Wait…what did you just say?"

"I said she's sleeping."

"No, not that. You said you bit her."

Hunter took a deep breath, forcing his pulse to remain even, tamping down his rage. The Alpha knew firsthand how demons forced their victims into hideous acts to survive. They'd likely starved Viktor.

"I won't judge you." Hunter shook off his own dark memories of Hell and what had been done to him. He turned to face Viktor, and sat on the floor, his back to the side of the bed.

"Of course you're going to judge me. But before you say another word, you don't know what it's like in there."

"Like hell I don't." The Alpha didn't elaborate because there was no fucking way he was talking about what had happened with anyone, let alone the vampire.

"What do you know about Hell?" Viktor challenged, his eyes locked on Hunter's.

"How do you think I got in and out so easily?"

"Are you for real? If you've been there before, why would you ever go back? What is wrong with you?"

"Why do you think I was there? I thought to myself, hey I haven't had a vacation in a while. Maybe I'll go somewhere with warmer weather. What better place to go relax than Hell?"

"Tell me you didn't go in on purpose just to get me?" Viktor pressed.

"What does it matter?" Hunter shook his head and glanced to the female.

"You and Quint really do have a hot bromance going."

"You're welcome, asshole."

Viktor's gaze drifted over the female. "The bites aren't

all mine. You know what's down there?"

"Yeah I know." *I've been bitten.* "What happened?"

"You know the drill. Torture. Starve. Revive. Torture some more." He paused, his expression solemn. "All I can tell you is that I didn't hurt her. I swore that to her and Ilsbeth…Jesus."

"No." Not the witch. Hunter closed his eyes and opened them. "Please just tell me you didn't drink from her."

Viktor went silent and averted his gaze.

Hunter leapt off the floor and lunged at Viktor, pinning him against the wall, crushing his throat with his forearm. With their gazes locked, he repeated his demand.

"Tell me you didn't drink from her," he gritted out. "Say it!"

"It's not like I had a choice," Viktor confessed, sliding down the wall as Hunter released him.

"Jesus fucking Christ, Viktor. What the ever-loving fuck were you thinking?" Hunter held up a hand, strode across the room, and stared out the window. "You know what this means, don't you?"

"I know. I thought the same at first but…"

"But what? I mean, really? You might have bonded with that bitch and you don't even know it. I don't care if she put on some crazy show down in NOLA after Jake found her ass in the woods. The fact is that she almost killed Dimitri."

"I know but she…"

"She…she…*she* bargained with a demon. Who knows which one? Could have been the one in New York or there might be more. And now, High Priestess in there is floating around with demon juju. Fuck me." Hunter blew out a breath and crossed the room to the female who still lay unconscious. She needed a bath but fuck if he was going to do it. When she woke up and shifted, all would be right with her world. Sort of. He knew differently but the good news was she was alive.

"Ilsbeth seemed different down there. She saved me. She saved her." He gestured toward the female curled into Hunter's bed. "If she hadn't allowed me to feed from her, that wolf there would be dead."

Hunter sighed. Exhaustion rushed over him as he realized he hadn't shifted since he'd returned above ground. Hell had sucked the life out of him. Regardless of the wolf, vampire and witch, he had a pack to run and was responsible for over a hundred wolves. He owed it to them to get his shit together before the entire pack sensed his condition.

Stripping off his clothes, he listened to Viktor, knowing full well that nothing was ever simple when it came to Ilsbeth. A debt was owed and would need to be paid. And while it wasn't his responsibility, he'd have to answer to Quintus.

"I've got this with Ilsbeth. It's going to be fine," Viktor assured him. "I'll take her…"

Hunter stripped off his pants, tossed them on the floor and stood naked. "You're not going anywhere, vampire. Oh no. You're going to help me figure out who the hell this wolf is and get her back to wherever she belongs. You fucking owe me too and don't you forget it. Fuck."

"I'm not a prude but…would you shift already? You and Quint might have a bromance but…"

"Get used to it, vamp. You should keep an eye on that slippery witch of yours."

Hunter called on his power, shifting into his beast. A rush of energy twisted through him. The second his paws hit the floor, he released a guttural howl, alerting the pack to his presence. He'd been gone far too long. Tonight, he'd run with his wolves.

Hunter caught sight of Viktor hovering over the injured female, and he growled.

"Seriously? I'm just…I think that something isn't right here." Viktor cocked his head in disbelief as the great wolf swiftly blocked him from edging any closer to the woman. "Something's wrong with her," Viktor insisted.

Hunter bared his teeth at him. *Vampire.* His beast blamed him for her condition. Hunter knew better but the last thing the she-wolf needed to see when she opened her eyes was the fanger who had attacked her.

"It's not like I'm an expert but don't you think she should've shifted by now? Maybe we should…" Viktor jumped back as Hunter instantly shifted back to his human form.

"Don't touch her!" Hunter yelled, glaring at him. The Alpha softened his stance when he detected regret in the vampire's eyes; he hadn't meant to hurt her. *Fucking hell.* Nothing was easy. "Don't take this the wrong way, Vik. I risked my ass to come get you. Some shit went down in New Orleans after they took you. Whatever. It doesn't matter.

Right now, this wolf…I'll take care of her."

"She'll tell you when she wakes up. I didn't hurt her."

"But you bit her."

"I had no fucking choice. Hell. I can't tell you what happened but I…" Viktor averted his gaze and speared his fingers through his hair.

"I know what happens in Hell." Hunter blew out a breath and shook his head. "Look, man. I've got a pack to run. Ilsbeth…Jesus I can't believe she's even alive…that you drank from her. And this one." His stomach clenched as his fingers brushed over her wrist. "She's my responsibility now."

"They did something to her. I don't know what. She's special." Viktor turned and slowly walked toward the door. Without turning back, he paused and gripped the doorjamb. "I know why you did what you did, coming for me in there. But the girl. Ilsbeth. I owe you."

"Just keep an eye on the witch. I'm staying with…"

"Ilsbeth isn't going anywhere," Viktor interrupted.

"Does she have a name?" Hunter asked, transfixed on the woman before him.

"No but I told you. She's special. More specifically, her blood tastes unique. I have my suspicions. But I'll defer to you. Ilsbeth rouses."

"But she…" The Alpha's fingertips tingled as he brushed them over her skin. "What is she?"

Without another word, the vampire disappeared from the room, and Hunter stood alone, silently watching the female. He knelt by the side of the bed and inspected her face. In the short time since they'd escaped Hell, her bruises had lightened as if she'd miraculously healed in her human form. No wolf had such powers, but Viktor had told him of her special blood. *Okay, what is she?* A hybrid? Something about her energy was extraordinary yet altogether familiar.

Hunter gently placed his palm on her forehead. Her skin emanated a unique blend of sophisticated vibrations. The Alpha concentrated his powerful energy, seeking her wolf. Yet as he called to her, he could not locate her beast.

She'd been to Hell. Anything could have happened to her while she was down there. Demons thrived on the innocent, stealing, manipulating their magick.

The Alpha focused on feeding her his energy. *Be well, little one, be well.* His thoughts roamed to her wolf, and he imagined a beautiful white creature running free. Her soft moan broke him free of his contemplation.

"Hmm…" She curled onto her side and winced. The blue bruising on her eye had morphed, improving but not yet gone.

"You're gonna be all right. You're safe now," he reassured her.

The beautiful stranger blinked open her deep brown eyes and gazed into Hunter's. "Don't let them take me."

Chapter Two

Willa's pulse raced as she opened her eyes and sensed the Alpha. His powerful energy twisted through her, stirring her to consciousness. Although grateful to be alive, she trusted no one.

For most of her life, she'd lived in secrecy. Her parents had been viciously murdered long ago. An ancient wolf, she lived rogue, living in isolation without a pack. As a physician, she worked with the disenfranchised, flying under the radar, until one day she was kidnapped and sold into Hell. Demons paid well for the pleasure of torturing her.

Her wolf had gone silent, beaten into near submission. Demon magick had been known to kill wolves, but her royal lineage gave her beast great powers. Although her wolf lingered in the shadows, she immediately sensed she couldn't shift.

Exhausted and traumatized, she was tempted to close her eyes and fall asleep. But fear set in, knowing both the demons and wolves would come for her again when they found out about her absence. She trembled, praying the wolf before her had benevolent intentions.

"You're safe now. No one is going to get you here," he promised, his voice low and smooth.

"I…I'm not safe. They'll come for me."

"Listen, sweetheart. You're a helluva lot safer than you have been. Whoever's coming for you has to get through me first."

"Where am I?" Willa's voice softened. Her focus was drawn to the cathedral ceiling, smooth cedar planks forming a steep apex. The warm masculine energy of the home calmed her nerves. As she settled her gaze onto the stranger who'd saved her, *Alpha* resonated in her mind.

"You're in Jackson Hole. Wyoming. You can stay here as long as you need to. I promise you my protection." Hunter sighed, aware of the reality of the situation. He'd just punched a hole into Hell. Stealing one vampire might go unnoticed, but he'd also poached a witch and a wolf.

"Who are you?" she whispered. "What kind of a man goes to Hell on purpose?"

"Long story…" Hunter glanced to her bite marks. "I needed to get someone out.'

Willa quickly tucked her arm under the blanket. Once she'd been untouched, no longer.

"My friend, he, uh…there was this zombie thing. She took him." He sighed. "Yeah, well…doesn't matter."

"And?"

"I got him too. I've gotta ask you…and I know it's hard, but how long? How long were you in there?"

"I'm not sure." Willa closed her eyes, her mind swirling with the torturous memories. "It seemed like years, but I don't know. I think more like weeks. I don't think I would have survived. I was put there. Sold."

"Jesus. Who? Who sold you?" Hunter asked.

"It doesn't matter. I don't want to involve you. They could come after you or your pack."

"I'm already involved. I just saved you. I'm not going to let some assholes take you back."

Willa averted her gaze. Her savior stood nearly six foot four, towering over her. His nudity didn't offend her, but without her wolf, a relationship with this Alpha served no purpose. As if he'd noticed her unease, he reached for a throw blanket and wrapped it loosely around his hips.

"I…the thing is, I'm not well," she confessed. "My wolf…I need a few minutes. I need to go but I…"

A surge of emotion tightened in her chest. She'd lost everything and had still somehow survived. But her great beast had disappeared, and she feared they'd come again. *Demons. The wolves.* Her tough exterior faltered as tears filled her eyes.

"Hey. It's gonna be okay." Hunter's expression softened. "I mean it. I brought you to my home. There's no one here who can hurt you. When you're feeling better, I'll help you get back home."

"I'm Willa. Willa Jacobs," she reluctantly offered.

"Hunter. Hunter Livingston. I'm Alpha of Teton Wolves. This here…I, um, I don't want you to get the wrong impression." Hunter glanced down and adjusted the throw. He scrubbed his hand over his cheek. "I've been away for a while, so I've got to take care of a few things…"

"Alpha." Willa heard the muffled voice of a female call for him, and her stomach dropped. Her panicked eyes went to his. If he were a mated Alpha, his partner would attack her. She shoved up onto the bed. "I'll get out now. I'm sorry."

"Hey now. Just take it easy." He held up his palms.

"I shouldn't be in here. I need to go. Your mate…" Willa wrapped the sheets around her.

"I'm not mated. It's just a friend. I've been away for weeks. Pack members are going to come snooping round."

"Are you sure? I can go." Willa exhaled a relieved breath. *He's not mated.* She quickly shoved the thought to the back of her mind, aware that even if he wasn't, there was no chance in hell she'd have time to get to know him further. Her mere presence in the pack put them all in danger. She would never forgive herself if they harmed any of his wolves.

"You can take a shower in there if you want. I'll see about fixin' you some clothes. Or um…wait a second."

Willa watched in fascination as Hunter crossed the room to an enormous armoire. He opened the heavy oak doors and retrieved a t-shirt, sweatpants and socks.

"It's kinda remote out here and it's not like I keep girls' clothing on hand. So, uh…" He returned to her bedside and set the clothing on the mattress. "Yeah."

"Yeah," she repeated, her mind focused on the fact he didn't have any women's clothing. *He isn't mated. Still doesn't matter. I'm leaving.* "Thank you."

The Alpha turned to leave but stopped mid-step. "For what it's worth…I'm sorry this happened to you. I know what it's like to be in Hell, and I'm not just talking about for a few days. I…"

"Alpha, you in?" The female voice grew louder.

"We need to talk about some things." Hunter paused. "I'll be back in just a bit, Willa. Just sit tight."

The door clicked shut. Alone, Willa broke down, her emotional walls crumbling around her. Although she'd survived Hell, the others she'd seen still remained. She didn't know their names. Innocent or guilty, the tortured souls suffered.

The Alpha, while well-intentioned, could not anticipate the level of evil searching for her. The rogues sold her for a price. Now that the demons had a taste of her, they'd pay even more to have her returned to Hell. The only way to defeat the wolves would be to provide them with an alternative item to sell or agree to be forcefully mated. Everyone around her was in danger.

No, she had to rally and get away from her heroic rescuer before they came for him, his wolves. She wiped the back of her hand across her face and shoved up onto her arms. A dull ache pulsed through her legs as she swung them over the bed. Her head pounded as her blood rushed to her toes. With her magick weak, her body hadn't healed properly.

To fully regenerate, she'd have to shift. But the wolf within had gone into hiding. The demons had spent the vast amount of their torture attempting to tempt her beast to the surface, but she'd crept further into her psyche, eventually disappearing.

Willa brushed away the tears from her eyes and steeled her nerves. She'd fight and find a way to survive.

She grounded her feet onto the stone floor. Its heated tiles emanated warmth through her muscles, making it slightly more tolerable to stand. As she crossed the room, she stopped cold, noting her shocking reflection in the mirror. A mere shell of her former self, fang marks mottled her skin.

She brought her fingers to her cheek and brushed away a blackened smudge of ash. Her entire body was covered in it as if she were wearing the devil's clothing. The scent of Satan filled her nostrils and she was reminded of the lashes that stung her back. She closed her eyes, willing away the memories.

Willa reminded herself she was no longer in imminent danger. *You're okay. Do what you need to do.* Time was short. After she showered, she'd talk to the Alpha, and secure passage to New Orleans before they found her.

Willa pulled Hunter's shirt over her head and brought the soft cotton fabric to her nose. She inhaled the masculine scent of the Alpha and closed her eyes. *Who is this man who rescues a total stranger from Hell?* She recalled his handsome face, but her mind drifted to the sound of his smooth sexy voice.

She'd been alone for such a long time she'd forgotten the pleasure of a man. As a girl, she'd dreamed of finding her mate, but it had all been forgotten as she learned her family's secret. What man would want a she-wolf tainted by hellfire?

Willa reached for the sweats and shoved her legs into them. *He thinks I'm going to fit into his pants? Well, maybe.* She smiled. The Alpha was tall, nearly six foot four. She gave a small laugh and proceeded to roll up the cuffs and then slipped on a pair of well-worn cotton socks.

She ran her fingers through her long curly brunette hair and tugged on its unruly locks. At least some things never changed. The demons had cut, burned and shaved her hair to no avail. While her body faltered after the blood loss, her beast fought back the only way it could.

Willa closed her eyes and searched once again for the great animal. A rustle in the darkness alerted her to its presence but it still would not surface. Deep inside, the hellfire burned, and she called on its power. As she opened her eyes, she caught sight of the sparks flickering under her skin. She reasoned she might not be able to shift yet but held faith her beast would soon return.

She lightly padded across the room toward the door. As she turned the doorknob and opened it, she heard the voices. She proceeded deliberately down the hallway, but with caution. The Alpha had been kind so far but just because he rescued her didn't mean he was trustworthy. She'd seen her fair share of wolves turn on her when they discovered her lineage. Her mother and father had always taught her to face the unknown with courage. Fear was an emotion for humans. Royal blood pumped through her veins, and her adventurous spirit had driven her far through life.

Willa paused as she approached the ledge of the stairs, the voices growing louder. Men. A woman. *The Alpha.*

Butterflies danced in her stomach as she stepped into the light. She blinked, her eyes adjusting as she proceeded. She curled her fingers over the railing. As she descended the voices dimmed into silence. The Alpha strode through the strangers. His familiar face wore a sexy smile. Her heartbeat raced as his eyes caught hers, and the most unfamiliar emotion curled in her chest. As if his gaze were a magnet, he drew her to him. Willa couldn't understand the attraction, yet she didn't hesitate, stepping forward, drawing upon her bravery.

"Hey. You're dressed." Hunter approached the intrepid she-wolf.

His smooth voice swam in her head. *Does he have an accent? Hmm, yes. A little. Maybe southern.* Her pulse raced. *Jesus, Willa. Speak like a grown up.* "Yes. Thanks for the clothes."

His smile broadened. "How do you feel?"

"I'm good. It's fine, really." *I can't shift. Not fine at all. Fake it.*

"Are you in pain?" Hunter's smile disappeared, his eyes locked on hers.

"No. I mean, I'll feel better when I can shift but right now…"

"Hunter," a female voice called from behind him.

Willa gave Hunter an awkward smile. She knew she was an outsider. One who needed to leave as soon as possible.

Hunter took her hand and pulled her toward him,

lowering his voice as he spoke. "I want you to stay."

Willa's smile broadened. The warmth in his eyes drew her in, and for a few seconds, she became lost in his gaze. She released a breath, and forced her eyes away from his, taking in her surroundings.

The large cathedral ceiling gave way to a wide-open family room area. Black furniture blended with the dark cherry floor. A grand piano sat in a corner and she wondered if he played. The entire back of the home was made of glass. The sun set in the distance, sinking into the mountains.

A touch to her hand brought her attention back to the commanding Alpha. Her pulse raced as his fingers wrapped around hers.

"You need something to eat. It'll help."

"I…" Her wide brown eyes met his.

Willa froze as he leaned into her ear, his warm breath teasing over her skin as he spoke. The sudden closeness caused her to be aware of his masculinity. Her cheeks heated as his chest brushed hers.

"I haven't told them anything. It's okay."

Just as quickly as he'd touched her, he released her hand. She brought her palms together, his energy tingling through her fingertips.

"This here is Janet. She's my assistant."

Willa gave a hesitant smile and nodded at her. The blonde she-wolf's closed smile spoke volumes as to her discontent. *Girlfriend?* All the more reason to be on her way. Packs were instinctively territorial. Willa surmised that a remote pack such as Hunter's would be even more so.

"This is the she-wolf? She looks unwell." The imposing stranger inspected her from a distance. "Why didn't she shift?"

Willa remained silent and crossed her arms, self-conscious of the bites. Yet she kept her eyes trained on the female, staring her down. Her royal instincts demanded respect.

"She's not feeling well. She just needs something to eat," Hunter responded, not missing a beat.

The brooding male approached and glared at Willa. "What was she doing in Hell?"

"Easy, Remus. Willa, this is my beta. That dude over there. Rafe." Hunter turned to his wolves. "Let me be clear y'all. Willa is my guest. So, play nice."

"You sure you don't need help with the female?" he asked.

"Yes, I can bring her something to wear if you…" Janet said, her lips still tight in a frown.

"I'm good," Hunter said, tension lacing his words.

"Nice to meet you," Willa managed. Her eyes darted up to the Alpha's.

"Hey guys, I've gotta get some food rustled up so if you wouldn't mind." He nodded toward the door. "I'll be out in a few and we can go for a run."

As the strangers reluctantly walked out the front door without saying goodbye, Willa relaxed. She wasn't in the mood, but if attacked, she'd fight to the death. The female had been less than welcoming, and she sensed they viewed her as a threat.

"I'm sorry I don't have much of a variety. I'm defrosting a few steaks and I've got some potatoes boiling. I haven't had a chance to order in food since I've been away. And unfortunately, I've been away from my house for a good long while." The Alpha crossed the room to a bar that extended into the living area. The curved wood had been intricately designed. Smooth curved planes of mahogany swirled on its surface.

He reached for a bottle on an overhead rack and retrieved it. "I may not have a lot of food right now. But what I do have is a shit ton of red wine. So, we're good on that."

"Works for me." Willa's instant response surprised even her. Something about Hunter seemed familiar. More than safe, his mere presence both excited and calmed her, but she resisted her attraction to him.

"Ah, a lady after my own heart." Hunter made quick work of uncorking the bottle, slipped two glasses in front of him and poured it. "The thing is. Hell." He exhaled and shook his head. "Bad things. Very, very bad things happen there. And you know, even though we're immortal, we certainly can die."

The Alpha paused and reached for a remote, pointing it at an enormous stone fireplace. As he clicked a button, the fire roared to life. He set it down and picked up the wine glasses.

Willa struggled to keep her eyes on his face. The wild, shirtless Alpha seemed unaware of his effect on her. As he approached, her focus painted over his broad muscled chest that led down to his ripped abs. He extended the glass, and she quickly lifted her gaze to meet his. She nervously accepted the wine as he handed it to her, giving her a knowing smile.

"Thank you." *Jesus, I'm an idiot.*

"Sorry, lost focus there a minute. Where was I? Immortal." He cocked his head. "Maybe that makes Hell all the worse. We don't die easily and when you get out, you don't forget."

"I'll be okay," she lied. Exhausted, the fear of closing her eyes wormed through her gut. The nightmares of Hell would linger in her dreams.

"Yeah, hmm, if you say so."

"I don't want to talk about it," she said, her voice soft.

"How about now, let's toast."

"Toast? Really?" She managed a small smile.

"Hell yeah. We're alive, aren't we?" He raised his glass into the air. "Here's to meeting beautiful strangers."

Willa held his gaze as her glass touched his, barely aware of the soft clink. With her eyes still locked on his, she brought the rim to her lips. The warm cherry notes danced on her tongue and she swallowed, her insides warmed by the drink.

"Come sit." Hunter nodded to the sofa.

Willa complied. Breaking eye contact, she surveyed the room as she walked. Something about his opulent home felt lived in, comfortable. She sat on the sofa and curled her legs under her. He smiled and fell back into an oversized chair and propped his feet on the ottoman.

"So, what's your deal?" he asked outright.

"I don't have a deal." Secrets maybe. "I'm just a wolf."

"And your mate?" he inquired.

"No mate." The corners of her lips curled upward. Was he interested?

"And your pack?" Hunter took a sip of his wine.

"I don't have a pack."

"You're a rogue she-wolf? I find that hard to believe."

"I travel often. I don't have time to belong to any one pack." It was partially true.

"You can travel and still belong to a pack," he challenged. "Where are you from? You have…a slight accent, yes?"

"I was born in Brazil. Most of my time in the States has been spent in New Orleans. About twenty years ago, I bought a home in the French Quarter. Logan knows of my presence."

"Does he know you're rogue? Because I'll clue you in on a little secret, sweetheart. I have a place in New Orleans, and no one's ever mentioned you."

"I keep a low profile. I don't run with the pack. Logan grants me permission to run." Willa ran the pad of her finger in circles around the rim of her glass.

Hunter raised a suspicious eyebrow. "And where else do you live?"

"Mostly central America."

"What are you doing down there?"

"I'm a doctor. I'm part of an international physician group that volunteers across the globe. Initially I was sent to Guatemala after a volcano erupted. I ended up staying a little longer. Did some research."

"You work with humans? As a doctor?"

"It's not that unusual. For wolves anyway."

"True. But for a rogue. Alone among humans. That is unusual. Rogues aren't usually the type to help others."

"I'm not all rogue." Tempted to tell him the truth, she bit her lip.

Hunter leaned forward and tilted his head. "So, listen. I've been thinking about this. I still don't have the full story but there's something about you. So, I'm just going to say it. I think you should stay with my pack for a while."

"I…" *I can't put your wolves in danger,* "can't impose."

"Tell me something, Willa. How did you get in Hell?"

"I…I was, um, sold there," she admitted. That much was the truth. "Ambushed. Then sold."

"I've gotta say I'm not an expert on the rules but that's also a little unusual."

Willa glanced down into her glass, remaining silent.

"Whoever did it could be coming for you again. Every time you leave, they say the demons get a little bit of a taste for your soul. Everyone who escaped…"

"Everyone?" Willa's focus drifted to the fireplace. The lick of the flames appeared to dance inciting warmth over her thoughts, yet in Hell, they screamed, tearing away the flesh of their victims. One of the many tools utilized to inflict pain. She recalled the torture, hearing her own screams in her mind. The others…the feedings. Her fingertips brushed over the newly healed skin on her forearm. Something had happened while she was there. The memories lingered just out of reach. Their faces and voices eluded her. "There were others."

"There were."

"I don't remember. I just know…awful things happen there." Her strength faltered, her voice shook. "But I can't stay." *I really want to stay.*

Willa hadn't been around an Alpha in such a long time. His powerful energy soothed the terrified wolf inside that still feared for her life.

"But of course, you can stay."

"I can't." Her eyes softened as they locked on his, tears threatening to fall. Willa swallowed the emotion back and brought the glass to her lips, taking a long draw of the wine.

"Willa." Hunter set his drink on the end table and moved to sit next to her. "You can."

"I'd like to but…" Her heart sped as the Alpha closed the distance between them. Her hand shook as she settled her glass next to his on the table.

"I know what happens in Hell. I know the kind of torture you've been through. And also, I know what it's like for a rogue wolf. It's probably why it was so easy for them to ambush you. You have no pack to help you. Look, I don't know what made you go rogue, but it has to be exhausting. You're on your own. I'm offering you refuge. Just stay a little while. Let me protect you."

Hunter reached for her hand, and her body pricked in awareness at his touch. The calloused pads of the Alpha's fingers told her he worked with his hands. She studied the contours of his face. Handsome, the scruff on his cheeks accentuated his strong jawline. While the sea of the truth lay between them, she fought the allure of the dominant Alpha.

"I appreciate your offer. It's just…the reason I was in Hell. I can't bring that to you. There's something I need to get before…" Willa stopped herself before divulging too much more. She needed to go to New Orleans.

"Then tell me the why."

"I can't. I can't put anyone else in danger. It's not fair to you."

"I just brought you out of Hell. Do you think I'm afraid of a little danger?"

"I'm not like you."

"I can tell that already. Your energy. When I touched you. I don't know what it is but it's different than most wolves," he commented.

"It's…" *Hellfire,* "unique."

"But what is it? Why are they after you, Willa?" Hunter exposed her palm and lazily drew a circle with the pad of his thumb on her skin.

"I can't talk about this. I…" No one outside of her family knew her secret. For it was the original magick of the wolves that danced in her blood.

Hunter brought her palm to his lips and she cupped his face. This man turned her inside out and she'd just met him. No, this couldn't be happening.

"I'll stay one night," she blurted out, unable to resist his spell. "I mean here. Not with you. Well yeah, with you but not with you. I'm sorry I just…you really make me nervous for some reason…I…"

"Shh. It's okay, Willa. There is a reason I found you when I did and I'm not letting you go. Not yet."

"One night, yes?" She wasn't sure whether she was telling him or asking. Her eyes fell to his lips and the energy between them sizzled.

"One night." He smiled.

Her gaze returned to his and he leaned in toward her. *Just one kiss. One night. I'll go tomorrow,* she told herself.

As she closed her eyes, his lips brushed hers and she moaned. Who was this man? He lightly kissed her and then brought her into his embrace, his warm breath upon her ear.

She relaxed into his arms, wishing she had time. Tick Tock. Tomorrow would come quickly and off to New Orleans she'd fly. But for this moment, she indulged. Her heart squeezed, knowing she was both safe and wanted.

But just as she relaxed against the strong Alpha, the energy in the room switched again. Her eyes flashed open and she screamed at the sight of the tall stranger looming above them.

Chapter Three

Hunter couldn't explain what drove him to kiss her. He knew it was wrong. *Jesus.* Six hours ago, they'd all met at a barbeque in Hell, and here he was tasting the lovely she-wolf he'd rescued. Lies rolled off her tongue yet he yearned to taste her mouth.

He didn't press her too much for the truth. If there was one thing Hunter knew, it was that secrets ate at the soul of a person. He'd watched her keep herself tightly wound, hedging, then telling one of her well-crafted answers. While it was clear she believed she put him in danger, she hadn't fully explained why.

Willa still hadn't shifted, something rare for a wolf. In his entire existence, he'd only seen a handful of wolves unable to shift after an injury. Unless they were about to die from a mortal wound or suffering the ill effects from dark magick, wolves could always transform, healing themselves.

Something about her felt familiar, as if he'd known her his entire life. Her unusual energy intrigued him. He should have walked away but with her in his arms, he indulged his desires. Her honeyed kiss lured him under her spell, her feminine scent stirring his wolf to rise. If only he could keep her.

Hunter gathered his strength, resisting the temptation to touch her further. As his lips brushed over her ear, his contemplation was broken. *Fucking vampire.*

"You know, I thought I was good, but you've got some sick moves, bro. No, no, no…keep going, please." Viktor gave a sly smile and winked at Willa. "She is smokin'. Or is that just Hell I still smell?" He pinched his shirt and sniffed.

"What the actual fuck?"

"What?" Viktor shrugged, fell back into a chair and propped his feet on the ottoman. "Jesus, this has been a long month. I really need a vacation."

"Where's Ilsbeth?" Hunter shot to his feet. "Tell me she's handcuffed somewhere. You did not just leave her upstairs."

"Do you take me for a fool?"

"Who's Ilsbeth?" Willa asked.

"Seriously." Hunter rolled his eyes. "Who here got captured and put in Hell?" He glanced to Willa. "No offense. I'm not talking about you. Although I know there's more to your story than you're telling me."

"She's indisposed." Viktor answered, his gaze drifting around the room. "Nice digs. It's not exactly my taste, of course…rustic. Fitting for a wolf. Classic in its own way, I suppose."

"What the fuck did you do with Ilsbeth?" Hunter's voice reverberated throughout the room.

"Who is Ilsbeth?" Willa sat straight up on the sofa.

"Why, she's the witch, of course," he answered

Willa's head snapped towards the vampire. "There's a witch in this house?"

"Interesting. She's worried about the witch." Victor dropped his fangs, giving her a broad, toothy smile. "You'd think she'd be more concerned about the vampire in the room."

"Who are you?" Willa asked.

"Where is the fucking witch?" Hunter demanded.

"I took care of things." Viktor sniffed again, this time into the air. "Is something burning?"

"It's the grill. Don't worry about it. Where? Is she?" Hunter struggled to control his anger at the vampire's nonchalant attitude.

"Ilsbeth is under control, man. Just chill. Like seriously, did you think I'd leave her by herself?"

"No, no, no." Knowing it would be counterproductive to saving his ass, Hunter resisted the urge to choke him. "You did not fucking let her go."

"Do you take me for a fool? We're talking about Ilsbeth. I took her where she belongs. New Orleans." Viktor stood and crossed the room to the kitchen, waving a hand in the air. "But don't worry."

"She threatened to leave, didn't she?" The Alpha rolled his eyes. "Of course, she did. That fucking bitch."

Hunter stormed across the room and slammed his fist onto the cold granite countertop. Willa flinched at the sound, but kept her eyes trained on the vampire.

"Yeah, about that bitch thing." Viktor glanced to the seasoned steaks that lay on a plate. He wrinkled his nose. "Something is definitely burning."

"I just told you. It's the grill, for fuck's sake."

"Let's get to it. Can't you see she is starving?" Viktor smiled at Willa, who sat across the room, wearing an expression of annoyance. "Please continue making sexy with the pretty wolf. Although you probably need to tend to that burning first."

"What do you know about wolves and hunger? You don't even eat." Hunter plowed his fingers through his hair. "Why the fuck did you take Ilsbeth back to New Orleans? I told you I needed to talk to her. I want to know her involvement in this. What was she doing in Hell? Who put her there?"

"I don't know the details, but I suspect whatever demon she'd traded favors with had come callin'. Time to pay the piper. Could've been for the black magick she used to try to trick Dimitri. Could be for something else we don't even know about. Who knows? Who cares?"

"Where exactly is she?" Hunter asked, keeping a concerned eye on Willa as she stood and walked to the fire, her back to both of them.

"Ilsbeth is where she belongs…in the coven." Viktor looked to Hunter. "I can cook if you let me. I used to be a chef."

"No, you didn't. Fuck off, vamp. The only thing you know about is blood. Quintus told me you don't eat." Hunter took a deep breath, restraining his anger. He reached for the plate of steaks and curled a finger around the door handle. As he slid the glass open, fresh air rushed into his lungs and he stepped outside onto the porch. He proceeded to fork the meat onto the grill, a hiss sounding as the hot metal seared the steaks.

Viktor raised an eyebrow at him, smiled and glanced to Willa. He closed the door, keeping his voice lowered to a whisper. "She doesn't remember me."

"She's struggling," Hunter sighed.

Viktor leaned against the door. "I meant what I said. I didn't hurt her. But her lack of memories? She's traumatized. It was Hell. Who knows how long she was there? And speaking of which, why hasn't she shifted? It would help. She still has a few bruises. Granted, they look like they're better but…"

"I don't know. I'm not sure what's happening." Hunter flipped the steak. "It's what you said. Something's different about her. She's special."

"I already told you that."

"No. I mean it. There's something else. I'm not talking about how she tastes."

"Well, this is interesting." Viktor laughed. "Are you smitten?"

"Smitten? Who the fuck even uses that word?" Hunter snapped.

"You are. Fancy that."

"Ilsbeth left the coven before," Hunter commented, changing the subject back to the witch. "What makes you think she won't get on her broom and fly the coop again?"

"Ilsbeth won't be going anywhere. And more

importantly, nothing will be getting in to take her. Samantha will take care of it. Don't worry yourself with the witch. Pay attention to the wolf you brought back. Willa, she's a lovely little…"

"What do you know of Willa?" Hunter's heart pounded as he said her name. "You fed from her. So fucking what? You have no claim to her."

"No, but apparently the thought of it really twists you up. Delightful as that is, I can't claim to know anything about her except she was used as a blood slave in Hell. I'm afraid that's it."

"She said someone is after her and I believe her. Going into Hell on purpose would be…"

"Stupid. Idiotic."

"Saving your ass? Yes, it was. I'm definitely questioning that course of action."

"Ah, but you care. Should we hug it out?"

"No, I'm good. I care about her. You? Not so much."

"You risked your life for me." Viktor put his arm around Hunter, who immediately shoved it away.

"I did that for Quintus. And you? Jesus, what is your issue?"

"Fine, but you'd better pay attention to the steaks because you're about to overcook them. They taste better mooing. Nice and bloody."

"Tell me more about Ilsbeth." Hunter caught sight of Willa crossing the room toward the kitchen.

"I didn't want to keep her here, around you and the girl. As much as she helped me down there," Viktor gestured to the ground, "I can't risk it. As soon as you wrap up things with the she-wolf, we can go back to New Orleans and deal with her."

"New Orleans?"

"You gotta admit, we could have a good time."

"Plenty of good times here in Jackson Hole. I need to stay with my pack."

"Don't be salty about me letting Ilsbeth go. You've got your hands full here. She's a complication you don't need."

"That fucking bitch. Let me tell you. Going into Hell? I sure as shit never expected to find her. I was only goin' in for you. But when I saw her. Fuck." Hunter shook his head and locked his gaze on Viktor. "You know Ilsbeth. I knew her back when. Long before she was the *High Priestess*. People who know her say she is a double-edged sword. She was never all bad. Maybe yes. Maybe no. I say it depends which side of the sword you're looking at and if she's shoving it through ya. But man, I could have killed her myself for what she did to Dimitri. And hey, I still get it. People didn't want her to be guilty. A million stories about the others she's helped over the years. Just because she fell for D. I don't know. She's a cold bitch in my book. Ah, fuck. I don't know. Down there in Hell, knowing you, knowing Ilsbeth, suspecting she'd helped you? I didn't think twice. Saved her ass too. But still, I've gotta know what she did with Dimitri. I want to ask her myself. And more importantly, I wanna know how and why she was in Hell."

"She helped to save your girl in there. That part is true," Viktor said.

"So you say, but I have some questions for her." Hunter forked the steak onto a plate and glanced to Willa who stood in the kitchen, her eyes on his. "There's something about her, yeah?"

"Ilsbeth? Well, she's certainly a force to be reckoned…"

"Not the witch. I'm talking about Willa. She's a doctor."

"Doctor, huh?" Viktor dragged out his comment with a cheeky smile. "I bet she has a good bedside manner."

"You're an asshole," Hunter snapped. He reached for the grill and switched off the gas. He stopped and glared at the vampire. "Look, Vik. Can you go easy? Willa isn't shifting. Like you said, she's traumatized. I want to give her some time to…." The Alpha glanced to her once again. His rogue she-wolf had begun peeling a banana and he silently counted the seconds as she slid the firm fruit between her lips. *Jesus, what is she doing to me?* "It's just she's not really ready to…"

"She looks plenty ready to me." Viktor laughed as Willa bit down hard onto the banana.

"She, uh, she…" Hunter caught sight of Willa smiling at him, her tongue brushing over her bottom lip. *Holy shit.* His hand shook as he lifted the plate.

"Oh yeah. She's ready all right."

"Shut the fuck up, vampire," Hunter responded, keeping his eyes on Willa.

"Stop being all sappy. You're going to make me sick. Move along. I'll come watch you eat meat. Doesn't seem right, cooking it so thoroughly. With you being wolves and all, I'd expect you to eat it raw."

"Quintus cooks. He eats. You know you might like it. Get with the whole 'I live among humans' program. I know it might be torturous for you, but you might want to at least try it."

"Quintus has gone soft. Not me. I'm a purist. It's been way too long for me to ever consider food. Sex and power. Now those are two things I can't give up." He laughed.

"It's not a pick one or the other scenario. The human experience is expansive. For us, even more so. I'm talking life. Be well-rounded, man." Hunter held the plate up to his face and sniffed. "Ah yeah. Now, that's what I'm talking about. Nothing like it. Go on. Smell it."

Hunter shoved the food toward Viktor. "Tell me you don't miss it. Don't lie."

"Fine. Fine." The blond vampire leaned over and sniffed briefly, then rolled his eyes. "Sorry, does nothing for me. Absolutely nothing."

"Don't just pretend to smell it. Go on," Hunter insisted.

Viktor raised an eyebrow and shook his head as he reluctantly acquiesced to his demand, inhaling its scent with a slight smile.

"That's right, Hollywood. It's good. So good." Hunter grinned in victory, aware he'd discovered the vampire's secret desire.

"It's just a momentary weakness. I'll be fine. Are there any donors out here in the middle of nowhere?" He sighed.

"Not many. I could call on a she-wolf I know. She's into being bitten. We've got a small blood club if you want to dine out. Probably your best bet."

"A wolf would do. I'm not picky." Viktor's gaze drifted to Willa. "She really doesn't remember me. Maybe she'd be interested."

Hunter stopped cold, his anger spiking at the vampire's implied threat. "If you ever touch her again, you're dead. You aren't drinking from her. Never. Ever. Again."

"Joking. Jesus, wolf. As if."

"We're clear?" Hunter growled. Willa's trauma had destroyed her wolf, and like fuck he'd let the blood sucker bite her again.

"Of course. It's not like I was really going to…"

"It's time to eat." Hunter ignored Viktor as he slid open the door, brushed past him and strode into the kitchen.

"That it is…I'll be back."

"Thank you. This was amazing." Willa brought the wine glass to her lips.

"I've thought about starting my own cooking show. I'm pretty sure it'll be a hit," Hunter joked, attempting to lighten the mood. She'd been quiet during dinner.

"If you make steaks this delicious, I'm sure everyone would tune in to see you." Willa glanced at her near empty plate, her smile slowly fading.

"Look Willa. I'm sorry…you see, the conversation I had with Viktor, he's the friend I went in to save."

"A vampire?" she asked, her tone soft.

"Yeah."

"And why does an Alpha save a vampire?"

"He's a friend." Hunter shrugged. "Maybe more like a friend of a friend. He was caught up in something. Kidnapped really. Well, technically, he went after the demon. She was more of a zombie really."

Willa stared at him wide-eyed with a closed smile.

"It's, uh, it's complicated."

"I bet." Willa took another sip of her wine and set it on the table.

"He's special." Hunter inwardly cringed realizing he'd used the same word to describe Willa.

"Yeah, he seems very…unique."

Hunter laughed. "You could say that."

"You make it a habit to go into Hell for vampires? You must be a pretty good friend."

"Quintus. He's from New York. We got in some heated situations together." Hunter's mind flashed to the ménage he'd shared with him and Gabriella, his mate, and decided to skip that discussion. "Let's just say we became close. And Viktor, well, he can kind of be a bit of an asshole but he's not all bad."

"And the disappearing thing he does?"

"It's an ancient thing. Like us wolves. The legends say…" As a child, he'd been told about an original family of wolves who sparked the legacy of their race.

"Don't believe in fairy tales," she warned.

"Real life isn't too far off from fairy tales. Quint. Vik. They're thousands of years old. So when I say 'ancient', they are the beginning of their species. I'm not saying they're the only ones. But those two…they're the real deal. Blood brothers. Same sire. They're close. Quintus just found his mate. There's no way I could let him go to Hell. He'd just found her, and she needed him. Open that portal and you never know when you'll get back. When Viktor was kidnapped, I had no other choice."

"We all have a choice. You made the choice to sacrifice your life. For your friends. For me. I'll always be grateful."

"I would never have left you." Unfamiliar emotions stirred in his chest as a shy smile crossed her face and she tilted her head, flashing her demure eyes at him. Hunter sucked a breath and rose, gathering the dishes. "Sometimes life is about doing the right thing. The universe placed you in my path. It's no accident."

"Let me help you clean up," she insisted.

"No way. You're a guest. Besides Paul will be by tomorrow, and he'll take care of all this. He usually watches my place when I'm gone. Since I've been away, he's been off seeing his cousins in New Orleans, but he'll be back tomorrow."

"A butler?" she laughed. "Fancy."

"Who? Paul? Sort of, but I like to think of him as more of an assistant. A jack of all trades. Keeps things in order."

"I can help you though." Willa reached for the silverware but stilled as Hunter placed his hand upon hers.

As Hunter's palm rested over her delicate fingers, his body stirred in awareness. He attempted to ignore it and focused on his words. "I mean it now. Not only are you a guest but you've had a rough go. I'm not going to let anything else happen to you. This will just take a minute and then I want to talk to you about this leaving business again. Go on now. Have a seat on the sofa and I'll be right there."

Hunter's chest tightened as she smiled at him, and he quickly removed his hand as if he'd touched fire. Jesus, there was something about her energy that drew him, confused him…aroused him.

Shoving the feelings away, he returned the smile and set off to pile the dishes in the sink. He began rethinking his grand plan to have her stay in his house. It'd been weeks since he'd been with a woman, and that alone should explain his attraction. But there was something about her that stirred his wolf. He didn't want to have sex with just any woman. The Alpha craved Willa, the hunger burning deep inside his gut.

He reminded himself that she planned to leave. His wolf urged him to chase her, but much as he was tempted, his responsibility was to his pack, not a rogue wolf he'd picked up in Hell. He should show her the guest room and go for a run with his beta.

The sound of tinkling piano keys caught his attention. He smiled as the familiar classical music began to fill the room. The beautiful she-wolf was full of surprises.

He studied her as he made his way over to the piano, watching her delicate fingers effortlessly drifting over the ivory. Her expression was relaxed, lost in the music. As he sat down next to her, she smiled at him. When the music ended, her hands rested on the keyboard.

"It's beautiful. Please. Don't stop."

She nodded and took a breath, her fingers depressing the keys. Hunter brushed his hands beside hers and began to play in unison. He'd learned the romantic duet nearly a hundred years ago. Willa's pace slowed as he joined her and she smiled, her eyes on his. Several minutes of pure bliss passed as their fingers moved in tandem. The rhythm danced, escalating into a crescendo, ending with a whisper of a note.

Deafening silence filled the air. Hunter's blood raced. As her pinky brushed his, his cock stirred.

"You play," she whispered.

"It's been a long time."

"Sorry?"

"It's been a long time since I've played…the piano." *Cared about a woman.* Hunter closed his eyes. The closeness of being next to her tempted him. *Fuck. No. Don't do this, Hunter.* He knew it was wrong. He'd just met her. She was leaving. Getting involved with a rogue wolf was trouble. There was always a reason they left a pack, and whatever it was, it wasn't good. *Tell her goodnight. Don't be stupid.*

As her eyes met his, his arousal spiked, and his judgment wavered. *Just a little taste.*

"Alpha." Willa lost her words as her gaze fell to his lips.

"Willa…" Hunter knew everything about kissing the beautiful she-wolf was wrong. But as his lips brushed hers, he was convinced nothing could be more right. His hands gently cupped her face, his mouth dancing with hers, his tongue probing. The sweet taste of her essence drove him wild. As he deepened the kiss, Willa moaned, her hands wrapping around him. Blood rushed to his cock and his hands reached for her waist.

His wolf sought hers. His beast told him this stranger, this gorgeous woman was pack. He shoved the piano stool back, devouring her mouth. The temptation to make love to her surged, and he lifted her by her waist onto his lap. She wrapped her hands around his neck, their lips crushed upon each other's.

As she writhed on his rock-hard erection, his cock throbbed in arousal. His hand drifted under the fabric of her shirt, finding her breast. Hunter grazed his thumb over her taut nipple. She arched her back, her chest thrusting toward his, and moaned.

What am I doing? Hunter knew he should stop, but his beast went feral as her lips moved to his neck, and she nipped at his skin. His palms slid down from her breast over her belly, teasing the waistband of her pants. Her hands gripped his shoulders as he slipped his fingers beneath the soft fabric and delved them into her slick folds.

"Alpha," she cried.

"You're beautiful," he murmured, his lips on her neck.

"Ah…I…" Her forehead fell to his chest as he plunged a thick finger inside her tight core.

Hunter smiled at how wet she was for him, yet he exercised restraint.

"Please," she begged, her hips thrusting into his hand.

The Alpha grunted as she shifted, her bottom grazing his stiff cock. Willa lifted her head, softly panting, her eyes on his. A silent connection sizzled between them, her electric energy surrounding him.

Hunter added another finger, sliding it deep inside her heat. His thumb teased over her swollen nub causing her to suck an audible breath.

"I...I..." Willa lost her words as she gripped his shoulders.

His mouth crushed onto hers as she splintered apart. He devoured her with his kiss, tasting the delicious she-wolf. She shook in his arms, moaning as he slowly removed his hand and held her gently.

Fucking hell, this woman was wild, feral as she bit at his skin. It'd be so easy to make love to her, to take her upstairs and fuck the hell out of her. But as familiar as her energy was to him, she emanated her own unique vibrations. She claimed to be wolf, yet she couldn't shift. None of it should matter. She'd be gone from his life as quickly as he'd discovered her.

Hunter groaned into their kiss, his cock throbbing as she undulated on his lap. *Don't do it,* his conscience urged him. *Fuck.* As he tore his lips from hers, she reached for his dick and he wrapped his fingers around her wrist. They exchanged a heated gaze, Hunter's forehead resting upon hers.

"Sweetheart, you tempt me but..." His words were interrupted by a familiar voice.

"You're seriously going to stop? Late to the party as always," Viktor commented.

Hunter took a deep breath, protectively wrapping his arms around Willa, sensing her tense beneath his embrace.

"What the hell are you doing here?" Hunter shot at Viktor.

"Ah well, you know I have the ability to move quickly. The perks of being a vampire. Just coming to warn you there's been a bit of a tiff here in quiet Jackson Hole."

"What are you talking about?"

"Your little resident blood club. Blue Moon. The name seems a trifle cliché, but I was able to find a donor there."

"What's going on?" Willa asked, her arms tight around the Alpha.

"I heard a rumor from a lovely little ginger. A human. She told me about a gang of thugs who roughed up her brother earlier today."

"I'm having trouble getting past the fact your donor is sharing information with you." Hunter desperately tried to ignore his painful erection.

"Unlike animals, I'm quite civilized," Viktor replied in a smug tone of voice.

"It could have been anyone."

"She said her brother was ambushed on his ranch. Gave him a beat down. Said they shifted into wolves."

Hunter released an audible sigh. Every now and then rogue wolves joined a pseudo pack of wolves, actively working together.

"They've come for me," Willa whispered.

"It's possible they're just another pack of rogues. They move through every now and then. We round em' up and scare them off. I can't have them fucking with the humans and drawing attention to the pack."

"I could smell the fear tonight in your little town. Your

humans are buzzing about scared."

"Viktor, I don't have time for hyperbole."

"I can also taste it. Her blood had a smidgen of fear in it. Can't say I didn't enjoy it. Gives it a little kick. Did I mention the brother got sent to the hospital?"

"Fuck all."

"Seems you may have an infestation. I'd be happy to help." His eyes fell to Willa and back to the Alpha. "Looks like you have your hands full."

"I do, which is why you need to stop that flashing shit and knock like a…"

"Human?" he smirked.

"Normal person," Hunter replied.

"I've got to go," Willa said, tugging away from Hunter.

"Willa." He knew he should ask her to stay but responsibility to his pack came first. As she slipped out of his arms, a sense of loss twisted through him. What was it about this female that stirred his emotions? His gaze lingered on her as she stood and fiercely stared down the vampire.

"Don't leave on my account," Viktor said blithely.

"Vampires don't scare me." She turned her focus back to Hunter. "The wolves that put me in Hell. It could be them."

"It could be any rogues. The fact is that we get them sometimes. They come through the mountains into the valley. The troublemakers have a false sense that they will be more protected, but then they get here and have to deal with my pack. And the ones not looking to cause shit, just stay a short time and move on."

"But they could be the same ones," she insisted.

"Or not. But one thing is clear, we've got a bad bunch who just roughed up a human. They could be a danger to other humans or even my pack. We've gotta round em' up and ship em' out."

"Or kill them. Yes, see how I fixed that?" Viktor walked around the piano and stood by the fire.

"If I leave Jackson Hole, they'll leave you all alone. I've got to get to New Orleans and then back to Guatemala."

"Hold on there, Willa. You aren't going anywhere without me. I know I agreed to let you go but I've decided it's not safe. Just give me time to take care of these assholes and we'll sort the rest."

"I don't have time. Your wolves are at risk and my…" Willa stopped short of finishing her sentence and raked her fingers through her hair with a sigh.

"Your what?" Hunter's curiosity was piqued.

"Nothing. It's just…well, my research. I need to get to New Orleans and pick up a few things and then I have to get a flight out."

"You're not leaving, sweetheart. Not tonight. You'll be safe here…"

"You can't keep me here like one of your wolves. I don't belong to you," she countered, defiance flickering in her eyes.

Hunter ignored Viktor's laugh of amusement. While he admired her fiery spirit, his little rogue wolf tested his patience. "Ah, you see that's where you're wrong. Every wolf that roams my land submits to me, as shall you."

"That's so not happening. I need to borrow your phone. I'm getting a flight out of here tonight."

"Sorry sweetheart, there's no flights going out of Jackson Hole this late. Please. Be my guest. Take a bubble bath or something. We'll be back in a few hours." Hunter stood and walked over to the counter and snatched his cell phone, tapping out a text message to his beta.

"You can't keep me here just because you decide that. As long as I'm here every one of your wolves is in danger. I'm leaving. They'll have trouble following me to New Orleans."

"The girl. Did you leave her at the bar?" Hunter ignored Willa's declaration. With rogue wolves in the area, it wasn't safe. There was no way he'd let her leave.

"Yes. A bite and a bang and she was on her way. Appears she was planning to dance the night away." Viktor caught Willa's look of annoyance. "I don't want to interfere with your little tiff, but I brought you clothing."

"What?" Willa asked, her mouth open in surprise.

"You brought her clothes?" Gratitude tempered Hunter's desire to strangle the vampire.

"I thought I could be of service. Made a quick stop at a boutique before it closed."

Fucking vampire. The Alpha angrily typed out the rest of his text to Remus, asking him to start a search of the territory. He would set out with Viktor to question the girl and her brother.

"Thank you." Willa smiled at Viktor, her voice soft. "I'm sorry I don't remember…"

"No worries at all, pet. If there is one thing I can do

easily enough it's flash in and out for an errand. If you ever decide to dump this wolf, I'd be happy to show you the rest of my tricks. Vampires do it with a bite." Viktor winked, flashing a flirtatious smile.

Hunter's jaw ticked as he stuffed the phone into his pocket. He'd called upon a few wolves to monitor the perimeter of his home and keep tabs on Willa. Her icy stare told him she had no plan of submitting any time soon.

"Perhaps you could do me one more tiny favor. Any chance you could get me to New Orleans?"

"Ah…well, of course but you see…" Viktor smiled broadly at Hunter. "I'm afraid I can't leave the Alpha by himself this evening. He tends to get into trouble. I'd like to think of myself as a…guardian angel."

Hunter forced himself to remain calm. The fucking vampire was deliberately irritating him. "You." He pointed at Viktor. "Number one. You're hardly angelic. And number two. You're kind of a dick." Hunter turned his attention to Willa, stalking toward her. "And you." As he came within two feet of her, his beast howled with arousal. "We have unfinished business. I'm not…" *ready to let you go,* "letting you go to New Orleans by yourself when I just rescued your sexy little ass out of Hell. You're right about one thing. Someone is after you, and they could be here or maybe they're just waiting for you to go home. No. No, I'm not letting you leave by yourself."

"But…" she protested, her expression softening. "Hunter…"

The sound of his name on her lips caused him to pause.

Jesus, what the hell is happening to me? The Alpha questioned his sanity, bringing the stray wolf into his home. And now instead of treating her as he would any other wolf, his judgement was clouding. This temptation, this gorgeous woman, distracted him from all else. He struggled with his emotions and attempted to shove them to the far reaches of his psyche.

"I'll help you get home once this is over. New Orleans. Guatemala. Wherever you want."

"I...I could help you."

"What?"

"Let me come with you. If you find the wolves, I can identify them."

"This could be dangerous. You can't even shift," Hunter said.

"I'll be fine. I know I'm having trouble but...well, Viktor there." She gestured to the vampire. Her voice wavered as she spoke. "He can flash me out if there's trouble and I can't shift. You can do it, right?"

Viktor laughed. "Why of course, love, but I'm afraid I'll defer to the Alpha."

Hunter raised an eyebrow at him, pleased that for once he'd respected his place. The Alpha quickly focused his attention back onto Willa.

"You can come with me tonight if you don't feel safe here. Vik can flash you back at any sign of trouble." As the words left his mouth, he wondered just what the hell was happening to him. "But I'm not letting you out of my sight until I know these assholes are caught. Going in and out of hell isn't an easy thing. So, let's get one thing straight. As long as you're here, you belong to me and I'm not going to let anything happen to you or any of my other wolves."

"I…"

"No arguing, doc. If you try to leave, I'm going to have your ass…" Hunter sighed, inwardly cursing his choice of words. Fuck, all he wanted was her ass and he suspected no matter what happened, his wolf would have her. He shook off the thoughts and continued. "I'm goin' to be straight with you. I don't know what you're hiding but I got a feeling whatever it is, you're not going to be able to get through it on your own. I know you want to protect other people, but this is my pack. My decision. My responsibility."

Hunter plowed his fingers through his hair. "At some point, you're going to have to tell me what secrets you're keepin'. Because I know you've got some. And before you tell me you want to go back on your own, consider this. Whether these rogues are the ones who took you or not, someone is probably looking to find you and put you back in Hell. I can tell you for damn sure that it's not easy getting in or out of Hell. Whoever put you there is on speed dial with some demon who's probably itchin' to get you back. I got lucky finding you. Chances are that if you go back, they'll hide you so far down you'll never get out. I get you've been living rogue. I do, sweetheart. But now is not the time to go runnin' off on your own."

"While I'd love to take your side pet, the Alpha is quite correct," Viktor added. "You will not survive a second trip to Hell. Even if they bring you back each time they torture you, your soul will die. You won't make it."

Hunter detected the flash of pain in the vampire's eyes, reminding him of the torture he'd endured. The Alpha knew the pain all too well. He reached for Willa's hand and pressed her palm to his chest.

"I don't know what they did to you down there, but neither do you. You don't remember today. But one day, one hour, one minute…you're going to snap out of whatever's protecting your mind from remembering and it's not going to be good. Trust me on this. Let me help you."

Hunter watched intently as her gaze fell, resigned to her situation. Her silence spoke although her lips never moved. While he'd like to think she'd agreed, he knew she hadn't given up easily. It wasn't a sign of submission, but one of temporary acceptance. A brief retreat from her fight; she'd rally. But for now, it'd have to be enough.

Hunter gently curled a finger under her chin. Her lids slowly opened, her gaze meeting his. "I know you've been on your own for a long time. And whatever you haven't told me, that's okay for now. But I'm not letting anything happen to you."

Hunter startled as she quickly wrapped her arms around his waist, hugging him tightly. Her chest rose against his and he sensed it was taking everything she had to keep it together. *Family. Love.* And he'd do whatever it took to give it to her.

Chapter Four

Willa sat on her bed and rested her forehead in her hands. She couldn't believe she'd almost made love to the Alpha. Desire drove her mighty beast to the surface, and she knew that she'd soon shift, her wolf running free.

Once she was healed, destroying the formula was her priority. After the task was completed, she'd have to move far away from Guatemala. Although she hated the thought of leaving her work, the humans she cared for, there was no other option. Using her blood had been a stupid mistake, but now that they knew, she couldn't afford for anyone else to discover how she created the experimental serum.

It had been a serendipitous accident. With a degree in archeology, she'd been drawn to the undiscovered Mayan buildings draped in the jungle foliage. Convinced the long-forgotten ancient civilization held the secrets to modern-day medicine, Willa sought to parse true remedies from myth. Within the confines of sacred stone walls, her discovery of a new plant species changed her perspective on human healing. But it was her own lifeforce that morphed her vision of a cure into a reality.

While slashing through the brush, the machete sliced her skin as well as the leaves. Covered in her blood and the secretions of the plant, the leaves regenerated. A few years of experimenting with the unknown herb led to the perfect ratios, for she'd secretly used it to regrow appendages on injured animals. The formula resulted in rapid renewal and growth of human cells.

After she'd used it to save a mortal life, she suspected the otherworldly event drew the attention of demons. Suspecting her heritage, a band of rogue wolves ambushed and kidnapped her in the middle of the night, killing several villagers during the rampage. Willa imagined the authorities would blame the massacre on drug traffickers. Like many foreigners, she'd simply gone missing. While they'd suspect she'd been sold into human trafficking, the truth was she'd been sold for a pretty price to a hungry demon.

Willa bit her lip and lifted her head, contemplating her enslavement in Hell. Whatever they'd done to her had been so horrific, her mind had gone numb. Although she had no memory of the vampire, his presence had stirred an odd sense of familiarity. But it was the Alpha that made her heart skip a beat.

Ah...the Alpha. Her thoughts were drawn back to Hunter, the way he'd played the piano, then her. Recalling his touch, gooseflesh broke across her skin, a shiver running through her body. *No Willa. Stop thinking about him. It's never going to happen. It's all a lie.*

What she hadn't told him was how she'd hated being on

her own. She'd never deliberately chosen to go rogue. The only choice she'd ever made was to protect her family. They'd all gone their separate ways so as to survive. If anyone ever found out their lineage…they'd be at risk.

Staying in Jackson Hole put Teton Wolves in danger. She'd leave in the morning as promised.

Willa released an audible breath and stretched her neck from side to side. She glanced at the small pile of bags near the dresser. Although she'd spent so many years away from civilization, she recognized the expensive brands. *Versace. Hermes. Chanel.* A small smile formed on her lips. The vampire did have a taste for things other than blood, that was for sure.

But as her fingers trailed over the healing bite marks, she remained guarded. Willa planned on keeping her distance and not tempting fate. No matter how nice he appeared, it was a vampire's nature to feed, and there was no way in Hell she was going to be on the menu.

"Where's the vampire?" She asked as they drove to the bar. Even with her shifter vision, the endless darkness of the plains gave the illusion of them disappearing.

"He prefers to flash." Hunter glanced toward Willa. "It's his thing."

She gave a small smile. "I want you to know…about me leaving. Today, what happened." Willa struggled to articulate her feelings. "It's just…I don't want anything to happen to anyone here in your pack. These wolves are going to come at me again. They..." *Know who I am.* "Know that I've been developing something."

"Developing something? Just what kind of doctor are you?" the Alpha asked.

"Some people fix cars. I fix people. It's what I do. It's what I've always wanted to do. I also have a degree in archeology, so I try to mix the two."

"A bit of an overachiever?"

"You know how it is as immortals. We live a long time."

"That we do," he agreed.

"When I decided to become a physician, there weren't many female doctors. But it didn't matter. I pursued it. Then I traveled the world. The more I traveled, the more I learned. Countries. Cultures. History. Humans. Paranormal creatures. But I always had the same intention no matter what I learned."

"And what was that?"

"I wanted to heal people. Humans are the same all across the world. They experience happiness. Heartbreak. They have strong spirits, but the reality is that they're fragile. They get sick. Die." Willa's thoughts drifted to all those she'd seen suffer, heaviness filling her chest. "Even wolves can be killed, I suppose."

"I get you but it's all the more reason to stay within the pack. There's safety in numbers."

"But what if you couldn't live in a pack? We all take different paths. Being rogue doesn't necessarily mean you're evil."

"No one said that. But it's true that a lot of rogues can't settle. The ones who can't manage to forge a connection with another wolf, they're often looking for trouble." Hunter made a sharp right turn down a single lane road.

"Am I looking for trouble? What about you?"

"First of all, I'm pack. I'm Alpha. And you're…you're," he stammered, "you're not evil."

"But you judge rogues as if you know everything. How do you know I'm not evil?" she challenged. "Who knows what Hell did to me? Maybe I was evil before they took me."

"This isn't my first time to the rodeo, sweetheart. There's two things I can detect. Evil and bullshit. And you're definitely not evil. I'm not sure about the second one just yet. No offense, but there's some missing pieces."

"You're an Alpha. There's a difference between bullshit and being cautious. I just met you. I don't know if I can trust you." A smirk crossed her face. "No offense."

"You trusted me enough at the piano," he countered.

"I…we…we were playing." The memory of his hands on her skin rushed to her thoughts and she fought the arousal.

"Yeah, we sure were. Or maybe I was playing you and you were…"

"Stop." Willa's cheeks flushed. "It doesn't matter." She sighed, her focus drawn back to the topic of conversation. "I'm not though. Just so you know. I'm not evil. But I am independent."

"Told ya. But as for the rogues? There's no reason to choose that life. Being rogue is not what we're meant to do.

Wolves weren't created to live outside of packs and be happy. It's not the way it works."

"Belonging to a pack isn't in the cards for someone like me. The world is my pack."

"I'm afraid we'll have to agree to disagree."

Willa didn't argue further. Although she longed for a pack, she knew where she belonged. With humans, the disenfranchised, with the dead whose secrets were yet to be discovered. She'd continue to provide ambiguous answers without outright lying to the Alpha. But divulging her heritage wasn't an option.

"A few ground rules." Hunter changed the subject.

"Such as…" His strict tone took her off guard. *Alpha*, she reminded herself.

"I know you're used to doing your own thing, but I need you to listen to me if things go south. This is Jackson Hole. This isn't some big city underground blood club we're going to. We don't have a strong vampire presence. A few regulars but mostly transients, many of whom are looking to let loose. It's not strictly vamps either. Witches, wolves. Every now and then we get a fae, but that's rare. You know how they are."

"I…uh, I don't know what you mean," she lied. Willa clenched her hands together, afraid the Alpha would sense the hellfire that lurked beneath her skin.

"Damn fairy almost killed me down in New Orleans a week ago. At least I think it's been a week. Time flies in Hell. And not because you're havin' a good time." Hunter cocked his head and continued. "But like I said, it's rare. To tell the truth, it's either really quiet round here or all hell's breaking loose. With the vampires, you just never know."

"Do you get..." Willa took a deep breath, keeping her voice soft, "demons?"

"We're just like any town really. You can't rule them out. But if you've got to worryin', you don't need to. No one's taking you back, Willa."

"I always knew..." *someone would find out about me*, "someone would want what I've been working on. But I never really thought...I mean I'm strong. But that day..."

"Don't blame yourself."

It's all my fault.

"It could happen to anyone. Not to beat a dead horse, but you were at risk being rogue. But I can promise you this. I'm never going to let anyone hurt you again."

"I knew it was dangerous. The jungle can be unforgiving. Jaguars, crocodiles, poisonous snakes, spiders. But I learned not just how to live there but thrive."

"What made you stay?"

"The people. Adventure. It's a beautiful place. There's thousands of undiscovered ruins within the jungle. I've helped out with a few archeological excavations. And the rainforest is a biodiverse treasure trove. Plants, animals, insects. Microorganisms. It's been theorized there could be a million undiscovered species. It's like nature's pharmacy. Potentially anyway."

"Humans are fragile. I know it's difficult to lose them, but I'm surprised you put yourself at risk like that."

"Wolves have been gifted by the Goddess to live

eternally, which is a double-edged sword when you watch their species struggle." She sighed. "I feel like it's my responsibility to give back."

"Even if it puts you in danger?" he asked.

"Yes. Who better to do it? If I get bitten by a poisonous snake, I shift."

"But depending on the injury, you could bleed out."

"Yes, well. I'm not entirely helpless. I've been around a long time. And before you ask, a lady never tells her age."

"What happened down there? How exactly did they get you?" he pressed.

"It was a stormy night." Willa closed her eyes, letting the memories rush forth. After the torrential rain subsided, she'd heard the squawking chickens. Within seconds, the howler monkeys went wild, their deafening cries alerting her that a predator had made its way into their territory. Although she suspected a jaguar, she knew local gangs had been working their way through the jungle.

It wasn't the first time she'd confronted drug traffickers. As wolf, she'd take them out with great precision, picking them off one by one. They'd barely hear the branches break under their own feet before she'd ripped out their throats. In the morning, it'd be blamed on a jaguar. With no lack of predators in the area, the remains often would be eaten before they were ever discovered.

That wet and tempestuous night, confident she could handle the situation, Willa left her home to investigate the intrusion and padded cautiously into the darkness. As she detected the sulfur in the air, she froze, the silver net instantly immobilizing her. Captured, she'd been forced to shift into her naked human form.

"Willa?" she heard Hunter ask, jarring her from the dark memory.

"Yeah...sorry. I was ambushed. I'd never had a problem before that night."

"Did they hurt you?"

"They, uh, the silver...a little. I wasn't there long." Willa blew out a breath. "There's things. Things about me. Whatever. It doesn't really matter. Whoever came for me the first time...this isn't over. And next time, I'm going to kill them all."

"Is that right now? Well I can't say I blame ya but if you'd open up to me, just a little now, you know I can help you."

"You got me out of Hell. I was distracted. I should have known better. It won't happen again."

"You're damn straight it won't happen again. I didn't just pluck your ass out of Hell to see you..."

"Alpha." Willa settled her nerves and kept her voice calm. "I appreciate what you did for me. I really do. But I don't want to see anything happen to your wolves."

"You ever hear about many people escaping from Hell? I'm not foolin'. Have you?"

The question took her off guard, but she remained true to her position. "Well, no. I've been around long enough to know they don't."

"For whatever reason I was meant to find you. And now that we've..." Hunter paused as he turned down a dark gravel road. Lights flickered in the distance, growing brighter as they approached, "played the piano."

Willa's cheeks flushed at the mention of their encounter and she fought the feelings that tugged at her heart. The Alpha could never be hers.

"You do recall us playing?"

"It was…" She shot a coy smile at the Alpha and quickly turned her gaze out the window. Her stomach flipped and she prayed she could get control of her emotions. "Unforgettable."

"So, I was thinking maybe after we round up these wolves, we could get to makin' a little more music." Although Hunter wore a smile, he kept his eyes trained on the road.

"I'm afraid that may have been a limited engagement."

"You play with others?"

"No. It's just…" Willa sighed, shaking off the memories. "I can't let these assholes come for you."

"As I've said, you're not alone anymore. We're coming up on things here, but I'm thinking we should have a repeat performance."

The corners of Willa's lips tugged upward. Out of the corner of her eye, she spied his flirtatious smile. *Don't go there girl*, she told herself. If you like him, you'll stay away. If the past had taught her anything, it was that anyone she cared about would die.

"Here we go. Up there," Hunter said.

Willa steeled her nerves as they pulled into a parking space, the headlights burning a hole into the darkness. Her thoughts raced. Seeing the same wolves who'd kidnapped her both excited and terrified her. She closed her eyes as another memory of her capture flashed in her mind. The silver scorched her flesh. She writhed in pain, screaming as they kicked her down to the ground, a heavy boot pressing her face into the dirt. Her wolf retreated, unable to shift from the poison. She stared at her attackers, refusing to let tears fall. As the earth cleaved open, flames shot out of the portal to Hell.

"Hey." Hunter's voice broke her contemplation. His gentle touch brought her back to the present and she turned to him. "Willa, I can't pretend to know all you've gone through. But I promise I'll keep you safe tonight, okay? You're not going back to Hell."

"You don't know that." *I want to believe you. It's my fault.* "I thought I was smarter…that night they got me…"

"Look at me." Hunter gently cupped her cheek, his eyes locked on hers. "What happened was not your fault. I know this has to be hard. It's likely these rogue wolves aren't anywhere near here. But you don't need to go with me into the blood club if you're not comfortable. If you want, I can have Viktor flash you back to my house. I'll get Remus to meet you there and keep you safe until I get back. I'll take care of this."

"No. I'm going."

"Listen to me one more time. No one is getting you tonight. Or ever. When I find these wolves who took you, and believe me, I'm going to make it my business to find them, I'm going to kill them. After we get done with this business with the donor and hear her story, you and I are going to have a long talk."

"Yes," she reluctantly agreed.

"All right. Let's do this." Hunter opened his door and exited.

Willa took a deep breath and blew it out, her eyes meeting Hunter's through the window. Her heart tightened with longing for the Alpha. As the door opened, she reached for his hand, unable to control the fiery energy that flowed through her veins. She was certain he'd feel it, but her nature could not be contained.

As they walked toward the entrance, she heard the muffled bass music filtering into the parking lot. The scent of dragon's blood incense hung heavy in the air.

The hair on the back of her neck prickled in awareness. She briefly hesitated and scanned the area but saw no one.

"You okay?" Hunter asked.

"Yes, I thought I heard…"

"Ah, glad you both joined me for the fun."

Willa jumped, a hand touching her shoulder, warm breath on her ear. She spun around on instinct, slamming her fist into the stranger's solar plexus. Viktor tumbled backwards, groaning with a laugh.

"What the fuck is your issue?" Hunter shook his head, his lips drawn tight with annoyance. "You're lucky she hit you and not me."

"Your girl's got a good punch on her." Viktor stood and stretched his arms.

"She isn't my…" Hunter paused. "This isn't a fucking joke. You're going to get someone killed with that shit."

"I agree with the Alpha. In my professional opinion,

there really is something wrong with you. You really should see a doctor about that. Oh, that's right. I am a doctor. I'm afraid there isn't a cure for being a jackass."

Hunter laughed.

"It's good to see you've got some fight in you, doc. It's about time," Viktor told her.

"I've killed vampires like you before." It wasn't as much a threat as a statement of fact. Not many over the years, but she'd withstood her fair share of fights.

"There aren't many like me, so don't test me, pet. I assure you, you will not win." His cool expression warmed into a closed smile. "That being said, I have no intention of hurting you. Always remember that. Even at my worst…" his eyes softened, "I will do right by you."

"I…" Willa stumbled over her words, struggling to remember him. The way he spoke was oddly familiar, as if he'd been a childhood friend she'd long forgotten. Hunter's warm voice brought her focus back to the club.

"Don't pay the vampire any mind." His attention went to Viktor. "I don't want you to go stirring up trouble tonight. We get in and out. If the human you spoke to is here, let's talk to her and get out without causing a fuss, got me?"

"But of course, oh great wolf. Ahroooo," Viktor howled with laughter.

"Fall in line, asshole."

"Ah, yes. Pleasant as always. Shall we?" Viktor extended his hand, ushering them forward.

"Ready?" Hunter asked Willa.

She nodded, and stole a quick glance back at Viktor, who wore an impassive expression. The sound of the heavy wooden door creaking sent her heart racing, and she took a deep breath, putting one foot in front of the other as they stepped into the bar.

A large woman approached, her black leather boots stomping across the room. Long rainbow-colored curls spilled over her shoulders. Her royal blue, shiny, latex corset forced up her ample bosom, flesh spilling over the edges of the tight fabric.

"What are you doing here?" she growled, a scowl painted on her face.

"Come to see you, beautiful," Hunter told her.

Willa's eyes widened with surprise at his statement.

"Come give me some sugar, Alpha." The burly woman stretched out her arms to him with a broad smile.

"No bitin' now," Hunter half joked as he hugged her.

"One of these days you're goin' to give me a go," she promised, laughing.

"Now, you know I'm not lettin' anyone bite me. Nothing personal, but I can't go about doing that, Cheryl."

"I'm just messin' with you. If I were Alpha, I wouldn't be puttin' my pack at risk for a good bite either. And you know I'm good. Real good." She waggled her eyebrows at him.

"That you are, that you are." Hunter wore a cool smile as he scanned the room.

"So, I know you didn't come down here tonight just to see me now, did ya?" Cheryl tilted her head, her gaze painting over Willa. "A new friend?"

"Yes, this is…a friend. She's staying with me a few days." Hunter set his focus on a group of humans who were huddled deep in conversation in a darkened corner.

"Hello." Willa nodded but made no effort to shake hands. Hunter may have trusted the vampire, but Willa didn't and preferred not to give her the chance to sniff her skin.

"A shy one. Well, it takes all kinds to make the world go round. This one here," Cheryl turned to Viktor and gave an audible sigh. "He's a troublemaker. Got to watch him, all right."

"Lovey, you know I'm just a friendly visitor in your establishment," Viktor cooed.

"You're always welcome, indeed," she responded.

As Cheryl gave Viktor a nod, Willa wondered why a stranger would look at him almost with reverence. Her focus settled on Hunter who'd craned his neck, eyeing two girls dancing near the bar.

"We're not here for blood. We're here for humans. Word on the street is a pack of rogues passed through town and roughed up a girl's brother."

"I don't want no trouble with anyone," Cheryl stated, her voice somber. "I'm not a gossip, of course, but I hear things."

"We need to see the girl. In private. We'll need a secure room," Hunter told her.

"I've heard a rumor the Smith boy on Hollow Bend got in a fight last night, but that's all I know. The girl, who goes by the name Shelley, told a few vampires. Can't trust the humans with their stories so I paid her no mind. She didn't say who the wolves were, but I suspected you'd either already know about it or be comin' to see her. Either way, not my responsibility, Alpha. I'm just a bar keep." She held her palms up to the air and smiled.

"You're much more than that, and you know it, but you're right that humans lie. So do vampires. And wolves. It's my business to know the difference. She's over there?"

"Yeah, yeah. The redhead with the blue hair extensions."

"Ah, but she did taste good, though. Like a fine year of wine." Viktor gave a closed smile, recalling his encounter. "Clean as can be. Like a mountain spring."

"He has a way with words, doesn't he?" She gave a hearty laugh.

"So, you've had no strange wolves through here?" Willa asked.

"Darlin', strangers are always passing through town, but rarely a rogue wolf the Alpha doesn't know about." She shook her head. "Now listen, I'd love to stay and chat, but you know I gotta keep tabs on the rooms. I have a few special headliners tonight. You should stay for the show. It's a human vamp act. She strips. He eats then does an artistic dance. I know, I know. It sounds basic. But I'm telling you, they've been getting rave reviews."

"No, thanks. I'm good," Hunter replied dismissively.

"Speak for yourself." Viktor shrugged with a devious smile. "I'm always up for watching a musical act."

Hunter shot him a glare. "No."

"Just like Broadway." Viktor turned to Willa who vacillated between amusement and disgust at his assessment of the situation. "See, she thinks I'm funny."

"I didn't say…" Willa crossed her arms protectively around her chest and guarded her thoughts. *How is he doing that?* No vampire had ever sensed her, let alone read her mind.

"Ignore him," Hunter growled at Viktor.

"The Avocado room is empty, but I think you'll be needing enough space for four, so you'd better take the Coconut room. Plenty of room for play if ya know what I mean. Just got in a new shipment of product from Fiji. You're gonna love it."

"What is she talking about?" Willa asked as Hunter took her hand and led her through a sea of bodies.

"Get the girl and meet me in the back." The Alpha shot out the command at Viktor, but never stopped moving.

Willa studied patrons as they made their way through the crowd. She could sense the humans, the scent of sex and blood filtering through the air. A labored cry tore into the din and Willa twisted her neck, catching sight of a nude man kneeling. His body shook as his mistress ran her long talons over his pale skin right before shoving him onto his back. The female vampire, dressed in a skin-tight purple satin jumpsuit with four-inch spiked heels, smiled as a trail of blood bubbled onto his skin. Willa's mouth gaped open as the man obediently lay flat onto the cold wooden floor and the vampire pressed her foot between his legs, crushing his testicles.

The sadistic mistress's cold eyes flashed to Willa and she hissed in displeasure. Willa stared down the vampire, holding her gaze until she looked away. When she turned to Hunter, she caught the momentary surprise in his expression. He quickly recovered, and his eyes narrowed in on a hallway hidden past the side of a stage.

As they entered, the walls appeared to dance; spiraling tubes of lights dangling from the wall changed colors. Willa imagined the humans might find the rhythmic pulsing unsettling, but she remained unfazed by its intensity.

"Here," Hunter said, opening a bright neon-green door.

"Wow. Okay." Willa's eyes widened as she studied the uniquely decorated room. Coconuts of various sizes and colors were placed about the room. The island-themed wall mural displayed palm trees. "Um…this is different."

"Yeah. Cheryl likes fruit."

"You mean she decorates all the rooms like fruit?"

"Nuts. Flowers too. She's got one for avocados, roses, peanuts. It's kind of a thing." Hunter shrugged.

Willa picked up a coconut, admiring the hand painting. A brightly colored crown adorned its outer skin. "Zulu?"

"Yes. I've brought her a few back from New Orleans over the years. She loves them. Always saying she's goin' home someday." Hunter scanned the room. "The vamps. They're odd birds. Look at Cheryl. She collects things. Human things. She never touches human food, but she's obsessed with…" Hunter gestured to a chandelier made of coconuts. "Stuff. Bric-a-brac. Then you've got a vamp like my friend, Quint. You'll meet him someday. He's a mad chef. Always cooking. Says it reminds him of when he was human. I can't say I blame him. I guess when you think about it, they were all once human. Can't imagine it really. One minute you're eating a slice of pizza, and the next, you're immortal and the only way to stay alive is drinking blood."

"Even wolves are born with the magick in our blood, but I can't imagine needing one specific substance to maintain my life," Willa mused, aware of her origin.

"Vik only drinks blood. Says he's a purist."

"That I do," Viktor exclaimed with a smile, ushering a young woman into the room. She nervously twirled a long blue lock with her finger. Her lips pursed tight, sucking a lollypop. "Ah, life can be so difficult. Perhaps the doctor needs to give me a checkup. And by checkup, I mean…"

"Ignore him," Hunter interrupted.

"Shelley, darling. These are my friends. This is the Alpha, Hunter Livingston. And this is Willa. Doctor to you."

"Hi," she responded, the candy still firmly lodged in her mouth. "I don't do kinky shit. One at a time. No orgies. Besides I can't donate any more blood tonight. I'm just waiting for a few of my friends."

"No orgy. No blood. I'm not a vampire and neither is she." Hunter approached the girl and gestured for her to sit. "Take a seat."

"I'll stand. I'm fine."

"Take. A. Seat," Hunter ordered, his voice laced with irritation.

"I didn't do anything," she whined. Shelley plopped

down onto the sofa and lowered her gaze, staring at a large purple coconut that sat perched on an end table.

"Where's your brother?" Hunter slid a few wooden bar stools toward the sofa.

Willa sat down, carefully studying the girl. She found it curious that certain humans sought out vampires whereas others lived in complete isolation, outright ignoring paranormals. Humans would always serve a purpose to vampires, and she supposed that as long as the supply outweighed the demand, risk would be minimized to their existence. A symbiotic relationship, sustenance in exchange for sexual release. Fair enough but there was always a chance of death, each and every bite.

"It's not the first time he's been beat up," Shelley told them.

"Where is he?" Hunter repeated.

"He's at home now. They released him an hour ago. His friend, Bud, said he's loaded up on painkillers." Shelley removed the red lollypop from her lips and held it up in the air as she spoke. "He's goin' to want me to wait on him hand and foot."

"Viktor here says you told him you saw wolves."

"Yeah, so? They weren't from around here."

"And just how do you know that?" Hunter pressed.

"They wanted to stay in our house."

"What do you mean?" Willa asked.

"I mean you shouldn't answer the door for strangers. They rang. And like a dumbass, I answered. They tried to bust their way in, saying they needed a place to stay.

Something about looking for someone. Can you believe that shit? Like what the fuck?" She rolled her eyes and exhaled loudly. "Ronnie shoved a few of them back out onto the porch and I went for the gun. By the time I got back, they were beating the shit out of him. I shot two. One in the shoulder. I pinged the other one in the knee. It was enough to get them to leave but fucking wolves man, they don't go down like a human would. It's not like I carry silver."

"They shifted in front of you?" Hunter asked.

"Yeah they fuckin' did. I always tell my friends, vampires are safer. More civilized, I say. Hotter too." She shot Viktor a sultry smile as she locked her eyes on his and slowly inserted the sucker back into her mouth.

"You heard it folks. From the mouths of babes." A broad smile crossed Viktor's face.

"Did they say anything about where they came from or where they're goin'?" Hunter ignored the vampire and continued his interrogation.

"Yeah, yeah, we had a whole convo. Seriously? Yeah, no. I just told you that they shoved their way in my house and attacked us."

"Any small detail might help," Willa interjected. "Do you remember how they smelled? What they looked like? Tattoos? Anything at all they said? Maybe a name?"

"Now that you mention it, they smelled like ass."

"Ass?" Viktor laughed.

"Like rotten egg?" Hunter asked.

"More like a whole dozen. Seriously smelled like ass. Disgusting." Shelley's nose cringed.

"Sulfur." The Alpha scrubbed the scruff on his chin, his eyes narrowed on the human.

"They're here." Willa's heart pounded in her chest, and she straightened her back. They'd come for her.

"Anything else?" Hunter pressed.

"Am I getting paid for this because I really would like another drink. My friends are going to be worried about me." Shelley stood and cocked her hip, fiddling with the stick in her mouth.

"I do believe we've all had enough, yes?" Viktor looked to Hunter who nodded. The vampire held the door open gesturing with his hand for her to leave. "It's been such a pleasure to see you again, pet. Happy trails."

As Shelley went to exit, she stopped to stare at Willa. "He was going on about finding a she-wolf. He didn't mention any names but said something about being on her scent. After what he did to Ronnie, I wouldn't want to be her. Just sayin'."

"As much as I love nature, I'm growing bored of the country. Perhaps I'll go to LA." Viktor yawned. "I need a vacation."

"No one's keepin' you here, vamp. You don't have to stay," Hunter told him as he stood. "My pack won't let them get any further. They have no place on our lands."

"I've got to get out of here," Willa insisted. "They're after me. Neither of you have anything to do with this. They've already hurt one human. He could have been killed. The only reason they didn't is because she shot them."

"They shifted right in front of them. They *all* shifted, not just the hurt ones. None of my wolves would ever do something like that. They want us to know they're here. It was a message. What they don't know is who they're dealing with."

"They're here for me. If I leave, you will all be safe." Willa paced and stabbed her fingers through her wild mane. "No, I've got to go."

"You're not going anywhere. We're all in this together."

Viktor picked up a plastic coconut and tossed it into the trashcan. "Can I suggest we retire? I'm so over this place."

"Why are you here?" Willa's expression grew somber, her limbs felt heavy as if they weighed a thousand pounds. She needed to shift.

"It's not my style to leave a friend in need," Viktor replied without emotion. His focus went to Hunter. "You ready?"

"Yeah. Let's get outta here," Hunter replied, giving a nod to Willa.

"Care to flash? We can skip out on the party without interference," Viktor suggested.

"Only out to the parking lot. We brought the car."

"Your wish is my command."

Before Willa had a chance to protest, the vampire touched her shoulder. She sucked a breath as she disappeared, disoriented as they landed outside the entrance.

With the soothing touch of the Alpha's palm on her back, Willa attempted to compose herself. Bent over with her hands on her knees, she struggled to focus on Hunter's face. His lips moved but the pounding in her head drowned out all sound.

"Jesus, Vik…what's going on with her?"

"Flashing is always a problem for wolves. You know that."

Willa coughed back the bile that rolled in her stomach, but soon lost the battle.

"Oh shit." Viktor jumped back, holding his hands up in the air.

"What the fuck did you do to her? Willa. Baby. Come on now." Hunter pulled her into his arms as she panted for breath. Closing his eyes, he concentrated, sending calming energy to his little wolf.

"I'm sorry. I'm so sorry," she repeated. The overwhelming vampire magick, dematerializing, had thrown her own energy off kilter.

"We could have walked," Hunter shot at Viktor, who rolled his eyes.

"How am I supposed to know how sensitive she is?"

"Next time go easy." Hunter looked down to Willa. "Can you make it to the car?"

"Yeah. I'm okay." She nodded her head, willing the fresh air to cleanse her lungs.

"You. We're taking the car." Hunter shook his head at Viktor who shrugged with a smile.

Willa heard the sound of the ticking mere seconds before the explosion. As they turned away from the door, walking toward the car, the force of the blast sent her flying into the air, landing on the grass. Grunting through the blinding pain, she clutched at the damp earth with her fingernails. All her breath rushed out of her lungs, and as she inhaled, the sulfur rushed into her nostrils. *Hell. Wolves.*

Hunter growled, and she lifted her gaze, catching sight of the vampire restraining him from rushing into the fire. They exchanged heated words, and as the Alpha shook him off, Willa screamed for him. *"Hunter!"*

Death hung heavy in the air even as the flames ebbed. Her head spun at the realization that innocents had been killed. Willa sucked back a sob, the blood of the humans and vampires on her hands. *My fault. I should have left.*

Willa grunted, shoving up onto her hands and knees. To no avail, she cried out to the Alpha, "No, don't go. Hunter!"

A firm hand rested on her shoulder. Her stomach tightened in anticipation for his attack. "No, no, no…I won't leave him."

"Come now, Willamina. He knows what he's doing. We've got to get out of here."

"What did you call me?" Splintered memories of Hell slammed into her at the sound of her name on his lips. She punched and clawed at Viktor as he wrapped his arms around her. Struggling, her ferocious energy surged, but she couldn't break free. "No. I'm not leaving him. Let me go."

"Sorry, pet. Consider this an order from your Alpha."

"No, no…" Her voice drifted as she disappeared into the night. *My fault.*

Willa curled into a ball, shaking. Her skin burned with hellfire, her stomach clenched as the room spun.

The fucking vampire had done it again. With her senses on alert, his familiar scent drifted in the air. Her eyes flashed open to see him staring back at her.

"Get away from me," she growled. Her limbs, heavy as rocks, wouldn't move, yet her mind began to race. *Hunter. Demons. Vampire.* "I've gotta go back."

"Forgive me, but I don't think you're going anywhere. If you'd just let me help…"

"No, don't touch me." He reached for her arm and she recoiled.

"You don't seem to understand how this works. I save you from danger. Then you are supposed to say, 'thank you'."

"Fuck you," she spat, bracing herself as another wave of nausea rolled through her.

"Thank you. Fuck you. Close enough." He shrugged. "I suppose they could be used interchangeably. Although I do prefer fucking." Viktor brushed the dust off his jeans and sighed loudly as he caught sight of her fiery glare. "Ah, well. Don't misunderstand. You're lovely but I'm afraid the Alpha would have my head if I touched you."

"As if I'd ever…ahhh," Willa cried, sucking a deep breath through gritted teeth. "What did you do to me?"

"As I explained, wolves don't do well with the transition, I'm afraid. You should be fine in just a bit. Might I suggest you breathe through it?"

"Are you kidding me? Oh Goddess. It hurts." She closed her eyes, fisting the sheets.

"Very curious how this affects you. I wonder if it's the blood." Viktor plowed his fingers through his blond hair.

Willa's heart caught in her chest, numb from his statement. "What did you just say? What about blood?"

"Um, nothing really. You know…my uh…" he stammered and turned to face her, "blood."

"What did you do?" she whispered, her curiosity piqued. The burning in her gut guided her toward the truth. *So familiar.* A memory lingered in the far recesses of her mind. "I know you."

"Well of course you do. We just…"

"*I know you.*" Willa shoved onto her forearms. "Come to me."

"Maybe we should get Hunter." Viktor stood firm.

"Come. Here." Willa's eyes locked on his as she sensed his acquiescence. "Give me your hand."

"Get away. Come here. Which is it, Willamina?" Viktor closed the distance between them.

"I know you." As his palm touched hers, her wolf rushed to the surface, howling. Memories of Hell churned in her mind. The slice of his fangs piercing her skin. Lying helpless as vampires drained her blood. Viktor, crazed and starved, shoving them away, sinking his fangs deep into her neck. She'd begged for mercy, slowly accepting death. In and out of consciousness, she woke to a room dead with silence. The starved vampire lay in the distance. She'd known then he'd saved her.

"I'm sorry, little wolf," Viktor said, his voice soft.

"You, you…you've had my blood." Her heart pounded against her ribs.

"I never meant to hurt you."

"My wolf." Her mighty beast woke, clawing to escape.

Willa's eyes flashed from brown to black, feral as she began tearing at her clothing. Overwhelmed with raw emotion, unfurled fury from her attack surfaced. Memories of the torture rushed over her and she struggled to stand.

"I'll get Hunter," she heard Viktor say but as she transformed, she refused to hear another word.

The vampire scrubbed his palm over his cheek as the angry wolf growled at him. "Well, then. That didn't go as expected."

Willa snapped, her beast wild, lost in the devastation of both captivity and torture. She'd been used as a blood slave, feeding savage creatures of Hell. Reality morphed into demon-fueled memories. As Viktor dematerialized, she paced, aware the rogue wolves roamed Wyoming. She had no choice but to leave. By tomorrow, she'd be gone.

Chapter Five

"Is anyone there?" The Alpha's question was met with silence. As he shielded his face with his arm, he coughed, ash coating his tongue. Red-hot embers crunched beneath his feet as he stepped into what was left of the bar.

He sensed the death all around him as souls left the bodies. Humans and vampires lay strewn among the rubble.

As Cheryl's face came into sight, he rushed to her side. Her lifeless eyes stared up at him as he reached for her. As he tugged the shard of wood out of her chest, he knew it wouldn't make a difference.

"Come on, girl." Hunter hung his head in frustration. "Ah, fuck. I'm sorry. This is some shit."

The familiar stench of Hell teased his nostrils, and Hunter gritted his teeth, his chest tight as he kissed the top of her head. *Fucking demons.*

He'd have to call the police department to claim the human bodies. With no particular vampire in charge of the others in Jackson Hole, he'd have his wolves help dispose of any vampires who weren't cremated by the flames.

A cold drop of water stung his face, the sky rumbling loudly. Lightning flashed across the plains, and he cursed as the torrential downpour commenced. As he headed toward his car, he growled, his mind racing. The wolves who had killed these innocents would suffer. He'd track them to the ends of the Earth and pick them off one by one. No one attacked in his territory and lived to tell about it. Death would come swiftly, and its name would be *ALPHA*.

Hunter sensed the lupine energy the minute he stepped into his home. "What the fuck?"

"Why does everyone keep asking that?" Viktor appeared out of nowhere.

"Where's Willa?"

"Yeah, about that. She's upstairs. She's fine. But…well. You see, we have a little…um, what you'd call a situation."

"I'm in no mood for your jokes, Vik. I've got over a dozen dead vampires being buried or sent to their next of kin. Dead humans too. If these assholes blew up a club tonight, who's to say what else they'll do? I need to consider what's going to happen next. All I know is either way, Willa can't stay here. She's in danger."

"You see. About her." Viktor hesitated. "Alpha, I say this with the utmost respect…your girlfriend…she's an animal in bed. And not in a good way."

"She's not my…ah, forget about it. Just tell me. What in the hell is going on?"

"You feel her, right?"

Hunter took a deep breath, concentrating on her energy. His eyes flashed to Viktor's. Relief coursed through him; he'd been concerned that her traumatized wolf refused to surface. "She's shifted."

"Yes. All is well. Now before you go to her, tell me about what went on after I left." Viktor changed the subject.

"I've got some of my guys out taking care of the vampires. Ones who have families. Whatever you all call them. Your friends? Coven...whatever. If they were close, they're going to find out. The vampires who live here are going to have to find a new place to go for blood. Cheryl handled all that shit. I'm going to put my beta, Remus, in charge for now until we find a new vamp, get a club going. They can't just go around biting humans that aren't donors."

"Technically you're not supposed to," Viktor said with a devious smile. "Accidents happen."

"Don't even fucking joke about it," Hunter warned.

"They wouldn't be wrong, tho. They blew up the whole damn building."

"I've got every wolf in the pack on alert. I've got to catch and kill these assholes. My bet is that they're on the run. We've got to get out there and start looking. They're going to want Willa back in Hell."

"Speaking of Hell." Viktor strode across the living room. He moved to the bar and began searching through the cabinets. "If you hadn't come to get me, I would have died."

"Make yourself at home. Don't be shy." Hunter knew Hell better than anyone. The Alpha fell back into an oversized chair and leaned his head on the cushion, staring up at the ceiling. Although he heard no noise from above, he sensed her energy, her anger. *Willa.* "I've got to convince her to stay with me. It's the only way I can keep her safe."

"Agreed. You know, I never meant to bite her." The vampire set a glass onto the counter and opened a bottle of whiskey, pouring a generous amount into it.

"Are we doing this now? Or should I say again?" Hunter fought long and hard not to live in the past. With his patience tried, he gladly reached for the drink Viktor gave him.

"I don't know how long I was gone," Viktor confessed.

"Over a month." Hunter didn't blink. He'd counted the days, carefully planning his rescue trip.

"I like to eat every day. The longest I've ever gone without….well…" Viktor's brows furrowed in thought. He sank down onto the sofa, lifting his glass to his lips. "My sire was a vicious individual. You know what he did to Quintus. Killed Mao. He drew great pleasure from seeing us all suffer. Days without eating, driving us to madness. He'd laugh as we nearly killed the unwilling humans he threw at our feet. It was all a show to him. He wanted us to kill. To be like him. To turn to darkness. To revel in those demonic tendencies that drove his very existence. But you see that's not how it works. One must have chosen this path in life in some aspect. Still it didn't stop him from trying."

"It's not like you and Quint are a couple of boy scouts." Hunter lifted the rim to his lips, the warm golden fluid gliding down his throat.

"We don't kill for sport." Viktor's eyes locked on Hunter's, his tone serious.

"Good to know." A corner of his lip turned upward, his tone laced with sarcasm.

"Demons. They enjoy the sport. They enjoy the death and torture. In Hell it's a free-for-all."

"I know better than you think." When he'd been trapped in the underworld, he'd lost track of time. He'd found out later he'd been gone for over a year.

"I've never gone longer than a week without blood and by that time, I'd been feral. So, when I saw Willa…"

Hunter slowly blinked, forcing himself to listen.

"I told you I didn't hurt Willa, but I fed from her."

"You could have drained her dry." As his hands tightened around his glass, he sucked a breath, forcing himself to remain calm.

"I won't deny it, but you can hardly blame me."

"No, I kinda can blame you. For all kinds of things. But…but…" Hunter held up a finger. "You did not ask to go to Hell. That I do know. Which is why I decided to come get you. Quint had his hands full. And so…"

"We digress. Willa. I didn't mean to drain her to the point I did, but there is only so much control I have. I did not hurt her."

"I don't want to know this part." The thought of Willa in the throes of sexual release angered him. She didn't ask for any of it.

"I know what you're thinking, but you know how it works. There is no other way. But if you're worried…I was in no condition to…well, you know…take things any further. And poor thing…she was in no condition either."

"What is your fucking point, Vik?" Hunter forced an impassive expression, concealing his relief. Thank the Goddess he hadn't touched her.

"Ilsbeth. I don't know why she was there. Or how she got there. But she intervened. She offered me her blood."

"Talk about a deal with the devil."

"No, there was something different about her. She wasn't Zella or whoever she'd said she was down in New Orleans. She was the high priestess. As real as you and I are sitting here. She whispered a spell upon Willa."

"Jesus Christ."

"I don't think it was a curse or anything like that. Willa simply fell into a deep healing sleep. Then she offered her blood and I took it. I can't explain it. I don't know how she got there."

"Samantha said she'd escaped the coven. But she also said that there was no way she could have left on her own."

"There you go. She'd been beaten when she'd come to me. She gave me her blood, but I'd given her my blood too."

"Jesus. You know better than to give that witch anything. What the fuck were you thinking?" Hunter shook his head. "Don't answer that. You weren't thinking, because you were in Hell."

"Nothing can be done about it now. I've had her blood and she's had mine. No harm no foul."

"Says you now. Next week when she turns you into her love slave, don't say I didn't warn you."

"I'm not daft, wolf. Ilsbeth is clever all right. She's literally danced with the devil and his demons. But she's not quite as old as I am. The truth of it is that sometimes your enemies become your friends when there is a greater enemy who is set on destroying both of you. You adapt. Survival of the fittest."

Hunter downed the rest of his whiskey and set his glass on the table. "Look, Vik. What do you need to tell me about Willa before I go up there? Because I'm getting ready to lock the wards down on this house and go to bed. You're welcome to the guest room."

"She's in your bedroom. Not that I've had the pleasure of being in your bed, but a man's dominion is quite easy to determine."

"You're never going to be in my bed either. Why are we even talking about this?" Hunter stretched his neck from side to side. "Willa. Tell me what happened."

"She remembers."

Hunter's stomach tightened, his lips drawn tight together. "Fuck."

"Yes, well. Before you panic…"

"I'm Alpha. I don't panic."

"Before you go storming into your bedroom."

That was exactly what Hunter planned on doing but kept silent, listening.

"She…um…well…"

"Spit it out."

"She was a little upset with me. You see she seems to have a bit of trouble with me dematerializing. So, this is an issue. We got to talking about this. She wasn't exactly pleased about her condition or leaving you. And I happened to mention that it could have been…maybe something to do with blood."

"Did someone drop you on your head while you were in Hell? Because for a thousand-year-old vampire or however old your ass is, you don't seem too smart."

"Don't be an asshole. Correct that. A big asshole."

"I'm pissed off. That you've had her blood. That you just told her what happened." Hunter snatched his glass and stood, walking over to the bar.

"I didn't tell her everything. Her memories. They're coming back on their own. It was inevitable. I may have filled in a few pieces but not all of them."

Hunter poured another drink and shoved it aside. He flattened his palms on the cool granite bar, reminding himself that Willa didn't belong to him. She was a rogue wolf he'd found in Hell, not one of his own. Still, anger coursed through his veins.

"I don't want anything happening to her."

"You saved me, yes?" Viktor strode to the bar and stared at the Alpha. "I owe you. And because I owe you, you will have the truth."

"What is it?"

"When we were in Hell. She tasted…powerful. Old. Her blood was different."

"She's a wolf."

"She's a wolf but I could have sworn there was something else. I've had many wolves over the centuries but her blood…she's hiding something."

"I know she's hiding something. Whoever is chasing her clearly wants something. Selling someone to Hell isn't an easy task. You risk getting your own ass fried. No." Hunter plowed his fingers through his hair, exhaling loudly. "They're in with demons. They're not everyday rogues."

"Her blood. Something about it. I know it was Hell. The sulfur. The rancid odors skew your taste. But she tasted… tainted."

"Like from a demon?"

"I don't know. It's not like I go around biting demons. It's just there was something unusual about her blood. Almost like a fae. But not really." Viktor's lips drew into a tense line as he looked toward the fire. "I don't know what's going on with her, but I know there is something off. I'm not letting you or her out of my sight."

Hunter's eyes widened. "She's not a demon."

"I didn't say she was a demon. I just said her blood is tainted."

"Willa is not a demon," Hunter repeated, his voice louder.

Viktor shook his head and turned to meet the Alpha's gaze. "You can't tell me you haven't noticed something. Something different about her. Anything."

Hunter clenched his fists. He'd detected her unique energy the first time he touched her.

"You have noticed. I know you have," Viktor insisted. "You're an Alpha. If she's your mate you'll find out some day."

"Mate? Hold up. Let me get this straight. First she's a demon and now she's my mate?" Hunter held his hands up. "This convo has officially gone off the rails. I think I've had enough to drink."

"Don't play me, Hunter. Your actions speak volumes. You brought a total stranger into your home. Your bed. You don't just pat her on her head, give her a few bucks and send her on her merry way."

"I would do that for anyone," he lied.

"I suggest that you be truthful with yourself before you go demanding honesty from Willa. Because if she's a demon, you'll have to kill her."

"She's not a demon. And the only people I'm killing are the wolves who killed all those people tonight. This ends now."

"Fine. Ignore me. But since I can see you aren't going to watch your own back, I'm going to be doing it for you."

"I have a beta for that. Remus will be back soon."

"I don't like him."

"You don't know him. And it doesn't matter. Remus will do fine to help me with Willa."

"No, he won't, because I'm here."

"Suit yourself." Hunter looked to the stairway, listening for Willa. "She's quiet. I've got to go talk to her."

Hunter walked from behind the bar, turning his back to the vampire. As he placed his hand onto the stair rail, the Alpha heard his voice.

"One more thing." Viktor chuckled.

"What?" Hunter's faced tensed in aggravation.

"She's not very tame," Viktor called to him.

"Wolves aren't tame. She's an animal."

"Ah, good then. It brings us back to my original statement about her being an animal in bed. Still funny."

"Not even a little bit."

"You're going to have your hands full. She didn't want to listen to me."

"You're not her Alpha." Hunter gave a small smile as he ascended.

The vampire had one thing right, he'd taken Willa into his pack, expecting her, a rogue, to submit to him. Yes, there indeed was something extraordinary about the she-wolf but he refused to believe she could be demon. Viktor may have been ancient, but he'd also been in Hell for over a month. All his time in Hell could have affected not only his taste but his mind. In the underworld, demons manipulated memories and perceptions of reality. They forced their victims to do horrible things they'd never thought they were capable of doing.

Secrets? Yes, Willa kept several, but he couldn't fault her sense of self-preservation. Her secrets had most likely kept her alive all these years, surviving on her own with no pack. Soon, he'd unravel them all.

As he strode toward his bedroom and wrapped his fingers around the doorknob, excitement pumped through him. Tonight, his beast would meet hers.

Hunter closed his eyes and reached for Willa, warning her of his intention to open the door. He smiled, realizing she'd blocked him. He'd extended her a courtesy, but his little she-wolf would soon learn he wouldn't be denied the truth.

He heard the growling as he opened the door. The sight of the majestic, spectacular she-wolf lying on his bed sent a shiver up his spine.

"You're beautiful." Hunter's heart pounded faster as he grew closer to her. "I think it's about time we had a talk."

Only one thing would convince her to shift, to submit. His beast paced, itching to be released.

"Easy, Wills. I hear you've been having some memories." Hunter began to peel off his clothing, readying to shift. "The vampire. Now I know what you're thinkin'. He can be a bit of an asshole, but I consider him a friend. Most days anyway. His brother, Quint, cares about him. It's why I went into Hell to grab his ass." As he unzipped his jeans, he focused on the white feral wolf, never taking his eyes off hers.

"I know more than anyone that Hell is a place of nightmares. You can't remember when you went in or when you came out. Time is relative. Your memories fail you, or your mind is tricked into believing things that never happened. The torture plagues you and you never think you can shake it, but then you do. You go on with your life. You find happiness again."

Hunter tossed his jeans on the floor, standing nude before her. "I know you're not going to come back to this world as a human and that's all right with me. Sometimes

Willa, we've got to go back to what we know. The most basic of our selves. Our truth. And right now, you're gorgeous and wild. But you're no longer a rogue. You may not be pack yet but you're mine."

Willa snapped and snarled in response.

Hunter smiled with a small laugh. "I know you're special. I know you have secrets. But there's something I need to tell you. You can't hide anymore. I'm Alpha."

Hunter sent his magick spiraling through his body, transforming into his beast. All his wolves would sense his infinite power. As his paws hit the floor, he released a deafening howl.

The Alpha set his sight on Willa. Her fur bristled in response, her haunches raised as she gave a low growl. The Alpha grew excited as he slowly stalked toward her. *Mine*, the wolf urged. His beast demanded her submission, but his humanity warned it was too soon.

The Alpha jumped on the bed and Willa barked at him. As he crept closer, she stood her ground, frozen as he nudged his muzzle into her fur.

The Alpha inhaled her scent, his wolf recognizing her as his. Her low growl drifted into silence as he circled around her. He noted how she kept her eyes trained on his every movement but didn't make a move to shift or run.

Hunter's heart raced as she studied him. The beast inside called to her. *Willa.* She blinked but showed no other sign of communication. Hunter slowly backed away, focused on the wolf. *Willa*, he called louder, his mind to hers, and she barked in response. *Yes. Come to your Alpha.* A rush of adrenaline pumped through his veins, and he quickly shifted back to his human form.

"I know you can feel me. I also know you don't want to get that close to an Alpha. My power…" Hunter deliberately released his energy, tendrils dancing around her. "All the wolves just felt it. Even the rogues, the ones who just killed everyone at the club. Even you."

Sitting on the bed, Hunter closed the distance, and he instinctively reached for her. Her intermittent low growl quieted as his fingers brushed over her fur.

"That's a girl. You're safe here. It's okay to just feel. To feel me. To feel in touch with my wolf." Hunter gave her a sympathetic smile. "It's okay to be angry about what happened in Hell. I wasn't happy either when I found out, but here's the thing…Viktor…I know he can be…" Hunter shrugged, "difficult. Arrogant. Ridiculous at times even. But he's got this part of him that's decent. I'm not saying he doesn't do bad shit, because I know he's Quint's brother and the two of them are a couple of bad asses. But he's not going to kill an innocent. It's just not his style."

Willa's muscles relaxed underneath his palm as he stroked her, his voice soft. "I know what Hell is like, Willa. Not just this time when I chose to go back. I've actually been there on a more permanent basis…kinda like you. It's not like I don't know what it feels like. To lose time. To not remember. Then to have flashbacks of the torture. I get it. And the only thing that got me through it was being around pack. Friends."

Hunter's heart caught as she transformed before him.

She quickly reached for the blanket, tugging it over her bare body. Wolves didn't usually shy away from nudity, yet she'd been secluded for so long from others, she'd adopted more human norms.

Willa stared at him, her long brunette locks draped around her face. "Is that what we are? Friends?"

Hunter chuckled. "Yeah, I'd like to think that, but we make nice music together."

"That we did." Willa gave a small smile. "About Viktor…"

"You don't have to talk about it if you don't want to. But if you do, I'm here."

"I don't feel a bond to him," she insisted. "I…I don't know why that matters. I don't want to be bonded to him."

"I've known a lot of vampires and they usually need to be close to someone to form a bond. And when they do, it's not a real bond like the one they form with their mate."

"I know that but it's just…I don't let others bite me. Not vampires." She averted her gaze, her lips tensed. "Not wolves."

"There's something about you, sweetheart. I know you're special. I don't know what it is."

"What's what?"

"Your secret. But I'm a patient man and a firm believer in having people make the right decisions themselves."

"What makes you think me telling you my secret is the right decision?" she asked.

"I risked my ass to get you outta Hell. And I'd do it again. You can trust me."

"I'm not trying to be difficult. You have to understand. The people who died tonight. That's on me. My fault. Not yours. Not Viktor's. My secrets are what put me in Hell. It's why these assholes are here, killing people. They know it. I know it."

"Look at me, Willa."

She slowly raised her gaze to meet his, and as their eyes locked, his pulse raced. This beautiful creature was in his mind and his bed, his wolf urging him to take her.

"I want your agreement that you'll stay with me for a while. Whether that's here or wherever we find the wolves who did this. You can come with me when I track them down and we'll go get whatever you need in New Orleans and Guatemala along the way. But I want your agreement on this."

"And if I don't?"

"I'm an Alpha. I can force you to stay here. I don't want to have to do that because I know you've been traumatized already but I can't…I won't let you run off on your own, knowing full well they could try to put you back in Hell. Now, I know you're thinking to yourself that I'm not *your* Alpha, that you're not in a pack and can do whatever you want. While I'd generally agree and have no say, I simply cannot let you go off alone. You…" *belong to me,* "are my responsibility."

"You're not my guardian angel."

"Make no mistake, I'm no angel, period. It's not in my repertoire."

"Why do you want to do this? Is this an Alpha thing?"

"Yeah, it's an Alpha thing, but if I'm being straight with you, this is a friend thing. This is about someone who cares about you. Someone who knows there's something different about you but who doesn't care what your secret is. Someone you can trust to have your back."

"It's not like I don't want someone to help me." Willa's face softened. "I just…what just happened. There will be others. They will do anything to put me back in Hell."

"Let em' try. I'll be waiting. But in the meantime, I'll be there for you, and when you're ready," *because she is going to tell me sooner or later,* "you'll tell me your secrets. Stay."

Hunter studied her as she took several seconds, mulling over his offer.

"I'll stay for a little bit, but I can't stay here long. I know I said I needed to go to New Orleans, but I've thought about it. I should go back to Guatemala first. There something I've got to take care of."

"All right. Then I'm goin' with. Whatever you've got yourself into is far too dangerous. If these rogues are using demon magick, they are going to be able to track you wherever you go."

Hunter noted the mystery swirling in her dark brown eyes, as she drifted deep into thought. He'd stepped into danger more times than he could count. It was precisely how he'd landed his ass in Hell the first time, but he'd be damned if he allowed Willa to go it alone. She'd learn in time that pack was more than family. It was home.

"I've been many things in this lifetime. A daughter. A sister." Willa exhaled slowly, her soft gaze drifting to Hunter.

In the moment of silence, the Alpha noted the sadness in her voice, and reached for her hand.

"A musician. An artist. A dancer. A doctor…ultimately a scientist." Willa gave a thoughtful smile. "We wonder why we are here. Immortal. Blessed. Some say cursed to live forever. There are days when I truly wonder what the meaning of this life is."

Hunter's eyes painted over her lithe body as he contemplated the question that plagued so many immortals. It was both simple and complicated. "Depends what you seek. I'm committed to this pack, to leading for as long as the Goddess sees fit. While we live forever, I do not believe we are infallible. The vampires tonight are proof of that. Tell me, Willa. What do you seek?"

"I'd never been happier than as a doctor. I used my skills to care for the humans as best I could. But like we talked about, they are so fragile. When I lived in Brazil, I spent time searching the Amazon for medicinal plants, but in Guatemala, I discovered something special. You see, the rainforest is ripe with undiscovered species of plants, animals, bugs. And so…"

"What did you find?"

"A plant. It showed potential on its own. Specimen Alyamya, it's just a name I gave it. It doesn't matter. What matters is that it had the capability to quickly heal skin, generating new cells on cuts and scrapes. But it wasn't like your average antibiotic cream. Within hours, a minor injury would heal."

"Like magick?" Hunter raised a questioning eyebrow.

"I just thought if it could heal skin that quickly…" She sighed.

"You asked for demon help?" he asked.

"No way," she protested, her voice raised at the prospect. "But I did alter it. I used my blood." Willa cringed, guilt settling in her gut. "Look, I know I shouldn't have done it."

"Wolf blood doesn't heal humans," Hunter challenged. "Vampire blood can for minor things, but you know they'd never allow that shit to go viral."

"I know. It's my blood…I don't want to get into it right now." *It's different.* "The bottom line is that it worked a little too well. It's not like I showed or even told anyone. No one but my friend, Janet. I only told her about the plant. She worked at the University in New Orleans."

"Wolf?"

"No. She's human. I met her at a conference. We attended a stem cell seminar together. I think something happened to her. She wasn't responding before I was kidnapped. Since I've been out of Hell, I haven't tried to contact her. It doesn't really matter because she didn't have the formula I used."

"You think she has something to do with the wolves attacking you?"

"I don't really know. I don't think so. But I do know that someone found out."

"Is it possible she told a pharmaceutical company? There could be big money in it. You know they're dippin' their fingers into the Hell fountain. Look at the kind of shit they do to the humans. Some of it's not so great. Many humans die because they can't even afford half the shit they sell."

"I don't know. When I talked to Janet, she wasn't all that impressed with what I told her. You know how scientists are. If you haven't studied it, proven it, it doesn't even exist. She didn't have any samples."

"Who else knows about this plant?" Hunter asked.

"Only one person from the village knew about the serum. Yoselin, my nurse. But there's no way she'd tell anyone. My memory is fuzzy, but she died that night. Before they shoved me into the portal, she came running out of the house. Screaming that others had been killed. When she went to help me, they ripped her throat out."

"You sure she's the only person who knew?"

"I had no choice. I couldn't let her die."

"Who?"

"Fatima. She's only five years old. Just the cutest little girl you've ever seen. She'd been out playing and fell onto a machete that'd been accidentally left in a field. The wound to her leg was severe. With the amount of blood loss…"

"You used the plant on her?"

"Yes," she admitted. Her voice wavered as she continued. "But not just the plant extract. It wouldn't have been enough to save her. I knew it wouldn't be. You have to understand. She would have died."

"What did you do?" Unlike vampires, wolves didn't possess the ability to save humans. Although she'd denied asking demons for favors, he suspected she'd engaged in some sort of dark magick.

"I'd experimented." Willa bit her lip and rolled to her

side, still holding Hunter's hand. "My blood."

"Your blood? You're not a vampire."

"No. But I'm not like other wolves. I told you. My blood is special."

"Willa. Wolves don't heal humans. Sometimes we can help heal other wolves, but never humans." *Tainted.* Viktor's comments echoed in his mind, but he refused to believe she was demon.

Willa moved to sit up but didn't release her hand. His arousal heightened as she placed her palm to his chest, gently guiding him onto his back. Hunter made no move to cover his nude body as she knelt next to him.

"Well, this has taken a turn for the better." Hunter flashed her a sexy smile. "But wolves still don't heal humans."

"My blood is special."

"You are special," Hunter told her. He couldn't deny the attraction to the creature he'd saved from Hell. His wolf urged him to take her, but he slammed down the instinct, focusing on her full lips as she spoke.

"I'm wolf. But my blood…it's different. You can feel me."

"Yes, I…" The Alpha's words silenced as her fingers trailed down his chest toward his abdomen. His skin tingled in their wake.

"What you are feeling is my blood. My power." Her lips curled upward. "It's magick in my blood. You can feel it. See it."

Hunter glanced down to his abdomen, astonished to see

a trail of light along his skin. "What are you doing?"

"These are the secrets I share with you tonight, Alpha."

Willa dragged the pad of her thumb over his hip. Blood rushed to his cock as her fingers teased lower down his abdomen.

"Who are you?" he asked, not really caring at the moment where she came from or the fact his skin was glowing.

"I do have a secret I will tell you." Willa leaned toward him, a whisper on her lips. "I…I…I want you."

Hunter's pulse raced as she drew closer, the heat of her body emanating onto his. The beast paced, his prey within reach. Willa's fingertips brushed the edge of his cock, and he lost control.

A moan escaped her lips as Hunter flipped her onto her back. Although logic told him to stop, to press her for the truth, he gave into his craving. His lips crushed upon her mouth, his tongue dancing with hers. She tasted like honey and fire, her mouth desperately seeking his.

Willa moaned into his kiss, and he lifted his gaze to meet hers, murmuring into her lips. "Sweetheart, I've gotta have you. Please tell me you want this."

She nodded, grasping at his shoulders. As her lips brushed his, seeking his kiss, she tilted her hips upward, grazing her pelvis against his.

"Let's make some music," she whispered, her sultry voice twisting through him.

His mouth went to her neck and she arched her back as he peppered kisses down to her collarbone. Her fingers tunneled into his hair as he continued his journey, his lips trailing down her chest and sucking her nipple into his mouth.

"Yes," she cried, her hands full of his hair. She sighed as he released her breast, his lips trailing down her stomach to her pelvis.

"Little wolf. Little wolf." Hunter sucked a quiet breath as he gently pressed her knees open, exposing her glistening pussy. The Alpha thrummed his thumb through her wet folds and over her clitoris. Her hands gripped his shoulders as he blew gently across her slick heat. "I'm going to devour you."

"Alpha…" Her words disappeared as his tongue delved through her labia, teasing her sensitive nub.

At the taste of her, his beast paced, warning him that this one was his. Feral, it sought its mate. Ignoring his wolf, he indulged, lapping at her clit. Devouring her as if he was a starved man, he teased his devilish tongue over her swollen bead, holding her hips firm as she began to tremble beneath him.

His fingers traveled under her bottom and teased toward her core. She arched her back, moaning in delight, as he slid a thick digit deep inside her, continuing to flick over her clit.

"Hunter…oh Goddess." As he brought her toward her climax, her nails dug into his shoulders. "I've got to…please…"

Her urgent cries for release stirred his beast. *I know her.* His cock hardened to concrete.

Easing a second finger inside her, he curled the tips along her sensitive strip of nerves. Lapping at her clitoris, he plunged his fingers inside her tight core.

"Now, please," she urged, shaking as her orgasm tore through her.

Her hands moved once again into his hair. The sweet sting on his scalp caused a sexy smile as he rose above her, in awe of her ethereal beauty. She wore a glow upon her skin, her hungry eyes drinking in the sight of him.

"You…you're…I…" she panted, unable to speak coherently.

"I've got to be in you now," he said, his voice low and sexy. Nothing could keep him from having her. This woman. This wolf. Something about her drove his savage instincts feral.

"Yes…yes." She nodded.

As he drove his cock deep inside her pussy, Hunter heard the whisper on her lips. "Mine."

He went still, his body electrified with arousal. Like a teenager with uncontrollable urges, he fought the wave of climax. *Mine. As in mine? She can't be my mate. That isn't what she said.* His wolf roared in his mind. *Fuck, no. Deal with this later. Oh shit. I am not coming. Don't…no!* He sucked a breath, forcing the suggestion to the back of his mind.

"My Alpha," she breathed, caressing his cheek. Her hips moved flush to his, her tight pussy accepting every hard inch of his shaft.

Convinced she'd read his thoughts, his lips went to her neck, nipping and licking as he pumped in and out of her. He couldn't face her in this moment, only lose himself within her arms. His wolf would betray his lust for her, its claim that she belonged solely to him, not just as pack but as mate.

His mouth on her breast, he bit upon a taut tip, eliciting a gasp. She moaned as he released her nipple, begging him to increase his pace.

"Harder…yes…please…faster."

The Alpha's lips brushed between her supple breasts. "Ah sweetheart, your wish is my command."

Withdrawing his dick, he gave her a wicked smile as she moaned in protest. Hunter reached for her waist, flipped her onto her stomach, and positioned her bottom toward him.

With one swift thrust, he slammed inside her. Willa cried in ecstasy as he filled her. She clutched at the covers, pressing her bottom toward him.

"That's. It. Ah…yeah. Fuck me…yes," she cried.

"You've got no idea what you're doing to me." He couldn't possibly tell her what was happening. Hunter's body tingled with magick, raw and feral energy twisting through him from the top of his head to his toes. This woman drove his beast wild, his humanity foreshadowed by the wolf.

Her pussy spasmed around his cock as he thrust inside her, his fangs elongating as he fought the release. Fucking hell, he'd have her all day long and it would never be enough for him.

Claim her, his wolf urged. And as he plunged inside her, coming hard, he leaned toward her shoulder. *No. Stop. Do not fucking claim her,* he told his beast, his teeth nearly grazing her skin. Turning his head quickly, he wrapped an arm around her chest and cupped her breast.

As the waves of energy rolled through him, his release subsided. The sound of her panting softly underneath him, giving a gentle moan of satisfaction, seized his chest. *What is happening? I found my mate in Hell? She can't be my mate. Shit. I'm so fucked.*

Hunter slowly removed himself from her and adjusted onto his side. He reached a hand around her abdomen and drew her closer to him and pressed his lips to the top of her head. *What am I going to do?*

"My Alpha," she whispered, drifting off to sleep.

And in that moment, he knew the exact answer to his own question. *Mate.*

Chapter Six

What did I just do? I want to keep him. But I can't. Willa's mind raced, her heart pounding. Making love to Hunter wasn't the plan. She should have been far away from Jackson Hole by now. But the Alpha had a way of putting her at ease. He filled her with warmth, his wolf driving her wild.

She'd rarely shifted in front of other wolves. But tonight, she'd deliberately revealed her beast to the Alpha. Immediately sensing his presence, she'd patiently waited. Demonstrating both her strength and her vulnerability, she allowed him onto the bed. When he'd shifted into his magnificent wolf, Willa thought her heart would burst. Lethal and loving, Hunter exemplified Alpha to the extreme. His power nearly matched hers, and her wolf told her he belonged to her.

As his teeth brushed over her shoulder, every cell in her body had gone into alert. *Mine.* She'd said it and heard his voice. Torn between screaming at him to stop or urging him to do it, she'd lost herself in her climax, feeling only him, ignoring the call to mate.

Alone for so many years, she'd thought it nearly impossible. The stories traced back to the genesis wolf pack. The Goddess generated the species, a small group of humans giving birth to first wolves. Their coveted blood was sought after a wolf was sold to Hell. The Goddess had ended the royal line with the Hellfire in which it was born. As a final member of the last royal generation, Willa would never mate or breed, living a life of solitude and service.

Willa snuggled into Hunter's embrace, reveling in the warmth of his body. She brought his fingertips to her lips and kissed them. Her wolf howled in celebration. For the first time in her life, she was no longer alone.

The dominant Alpha had shown her trust, mastering her body. Making love to her in a way no man had ever done, Hunter had broken through her barrier. While she hadn't divulged all her secrets, she'd softened and shared more than she'd thought possible.

Willa shoved doubts and fears to the back of her mind. Tomorrow, she'd return to her senses, she'd go back to the jungle and destroy the formula. But for the next few hours, she'd steal time within Hunter's arms. *My Alpha.*

The warmth of the sun on her face woke her long before she heard the voices. Dreams of her Alpha chasing her through fresh fallen snow danced in her mind. Safe within her fantasy, Willa fought opening her eyes. Tightening the sheet into her fist, she curled it against her chest and rolled to her side. Her Alpha's scent lingered on the fabric and she smiled.

Shouting male voices jolted her from her dream, and she shot upward.

Although tempted to leap from the bed, she stilled, listening intently. Her eyes drifted to the empty space next to her. Hunter had left her without saying a word. Doubt crept into her thoughts, her stomach tightening. *Did he just want to fuck me? Did I imagine the call of my wolf for his? Shit.*

Reality set in and her lips drew into a tight line, her heart sinking. Why would an Alpha mate with a rogue? He said himself they were trouble. He had no reason to trust her.

She was a liability to him and his pack. Once he found out about her lineage, he'd never want her.

The shouting grew louder, and her heart caught in her chest. *Oh Goddess. It can't be him.* While they hadn't spoken in years, she'd never forget the sound of his voice. Irmão. *What is he doing here?* Panic raced through her veins as she sprang from the bed and reached for a robe that was draped over its frame. Willa stabbed her arms through the sleeves and quietly padded across the floor. She wrapped her fingers around the door's brass handle, pushed it open, cringing as its hinges creaked loudly. As she stepped into the hallway, she heard a door slam, the voices becoming distant. With stealthy agility, she ran down the staircase.

She peeked around the corner but saw no one. Catching a flash of the Alpha through a window, she ran to the sliding glass door and peered outside. Two males struggled to break free as Hunters' men restrained them. *Irmão. What is he doing here?* Without thought to her own safety, she slid open the door, and bounded outside.

"Tie them up," the Alpha growled.

"Kiss the ground, asshole." A large muscled male, who she recognized as Remus, grunted, shoving the bound male to his knees.

"Stop," Willa cried. She should have been calm. Played it cool. But as her feet carried her to him, her heart raced.

"Willamina?" he asked, blood dripping from his lip.

"Irmão," she cried. Tears spilled down her face. It had been years since she'd seen him in person.

"What are you doing?" Hunter rushed toward Willa. He reached for her and attempted to lift her onto her feet, but she batted him off, caressing her palm over the cheek of the rogue wolf. "What are you doing? This man killed a wolf tonight."

"No, no…" she repeated. Willa had known him her entire life. "If he hurt anyone, it would be for good reason."

Her gaze drifted to the other man who leered at her.

"I see the bitch got her some Alpha dick. Hope you enjoyed it because you're goin' back to Hell soon," he spat at her.

"Fuck you," Willa screamed. With her heart pounding, she jumped to her feet and swung her fist at him, landing it square on his jaw. Blood sprayed in the air, his head thrashing to the side. As she went to punch him a second time, firm hands wrapped around her waist, pulling her away.

"We need to question him first, Willa," the Alpha told her.

"No, he's mine. None of the rest of you will touch him."

"They don't know about you, Princess." A diabolical, bloodstained grin flashed across the rogue's face.

"I'm going to kill you," Willa threatened as she attempted to break free. "Let me go this instant. I have every right to kill him."

"Nah, bitch. None of youse is going to have the pleasure. I'm goin' to Hell and none of you gonna stop me."

"You're going to die," Willa screamed, lunging toward him. But she was no match for the Alpha as he tightened his grip.

The wolf broke free of the others, shifting before they had a chance to grab him. Hunter immediately released Willa and transformed, his dominant black wolf snatching the enemy by its neck.

Viktor flashed behind her, instantly restraining her from going after the rogue. "No!!!"

Without hesitation, the Alpha clamped his jaw upon the wolf's neck and violently shook it, tearing away a chunk of its flesh. Blood sprayed into the air as he thrashed its dead body from side to side.

The Alpha spat the corpse from his mouth and circled around to face the pack of men who had gathered. He gave a victorious howl into the crisp morning air, a warning to any rogues that their death would come next.

Willa's heart pounded in her chest, both grateful he'd killed her attacker but angry he'd deprived her of justice, wanting to kill him herself. The sight of his spectacular strength, the dead wolf at his feet, called to her beast. *Alpha.* The word resonated through her as if he'd spoken it out loud.

Her focus shifted to the man on his knees. She wrenched away from Viktor and fell to the ground at his side.

"Julian."

"Willamina. We've got to get out of here. What are you doing here with this pack?"

"She's mine." The Alpha transformed, towering over them.

The dominant tone of his voice sent shivers through Willa, but she concealed her reaction. "Let him go. I know this wolf. He's not capable of whatever you are accusing him of doing."

"I'm plenty capable," Julian challenged. "I restrained this asshole who just had his throat rearranged. I was on my way to bring him to the Alpha when meat head over here," he glanced at Remus, "and his goons decided to attack me. What are you doing with this guy, anyway?"

"Julian. Give me a minute." Willa lifted her gaze to meet Hunter's hard stare. "Trust me. Hunter. Alpha." She lowered her eyes. "I swear to you on my life. I know him. He's a good man. Please release him. I need to talk to him now." She turned her head and glared at Remus. "Alone."

"What are you doing here? Oh Goddess…look at your face." Willa reached for Julian, gently touching the red welt on his lip.

"It's nothing. I'll shift and I'll be fine." He winced and batted her fingers away.

"But you're hurt."

Julian sniffed and went still, his eyes trained on hers. "You're different."

"I don't know what you're talking about." Willa crossed her arms. She turned toward the window and walked away, her thoughts drawn to Hunter.

Although she'd convinced him to release Julian, he refused to let him leave Jackson Hole. She hadn't divulged the details of their relationship but simply told Hunter they were close, and that Julian would never hurt her, insisting she needed time to speak with him privately.

"I know that look. You're in trouble. You can't hide from me, Irmã." Julian's voice broke her contemplation.

Memories flooded back as he spoke their native tongue. "Irmão. It's been too long, but with good reason."

"What have you been up to, Willa? You haven't texted in over a month. What are you doing in the States?"

"It doesn't matter, Julian. What matters is that you're here. Those rogues. They could've killed you." Or he could kill the Alpha. His powers had always been lethal. If pushed, he'd lose control.

"They'd never be able to kill me, and you know it. What's with the Alpha? How well do you know him?" Julian shoved off the bed and leaned on the dresser, inspecting the swelling on his face. "I'm gonna have to shift."

"I met him a few days ago."

"Moving quickly, aren't you?"

"Whatever you thought you saw, you're mistaken. You need to leave here." She concealed her expression, concerned he'd suspect the Alpha was her mate.

"Your scent…"

"I've been to Hell. The Alpha rescued me and was kind enough to let me stay here a few days. I'll be on my way soon, as should you." The lie rolled off her tongue easy enough. Confident with her half-truth of a declaration, deflecting talk of Hunter, she turned to face him. "He doesn't like rogues. Just tell him what he wants to know and I'm sure he'll let you go."

"Whoa, hold up. Willa. Why didn't you contact me?" Julian strode over to her within seconds and took her hand. "I was up in Idaho when I heard about the explosion. Something about it didn't sit right with me so I thought I'd check things out. I found that rogue just over the border. It doesn't matter. What matters is that you didn't contact me."

"We agreed not to contact each other often. It's too dangerous. Besides, I didn't have my phone and…" The air deflated from her lungs and she debated how much to tell him. "You know I haven't been to the States in years. My work in Guatemala…I've been busy. I'm helping humans. Staying well hidden. Or at least I thought so." Her lips drew into a smile that didn't reach her eyes. "Something happened. And before you say anything…I'm going to fix it."

"Who put you in Hell, Willa?" he asked, his voice stone cold.

"I don't have names. All I know is that they're rogue. That guy today. He was one of them. But there were at least five, maybe six. They took me by surprise. But I swear before that it'd been safe. Quiet. No one was ever looking for me and if they were, I always knew hours before they ever showed their faces. The villagers often knew about strangers before I did."

"You let humans protect you?" he asked with a smug air.

"Of course not, but I absolutely used them as a check as to who was in town. Besides, the jungle is a big place and if evil wants to visit, they can always orb in. I live in a pretty remote place. Aside from drug and human traffickers, I haven't had to kill too many people. Just the bad ones." *Not sorry.* "It's been decades since I've detected any kind of real danger. The paranormal kind. Look, I don't know how the hell these guys got past the villagers. There were no signs."

"What did you do?"

"What do you mean, what did I do? I fought them of course. But they nabbed me with silver. I couldn't get free. My wolf, she couldn't fight them. The next thing I know I'm in Hell. I don't remember much of it." *Vampires. Demons.* Teeth ripping into her flesh, her skin flayed open. She shivered at the nightmarish thoughts, closing her eyes briefly and then reopening them, forcing her rapidly increasing pulse to slow down. "Hell doesn't matter. What does matter is that Hunter saved me."

"I'm not talking about that. What did you do? Something must have attracted them. Please tell me you didn't…"

"I experimented with my blood." Willa bit her lip, anticipating his wrath.

"Now why would you do that? You know full well that demons would like nothing better than to use you up. The wolves were just looking for a payout."

"I'd discovered this plant that accelerates the regeneration of cells. I'd been experimenting just to see if I could duplicate the characteristics of my blood without drawing new samples. I used a drop of my blood. I extracted and manipulated it. I'd refined the technique, adding it to a serum I'd developed from the plant."

Julian plowed his fingers through his hair, promptly scrubbing the scruff of his jaw. "This is not good."

"There was this child." She lifted her gaze to meet his; anger flared in his eyes. "Don't judge me, Julian. There was a little girl. I couldn't let her die. I attempted every human technique possible. The only other way someone with her injury could have survived is if maybe a vampire had been present…which there wasn't. I'm sorry but it was the only way. You don't know what it's like with the humans."

"You saved her?" His cold expression softened.

"Yes, it worked, but somehow the rogues found out about me. Or demons. You know how they are."

"I can't believe you did this. You're going to be more exposed now. You'll have to go into hiding again. Preferably somewhere off this continent."

"No. I can't go. Not yet." *Hunter.* "I have to destroy the formula. I have to go back to the village. And then maybe I'll go to New Orleans where I can blend in. I'm not leaving the States until I find every last wolf who did this to me and kill them. I'm going to make a statement to anyone else who thinks they're coming at me. I'm not running anymore."

"Fine." He blew out a resigned breath. "But you're not going without me."

Willa gave a sad smile, her heart tightening at his words. Always protective, always her Julian. "You'll be in danger."

"We'll be in danger," he replied.

"I know I fucked up. But these humans…when you see a child…"

"You've always had a big heart."

"Hell will put a bigger bounty on our heads if we are together."

"It's been over a hundred years. Let em' come at me."

"The Fae. Some of them won't like that I walked away."

"You didn't walk in and out. No, it sounds like that'll be on the Alpha's head if any of them have a problem with it. Besides, now that you've been in Hell, they're not going to just let you go anyway. I don't know what demons got hold of you, but they'll want a taste. You're like retribution for our entire species."

"We could make a deal with a Fae. They could bargain on my behalf," she suggested.

"It's like dealing with the devil. No. You'll owe them forever. We need an ally. Someone who has the ability to wield dark magick but hasn't quite gone all bad."

"How about a vampire?"

"We'd need an ancient, but I don't know if we should do that. They can be just as dangerous as demons."

"Hunter rescued someone in Hell. He's here. He actually was there…outside with us just now." *Viktor.* Willa inwardly cringed, immediately regretting her suggestion.

"What did you just say?" His eyes widened at her statement.

"It's why Hunter went to Hell. He was there for Viktor." *Who drank my blood?* Better to leave out that tidbit of information. "He's friends with him."

"I don't like the idea of it. They can be dangerous." The corners of his lips drew upward into a devious smile. "But I do know a powerful witch who owes me a favor. She can help us give something of value to the demon, something better than you. The only reason Hell wants us is because the Fae is pissed about something our ancestors did a thousand years ago. If we can appease them, we'll be free to live as we want."

"I'm not sure I would live any different." Willa reflected on her solo travels, her kindness toward humans. "This world needs our help."

"We are all born as we are. Humans must walk their own path. But if we do this…go to this witch, we can at least have a choice again."

"I've got to go to Guatemala first. I need to erase any trace of what I've done with my blood. The plant alone, though…the research must continue. I have to make sure it falls into the right hands."

"Where's your research?"

"In the jungle."

"What about these rogues? Do you remember anything

else? Something they may have said?" he asked, changing the subject.

"I don't know. The only person who knew about it in the village was Yoselin and she's dead. But I know full well that a miraculous recovery would stir people to talk. The only other person who knew about the plant is a colleague of mine in New Orleans, but it wouldn't make sense that she told anyone. Scientists make plant and animal discoveries all the time where there is *potential* to cure disease. I guess what I'm saying is that it's nothing unusual. Nothing that would scream paranormal to a human. It's not like we talked often. Obviously, I don't have my phone here, so I haven't been able to try to contact her. I've been in Hell for a month. I could ask Hunter if I can use his computer and log in to my email. Even if she was the one who outed me, it's likely she's dead. It's not like the wolves or demons are going to leave her alone."

"We'll worry about her later. I agree. First, we've got to get rid of any evidence you still have that you used your blood. So, if it's written down somewhere…"

"It is. You have to understand. I was doing research. I wasn't stupid enough to leave the papers in my house though. I have them hidden." Willa turned to him, knowing he wouldn't accept the Alpha in her life. "I've promised he could go with me."

"What are you thinking? If you've got some idea about you and the Alpha, you know we can't mate," Julian stated with no emotion in his voice.

Willa noted the sadness flickering in his eyes. He quickly

recovered, the hint of his pain disappearing as if it had never existed. She knew all too well the familiar sense of loss. She'd long ago accepted her fate, but her entire world had shifted last night within the Alpha's arms.

"Our lives have been fulfilling, yes? Whatever we have done has been our destiny." She deliberately withheld sharing her suspicions about the Alpha. *Mate.*

"It's been too long, Willa. I've missed you."

Julian wrapped his arms around her, and she fell into his embrace. *Home.* Tears rolled from her eyes, the comfort of family. He'd been everything growing up, and her separation from Julian had broken her heart.

"Goddess, I can't let you go again even if I wanted to. This has to end. We'll find a way," he assured her.

"No more running for us. No more hiding."

Julian was back in her life under the most unexpected circumstances. Willa reined in her emotions, swallowing a gentle sob. As she clung to him, she never heard the creak of the door.

"What in the hell? Step away from the female or you die," she heard Hunter growl. Waves of his anger rolled through her as if they were her own. She startled, breaking free of the embrace. She threw herself in front of Julian, shielding him from the feral Alpha.

"He's not hurting me," she told Hunter, defiantly glaring at him.

"I don't care what he's doing. No male should be touching my…"

Willa's stomach flipped as his words lingered. *No, don't*

say it, she inwardly willed. Her pulse raced. *This is not happening….not in front of Julian.*

"Your what?" Julian asked, his voice equally terse. "You just met her. She's nothing to you."

"She's my responsibility. Whoever you are…"

"A friend," she lied. "He's a friend."

Hunter's heated stare painted over both of them, his face tensed in anger. "I don't care what he is. You're mine and I want him away from you." He cocked his head, studying Julian. "Lying doesn't become you, doctor. This wolf is more than a friend. Who he is I don't know yet, but I don't care. He's not staying here. I should have never made the mistake of leaving you alone with him."

"I told you I know him. That's reason enough. Besides, you can't tell me what to do." Willa released a pensive sigh. "Look, I appreciate you saving me, but you can't start telling me who I can and can't see."

"I don't have time to play games. Over a dozen vampires were killed and we've got significant human casualties. The one wolf who knows where his buddies are is dead by my own hands. And now this. You in *his* arms. I won't have it."

"What is wrong with you? Just because we had sex, that doesn't give you the right to…" Her voice trailed to silence, inwardly cringing at her choice of words.

"Did you just say you had sex with this asshole?" Julian asked, his eyes widening in surprise.

"I…it was just. Julian, don't…" Willa stammered.

"You fucking touched her!" Julian lunged for the Alpha. Willa's heart pounded as he charged forward, ramming

Hunter against a wall. The Alpha shoved him away, flipping him around and strangling an arm around his neck.

"No," she screamed. "Don't hurt him. Please."

"You wanna challenge me? Do you? I've already killed one wolf today." Hunter tightened his hold as the wolf flailed, attempting to break free.

Willa rushed to the Alpha from behind. She gripped his arms, but they wouldn't budge. "Please. I'm begging you to stop. Don't do this," she pleaded. If Julian released his power, he could kill Hunter.

"Who is he to you? Your friend? Your lover?" The Alpha tightened his hold.

"He's not my…"

"Your what?"

"Julian." Willa sucked back a sob, releasing her grip. As she shoved away, her reddened eyes locked on Hunter's. "You can't kill him." *He could kill you first.*

The Alpha refused to release him as Julian continued to struggle. "Why is this wolf so important? If he's not your lover…"

"He's my brother," she confessed.

"What did you just say?" The Alpha loosened his grip, and Julian sucked an audible breath of air.

"My brother," Willa repeated, her voice shaking. "Irmão."

Hunter released Julian, shoving him toward the wall. "What is your name, wolf?"

"Louvière" The wolf coughed, regaining his composure. "Julian Louvière."

"No." Hunter plowed his fingers through his hair and shook his head. "This can't be. I would've known."

"I'm her brother. Now don't you fucking touch her again or I'll be the one killing you. You have no idea what I can…"

"Julian. No." Willa shot her brother a glare. She couldn't risk telling Hunter everything. Not yet. Not this way.

"You were in Acadian Wolves? I would have known if you were Jake's brother."

"Guess you aren't as smart as you think you are."

"I'm going to fucking kill him anyway," Hunter told Willa, his attention focused back to Julian. "How can you be both her brother and Jake's? None of this makes any sense. Jake's never even mentioned Willa."

"I'm not his blood brother. His parents weren't part of the pack when I met his Mama and Pa and joined up with their family. We're brothers no matter how we came together. I eventually had to leave the pack, went rogue. I was only in New Orleans for a few years. Flew under the radar. But Marcel knew."

"You're telling me your name's not really Louvière?"

"I didn't say that." Julian lay back onto the mattress and winced. "Jesus Christ, I need to shift. Was it necessary to choke me? You're a Neanderthal."

"You came at me, asshole. And for the record, I'm only letting you live because of Willa."

"Fuck off. You're the one who hooked up with my sister. I should have killed you. You've got no idea who you're messing with, pal."

"Louvière isn't Willa's last name."

"What?" Julian groaned.

"Louvière is not her last name."

"I said it was mine, not hers. It's the name I adopted when I was taken in by Jake's parents."

"It's true. We're siblings," Willa admitted, her body tense. It had been a lifetime since she and Julian had admitted their relationship.

"This doesn't make sense," Hunter insisted.

"It's a long story but we were forced to separate. He went with Jake's family. And I went..." She hesitated. "It doesn't matter what our names are. What matters is that we are blood. He's my brother."

"Two rogues. Isn't that rich?" Hunter glared at Julian. "Tell you what. I'm callin' Jake. And if your story doesn't sync with his, you're done. I don't care how many tears your so-called sister cries. Too many people have died, and you were found with one of the wolves involved."

"Why would I lie about him being my brother?" Willa's temper rose. She grew tired of the Alpha's dominant nature. "And even if I did, there's no proof he did anything wrong. He brought the wolf to you."

"No need to defend me, sis. I got this." Julian shot Hunter a wise smile. "I'm the one who found that rogue, not your wolves."

"I'm sick of this shit. I can't do this anymore." Willa's lips pursed tight, her arms crossed. "I appreciate you rescuing me, but this is where I draw the line. All three of us have secrets. Hunter, I literally just met you. Just because we…" Her cheeks heated as the memory of them making love flashed in her mind. She shut it down and doused the arousal, refocusing. "It was nothing."

"You shagged my sister," Julian spat out. "Fucking Alpha."

"Shut up," Hunter and Willa replied in unison.

"It's irrelevant what happened between us," she lied. "I have work to do. I have to fix what I did."

"Irrelevant? Hmm…is that what you call what we did?" Hunter asked, ignoring the rest of her statement. "Yeah okay. Nice."

"TMI people." Julian held his palms up and shook his head. "Don't want to know."

As the Alpha strode toward her, Willa stood her ground. She tightened the tie on her robe, reminding herself she was naked beneath the fabric. His energy washed over her, and she resisted the urge to reach for him.

"This. Whatever's going on between us…" Hunter locked his eyes onto hers. "was *not* irrelevant. You know it and I know it. You can try to go rogue. You can live alone in the middle of the rainforest. But this thing…us…it can't be undone. It's far from irrelevant. I suspect the opposite is true."

"I…I…we shouldn't discuss this. Not now." *Not in front of Julian. Not ever.* If she spoke the words, it might confirm her suspicion about the Alpha.

"I need you to come with me. You can talk with your brother later. Until I check this out with Jake, I don't want you here with this guy."

"You can't separate us." Willa stepped backward, putting distance between them as her traitorous body tingled in arousal, her wolf craving him.

"You're wrong, doctor. I'm Alpha. This is my house. My property. My wolves. I may not be able to keep him from trying to escape but under no circumstances am I going to risk your safety by letting you stay here." He pinned her with a hard stare as her defiant eyes flashed back at him.

"Save that anger for whoever else put you in Hell. Not for me. Now come along, Willa," he ordered.

Rage boiled in her gut. She took a deep breath, attempting to calm her emotions. She shot a look at her brother, who smiled. Her eyebrows crinkled in confusion. "Is something funny?"

"Ah little sister, something brews between you and the Alpha. This is an unexpected turn of events. If I weren't so happily flying solo, I'd almost be jealous I'm alone but last time I checked…" Julian paused, his gaze in thought. "No. Single works. Yeah, I'm good."

"There's nothing funny about this," Willa snapped at her brother.

"Go with the Alpha. I'm not going anywhere. Jake will vouch for me."

"Fine." Willa took a large step around Hunter, ignoring him as she headed out the door.

"She's going to be a tough one. Good luck there, Alpha," Julian laughed.

"I don't need luck. You should be worrying about yourself."

Willa quickly exited the guest room, striding through the hallway, toward the staircase.

"You can't outrun me," he called after her.

"You don't have any idea what I can do. I need to borrow your cell phone. Now. I'll have money wired to a local bank, so I can get us out of here."

"Us?" he questioned.

"Us." Willa spun on her heels to face him, her heart pounding. "As in Julian and me. I don't know what that little display was back there but I'm a grown woman. I've survived on my own without you or any other wolves. Especially not an *Alpha*." She mimicked quote marks in the air with her fingers. She shook her head and pulled her long hair into a ponytail, twisting at it.

"You can't just leave," he told her.

"No. I actually can. You can either let me borrow your phone or I'll shift and run as wolf to the closest human police station and claim I've been abducted. Or have amnesia. Any excuse. I need to go. You should trust me."

"And why should I do that exactly? Because we had sex? Sorry sweetheart but it's not my first time at the rodeo. That guy in there. He could be your brother or not. I must have lost the good sense I was born with to think we…"

"Don't even say it. I know…" *Sex? That's all it was to him?* "You probably do this all the time, but I don't."

"What's going on between us. You and I both know what happened back there," Hunter glanced to his bedroom and back to Willa. "But you're not going anywhere. And neither is he. You can use my phone to make a few phone calls but it's not safe for you to leave."

"Julian and I can go." Willa sucked a deep breath, attempting to remain calm. "What happened between us. It was regrettable."

"Regrettable is it now? You go from screaming my name like I'm a God to calling what we did *regrettable*? Wow, okay then."

"There are things about Julian and me you don't know. What I did with the serum must be addressed as soon as possible. I can't wait until you straighten things out with the humans and vampires. I'm quite sure the wolves who captured me have moved on." *Because they know I'm going home.* "I appreciate you saving me, but I'm not part of your pack. You can't tell me what to do like you do your other wolves. Whatever happened with us…" Sadness danced in her eyes and she struggled to control her expression.

"Was regrettable," Hunter gritted out. "Got ya."

"I'm sorry." Willa's mind clouded with at least ten pithy replies yet all she could do was apologize. What the hell was happening? Her senseless attraction to the Alpha hindered her judgement.

"You need a phone? There's one in my bedroom on the nightstand." Hunter gestured down the hallway. "I suggest you get dressed, come down and get something to eat. Nothing's changed as far as I'm concerned. You promised earlier that you wouldn't run. We'll go together. You're right about one thing. I'm not your Alpha."

Willa opened her mouth to interrupt but the words never came. Her chest tightened. *My Alpha.* That's what she'd called him in bed.

"But right now, you are my responsibility. Look, phone's over there. I'm headed downstairs to call Jake and meet with my beta and Viktor. I'd like you down there with us." Hunter strode toward the staircase, stopped at the landing and turned to her. "If you won't take an order, then do it as a favor. Stay away from Julian until I have a chance to check him out."

"He *is* my brother." Willa suspected he knew she was telling the truth, but his pride kept him from admitting it. "I want you to know that I don't want to lie. Everyone has secrets, Hunter. We all do. But some secrets are the kind that can get you killed. What happened between us," she bit her lip, her body tensed with frustration, "it meant something to me. It's just that I'm not ready to talk about what's going on. And just so you know, I've had good reason to keep my relationship with Julian a secret from others. He's deadly, no doubt. But he's no murderer and there's no way he'd ever help wolves like that guy out there. And for as much as he was acting a twit with all his smirking, he'd never in a million years hurt me."

"Get dressed. We'll talk later. But know this, Alpha or no Alpha, you're not going this alone."

Chapter Seven

Hunter stomped down the stairs, rage seeping from his pores. His mind spiraled, as he attempted to process his conversation with Willa. *How could this woman be my mate?* Ever since they'd made love, the question had been repeating in his mind.

"Jesus fucking Christ. Really? Leave it to me to find my mate in Hell," he grumbled under his breath. "And a rogue. What the fuck?"

What the hell was he supposed to do with a wolf who'd never become pack? She'd been fairly adamant that she wished to remain on her own. The pack was his life. If word got out he'd mated a rogue, they'd likely challenge his loyalty to the pack. *Fuck me.*

He rolled his eyes and headed toward his office. She'd called their love making irrelevant, regrettable. Her fingernails digging into his shoulders while she screamed his name told him otherwise. His beast demanded he claim her, but he refused to indulge it. No, this whole fucking mating thing had to be some sick demon joke.

Walking away from his mate might kill him, but he would survive. He'd been through Hell already, so what was a little more torture?

No doubt Willa radiated a unique power. Glistening skin set her apart from any other wolf he'd ever encountered. But she'd made it clear she didn't need him, insisting Julian would protect her. Jealousy flared when he saw them together. *Siblings.* Although she'd appeased his wolf with her explanation, a darker secret bound them together, excluding all others, especially him.

There was only one way to know for sure if Julian was legit. Hunter reached for his cell phone, quickly tapping in the digits.

"Yo," Jake answered.

"Hey, bro. How's it going in San Diego?" Hunter asked casually.

"'Bout to catch some waves on this beautiful California morn. What's up?"

"Some shit's been going down since I got back from…" the Alpha coughed, aware that it sounded insane, "Hell."

"Hell?" Jake laughed. "Because everyone goes to Hell for a quick vaca. Guess it's more of a staycation for the demons. Nice and hot."

"Yeah well, I was busy saving a vampire." *I sound completely certifiable now.*

Jake laughed harder. "Stop fucking around. I've gotta roll. Swells are sick today."

"Nope." Hunter released an audible breath. "It's true. You know that vampire you rolled in with. Your buddy,

Quint. He, uh, he's got this brother." *Jesus, it sounds worse.* "Viktor. Had to get him out."

"Come on. Stop fucking around."

"I know it sounds crazy as fuck, but this is my life."

"You seriously went to Hell to save someone outside pack? A vampire?" Jake's voice raised in disbelief.

"Yeah, I did." The Alpha pinched the bridge of his nose. "It's a long story but that's exactly what happened. Viktor. I managed to get him, but I also picked up a couple more folks on the way out."

"Are you trying to get killed? Because going to Hell for any reason will get you dead on its own. Now you picked off a few more souls. Jesus, Hunter. You know they're gonna come after you for shit like that. You're lucky you're even calling me right now."

"Look, I know it was dangerous but it's just something I had to do."

"Who else did you nab?"

Hunter cringed as he said her name. "Ilsbeth." *There. He knows.*

"What the fuck? Are you kidding me? She was in Hell? Now wait. You brought her out? You know she messed with demons."

"Last I was in New Orleans, Samantha told us that she'd gone missing. Zella flew the coop. Sam suspected she was taken and didn't leave on her own. I don't know. Whatever. That witch has got more lives than a cat. She's back in New Orleans now. Vik took her back to the coven. But I've gotta say. The Zella shit is done. I mean, she didn't mention one word of it. She was as cool as a cucumber. Every bit the high priestess she used to be. Word from Viktor is she helped save him from killing the other wolf."

"What other wolf?" Jake asked.

"Yeah well, that's the thing. I rescued this doctor. Willa."

"Ah…a female." Silence.

"She's…" Hunter debated his choice of words, knowing Jake listened carefully, "special."

"Special, huh? Special as in demon? Or special as in hot as fuck?" Jake laughed.

"Well, yeah. I guess you could say she's attractive." *Hot as fuck.* His dick twitched, as his thoughts drifted to making love to her. "This isn't about how she looks. It's more about this thing she does. Her energy." *Here we go with the crazy again.* "Ya see, she does this glowin' thing sometimes. Not like a fae or anything. She's a wolf. All wolf. I know because I've seen her shift. She's…" *Beautiful. Trouble. My mate.* "A rogue."

"That's goin' to be a tough one."

"Tougher than you think. Got some issues with a pack of rogues that sold Willa to Hell for a ransom. Now that she's out, they're itching for trouble. They roughed up a human in town here looking for her. They also blew up the blood club. Murdered vamps and humans. A real fucking mess. I killed one of them but the other five are still on the loose. And there happens to be this other wolf. Yet another rogue. Says he had a hand in catching one, that he's not involved."

"Yeah?"

"So, Willa is telling me this dude's her brother."

"Okay. What's up?"

"You know I've been in Wyoming a long time, yeah. Eighty years ago or so, I left NOLA. I've got the house, but I'm not involved with Acadian Wolves or Logan's pack business. There were years I was gone I may have missed a few things. Now, I usually make it my business to know what's doin', but I understand you had a brother. And this wolf. There's no easy way to say this but he says his name is Julian."

"I gotta tell you I don't see him often. And by often, I mean I don't usually know where the hell he is. But he texted recently, maybe two or three weeks ago, which is pretty unusual. Said he's out our way. Montana. No, Idaho."

"This Julian can't be the same Julian because I know you'd know Willa." Hunter's patience drew thin as his words were met with silence. "What? What is it?"

"Now listen. I don't know if this wolf is really him, but Julian is my brother. Not by blood though. So, it's possible he's got siblings or family I don't know about. It's not like Ma would tell me if she had a good reason not to. That being said, I don't have any direct knowledge of him having a sister. But who the hell knows?"

"What?" Hunter asked, his blood pressure beginning to rise.

"Yeah, you know Ma and Pa. They loved a good cause. And Julian was nothin' but. My parents moved around a lot. We weren't always with Acadian Wolves. And Julian. I don't know. He was always special. Strong as shit. The thing with the skin? Ma swore us to secrecy about that trick. She'd whip my hide now just for talking to you about it. There're some family secrets you just don't tell. I know the Alphas knew. Marcel was in on it but that don't mean he went around tellin' everyone. If this Willa's glowin', maybe they're related."

Hunter's stomach clenched. *Willa.* "She's still in danger."

"I don't know what to tell ya. Ma was kind of hush hush about things."

Hunter closed his eyes, a rush of air escaping from his lungs. Their elders kept secrets. As an Alpha, he'd thought he'd earned the right to know all. After all these years, apparently, he didn't. *Shit.*

"You don't think your mom would care to elaborate at this point?"

"Hunter, my man." Jake laughed. "You know there's no way Ma is goin' to tell you. She'll tell you a million stories about Jules, but that's about it. Even after his ass went rogue, she wouldn't hear a negative word. Special. Unique. Blessed. That is what she'd call him."

"And what would you say?"

"I'd say I was pissed. He's my brother. I loved him. And then one day he just ups and leaves us. Doesn't want to run with pack. Doesn't even tell me where he went. I don't know. I guess I see it a little differently now that I'm older. What if he thought he'd challenge the Alpha? Maybe he thought he'd kill Marcel? I still think that's why he left. I know how that feels and lemme tell ya something, Hunter.

HUNTER

It sucks. You and Tris off and went to other packs. When you don't have any prospects, and something is tellin' ya that you're supposed to be Alpha when all you really want to do is stay with your family…it's not easy."

"Yeah, I hear ya. I guess for me though, I never got going rogue. I had a buddy go off a year before I left. He never said he got the call to challenge but one day he was gone too. But not everyone leaves because of that. Some choose to run rather than consistently submit. These aren't good people."

"For sure, but Jules is different. He's got good intentions but the boy's hellfire. He's got this special thing going on. Trust me, if he's staying in your house right now it's because he wants to stay, not because you can keep him there. He's not going to kill anyone if that's what you're worried 'bout. Without reason anyway. I would like to hear more about this Willa chick. She's essentially my sister."

"Exactly. So, the next time you refer to her as hot, you might want to rethink that." No one was going to think of her as attainable, because she was his.

"Hey, you don't need to worry about me, bro. I'm mated. But you? You sound wrapped up in this she-wolf for only knowing her a few days. A little somethin' going on?" Jake laughed.

"Yeah, no." *Definitely, yes.* "Hey. I appreciate your help."

"You bet. Tell Jules I said to get his ass to San Diego. He's not that far."

"Yeah, yeah. Will do."

"Listen Alpha. If you need any help there, I'm not too far away, ya hear?"

"Thanks. You enjoy those waves."

"You bet. Later."

As Hunter clicked off his call, he heard shouting. "What the fuck now?"

He took off toward his study, the arguing between Viktor and his beta growing louder.

"Ah, there's the boy wonder," the vampire remarked as the Alpha entered his office.

"What the fuck is going on?" Hunter asked.

"Someone's missing," Remus yelled, fire in his eyes.

Hunter stopped cold, anger coursing through his veins. "Who?"

"Maggie Owen's son, Adam," Remus told him.

Viktor turned his attention toward the Alpha. "I've been explaining to the Neanderthal that while the rogues may have taken the child, you can't trust everyone. The mother appears to have gone missing as well. He could be with her."

"Is this true?" Hunter asked Remus.

"Yeah. I drove by and she's not at her house. I stopped in town at her shop and it's closed."

"Witches aren't the only ones influenced by evil," Viktor noted.

"Did you stop by her house? Is it locked? Her car?" Hunter asked.

"She's gone," Remus responded. "I tried texting her but she's not responding."

"I asked you to have two guys run the land. Have there been any more reports of rogues in the area?" Hunter rounded his desk and fell back into his leather chair. As

Alpha, he could sense all his wolves. No one in his pack appeared to be in peril. "If there's nothing amiss at her house and her car is gone, she's probably left to see her family. You know she goes to see her family in North Dakota every now and then. I'm not going to keep every pack member on a short leash. I've known Mags for a while now and she's pretty independent. I also know you and she have been sniffin' 'round each other for a while. Did y'all get in a fight?"

"She's not my mate," he growled.

"I'll reach out to her. I can tell you that as her Alpha I'm not feelin' she's in immediate danger. My wolves are good. But the ones I'm looking for…"

"We followed the scent of the rogues down to Munger Mountain. They either air lifted out or maybe took the Snake River." Remus changed the subject.

Hunter glanced at a text that flashed onto his cell phone. "Sherriff says the human deaths are being investigated by the FBA. They're classing it as a terroristic act."

"Vampires are laying low?" Remus remained standing and rested his elbow onto the heavy stone fireplace mantle.

"Hope you don't mind, but I checked on a few of the ones I met at the club. The ones that are alive." Viktor sat in the chair across from Hunter's desk.

"Obviously. Do we really need this joker?" The beta asked, a stone-cold expression fixed on his face.

Viktor flashed, materializing behind the beta. With his arm wrapped around his neck, the vampire's fangs descended, grazing the wolf's skin. "Don't even think of shifting. I'll drain you before you have a chance to shift. I'm going to say this once. Behave like a good doggie or I won't think twice about killing you."

"Jesus, Alpha. Get the bloodsucker off of me," Remus coughed. He struggled to break free but couldn't shake Viktor.

Hunter shot to his feet but didn't make a move to intervene. "I don't have time for this bullshit. Remus. Knock off the digs. Vik here is an ancient. And if you don't know what the fuck that means I'll spell it out for you. He can kill you within seconds and honestly as much as we've been through the past couple of years, you're acting like an asshole. I just risked my damn life to get him outta Hell and I don't need your shit. And you." Hunter glared at Viktor. "Get the fuck off him. I need you to focus for five fucking minutes."

"I don't like him." Viktor held tight to Remus, stroking his palm over the top of his head. "Saved by your Alpha. You'd better heel, or I'm afraid next time I won't be so restrained."

"Stop fucking around and let him go," Hunter ordered.

"I'm going to give your boy there the benefit of the doubt but if he throws me any more shade, he's going to be on his knees." Viktor released the beta and instantly flashed back to the seat. He dug his fingers into the arms of the chair, glaring at Remus. "You need to send your dogs to behavior school."

"Vik." Hunter slammed his palm onto his desk. "Focus. Now."

"Yes, yes." Viktor casually brushed a wolf hair off the arm of the chair. "Continue."

"Willa needs to go to Guatemala. I need you to flash us there then to New Orleans." Hunter turned to address his beta. "I need you to keep things running while I'm away. I'll be gone a day. Two tops. The rogues are going to keep after Willa, so they probably won't be back."

"Guatemala? Where in Guatemala?"

"Doesn't matter. You're staying here."

"I'm no detective but I'm pretty sure returning to the scene of the crime isn't going to be a good idea," the beta challenged.

"I hear you. But she's got some business she has to attend to before we do anything else. She was doing research. Sounds like someone might be after it."

Viktor's eyes grew darker as he thought on the Alpha's statement. "Something they wanted? I imagine it must have to do with Hell. Why else would the wolves want it?"

"The details aren't important right now," Hunter hedged. "What's important is that she destroy it."

"No worries. I'll keep the pack safe," Remus told Hunter.

"I need you to keep watch over Julian. He checked out with Jake, but I don't trust him. That said, I don't want him harmed. Got me?"

"Yeah, all right." Remus stared blankly at his Alpha.

"Just keep him here in the house. If he leaves, don't follow him. I don't want any trouble." Hunter scrubbed his beard.

"I sense an issue, oh great one. Do tell, do tell." Viktor's face flashed with a devious smile.

"Look, you're both gonna find out sooner or later." Hunter sighed, his eyes on the vampire. "Julian is her brother."

"What the hell? No, that dude needs to go," Remus insisted.

"I don't trust him, but I've got no choice. The bottom line is that he's not just her brother. He's Jake's brother too. Julian told me he helped catch the rogue. Is that true?"

"He was with him. Fighting. But still. Just because he had him pinned to the ground, that doesn't mean he's innocent. He's playing us."

"We'll soon see," Hunter began. "Keep an eye on him. If he's Willa's brother…"

"Willa is some bitch you rescued in Hell. Now that she's fucked you, she's got your mind all screwed up," Remus challenged.

The Alpha sprang to his feet and rushed toward his beta. He grabbed him by the collar of his shirt, slamming him against a wall.

"Don't you ever talk about her like that again. Am I making myself clear?" the Alpha growled.

"Yeah, sure." Remus broke free of Hunter's grip and rubbed at his chest.

Hunter turned around and averted his feral gaze, aware of his exaggerated response. *Fucking hell, what am I doing? What's wrong with me?*

"This really is going to be interesting to watch." Viktor gave a small chuckle.

"Shut it, vamp. I've got enough issues going on without listening to your shit."

"Hmm…let me think on it." Viktor cocked his head as if he were deep in thought and gave a broad smile. "No."

"You're an asshole, you know that, right? I should have left your ass in Hell."

"Ah, my dear Alpha. You don't know me very well, but I am loyal to a fault. While I do appreciate your heroic actions, I'm not going anywhere." The smile disappeared from his face, his expression serious. "I owe Willa. I could have hurt her."

"But you didn't."

"I'll never be my sire. Willa has my loyalty. Perhaps even more than you do."

"So, let me get this straight. You're going to take fang boy with you to Guatemala?" Remus shot Viktor an icy glare.

"Yes, he's going. But Willa seems to be getting pretty sick when she dematerializes. Even for me, it's not the best way to go. Think it's best to take the PJ. I've got Ty and Vince on call."

"You both need to toughen up. Wolves." Viktor rolled his eyes.

"Remus. I need you to go over to Maggie's house and check it out one more time. I want to be one hundred percent sure that something hasn't been overlooked."

"Like what?"

"I don't know. A note? Anything. No offense but if you're not mates, maybe she was seeing someone else. Give her mom a call. Let's find out if anyone's heard from her. I have a feeling there could be something else about her unrelated to the rogues."

"I'll go but I already…"

"This isn't a request." A loud ding from Hunter's cell phone interrupted his train of thought and he lifted it to read a text from one of his wolves, Rafe.

Got a situation out here. Caught me a fae.

"It just keeps getting better and better." Hunter laughed. *What the fuck?* He tapped out a message to Rafe. *Where u at?*

Out riding Two Ocean Pass. I'll head in. Got him tied up.

"No, no, no." Hunter tapped as he spoke out loud. *Too dangerous. Keep him grounded & we'll head out. He's goin' back in the pit.*

"We've got us a problem. A fae." Hunter looked over at Viktor. As long as he had the vampire around, he might as well use him. "I'm gonna need a ride."

"Look how adventurous the Alpha is. He spins but he's ready to fly again." Viktor clapped his hands together with laughter. "All right then. I'm game. Fae. Nasty little beasts."

"Remus. I need you to stay here and guard Willa and Julian. I'll be back in an hour and then I want you to swing by Maggie's house one more time. I also want to speak with the entire pack before I go. It's a Saturday so it should be easy enough to get everyone together for an emergency meeting. Start sending notifications. I'll be back."

"You got it, boss." Remus nodded.

"Stay away from Willa," Hunter warned.

"Absolutely."

"Julian too." He nodded at his beta, his gaze firm.

"That wolf is trouble."

"He may be. But he's Willa's brother. And Jake's. So, leave him the fuck alone. As soon as I get things sorted with Willa, he'll be on his way."

"If you say so, Alpha."

"If Willa asks…"

"Back in an hour. Got it. You be careful. Fae ain't no joke." Remus gave Viktor a dismissive stare before he exited the office.

Hunter rubbed his eyes and shoved his cell into his back pocket. "Rafe is out on a trail with his horse."

"What do you have in mind? I can flash to him. Think about where we're going, and this should work well enough." Viktor stood and stretched his arms into the air. "Ah, I love a good adventure."

"Let's do it."

Hunter approached Viktor, readying to dematerialize to Rafe. He hated the feeling of being torn apart and flashing like a ghost, but time was of the essence. "Rafe said he was about thirty minutes down the trail. You think you can handle that, fly boy?"

"Your flight is now boarding." Viktor smiled, his eyebrows raising in delight.

"Did I ever mention how much I hate fae?"

"They're sneaky little devils. No worries. Uncle Vik is here with you."

"You're an asshole."

"That's why I'm the best."

"Let's go find out what this dickhead is doing on my land."

Hunter's face tightened as he placed his hand on the vampire's shoulder. Nausea rolled through his stomach, and the familiar darkness blinded him.

***

"Goddammit." Hunter spat onto the ground, his hands on his knees. "Woah! That shit is not right."

"Take a few breaths. You seem to do much better than your…"

"Don't fucking say it." *Mate.* Jesus, even the vampire knew.

"Hottie houseguest?" Viktor laughed.

"Shut it." He brought his hand to his forehead, willing the spinning to stop.

"Sexy she-wolf. Yeah, I heard you go at it."

"Shut. The fuck. Up."

"Oh, Alpha…" Viktor's high-pitched voice bored into Hunter's head.

"I swear to the Goddess. This place has nothing but wood. I'm gonna find a nice sharp piece and stake your ass."

"Oh yeah. Harder," Viktor grunted.

"I told you to shut up!" Hunter sucked a deep breath and came round, swinging a hard left into the vampire's gut.

Viktor laughed, falling backwards onto the ground laughing. "Pussy."

Hunter closed his eyes and licked his lips, drawing in another gulp of air. As he blew it out, the nausea passed and his focus landed on Viktor, who shoved back up onto his feet. "You're an asshole."

"A little anger always manages to dislodge whatever discomfort one is feeling. Better, pup?"

"Call me a pup again and I'll punch all of those veneers off your fangs."

"You do need to be a little more appreciative of all my efforts." Viktor brushed the dried leaves off his jeans and scanned his surroundings. "Where are we anyway?"

"Near Moran. Up toward Two Oceans Pass." Hunter reached for Rafe in his mind. "He's close. I'd say about a half mile. This way."

"I'm not exactly wearing hiking shoes. I just bought these fly Futurecraft." Viktor glanced to his feet. "They're expensive."

"Too bad, Hollywood."

"We don't have to hike, you know that, right? I could just…pow…wham…flash us right there. My kicks are brand new, yo."

"You need to stop. Right now. For real I'm going to punch you in the face."

"Don't hate on me. You know I'm right."

"You're a pain in the ass. Almost always. Definitely now." Hunter sniffed. The scent of sulfur laced the air. "Up here."

"I only put up with this because I find you amusing." Viktor carefully trekked through the forest, avoiding the mud. "I don't know why I do this to myself."

"You do it because I saved your ass," Hunter replied.

"True. True."

"I smell fae," the Alpha growled. His long strides

increased as he pressed through a thick brush. He stopped short as the devious fae came into sight. "Kellen."

"You lived?" he spat.

"Hey, Rafe." The Alpha nodded, stepping around the fae. The last time he'd seen Kellen, Hunter had been in a bar on Frenchman Street, dying from demon poison. He looked over at the usually cool as a cucumber fae who lay hog tied in the middle of the woods. "Karma's a bitch."

"Alpha." Rafe nodded toward the struggling fae. "Surprised him from behind. He must have been worshiping or deep in thought because he never saw me comin'. His fire's over there. I stoked it just in case he's going back."

"Oh, he's going back all right." The Alpha was careful not to make any deals as the fae were always looking to make a buck off of information. The unique creatures could easily pass between earth and the netherworld. They could not possess or curse, yet they'd been known to kill or trade souls to Hell in exchange for favors.

Hunter knelt, making eye contact. "How's it hangin', fire boy?"

"You treat me like this after I helped Quintus? Never again will I do a favor for the lot of ya. Never. Fuck you and your wolves."

"Someone seems to be havin' a bad time of it." Hunter glanced at Viktor.

"And this was worth getting my new shoes dirty? Now I'm in a bad mood. Do you hear that, fae? My patience is thin."

"How's about you tell me exactly why your hairy ass is

trolling about in my territory?" Hunter glared down at the bound fae.

"I like the wilderness." He laughed, saliva spraying from his mouth. "I've got a right to go to Yellowstone like anyone else."

"Got news for ya. You're not in Yellowstone. You're running on pack lands now. You remember nawlins, do you?" The fae had enjoyed watching him suffer as the demon blood spread throughout his bloodstream, nearly killing him. "All you wanted was money."

"You pay for information. I give it. That's how it works." Kellen laughed.

Hunter leaned forward, coming within inches of his face. "That's right, asshole. That's exactly how it works. The way I see it is you've been campin' out here on my property. Possibly for days."

"Days? Well, that's going to be expensive," Viktor said, with a coy smile.

"Yeah, you know property out here is pretty pricey. Rent's been goin' up," Rafe added.

"Now I'm willing to bargain. But you're going to have to pay to even things up." A cold smile crossed Hunter's face.

"But I've only been here for a day," the fae protested.

"Well isn't that a shame, guys," Hunter laughed and stood up, towering over him. "Ole Kellen here has to pay even though he's only stayed a day. But rent ain't free, bud. Nope, 'fraid not."

"You owe the Alpha," Viktor told him.

"Ah…you both can go to Hell!" Daggers shot from his eyes as he glared at Hunter.

"This guy interrupted my ride. Damn inconvenient for me, Alpha." Rafe leaned over and picked up a few sticks and threw them into the pit, the flames licking up into the air. "Could've started a forest fire."

"See now that's gonna cost extra. I don't make the rules. Fair is fair."

Kellen squirmed, attempting to pull apart the iron chain that wound about his wrists. Unsuccessful, he winced as it burned his skin.

"Information's the name of the game. Even up. Tell me. What's an urban fae like you doing snooping out here in the woods?"

"A couple of wolves owe me," he confessed. "They sold a soul to Hell. She got out so now they can't keep the reward. No, no, no. The demon will have its due if the money isn't back soon."

Willa. Hunter's stomach clenched at the thought and he resisted the urge to kill the fae. While she'd been in Hell suffering, this bastard was out to make money off of it.

"I want to know the names of the wolves who owe you," Hunter demanded.

"Whaddya mean? Names. No names in this business."

Hunter lost control and lunged at the fae. He rolled him onto his back and straddled him, wrapping his hands around his throat.

"Now you listen up, Kellen. I want the truth now, not some bullshit fae story. Names. I want names. I don't care if they gave you real or fake ones, but I know a slippery one like yourself doesn't do business without having a name to be paid or owed. It's not in your nature."

Kellen choked as Hunter tightened his grip. "You can't kill me."

"I won't kill you. Might bring demons crawlin' out of the woodwork for all I know. But believe me when I say I can and will keep you tied up. For as long as I want. Consider me the sheriff of your debtor's prison. This is my territory, not yours. You want out? Names. Now!"

"I don't know, I don't know. Maybe Jerry. Jack. Jermain. No. Jerry. He came with only one other wolf. Connor was his name. They're rogues. But they have this sort of makeshift pack, he says. Not my business. I only work the deals."

"Where are the wolves from? Where are they going?"

"How am I supposed to know? Met em' in New Orleans just like you and the blood sucker."

"Easy." Viktor nudged Kellen's chin with the tip of his toe. "I'm not as nice as my brother."

"Tell me about the soul. Who is she?" Rage boiled inside Hunter, yet he kept his voice calm.

"She's a special one. But you already know that, don't you? Now get this iron off my wrists. It's gonna kill me."

Hunter paused and nodded to Rafe who made quick work of releasing the fae. He pushed onto his hands and knees, grunting as he stood, dirt marring his face.

"Tell me about her," he pressed.

"Can't you feel her? I can feel her now as I scan for

energies. I know you took her from Hell. She's still with you, isn't she?"

"I'm not the one answering questions. What is she?" Hunter asked, ignoring his question. "You owe me."

"She's wolf. She's origin. She's everything. Her power is special. Ancient pedigree, I tell ya. Took special fae magick to subdue her, I hear. But was all paid for. What people do with my magick isn't my business. I can't be responsible. It's all business."

"Why is her power special?" Hunter asked. "Why is she so important to sell?"

Kellen smiled broadly, his laugher echoing in the forest. "How can you not know what she is? She's wolf. *The* wolf. I cannot tell you more. I am forbidden to betray, I'm afraid. Demons want her. Wolves want her for the sale of her flesh. And you, Alpha, what do you want her for?" Kellen revealed his brown crusted teeth.

"I saved her from that cesspool you crawl in and out of. She's my wolf now," Hunter insisted.

"Not possible," Kellen insisted, his voice raised. "She's rogue. She'll never be pack. She'll never mate."

"What do you know about the ways of the wolves? If I say she's mine, she's mine. So, go ahead, you can call your demon buddies…"

"No…demons! No demons," he said, circling the fire.

"You're in and out of Hell all the time. Just staying long enough to get a taste. You'll never get enough of your fix. I see you for what you are, Kellen. You're a junkie. You may look the part, blending in with the humans, but you're as evil as they come."

"You don't know anything about me." He waved his hand at him.

"I know you walk with demons far more than you walk with immortals or humans. I know you helped these assholes kidnap her. I know you traded an innocent soul for money. All of these things are reprehensible."

"This is our purpose. The Goddess has a purpose," he told Hunter, dipping a finger into the hot coals. "We earn money for our favors, but the deeds are not ours. The Goddess allows us to move freely, not the demons."

"Whatever you gotta tell yourself to sleep at night but as far as I'm concerned, you're a lowlife scum, sucking off the sins of humans and others, waiting for your next deal. Before you jump back into that firepit you got going there, I'm warning you. Willa is off limits. To you or anyone else who's fixin' to hurt her. Put the word out that she belongs to me. She's my pack now. She's not alone. Those wolves, Kellen. One of them is dead. I'm gonna kill the rest when I find them. It's just a matter of days. So, when your ass lands back in New Orleans, you keep in mind who's going to be around. Choose your sides wisely. Next time you cross me, fae magick or not, you'll be dead too."

"I'm innocent. Come and go as I please. I may owe you for the time, but nothin' you can do about it."

"You're nothin' but a flea and it's time to flick you the fuck off my territory." Hunter shoved Kellen toward the fire pit. "Time to go home."

Kellen's eyes transfixed on Hunter's as he leaned back and fell into the flames. His entire body disappeared into the ground as if he'd dove into water. Sparks danced into the air, the fire smothered in magick and hellfire.

"Fuckin' fae." Hunter kicked at the dirt, spraying it over the fire.

Rafe dug his fingers into the earth, dousing the flames.

"Kellen is quite a piece of work. I'm not sure how Quintus manages to deal with his sort. But then again, I have my own informants," Viktor mused.

"If you don't mind me askin', Alpha, what's going on with the girl you brought back from Hell?" Rafe wiped his hand across his forehead and spat onto the ground.

"Nothing. He's lying about her." The Alpha inwardly questioned Kellen's claims about Willa. She was extraordinary, almost otherworldly. He'd seen her gorgeous wolf, and while he suspected a hybrid of some sort, she was not evil. "It's just that Hell…it affects people. Any species can be contaminated by it. Humans. Vampires. Witches. Wolves even. They choose evil. But the fae are more susceptible. If you walk through Hell one too many times…"

"Haven't met many fae to be honest." Rafe made quick work of mounting his horse.

"Best you don't. Ya don't want to be caught up in a bad deal. It's what they do. Kellen's a motherfucker. But he's pretty visible. That's why Quint uses him."

"Yes, but Quint still should have killed his ass." Viktor sighed and gestured toward his feet. "Now would you look at that. How am I ever going to get this mud off my shoes? Did I mention they were brand new?"

"Gotta roll, Rafe. Have a good ride," Hunter told his

wolf, ignoring the vampire's complaint.

"That I'll do, Alpha."

Hunter stilled as he turned to Viktor, shock rolling through him. *Willa.* As if someone had stolen his lifeblood, his hands turned icy. He closed his eyes, focusing, searching for her.

"What's wrong now? Don't you see how dirty my…"

"Willa's gone." His eyes locked on Viktor's.

"What do you mean she's gone? She's back at your house. With Julian."

"No. I can't feel her. I've gotta get back now. If she ran off with that loser brother of hers, I'm gonna spank her ass."

"Now that is something I would like to see."

"Now vampire," the Alpha ordered, setting his palm on Viktor's shoulder. "Let's go."

Chapter Eight

Willa's mind swarmed in confusion, her conflicting emotions warring. She'd always remained in control of her beast…until now. Overwhelmed, she stood in front of the bathroom mirror, staring into her bloodshot eyes, her face puffy from her tears. After she'd dressed, she let her mind wander, reaching for Hunter, but he was gone. The Alpha had left without so much as a goodbye. It was what she'd wanted, yet now that he'd gone, she thought of nothing but him, making love, lying safely in his arms.

Believing she'd never mate, Willa never considered the consequences if she found one. The attraction to the Alpha was palpable, like an addiction she couldn't deny. Craving her next fix, she prayed to the Goddess to make it go away.

Children. Before she could stop the thought, the word streamed through her mind. *No, no, no. Stop it, Willa. You cannot think of this. Just get going with your business. Worry about the Alpha later.*

Willa startled at the sound of the bedroom door swinging open, heavy footsteps treading across the floor.

Not Hunter. Not the vampire. Not Julian. Dark energy sent her wolf on alert. Willa picked up a hand mirror lying on the counter and smashed it. With a towel she picked up a shard, readying it as a weapon. Willa quickly stepped into the bedroom from the bathroom, holding it tight. Poised to stab the intruder, she caught sight of Remus.

"What are you doing in my room?" Although she relaxed her arm to her side, she kept a firm hold on the glass.

"Just thought I'd check on you. Alpha's gone to check something," he said, his eyes painting over her.

"What do you want?" Willa took a step back, increasing the distance between them.

"What do I want?" Remus cocked his head and sat on the bed. "I want to know what you are. I want to know what Hunter brought back from Hell." He sniffed the air then shot her a cold smile. "I can smell it on you. Like a filthy demon whore. Yet he claims you're a wolf."

"I am a wolf." Willa's grip tightened around the towel.

"You know what I think? I think you and your so-called brother in there aren't really wolves. You may look like a wolf, run like a wolf, but you're dirty. I think," he smoothed his palm over a wrinkle in the comforter, "you're not who you say you are."

"It's none of your business who I am or who I'm not. The Alpha is the only one who needs to know. That's the advantage of not being pack."

"I'm the beta. He's not here. I'm makin' it my business."

"Where is the Alpha?" she demanded, her heart pumping faster as Remus stood and approached her.

"I told you. He's busy."

"Why didn't he tell me?" *Because you don't matter to him.*

"Because you're not pack. You're a visitor. An outsider who has no reason to know about pack business."

"I think you should leave now." She glanced to the door, which she noted he'd taken care to completely close.

"The Alpha and I share everything, you know." He licked his lips and smiled. "We lead together. We run together. Fuck together. What do you say? You want to have a go? I bet your pussy is tight as a drum after being in Hell."

Remus snatched her wrist and pulled her to him, the stink of his foul breath wafting into her nose. She attempted to pull away, but he held tight.

"I bet you like it in the ass, don't you? A bitch like you wants it hard and rough. I'm just the guy to give it to you."

"No!" Willa screamed as he shoved his hand between her legs. Without pause, she swung the blade at him, slicing open his cheek.

"Bitch!"

As the back of his hand landed across her face, pain shot down her neck. She rolled onto the ground and swung her leg under his, causing him to fall. Clammy fingers wrapped around her ankle. Willa struggled to get away, kicking her boot at his gut. He growled and tugged her closer to him.

"Get the fuck away from her." The sound of Julian's voice filled the room and within seconds, her foot was free. As she rolled onto her back, she caught sight of Julian throwing Remus across the room. The sound of glass shattering shook the room as the beta fell through the window, his body landing with a thud onto the ground below.

"Oh Goddess. Julian," Willa cried, rushing to his side.

A cool breeze rushed over her as she peered through the broken glass. The mangled body of the beta lay motionless on the grass.

"Is he dead?" she asked.

"Doubt it, he's a wolf. But we're not sticking around to find out. It's time to roll, lil' sister."

"How are we going to get out of here?" she asked.

"I've picked up a few tricks since I last saw you. We're going to Guatemala?"

"If we can get to the main city, I can arrange for a…"

"Just think of the place you want to go."

"What?"

"Just think of the place, okay? Picture it. Now close your eyes." Julian winked.

"Are you making this up? Because I swear to the Goddess, Julian, this is not the time to screw around. We've got to get out of here before Remus wakes up or the pack finds him. We should just look for the keys to the car and take it. We can hop a flight in Idaho Falls. By the time they find out we're missing, we'll be long gone."

"Trust me. Just close your eyes. Think of your village, okay."

"Fine but I'm telling you if you're fooling around, I'm going to kick your a…" Willa's words disappeared as she spiraled into the darkness, dematerializing away into nothingness.

Willa breathed in a deep breath of air as her feet hit the ground, the pungent scent of the rainforest vegetation engulfing her senses.

"Where did you learn that?" she laughed, slapping her brother's arm.

"A magician never reveals his tricks. You okay?"

"Are you a vampire?" she asked, her face falling flat. *Viktor.*

"What? Why in the world would you ever ask that? As if I'd ever let one of those bloodsuckers have at me. No fucking way."

"Because. Viktor. He can do that as well but when he did it, it made me sick."

"He's drawing on ancient magick that isn't derived from wolves. Our magick is within us."

"But how do you have it and not me?" A tight jab of jealousy poked her.

"You have it too. Right here." He gently placed his palm on her head and brushed his thumb over her forehead. "Your third eye will lead you, lead your light. You have spent far too much time with humans, suppressing and hiding your nature. But don't worry, we'll correct all that."

"I don't think so. I'm not staying with Hunter. Especially after what just happened." Willa took a step into a well-worn path. "This way."

"We are headed toward the village?" Julian hesitated, gesturing in the opposite direction.

"As much as I'd like to see everyone, I keep my notes hidden within the lost city. It would be far too easy for someone to find them while I'm not in my house. The formula had to stay here."

"Where exactly is here?"

"In the rainforest."

Julian tugged on a leaf and plucked it. "Yeah I can see that."

"There was once an ancient Mayan civilization. A lost city. It's here. Beneath the canopy. Literally thousands of structures."

"Society never ceases to amaze me."

"Our ancestors knew of these things, I'm sure. You never paid attention to Mama's stories."

"Who's the one disappearing? Oh yeah, that would be me. I listened well enough to that part."

"I listened too." She shoved at his shoulder with a laugh. "Who knows what we are supposed to believe? One day we are living in a pack. The next, our parents are dead, and we've all split up. Until today. Now, it's just you and me. I was told we would never mate and now…well." *Hunter.* Willa's face tensed, and she kicked away at the brush with her feet. "The path ends up here."

"I suspected it wasn't all a lie. They knew if we spent too much time within a pack, we'd attract the attention of others. And not the good kind. As it is, the rogues managed to nab you and you were experienced. Problem is that even though you've been running as wolf, you aren't experienced in fighting. Your instincts failed you that day."

"Thanks a lot, Jules. As if I wasn't feeling bad enough."

"I'm sorry, Willa, but we're a product of our environment,

not just our genetics. Mama and Papa did everything to protect us, but they discounted the need for us to be with other wolves."

"Yeah, well, what makes you so special? You're rogue too."

"I've spent a lot of time with wolves. Not here in the Americas but I've traveled the world. I never spend enough time in one place to join a pack. I've been in thousands of fights, rarely losing."

"Is that why you left Jake and his parents? It wasn't fair to them."

"Jolia was a second mother to me. They took me in, and I loved them. But what's inside me, I couldn't stay in New Orleans. Challenging Marcel wasn't a path I could choose."

"How is it you didn't spend time with Hunter?"

"I didn't draw attention to myself. He's older than the others. I'd been with Jake's family for a long time and they'd moved round. By the time I landed in Acadian wolves, Hunter wasn't around. He was off establishing his own pack."

"Nice pack he's got. His beta is an asshole. How could he not see that?"

"I don't know. He might have been a good actor."

"You'd think the Alpha would know."

"You can tell me, you know?" Julian stated, wearing a sly smile.

"Tell you what? Shit." As the eight-legged creature landed on her, Willa jumped backwards, bumping into her brother. "Get off me!"

"It's just a bug." Julian swatted it off her arm and laughed.

"I'm fine with bugs. Not spiders. I hate spiders."

"Tell me about the Alpha. Your scent was all over him. And you're wearing his. You haven't known him that long which leads me to believe something is up. I'm not gonna say it."

"There's nothing to say." *Mate. Mine.* "We were together. He's…okay." *Amazing.* "There's a lesson I learned long ago. Sometimes we can't have everything we want."

"Yeah, okay. I still can't believe this is happening to you. This is awesome news, yeah? It wasn't supposed to happen to either of us."

"Nothing is happening," she insisted, her voice terse as she pressed through the deep brush.

"The thing is once 'it' happens, there's not a whole helluva lot you can do about it. Your wolf. You will crush her if you deny her her…"

Willa spun on her heels, pointing her finger at her brother. "Do not say it. Do you hear me? Don't say it. Don't. I can't let myself go there. I just can't." Her voice wavered, emotion bubbling up through her words. "He left me back there. With his violent beta." She shook her head, her hands on her hips. "No. I'm not going to be with someone who can't value me enough to…Ah, why am I even talking about this? There is no way he can be my…you know. I am not saying the words, Jules. If I keep this quiet, it will go away. Right now, I need to focus, and I can't do that if I'm thinking about him." *My Alpha.*

She sighed, and spun around, again making her way through the thick jungle. "This is going to take us all day. Maybe we should shift and run the rest of the way."

"If you're okay with goin' au natural and leaving our stuff here."

"No, I'm not crazy about doing that in the jungle. Besides it's not that far. What I really need is a machete."

"I could make this easier for you, dear sister. That's if you want to know."

"Know what? How to materialize a machete out of thin air? Because if you know how to do that, please do."

"Don't you realize you have it inside you already?"

"Stop screwing around, Jules. Either go flash somewhere and get one or let's just get through this the hard way and be done with it."

"I'm not fucking around. Listen. Part of our legacy is power. Power other wolves don't have. You're never going to see any wolf do what I can do."

"Viktor can."

"He's a vampire."

"True, but the magick is similar. Viktor doesn't say how old he is. But my guess is thousands. And when did the first hybrid begin? Mama said the Goddess created them to be one with nature, from the very beginning of time. But was it? May have been before. Or after. But the very essence of the magick bestowed in our bloodline is royal." Willa's lips drew into a tight line. "While I don't deny our heritage, I can't say anymore what that even means. I did everything they told us. Our blood is different. We'll be the end of the line. I'll never have children because I'll never have a…" Tears brimmed as she balled her fists. "Mate."

"Willa." Julian's voice softened. "I'm not saying that everything they said was true. But the power within you is already there. Your light. Give me your hand."

Willa's eyes flashed to his in doubt.

"Come on. Just indulge me."

She extended her hand, placing it in his. He turned it over to expose her palm.

"Your skin." He traced a finger up her wrists. "You don't just sparkle."

Her heart squeezed in her chest, his words conjuring long-lost memories; running in the dark through the fields, she'd allow her skin to glow. She'd insist she was a star, her brother a warrior sent from the heavens, protecting the galaxy so she could shine bright.

"Show me," he told her.

Willa smiled at him and sent the magick to her blood. Her arm tingled, the light dancing over her skin.

"You've only ever seen light within your veins. But my dear sister, your energy is so much more than that. It's power."

"I'm like a glow stick." She laughed and went to pull her hand away, but he held firm to it.

"It's more than that. You just have to focus your magick. Let it flow from your skin to the object as if you're touching it yourself. Start small and you will grow stronger. When I came into mine, I could only dematerialize short distances. Over the years, I honed my powers. Now there is nowhere beyond my reach."

"You're serious?" Willa cocked her head in disbelief. "Julian, I may have been able to light our way in the dark like a firefly but that's a far cry from what you're suggesting."

"Indulge me." He released her hand and glanced to the brush she'd been attempting to clear with her feet. "That over there. Start with the enemy at hand."

"You're joking, right?"

"Do you want to get what you need or what?"

"Okay, fine. But we're just wasting time. You could just flash and get me a machete. I'll be fine while you go. It's not the first time I've spent time out here by myself. It is, however, the first time I've been completely unprepared and didn't have my gear with me."

"You've got everything you need. Now focus. Reach for the weeds and move them. Whack them."

Willa stretched out her hand towards the brush. She attempted to concentrate but the thought of doing so struck her as funny. She bent over, laughing. "This is ridiculous."

"What are you doing? Have you gone mad?"

"This is crazy." She raised her palms up toward the sky. "Do you hear that, Goddess? Julian says that after years of running around glowing, I've got a superpower."

"Not technically a superpower." He shrugged. "More of an enhancement to your current power."

Anger boiled inside her chest. Sick and tired of running, hiding from evil, she yearned to live her life in the open with her family. Hate for the wolves who'd kidnapped her burned deep in her belly, and her eyes went wild with rage. Tortured, used as bait for rabid vampires, she'd suffered at the hand of demons. A lifetime living a lie. Discovering she had a mate….one who'd left her alone with his violent beta. And now, trudging through a hotter-than-hell jungle, sweat drenching their bodies, they had no choice but to manually clear a path.

Fuck this. Fuck all of it. She spun around toward the brush and sent her energy sizzling through her body. With nothing left to lose, she stretched her hand out. Rage tore through her mind, a jolt searing through her fingers. An invisible force whipped through the air, the plant stems snapping as if on cue.

Willa stumbled back into her brother's arms, stunned.

"Fantástico, Willamina!" Julian clapped his hands together. "I told you you could do it!"

Willa's heart pounded in excitement. She stared at her hands, realizing the implications. *A new power.* She smiled, hope sparked. Retribution would be hers. The wolves who sold her to the demons would pay.

With a flick of her wrists, she whipped her hands toward the path. The scent of fresh cut greenery filtered through the air. She turned back to Julian who stood with his hands crossed in front of his chest, smiling.

"You coming?" she asked, with raised eyebrows. The leaves crunched underneath her feet as she strode ahead.

"Lead the way, princesa," her brother said, allowing his Brazilian accent to blend into his words. "A majestade."

"Yeah, that's me. Royal as fuck," she joked.

"Don't take this the wrong way, Willa, but I gotta say," Julian stared up into the jungle canopy, "this is a little anticlimactic."

"I'm sorry this incredible, mostly unexplored lost civilization has disappointed you so greatly, irmão," she said, sarcasm lacing her words.

"All I see is trees. Snakes. And bugs. Don't get me wrong. I love bugs." Julian flicked a buzzing mosquito away from his face. "Where the hell are we anyway?"

"Petén. Northern Guatemala. What are you complaining about? We grew up exposed to the rainforest. You always wanted to trek when you were a kid." Willa smiled, recalling how Papa had warned them to stay in certain areas. She and Julian always pushed further and further, often getting in trouble.

"Brazil is different. It's home." He sighed. "Besides, I've spent a lot of time in the city. I guess you could say I'm more of an urban wolf. It's more my style."

"Oh, really, city boy. Where's that?" She laughed, having a hard time picturing him without open land.

"Miami. South Beach, baby." Julian followed his sister as she continued to cut a path through the jungle.

Willa turned to her brother, stopping but only for a second before delivering a fresh whack to the weeds. "We're almost there."

"I know that look. I'm not crazy. The weather's nice and warm year-round. None of that snow bullshit your boyfriend likes."

"He's not my boyfriend."

"Nightclubs. Beaches. Parties. Boats. Did I mention beaches?"

"And where does a wolf like you run in the big city?"

"Everglades. It's not as great as home but I like it. It's spicy." Julian waggled his eyebrows. "I love a good bachata."

"Yeah I bet it is. I know where you're going with this and I'm good. I don't need to know all your sexcapades."

"Don't be a prude."

"I'm not a prude. I just don't want to hear it from you."

"Truth is, I travel all over the world. But in the States? Miami's my favorite."

"I haven't been gone too long, but the plants grow quickly." Willa sliced through a thicket of branches, revealing a stone wall. Covered with vines, the ancient structure was barely visible. "Let's go this way. We've got to get to the front of the building." Willa continued whacking at the weeds, until they reached a small clearing.

"Jesus, Willa. This place really is in the middle of nowhere."

"That's because it is."

"Where's the door?" Julian studied the crumbling pyramid-shaped ruins.

"The door is more like a tunnel." Willa glided her palm down the wall, settling on a raised circular pattern that had been carved into the stone. Locating a small hole, she inserted her finger and depressed the hidden lever.

"What are you doing?"

"It's kind of like a super-secret lock. I might need help with getting this stone out. Sometimes it gets stuck."

"Don't you remember what Pa said about getting your tail bitten off?"

"He was talking to you, not me. You're the one who always had to go in the river. You just about had your tail bitten off by bull sharks and piranhas."

"Ah, the good old days." Julian reached for the stone as Willa struggled to remove it. "Let me help."

"Be my guest." She gave a tight smile, aware she'd sealed the entrance a little too well.

"Can't we just flash inside?"

"It's protected by ancient Mayan wards. This will just take a minute."

"If you say so." Julian effortlessly slid the stone out of the wall and set it aside onto the ground. He stared down into the small opening. "What's next? You expect us to what? Oil up and slide inside this hole? There has to be an easier way in."

"Suck it up, Jules. It's only a few feet." Willa inwardly laughed at her brother. He had always been her hero, one of the bravest wolves she'd ever known. And he still was except for one weakness, his fear of enclosed spaces.

"More like suck it in. Ladies first." Julian gestured toward the hole.

Willa didn't hesitate. Headfirst, she shimmied inside and navigated the claustrophobic passageway crawling on her forearms. She held her breath as a cockroach scampered over her wrist and down toward her legs. "Incoming!"

"Jesus Christ." Julian followed behind her, scrunching his nose as the insect darted through his hair and down his back.

"You're doing great." With a grunt, she hoisted her body

out of the tunnel hands first. Her legs quickly followed, and she shoved up onto her feet, turning to her brother.

"A little help?" Julian's hands dangled out of the hole.

"I've got you." Willa laughed and grabbed hold of his forearms while he settled his feet onto the floor.

"I could've gotten stuck inside there. You're this little thing and then there's me."

Willa stared up at her big brother, realizing she'd forgotten how tall he was. At six-five, he towered above her.

"Sorry. But it's the only way I know how to get in here." Willa sent her energy to her hands until they glowed bright, illuminating the vestibule. "It's a little tight. There's a small tunnel here, but I promise, it opens up. This way. It's not too much further."

"More tunnels. Awesome." Julian brushed the dirt off his jeans.

"I discovered this place about ten years ago. For the longest time, I used it as a sanctuary of sorts. Archeologists discovered the city this century, but it's far too vast of an area for them to excavate all at once. There's actually only a few digs in the entire area."

As they emerged from the passageway and entered the main area, Willa smiled. Hundreds of needled sunlight beams pricked light onto the floor. Vines climbed the walls, colorful flowers blooming along the edges of the room's perimeter. To the far-right corner, a spring percolated from the mouth of a triangular symbol that had been carved into the wall.

"What is this?" Julian asked in wonderment, scanning the interior.

"It's a Pibna. A sweat lodge. It's about healing. This building though. It's unusual. The pibna does not sit alone. It sits within this magical structure." She gestured to the spring water. "It's good. I've drank from it. It must filter through from a local cenote. There's one a few miles from here." Willa stepped toward the ivied wall and slid her finger over a leaf. "I suspect most of these plants grew organically, perhaps a seed flying through the wind, or birds. But these ones here." She bent to sniff a bright fuchsia-colored flower. The size of a dime, its delightful fragrance filled her senses and she smiled. "I believe they knew of its healing power. Not only that, I believe they cultivated fungus." She pointed to mushrooms sprouting across one of the walls. "Psilocybin."

"Well, hello there." Julian gave a broad smile. "Magic mushrooms."

"Peyote. Other hallucinogens were probably used during rituals."

"I can feel a buzz all right. But it's more of the woo woo kind," Julian commented.

"I feel it too. Because that's what's in this place. All around us. Infused in every molecule of those plants. There's a small bush outside the building. It's how I discovered it. Nature or magick both have a way of spreading." Willa sighed and put her hands on her hips. "The villagers understand that I often use natural ingredients as well as western medicine. The day the child was injured, I had to do something. She would have bled to death."

"You've always had a big heart, minha irmã."

"Doesn't matter at this point, because I'm destroying the formula."

"Maybe you should destroy all these plants too? I know you don't want to, but you could torch this whole place, and no one will know."

"Are you crazy? I'm not doing that. This entire site is a historical treasure. It's a wealth of information about an important ancient society."

"You know all this magick here, whatever spurred these plants, it could be from Hell."

"I suppose that's a valid theory. They did engage in human sacrifices. The bones of the victims are sometimes found in the cenotes."

"And you drank the water?"

"Stop it already. None of that is important. What's important is that I destroy the formula, so no one will know how I did what I did."

"Okay, on with it."

"Over here." Willa made her way to a stone hearth. A structure within a structure, the bricked area stood off to the side. "They used to make fire in this pit. This Zumpul-ché. A Temescal. Inside there are rocks that would have been heated. It's like a sauna. They still have them today."

"Right on. Sweat it out."

"All kinds of people used them. The sick. Athletes. Mothers who'd given birth."

"I do love a good steam bath."

"Jules. Focus. Don't you see? This structure. It may have been used to heal. The plants. The steam bath."

"All very interesting, but time is of the essence. Perhaps you don't realize the implications of leaving the ranch," he said in his best southern accent. "Your boyfriend is going to lose his shit when he finds out you're missing. I don't mean to point out the obvious, but he's an Alpha. And I know you don't want to hear the m word but it's on the tip of my tongue."

Willa whipped around wagging her finger at him. "Don't you say it."

"Mmmm…." He laughed.

"Stop. He doesn't even know where we went." She quickly withdrew her hand, with a shudder, suspecting her brother was right.

"Let's just put it this way. If he marked you while you were doing the dirty deed then…."

"I don't bear his mark because we aren't…" Willa couldn't bring herself to say the dreaded word.

"Just because you can't admit what's happening doesn't mean it's not true. It may have been a long while since I've been pack but I'm sure as hell that Hunter's coming after you. He'll make it his business to find you and it won't be hard to get here because he's got Viktor the super vamp at his beck and call."

"Even if he gets here, I'd dare him to find me. We don't even know he's my…why are we even talking about this? I need to do what I came here to do. Just hold on a minute while I get the formula."

Willa reached inside a hole next to a mantle and retrieved a wooden container, a horned creature intricately carved into its surface. She lifted its lid and peered inside it.

"You kept a locker?"

"It's just a few things. I told you I spent a lot of time here. I found this artifact and I used it."

"You should have been an archeologist instead of a doctor."

"I may do that someday but for now it's more of a hobby. I've read these types of boxes were sometimes used in rituals for the dead, often filled with gems."

"Now you're talking."

"Don't get too excited. The only thing in here is…ah…" She set the lid aside and retrieved a piece of paper and unfolded it. Her handwriting was scrawled across its surface in crimson ink. She glanced at her work, sadness in her eyes. "I had good intentions. I should have known better."

"It's not your fault. You've always had a good heart. It's why you're a healer. Watching the humans die. It's never easy. But you know more than anyone it's why we need to limit contact. At the very least we need to attempt to keep relationships purely professional."

"I just wanted to help," she said, a reflective lilt in her voice. "I loved working in Guatemala. Living here was perfect. Almost."

"I know you're trying to do the right thing but if you torch this place, the stone will hold, and you'll leave no trace of your energy or these damn plants."

"I'm not destroying the interior of this ancient structure. Are you insane?"

"I'm not the one who spent time in Hell. Just sayin'."

Willa retrieved a lighter from the box and held the paper between her fingertips. "This had a small spell in it too."

"What?" He raised his eyebrows at her.

She cringed, her nose wrinkled, the corner of her lips turning upward. "Well. It's not like I'm a witch. It's just an amplifying spell I'd learned a really long time ago in Peru. Whatever your intention is, it's supposed to draw the forces from the universe. Helps give it a kick."

"Dear Goddess above, your Alpha is going to have the time of his life with you." Julian laughed, shaking his head as he paced. "Wolves aren't supposed to mess with magick."

"I'm a scientist. A healer. It's all magick to me."

"You're dangerous."

"I'm brilliant," she laughed. "I simply made a mistake. We all make mistakes."

"Let's get on with it. Your Alpha will be here soon. I'm not looking to get into another fight with him."

The pad of Willa's thumb rolled over the rippled edge of the lighter, igniting the flame. She took a deep breath, ready to destroy her discovery. "I release the magick back into the universe with good intention."

Willa gasped as the paper caught fire. As the flames grew closer to her fingertips, she let go of it, watching as it curled into ash.

Julian smiled and clapped his hands together. "Well that's that. Shall we go?"

"Yeah. I guess that's it so…" She lost her words as the earth shook beneath her feet. Rocks shifted above, raining rubble down onto the floor. "This isn't good. We've got to get out of here."

"Earthquake," Julian explained.

"No…" Panic rose in her chest as she caught sight of black smoke billowing out of the domed sweat lodge, the scent of sulfur fresh in the air. *Demons.*

"We've got to get out of here. Now!" She dropped the lighter and ran to the wall of plants, gently uprooting a sapling. "Can you flash?"

Julian moved to Willa and set his hand on her shoulder. "It's not working. Must have been right about those wards."

"Could be the demons."

"Let's not stick around to find out."

They ran through the passageway toward the vestibule. "You go first," Julian insisted, gesturing to the hole.

"No. This is my mess not yours."

"I'll be fine. Just go, Willa. We don't have time."

"Jules, please." Moisture welled in her eyes as the smoke grew thicker. She coughed, the scent of Hell growing stronger.

"Stop arguing. The demons are going to be here any minute. I'm gonna use that spring water over there to help ward them off."

"Water?" Tears streamed down her face as she shuffled forward in confusion.

"You're not the only one who plays with magick, minha querida irmã. Now go," he growled.

"I thought you said we shouldn't play with…" Willa's words trailed off as Julian lifted her by the waist, shoving her headfirst into the dark opening. With barely room to turn, she glanced back to her brother, the black smoke creeping up around her shoulders. "Julian! Hurry!"

"Don't stop moving! Go! Go!" he yelled at her.

She scurried faster as Julian's powerful energy touched her mind, urging her to flee. *No, no, no. This can't be happening.*

Willa's heart pounded against her ribs as she scrambled through the stone tunnel. A stabbing pain shot through her as a jagged rock tore through her jeans, slicing her knee. Her adrenaline kicked in, blocking the pain. Light blinded her eyes, fresh air rushing into her lungs as she emerged from the passageway. She tumbled into the brush, her hands plowing into the muddy earth.

Willa quickly shoved to her feet and peered back inside the hole, screaming for Julian. Thick smoke billowed from within, and she choked back the sulfur-tainted fumes. In a futile attempt to illuminate the tunnel, she forced her power to her hands. "Julian! Where are you? I can't see you. Julian!"

Her stomach rolled as seconds ticked by. A deafening scream emanated from within, the dark howl of the demon beckoning her to Hell. The deathly sound overwhelmed her, and her head began to spin. Disoriented, she lifted her head, smacking it onto the passageway's stone ceiling. Stumbling backwards, she struggled to stay conscious.

"You're goin' to be okay." Hunter's words registered as her vision blurred. Falling, she gasped as his strong arms caught her. Her limbs went limp within his embrace.

Julian. Help him. She screamed in her mind, but as the dizziness slammed into her, no words left her lips.

"Demons." Hunter shook his head at Viktor.

Demons. The sting of the tears streaming down her face

and her throbbing skull were the only things reminding her she was still alive. As the darkness tunneled in, she succumbed, unable to fight. *Julian.* Hell had taken him.

"Why, Willa?" Hunter whispered.

Willa's heavy eyes refused to open but the Alpha's calming presence surrounded her. The weight of his strong arms around her kept her grounded. *Safe.* Skin to skin, the warmth of her Alpha protected her.

"I'm sorry. I didn't mean to make you run. I shouldn't have left you alone."

Where is Julian? Demons. The jungle. Where am I? A fire of panic burned through her thoughts as she struggled to awaken. She attempted to shake off the fog.

You're in my home. New Orleans. Hunter pressed his lips to the back of her head. "You're safe."

"Julian," she managed in a whispered cry, blinking her eyes open.

"He's going to be fine."

"No," she moaned. "They'll kill him. We have to go back to Hell."

"I promise we'll find him. We can't go back right now but I swear we will."

Willa's swollen eyes burned as she opened them. The gentle flame of the candlelit room made it easier to adjust to the dark. With no memory of leaving the jungle, she didn't know where she was, but the comfort of his body surrounding her soothed her wolf. With her bare skin against his, she was reluctant to move.

"I destroyed the formula, but he wouldn't come with me. He said something about the water. And magick. Why didn't he just come with me?'

"Because he was protecting you."

"But he could have escaped."

"Viktor has gone to look for him. But Willa, you should have waited for me," Hunter told her, his voice firm.

A streak of anger shot through Willa, recalling how he'd left the house without saying a word. "Wait for you? Are you kidding me? You left me with a stranger."

"There was a fae in my territory. A dangerous one. I had to take care of it. Leaving you with Remus…"

"He attacked me. He tried to rape me. If it weren't for Julian…." Willa spun around to face him, her palms flat on his chest. "We had to leave."

"He was gone when I got back. The room was torn up, but I assumed Julian…"

"Julian saved me. He threw him out the window. Then we left for Guatemala to destroy the formula."

"I can't believe this. I've trusted him with the pack in the past and I've never had any issues. He's always been a little hardheaded, but he's never attacked anyone before. I specifically ordered him to leave you alone. And Julian. This doesn't make any sense." Hunter's expression softened. "I'm really sorry, Willa. If I had known…"

"I'm fine but Julian…" Guilt twisted in her gut at the thought of him fighting the demons alone, dragged into Hell.

"Your brother's strong. He's going to be okay. Viktor sensed the magick he used to flash you. It's how we found you. When I first saw you with him, I thought you were…"

"Lovers?" she interrupted, regretting her choice not to divulge their relationship. She'd been less than candid with regards to her brother's identity.

"I want to believe you, but little wolf, you've got all kinds of secrets. I know you haven't told me everything. Julian flashed. How does a wolf do something like that, Willa? It's not something we do. Not ever. If I'm going to help you, help him, I've got to know the truth."

"Are you sure you can handle the truth?" *He'll reject me.*

"I can handle anything if you just let me in," Hunter promised.

Willa's heart raced as his fingers gently cuffed her wrists, and his eyes peered into her soul. There was something about this man. He'd saved her and asked for nothing in return.

"You ask for the truth but what if it changed how you felt about me?" Tears welled in her eyes as the loss seized her chest. "Julian is the only one left in my family."

"We'll find him. If he didn't get out, I'll go back to Hell and get him. But you have to tell me the truth about what's happening. There's too much at risk. I just had a dangerous fae, one reeking of Hell, show up on my land. I can't have that. If you don't tell me what's going on, I'm going to have a hard time helping you and keeping everyone else safe. No more lies."

"The truth?"

"Yes. The truth. I swear on my life you can trust me."

Willa took a cleansing breath and summoned the courage to tell him. "I am Aline Ermenjarta Lobo. Princess Aline Ermenjarta Lobo. I am from the ancient clan of Lobo. Lupine origin. For years, the pack remained largely isolated in the heart of Brazil. With caution they allowed other packs to splinter off and prosper, to dilute the genes of the original wolves. The people of my pack dispersed long ago, realizing the danger of their strength, and their numbers dwindled. My parents were murdered. My brother and I, the purest of breeds, are rare. Rare is coveted. Rare is hunted. We separated and disappeared."

"Are you telling me that you're from Lobo? Now wait. There's no way. Lobo is dead."

"Lobo is hidden."

"Lobo is first of the wolves. Royalty. The stories... Willa..."

"I have been reinventing myself throughout the years, but I belong to no pack. Our family broke apart because when we are together our blood draws the attention of others." *Please believe me.* Her stomach tightened as the truth spilled from her lips. "The magick of the wolves. Shifters. Its origins come from both the Goddess and the glow of the underworld. Through generations of breeding, only the pure magick of the wolf remains. But the Lobo. The elemental wolf. Our blood remains different." Willa closed her eyes, terrified to say the words, to admit the forbidden truth.

Hunter took her shaking hands into his, rubbing her

palms. "Whatever this is. This truth. There is nothing we cannot handle together."

"Why do you do all this? We just met. I…" Willa's heart squeezed. He'd come for her and wasn't running despite what she'd told him. *Trust.* It was a concept she'd long abandoned…until now.

"It's okay," he encouraged.

"Wolves. I'm sure you've heard the lore from your parents, pack elders. Wolves are born of the Goddess, you've been told. A wolf shaped into its human form. The magick is strong. Pure. This." She wiggled her fingers, eliciting a glow on her skin. "This…is…" She took a deep breath and blew it out. "This is hellfire."

"You aren't fae," the Alpha responded, not flinching at her statement.

"No, but the hellfire lives within my blood. It's not something I can change or stop. This is an elemental ability. It's why my blood heals. It's why I glow. It's the reason my brother has the power to dematerialize. It's also the reason why the demons can sense me. And all of this is why a pack of rogues think they can make a buck off of kidnapping me or any member of my family."

"You aren't a demon." Hunter kissed the tips of her luminescent fingers.

"Aren't you hearing me? My blood. It's tainted with the same magick the fae uses. Hellfire. I'm pure but to you…I'm like a demon."

"Sooooo, you're saying I'm dating a princess?" A broad smile broke across Hunter's face.

"Is there something wrong with your hearing? I just told you about the hellfire."

"Do you get a crown or is it just a rumor?"

"No. Wait. What is wrong with you?" A curious smile curled onto her lips. "I have hellfire in my veins. You know. From Hell."

"Yeah, yeah. I got that part. I have to say I always thought Lobos was some kind of a mythology."

"Hellfire," she repeated louder, her eyes widened. "Why aren't you running for your life?"

"Run for my life? You do remember I broke in and out of Hell, right? Hell is my bitch."

"Your bitch, huh?" she laughed.

"So what? My girl's got a little extra fire in her blood. No big deal. You're royalty, Willa. You've given a lifetime of sacrifice for something that was beyond your control."

Willa searched his eyes, thinking there had to be a catch. If any other wolf knew, they'd be leery of the trouble she'd attract.

"You can't possibly want me." Her smile faded, emotion twisting inside her chest. Her wolf howled in protest. *Mate.*

"Being immortal gives us a lot of time to think about what's really important. And despite knowing the Goddess has the final say, we often try to control fate. It's a fool's game. We're no better than the humans when it comes to controlling destiny."

Her heart beat faster as Hunter wrapped his hand around her waist, drawing her closer until their lips nearly touched. She lowered her gaze. "You have better choices than me. I'm ancient. I'm royal. I bear the sins of our creation."

"I think you already know the answers. Search your wolf and she'll tell you what you need to know."

"What kind of man sees nothing of my past? Who are you?" Her pulse raced, his powerful energy rushing through her.

"I'm your Alpha." As his mouth claimed hers, Willa melted against him. The electricity in the air sizzled as their bared bodies wrapped together. He tore his mouth away, resting his forehead against hers.

"You belong to me, Willamina," he growled.

"It's impossible." She denied it, but her wolf rejoiced.

"The truth lies within you. No matter what you've been told, it's true. Something about you. It's as if I've always known you."

"No," she half protested.

"Time to prove it to you. Don't say I didn't warn you."

Hunter reached between her legs, dipping his finger into her slick heat. Willa cried aloud as the pad of his thumb circled over her clit. Her mind told her to resist, but her body ignited with arousal, her wolf claiming her mate.

His lips crushed upon hers, and Willa moaned into his devastating kiss. She tilted her hips as he delved inside her pussy. Her breath quickened as his mouth found her neck, his tongue teasing the skin behind her ear.

"Hunter," she cried, her body on fire with arousal.

He palmed her breast, gently rolling her nipple between his fingers. Willa moaned in response, the gentle pinch igniting desire throughout every cell in her body. She trembled as he added another thick digit inside her slick core, stroking her sensitive strip of nerves, bringing her closer to climax.

"Goddess." She wasn't sure if she was begging or praying but her Alpha certainly acted like a God. As he stroked her clit, she lost control.

Willa's orgasm seized her, and she panted, her eyes on his as he withdrew his fingers. She sucked a breath as he rolled her onto her back. His intense gaze bored into her soul, and Willa's heart pounded as his dick pressed through her wet pussy, breaching her core.

"You're mine, little wolf," he growled in a low, sultry voice.

Panting for breath, Willa nodded in agreement. *My wolf. My Alpha.* Hunter's dominant energy overwhelmed her senses. Her savage wolf clawed for her mate, demanding she claim him.

She wrapped her hands around his neck, sucking a breath as he thrust deep inside her pussy. Feral with lust, she submitted, wrapping her legs around his waist as he drove himself deeper. As he stretched her open, her head tilted backwards, exposing her neck. His lips trailed along her collarbone, and her wolf howled in delight.

"Yes, oh Goddess, please," Willa cried as his pelvis brushed over her clit and her climax drew closer.

"Hunter…I need…" *You.* Passion swirled in his eyes as she pleaded for mercy. "Please…I'm going to…yes, just like that. Hunter, please."

"Willa," he growled.

"I'm so…oh Goddess." Breathless, she arched her back, tilting her hips upward in rhythm with his. She struggled to keep her orgasm at bay, utterly immersed as his thick cock filled her.

"You belong with me. Do you feel it? Ah, Goddess, yeah." His lips traveled to her shoulder.

"Hunter," Willa cried out loud. She bared her neck, willingly submitting to the Alpha. As his teeth clamped down onto her shoulder, her orgasm tore through her. She writhed beneath Hunter, taking in every hard inch of him. Willa's fingernails stabbed into his skin, her pussy tightening around his cock as he slammed inside her once more. She trembled, her body tingling from her head to her toes as waves of her orgasm rushed through her.

Mate. She'd submitted. He'd claimed her. Emotion twisted through Willa as her mind spun with the implications. There would be no turning back. Hunter was forever hers.

Chapter Nine

His name on her lips rung in his ears as he slammed inside her tight pussy. The sting of her fingernails drove him to thrust harder. As she shook with orgasm beneath him, he thrust a final time, coming hard. Her ethereal energy rushed through him, his Queen demonstrating her power.

Fuck, fuck, fuck, he inwardly told himself as he stilled, shivering from the last tendrils of his orgasm. Hunter released his bite and buried his face into her chest. Challenge accepted; he'd taken his mate. Only for a second had he considered the ramifications of his actions, but the fierce instinctual urge won out over logic.

Hunter rolled onto his back, bringing her with him. He panted for breath, brushing a kiss to the top of her head.

"Alpha," she whispered, her warm breath grazing over his chest as sleep claimed her.

Hunter slowly released the air from his lungs, staring up at the pressed tin ceiling, his mind racing. *Royalty.* Willa's confession brought back childhood memories. Hunter's parents had told them the tales. A family who begot the origin of wolves. While some had believed them to be hiding in seclusion, others simply discounted their existence. And now, the princess lay sleeping within his arms. *My mate.* He'd lost control and marked her as his own.

Doubt seeded in his mind as it spun with the ramifications of his actions. It wasn't the hellfire flowing through her veins that concerned him. *Rogue.* She'd lived a life on her own without pack for over a hundred years. She'd chosen to live in solitude among humans. Strong willed, she'd do as she wished, and he questioned if she'd ever truly submit. Sexually, allowing his bite was instinctual. Within the context of pack, she'd be tested and could easily choose independence over the family of wolves.

If he was forced to walk away from her, he suspected his ability to lead could falter. Logically he told himself it didn't matter. He barely knew Willa, yet it could kill him to abandon her.

Hunter shoved away the negative thoughts, embracing the exhilaration that coursed through his veins. As he drifted to sleep, he breathed in the scent of his mate, his beast content.

Suspecting they'd be making a trip to New Orleans, Hunter had arranged to have his home stocked with food while he was in Wyoming. Although he owned a home in the bayou, he'd decided to stay at his home in the French Quarter, closer to Samantha's coven. He'd always loved the multicultural city, partaking in both its music and art. He excelled as a concert pianist, but it was the Alpha's cunning skills collecting and selling antiques that had earned him his fortune over the years.

Hunter's stomach growled as he opened the refrigerator and searched for something to eat. He selected a few blocks of cheese and some prosciutto, his thoughts returning to Willa. Claiming her hadn't been so much of a plan as more of an instinct. He could have cared less about the hellfire, but his pack would bring scrutiny. Her claims of royal blood might breed jealousy and challenges. Without seeing her fight as a wolf, the outcome was uncertain.

Hunter placed the food on the counter and turned to the pantry, retrieving crackers and a soft plastic honey bear. He eyed the fresh loaf of French bread he'd had delivered and reached for a serrated knife. As he heard the creak on the wooden floor, he spun fast as lightning, withdrawing a razor-sharp chef's knife from the block and pointing it at the intruder.

"Miss me?" Viktor asked with a smile.

"Jesus Christ, you need to stop doing that." Hunter set the knife on the counter and continued his task. He reached for wine glasses and set them down onto the black granite.

"You always seem surprised. I really don't get it. You're friends with my brother. You know how it works. Flash in. Flash out."

"Yeah well, it appears I've picked up another blood sucker."

"When you put it that way it sounds quite nice. You sure are a sweet talker."

"If the shoe fits."

Viktor cocked his head and rolled his eyes, noting Hunter's lack of clothing. "Wolves."

"What's your issue?" Hunter opened the wine vault and sighed. "Hmm. Domaine Leroy Richebourg Grand Cru?"

"The wolf doesn't wear pants, but he knows his wine."

"Chateau Petrus Pomeraol?"

"The pinot noir." Viktor glanced at the cheese and turned his nose upward in disgust.

"Quint cooks. What's your issue? Food is good."

"Food *was* good." Viktor picked up the pie-shaped chunk of brie, inspecting the package. "My brother doesn't need food. He's weak. Insists on cooking this human shit as if he is one. *We* drink blood. Preferably human. A witch or wolf every now and then is fine, but a human? It's as natural as you eating this." He tossed the cheese block onto the counter.

"Don't let Quint hear you talk that way. He'll kick your ass."

"He'd try," he grumbled.

"He would."

"He depends too much on this human sustenance and now that he's with Gabriella," he sighed, "I'm afraid he's gone even softer."

"It doesn't make you weak to eat food."

"We all make our own choices, Alpha. Vampires are reborn. And the moment it happens, we're stripped of our human privileges. We must embrace what we've become. Adapt or die. If we spend a lifetime remembering or worse, lamenting, the evolution of ourselves, that serves no purpose."

"No offense but you're an old dude. You'd think you'd be good with it by now." Hunter opened a drawer and rummaged through it, searching for a corkscrew.

"Of course I accept it, but I cannot allow myself to reminisce about my human days. They're over. I'm vampire. It's all that I am now."

"Well…ah, found it." Hunter smiled and held the tool up in the air. "I'm just sayin' maybe it's time to let this thing go. Relax a little."

"Tell me about Willa," Viktor said, deliberately changing the subject.

"She's amazing." Hunter smiled, making quick work of uncorking the bottle.

"Look at me," Viktor demanded.

"What?" The Alpha shrugged, a silly smile forming on his lips.

"You are like a girl."

"Girls are amazing."

"You didn't?" Viktor sniffed into the air. "You've mated, haven't you?"

Hunter laughed and began opening the cheese.

"You wolves be droppin' like flies."

"I didn't mate her. I marked her. Big difference."

"So, you peed on her then? I licked her she's mine sort of thing? You wolves are animals."

"Fuck off, Vik."

"Ah well, all of you can live in bliss. Poor me will have to fuck a different hottie every night. I'll suffer but someone's gotta do it." He slid a chair out from the table and sat.

"It's not like I have control over these things. I didn't go looking for her. I was looking for your ass."

"You found ass, that's for sure. And it wasn't mine."

"What's done is done. The Goddess determines fate, not me. If I hadn't marked her, my wolf would have gone berserk."

"You blame it on the animal? Pfft. I've seen the way you look at her."

Hunter grinned and held the bottle up to Viktor. "Do you want a glass?"

Viktor shot him a hard glare.

"I'll take that as a no."

"Where is she?"

"Upstairs. She needs to rest. I want her to eat something and get a good night's sleep before we go tomorrow."

"The witch?"

"Yes. The witch. Ilsbeth."

"Friend or foe?"

"Foe. Definitely foe. But she saved you and Willa. So off we go."

"She's got a long history of riding the fence. Demons. You play with fire, you get burned."

"And burned she did. Dimitri almost lost his beast. She did that."

"Bargained for black magick. There's always a price."

"It could've killed him."

"He must have some game in the bedroom to drive a witch like her to do something so batshit crazy."

"She liked the D." Hunter shrugged and smiled. "I don't know. Maybe I shouldn't be so harsh. It could've been more than that, but we all know the score. Including her. Wolves can only mate with wolves. Sometimes a hybrid. But never a witch. Or a human or vampire for that matter. It's just our nature. If we're going to breed, which we choose to do when we want, we have to have shifter blood."

"And your girl?"

Hellfire. "She's special."

"Do you care to share why?" A wry smile tugged on Viktor's lips.

"It's not my place to tell you."

"So that's how it's gonna be?" Viktor's gaze went to the ceiling, the sound of footsteps above. "She'll tell me eventually. I've had her blood."

"That's all you're ever going to get," Hunter growled. The thought of anyone hurting Willa spiked his ire.

"I thought you wolves liked to share," Viktor countered.

"Yeah, well. Not me." In truth, Hunter hadn't considered it but as long as they remained unmated, sharing her with another, even for her pleasure, simply wasn't an option.

"Pity. She is lovely."

"Vik. I just got done marking her. It wasn't exactly very well thought out. It just kind of happened. Can you cut me a break?"

"Perhaps. Depends on the secret."

"All I can tell you is that the price on her head still stands. The demons will come for her again through these assholes."

"Demon issues can be solved by demons."

Hunter stopped mid-slice of the cheese and set the knife down on the counter, turning toward the vampire. "Do not summon a demon. I'm fucking serious, Vik. We will handle this. Ilsbeth…"

"Ilsbeth deals with demons. We don't even know if she's clean or what the hell is happening with her."

"We'll find out soon enough. Tonight food. Sleep. She's had a rough go of it." *Julian.* "What happened in the jungle…"

"I haven't found him yet. I looked," Viktor offered. "There was nothing inside or outside of that building."

"Are you reading my mind or something?"

"You have your secrets. I have mine." Viktor flattened a palm onto the table. "He could be in Hell, but he could have flashed somewhere safe. Speaking of which, I sensed that he flashed when we were back at the house. It does leave this tangible energy in the air. We didn't have time to discuss it, but don't you find it odd? A wolf with that sort of power? In all my years, I've never met a wolf who could do that. A witch every now and then. This wouldn't have anything to do with Willa would it?"

"If he flashed away, then why isn't he here right now?" Hunter ignored Viktor's question. *Hellfire. Royals.*

"I was able to flash in, but the entire thing had been burnt to a crisp. Fucking demons. Maybe he's got a tail on him. Can't shake it and doesn't want to bring it our way."

"Hopefully it's that, because I sure as shit don't feel like taking another trip to Hell."

"What was your girl doing in Guatemala anyway?" Viktor set his attention on Hunter, who was carefully arranging crackers onto a plate.

"She got into some trouble."

"What kind of trouble?"

"Human trouble."

"They can be quite difficult."

"The short of it is that she found a rare plant." Hunter popped a piece of cheese into his mouth and continued. "There was a kid who was going to die, and she used a special serum to save her."

"And?"

"She used her blood in the serum." Hunter sighed. "Even you vamps don't go around saving humans with blood very often."

"Some have. It's a rookie mistake. Your girl is no rookie though. And besides, wolf blood won't do shit to save a human, which means there really is something special about her. And since you're being cagey, let me guess. It has something to do with her blood."

"She went to Guatemala to destroy the formula."

"I've had her blood," Viktor mentioned casually.

"Yes, I know. You said it was tainted. We've discussed this."

"Now I know it was Hell so things are a little fuzzy but there was something about it." He scratched his head.

"I told you. She has to tell you herself. With Julian missing…" *Possibly dead.* "Just give her a night before you ask her, okay? Tomorrow we'll see if Ilsbeth knows if there's anything we can do to get the price off Willa's head. She's neck deep in demon shit and I know she probably has an idea how to deal with them. Assuming Ilsbeth is operating with a full deck. I wasn't there when you dropped her ass off at the coven so who the hell knows? But I know the old Ilsbeth. That one? She knows demons." He set the cheese plate onto the table. "We should buzz Samantha. She'll know what's up."

"About Ilsbeth. You're not going to like this bit of news that I have." Viktor's voice morphed into a serious tone.

Hunter's stomach tightened. "What now?"

"Now don't panic because I did get a text from her."

"What happened?"

"She refused to stay at the coven and flew the coop."

Hunter slammed his hand down on the counter, rage tearing through him.

"Easy now. Just listen. She's going to meet with us."

"I told you not to take her…"

"Perhaps you were right about that bit but…"

"Where is she?" Hunter demanded.

"I don't know yet. She's going to message me the location."

"I hate that witch." Hunter exhaled loudly, and reached for his wine, taking a long draw.

"She's what I'd like to call a necessary evil. But let's not focus on that tonight. I promise we will meet with her tomorrow or I will track her down myself and drag her back here on her broomstick. Now about Willa. Is she okay with meeting…"

"She," Hunter went still, hearing the floorboards creak above his head. He pointed upward, "is awake so mind yourself, vamp."

"I do like her. And not just her blood." Viktor shrugged. He reached for a piece of cheese and sniffed it. "She's a fighter."

"Let's hope she is."

"And that means?"

"It means she's going to be pack."

"Ah, you beasts are all about dominance. I suppose we are the same. But we aren't loyal to a band of vampires."

"Kade is."

"Yes. He rules New Orleans, but in general, ancients like me? I have no time for assholes. I just kill them. Listen or die. Easy choice."

"She's coming. I…" Hunter lost his words as a white wolf padded into the kitchen. He smiled, admiring her confident stride.

"She shows herself again," Viktor commented as she passed by him.

"My beautiful wolf." Hunter reached for her as she approached him, running his fingers over her fur. "Are you hungry?"

Willa whined, laying her head into his palm.

"Oh Goddess, she is adorable. I changed my mind about wolves. I want one," Viktor told him.

"Wolves don't mate with vampires."

"You never know what I'm capable of, friend. I've lived a very long time and no woman belongs to me as of yet." He reflected in silence. "Perhaps I'm cursed." A sad smile crossed his face. He quickly recovered and placed a cheese cube inside his mouth.

Hunter watched in fascination as the vampire slowly chewed, his gaze settling on Willa. Tempted to make a sarcastic remark, he restrained himself, his lips drawn tight.

"I must say this cheese isn't horrible," Viktor remarked. "It's been over five hundred years since I've tasted food."

Hunter's eyes widened, a smile on his lips. "Are you telling me that you picked today to eat something?"

"I'm not myself after that trip to Hell." His eyes softened as he glanced at Willa. "No worries. I'll be right as rain with a few more sips of blood."

The Alpha detected her magick shift as her fur transformed to skin. Willa slowly stood, her nudity mostly hidden as she stood behind the kitchen island. The locks of her hair dusted over her nipples.

"You're beautiful." His cock jerked at the sight of her. *I'm so fucked.*

She smiled, her cheeks blooming pink.

"Ah, the wolf is gone. From beast to beauty." Viktor smiled.

"You had cheese," she said.

Viktor shrugged. "Yes, I suppose I did. I'm not exactly myself. Could be Hell."

"Viktor." Her smile disappeared, concern rattling her voice. "My blood. Is it changing you?"

"Your energy is like the sun, my dear Willamina. Nothing about your blood would ever harm me." Viktor reached for an almond and rolled it in his fingers. "I'm susceptible though to Hell, demons. My sire, Baxter. He was brutal. He tried to destroy any goodness within us. The darkness in him was overpowering. Only demons conjure that kind of evil. If I didn't know better, I'd think he'd been in Hell with me. That laughter. I'm not sure if you remember it."

Willa shook her head, but Hunter knew the diabolical cackling all too well. The voices, encouraging the torture.

"It doesn't matter. What matters is that I bit you without consent. And while I've killed and will do so again, I don't harm innocents."

"It's not your fault," she responded, empathy for the ancient vampire in her voice. "You had no choice."

"The Alpha keeps the secrets of his mate."

Willa's eyes flashed to Hunter's and quickly returned to Viktor's.

"Why are the demons after you?" he pressed.

Her spine straightened as if she wore a crown. "I am Aline Ermenjarta Lobo. Princess Aline Ermenjarta Lobo."

Viktor gave a knowing smile. "Your parents?"

"Aren't alive. My lineage is why the wolves kidnapped me. They knew they'd get money. Like trophy hunters hunting a rare animal, they snatched their prize. Julian is my brother." Willa held out her hands, sending light to her fingertips. "I have hellfire in my blood."

Viktor shook his head. "Fucking demons. Always

thinking that they'll have the last laugh. Now I'm finding out that you were sportin' hellfire."

"I wasn't exactly in the condition to tell you."

"No wonder I'm not myself."

"I think it's why I don't react well when you dematerialize. Something about my blood. It could be you. Or it could be me. Julian…"

"He's a Lobo too. Prince." He shook his head. "His power."

"Yes. I didn't know he could flash like he did. It's not like wolves…well…you know we don't do that."

"But you aren't just any wolves. You're royalty. Still holding onto that teensy tiny bit of hellfire. Like the missing link."

"It's not as though we can control it. In the jungle. I…I…" she stammered.

"It's okay, sweetheart. Nothing's going to hurt you here." Hunter wrapped his arm around her shoulders, and she relaxed against him.

"I can move things. Like if I focus all my energy."

"Telekinesis!" Viktor clapped his hands together and laughed.

"Like witchcraft," she said.

"Like an original wolf," Viktor replied. "Or," he locked his gaze on hers, "an ancient vampire."

"How do you mean?"

"He's just saying that the powers within you. They develop so to speak."

Viktor nodded.

"Vik probably didn't start flashing right away. The vamps are like little babes in the woods when they're first turned."

"Easy." Viktor grimaced at his words.

"Whatever. You're a fledgling. It's why his master could be such a dick to them for so long."

"It's true. I didn't flash right away but neither did Quintus. He tells everyone he did it first but he's wrong. I just didn't tell him. He'd be quite jealous."

"Someday Quint is gonna hear you talkin' shit about him and kick your ass."

"Blah, blah, blah. We've already worked out our squabbles. I've got style. He's got…I don't know. A skill for killing people. Let's face it. It's not like he was always good. He killed people. For a living. Why do people always assume he's the good one?"

"Because he's a badass. And they'll tell him whatever he wants to hear."

"Okay, he does have that special power too," Viktor held up his fingers, making air quotes. "But, ah, dear friends, I can do things he can't. Which before you ask, I'm not telling either of you, but it does bring us back to Prince Julian."

"That's not his real name," she told him.

"But of course it isn't." Viktor sighed. "My point is just that when you are ancient, when you are origin wolves, you get special powers too. Things others don't get. But it takes time to develop them and you," he blew out a breath in disgust, wrinkling his nose, "you spend entirely too much time with humans. What were you thinking?"

"That I'm saving lives. That I'm a humanitarian."

"But you're not human. And that's my point. Whatever little trick you did with your blood is drumming up all this nonsense. The demons probably all have their pointed little tails in a bunch over losing your special soul. Someone got paid."

"And they want me back."

"But they're not getting you back. The assholes who took you are going to die. It's the only way. They've already killed humans and vampires. My beta is missing. It's just a matter of time."

"Your beta is not a good person," she insisted.

"He's not. But he is missing. I don't know what his involvement is in all this, if any, but he's my responsibility and I have to deal with him too."

"Tomorrow will be the day."

"Ilsbeth." Hunter's expression flattened in anger.

"You cannot let her get to you, Alpha," Viktor warned. "She's cunning. I don't trust the demons have not gotten to her."

"She saved your ass."

"Ilsbeth works in trades. Tit for tat. It's what she does," Viktor explained.

"You owe her." Like the fae, Ilsbeth would see it as a debt. "But she owes me, and she owes Dimitri. I could call him in if I have to, but I think it's best we keep her away from him. I don't think Logan would go for it and frankly as an Alpha, I wouldn't allow it either."

"I hate owing that bitch, but she saved my life."

"And mine. In Hell…" Willa's voice faltered as if she were in a trance. "With you…I remember flashes you know. It's like a movie. Even with Ilsbeth there, you could have killed me."

"I barely had control, but I tried not to hurt you." Viktor sighed and glanced toward the ground. "My entire life I've stared into the face of evil. Baxter. If you didn't know him, you'd think he was Satan himself. When I was first turned, the thirst for blood was so great I could have killed for it. He'd chain us with silver just for the hell of it. Quint and I…so many days we wanted to stake ourselves. But you can't, you know. His laughter. I can still hear it. He'd bring in a human, draining them dry right in front of us. One after another. Like wild dogs, we'd pant, tugging so hard at the silver the entire room smelled of burnt flesh. When he'd release us…oh Goddess. Death. It was all I could think of. Not one time though." Viktor shook his head, his expression somber. "I could not do it. I'd take what I needed, and escape, running so far into the night, until I couldn't go any further. All the while knowing he'd never release me from his mental hold. When I close my eyes, I can hear the screaming. The kind of screaming that punches through your chest, wraps around your heart until you can barely breathe. He'd kill them all. I wasn't strong enough. Neither was Quint. We'd learned restraint. All the time growing stronger and stronger until we could break free of Baxter."

As a pregnant pause lingered, Hunter recalled Quintus' recollection of their brutal sire. A mercenary, the ancient vampire had killed for money, claiming he'd enacted retribution on those who embraced evil. Yet the lethal nature of the vampire edged darkness despite his leaning toward goodness.

Viktor, seemingly unaware of his brief silence, continued. "The souls in Hell who are destined for an eternity of torture? Some made their choice while they lived on this plane. Maybe they chose evil. Maybe, like our dear high priestess, they made a deal with a demon. Even when you have nothing left to give, you can still make the right choice. And then the souls who've been stolen? Like you." He lifted his gaze to meet hers. "Or me. Or perhaps even those who are as foolish as our Alpha, who risk going into Hell for any reason. We continue to make the choice over and over again until we are released of our misery or give in. I made a choice Willa. I chose you. And Ilsbeth? She also chose you. This is why you felt no pain."

"I'm sorry," Willa offered.

"Ilsbeth, if she's truly trying to change, she owes the Goddess. I'm sure it wasn't the first time she's traded with demons, but she got in over her head with whoever she played with," Hunter said. "I've been thinking about this ever since I rescued her. I just can't help but think whatever she did, I think it was more than just bargaining for Dimitri. She's been around a long time. Something's bothering me about it. I don't think it's as simple as screwing up over wanting a wolf."

"I agree. And so," His expression lightened, a small smile crossing his face. "We must be careful tomorrow. Whatever took her from the coven, which I'm believing they absolutely did take her, could be waiting for her."

"They'll be after her again," Hunter warned.

"Possibly. We need to talk to her, but I'm letting both of you know right now that if we need to flash, we're all out of there. Sorry pet, but no taking the car."

Willa smiled. "Only if we have to. I can't risk getting any sicker. There's something about when you dematerialize. It seems like it's taking me longer and longer to recover."

Hunter kissed the top of her hair. "We'll drive."

"Ah, the wolves are going soft."

The touch of her palm on his chest ignited a fire within him. "Yeah, I don't think that's happening."

"Seriously. I cannot take mated wolves." Viktor rose and brushed his palms over his jeans.

"We haven't…" Willa twirled a long lock into her fingers, inadvertently exposing her shoulder.

"Ah, no worries. I've really got to go get something decent to eat."

Distracted, Hunter caught a glimpse of the colorful design on her skin. *His mark.* His cock hardened like concrete at the sight of it, his wolf urging him to fully claim her. His emotions warred silently as she spoke to Viktor. Two days ago, he was just an Alpha doing his thing, albeit in Hell, and now his entire world had been overturned.

He glanced down to his stiff erection, that remained well hidden behind the island. "We'll be here until dawn."

As Willa's hand wrapped around his shaft, his eyes flashed to hers and she gave a sexy smile, ignoring the vampire. Goddess, she'd kill him.

"Wolves," Viktor mused, stretching his neck from side to side. "I've got to get myself a meal."

"Hmm…yeah I'm really hungry," Willa said.

Hunter bit his lip as she stroked his cock. *What the fuck is she doing?*

"I find myself parched. Some sweet blood and flesh will do nicely," Viktor told them.

"I could not agree more." She smiled and glanced up to Hunter.

As she tightened her grip, his palms flattened onto the counter. He sucked a breath, her thumb running over his wet slit.

"Don't you agree?" she asked.

"Yeah, yeah. Food. Good." *Jesus, I sound like an idiot.* The vampire would know what they were doing. "Need food."

"What the hell is wrong with you?" Viktor plowed his fingers through his hair. "I'll head out to Frenchman and shoot Quint a text. That mated fool might be hard to reach."

"Hard. Sure will be." *Fuuuuuccck.* Hunter's lip drew tight as Willa shifted against him, dragging the tip of his dick along her hip.

"Tomorrow." Willa gave her Alpha a quick glance. "I am starving."

Sweat beaded on Hunter's forehead. Did she want to be seen? What the hell was she doing?

"Eat then. I'm not stopping you." Viktor cocked his head, his eyes narrowing as he studied them. "What are you two doing?"

Hunter cracked a broad smile. "Nothin you need to be worryin' about, vamp."

Willa laughed. "I'm handling things here."

"Fuck you two." Viktor shook his head, the corner of his lips tugging upward. "Fuck me. I've gotta get something to eat."

"So do I." She winked at Hunter.

"I'm done with both of you. Peace out, bitches." Viktor snapped his fingers, disappearing into the air.

Hunter spun, taking his dick into his hands. The sounds of her laughter sent blood rushing to his cock. He stepped back, keeping just out of reach of his devilish temptress. Inwardly he laughed, his eyes painting over her. While he'd allowed her to take control, she'd officially lost the reins.

"You're hungry, huh?" He laughed, sliding his thumb down his shaft.

"Ravenous," she answered, her voice husky.

"On your knees, mate."

Her eyes widened along with her smile. "Mate?"

"Now," he ordered, his smile fading. Fucking hell, he wanted her, but this time there'd be no quick sex. He planned on taking his time exploring every part of her.

Willa kept her fiery eyes on his as she dropped down before her Alpha.

"You like playing while the vampire watches, do you?" He inched closer to his mate. Her cheeks flushed in response to his question. "Is that how you like to play, little wolf?"

She licked her lips and shrugged.

"All right then. You're a little bit of a freak now, are ya?

This is an unexpected development. How about you open up those lips for me, sweetheart. You're hungry, you say? I've got a little bit of something for you."

As her lips slowly parted, Hunter's heart pounded in his chest. He'd push her to her limits and then some and enjoy every fucking second of it.

She lifted her head, her sultry gaze penetrating his. He dragged the tip of his cock along her bottom lip. She remained still, as if waiting on him to command her. He reached for her mind, testing the new connection with his mate. *Open, princess.* He smiled as she responded, guiding his cock into her warm mouth.

Willa's hands reached for him. *No hands. You're for my pleasure now.* She complied, withdrawing them. *Good little wolf.*

He shivered as her full lips surrounded his dick, sucking him as he plunged inside her. His fingers speared through her thick hair, his palms gripping her head as he thrust in and out of her mouth. A surge of her energy spiked through him, and he sucked his breath, his orgasm teetering toward explosion.

Hunter groaned, pulling his dick from her mouth. His cock ached at the sight of her wet lips. "I'm gonna come right now if we keep this up and we've got some eating to do."

"What?" she asked, her voice breathy.

Without explaining, he reached for her waist, lifting her from the ground up into his arms. He briefly eyed the kitchen table and the counter, but for his plans he needed a soft surface, a play space where he could take his time.

"Where are we…"

"One thing about my NOLA home, it's built for comfort." Hunter cradled her to his chest, his erection springing forward as he made quick work of bringing her into the family room. He carefully laid her onto the sheepskin rug, devouring her with his hungry eyes. As much as he wanted to fuck her right there, he'd savor every minute with her. Tomorrow they'd fight all day, but tonight was theirs.

"Stay right there," he ordered, and she giggled in response.

"I'm still hungry," she called to him.

"Don't you worry," he laughed. Hunter quickly brought the wine glasses and cheese tray, but not before setting the plastic honey bear atop it.

"Hmm, so hungry," she purred. "But I don't want cheese."

"I'm seeing a new side of you. You're feeling feisty, huh?"

"Horny."

"Good things come to those who wait."

"Maybe I don't want to wait."

Hunter placed the glasses onto the hearth and flipped a switch, igniting a fire. "Maybe you're going to have to learn how to submit, first, mate."

"I still don't believe this is happening." Her fingers drifted to her neck, tracing the mark. "I was always told I couldn't. It's not that I didn't want it, you know. I was raised in a pack. It was small but I had one. Aunts. Cousins. Julian." Sadness shone in her eyes.

"He's going to be fine."

"I don't feel him, but I know in my heart he's okay. When we were kids, we just knew what each other was thinking. It's kind of like how I'm feeling you. Except your energy…it's so intense. When I'm with you, my wolf, she's…she wants to claim you. To complete the mating. It's crazy, really. Isn't it? We've just met."

"Those are human reactions. You're a wolf, Willa. This cannot be explained in human terms. Our beasts, they know." Hunter reached for a piece of cheese, slid it atop a cracker and held it close to her lips. "Eat."

Willa parted her lips accepting the crispy treat. "Hmm… okay…"

"That's it. A little something in your belly will be good for you. I can order some take out later. For now, though, I plan to eat you."

"Is that right?" she laughed.

"You're very tasty." Hunter reached for the glass and put the rim to her lips, smiling as she sipped her wine.

"You're very tasty too, but you're a tease. I'm suffering. I need you." Willa feigned sadness, her lips pursed in disappointment.

"You'll get me, sweetheart. But first, did I mention I have a sweet tooth?"

"And what do you plan on doing with that?" Willa's eyes widened as he picked up the honey bear, her lips in a broad smile.

Hunter placed a dollop of the syrup onto a piece of cheese and placed it in her mouth. He selected several more pieces and studied her. "I think, though, you'd make a nice serving dish."

"What?" she said, nearly choking.

"No moving now. You'll disturb my dinner." Hunter placed a small slice onto her stomach and hips. "This." He held up the bear. "I do enjoy it sticky sweet. I bet you will too."

Willa tilted her head, opening her mouth, moaning as he squeezed a tiny drop onto her tongue and lips. She sighed as he trailed it over her nipples, squeezing a few more droplets onto the cheese. Hunter gently settled in front of her, spreading open her knees.

"Much better." The Alpha leaned over her and dragged the tip of his tongue over her lower lip. "Delicious."

His mouth crushed onto hers, tasting his mate. She brushed her hand ever so slightly onto his cheek, sending her powerful energy spiraling through him. In all his days, he'd never met an equal, someone who could transcend her vibrations.

His forehead rested upon hers as he tore his lips from hers. His breath heavy, as if she'd stolen his heart, he blinked open his eyes to gaze into the mysterious soul of his mate. His cock brushed over her stomach, igniting fresh arousal, and his devious smile was all the warning she would get as to what he'd do next.

"I'm famished," he growled.

Willa's fingers speared into his hair as he peppered kisses down her breast. Hunter lapped his tongue over a taut nipple, sugary sweetness dancing in his mouth. He flicked at her tip once before taking a firm suck, then quickly moving his attention to her other breast.

"Oh Goddess," she moaned in response, her hips rising to meet his.

"You're fucking amazing," the Alpha groaned as her pussy brushed his cock. He resisted the urge to slam inside her, filling his mate to the hilt. *Patience*, he silently told the wolf within who sought to devour its prey, sinking its teeth into her flesh to seal their bond.

"Don't ever let me go." Her desperate breathy words wrapped around his heart.

His mouth explored her body, tasting and licking, leaving a trace of his kisses in their wake. He memorized her every curve, ever so lightly, teasing as he rested between her legs. She moaned in response, as his hands found her soft breasts. His heart pounded in his chest, his wolf howling, restless for its mate.

"This," he whispered, his fingers trailing down her stomach, settling on her hip. With his lips mere inches from her pussy, he raised his gaze. Her dark eyes swirled with passion, flecks of light dancing in her pupils. "You will never be alone again. We have a lifetime to explore, to grow together."

"My Alpha," she whispered. "You're mine."

Chills danced over his skin at the sound of her sultry voice claiming him as hers. Whether he'd expected it or not, Willa had stormed into his heart, commanding his wolf to attention. Everything he'd ever known was forever changed.

Slow and deliberate, holding her gaze, he dragged the tip of his tongue through her pussy, and licked his lips, savoring the sweet honeyed taste of her. She bit her lower lip, and all he could think about was devouring every last bit of his mate. He wore a smile as his fingers trailed down the crease between her mound and thigh, teasing the sides of her labia.

Setting his focus on his prize, he pressed his mouth to her pussy, driving his tongue into her ripe flesh. He lapped at her clitoris, driving a finger inside her. She bucked up into his mouth, her fingers clutching at his shoulders. The sound of her moan was like music to his ears. His broad flat tongue grazed over her sensitive nub as he sucked it into his mouth. She shook beneath him as he added a second finger, penetrating her core. Stroking in and out of her, he increased his pace, flicking his tongue over her clit, her cries becoming louder and louder.

"Oh Goddess…Hunter. Fuck. Yes. Don't stop. Ah…"

As he cupped her ass, he teased her cleft, allowing his pinky to brush over her ass.

"I…I…Yes, yes, yes…That's it," Willa panted.

Her response to his touch was a welcome discovery. "Fucking come, baby," he murmured, his lips sucking her clitoris into his mouth.

"I need you in me. Yes! Yes!" she screamed, her body shaking in release.

Hunter lapped her pussy one last time and pressed onto his knees, watching his beautiful mate come. He took his dick into his hands and speared it through her wet folds, teasing her clit one last time before he sated his desires.

As Hunter slid inside her hot sheath, he sucked a breath. Her quivering channel tightened around his cock. *Oh*

Goddess. So fucking perfect. Everything about her. She arched her back and tilted her pelvis, forcing him in deeper. *No. You've got this. Jesus*, he inwardly cringed, realizing he had to talk himself out of coming right then. As he caught her knowing smile, his heart caught in his chest. This woman would turn him inside and out and he'd crave her for the rest of his life.

He leaned over Willa, his arms caging hers. Easing in and out of her, Hunter dipped his head, capturing a taut nipple between his lips. Willa moaned, wrapping her legs around his waist. Her fingers tunneled into his hair, clutching him to her chest.

"Don't ever stop," she pleaded, her hips meeting his as he thrust inside her.

"Never," he promised.

As he made love to her, twirling the tip of his tongue over her taut peak, he smiled at their perfect fit. Her legs tightened, and he allowed her to roll him onto his back, her hair brushing over his chest. He marveled at her beauty as she threw her head backwards, her long locks spilling over her shoulders.

Willa impaled herself onto his rock-hard cock, grinding her hips, undulating on top of him.

"You're going to kill me, woman," he growled, gripping her ass.

As she brought her hands to her breasts, rolling her nipples between her fingers, she smiled. "You sure you're up for me, Alpha?"

"Do I feel up to it?" He drove his hips upward.

"I seem to have lost all sense around you…Ahh…" Her hands drifted to his chest.

Willa's head lolled forward, her hair grazed over his skin as she leaned over him. A low growl emanated from her throat, her lips brushing his chest. "My wolf. Fuck me. Fuck me hard, Alpha."

Her words stirred Hunter's beast. Suspecting Willa was far more Alpha than she'd let on, or perhaps knew herself, she'd push him further. His cock lengthened as her mouth drew closer to his neck.

Fuck, they'd never discussed the time of their actual mating. Yet it hardly mattered. With his dick so far in her he thought he'd never leave the bed again. No, his wolf would have her one way or another. In all ways. Sweet nothings or silence. Rough or gentle. All day. All night.

"Do you know what it means, Hunter? To accept to be my mate?"

Hunter could barely understand her question, her hips undulating on his. He speared his fingers into her hair, lifting it so he could see her face. The soft brush of her lips over his nipple contrasted with the bite of her fingernails stabbing into his shoulders.

"What? Ah…fuck…Willa, you test me." He thrusted up into her, her slow deliberate teasing mouth torturing him.

"My Alpha." Her whisper sounded like thunder in his ears.

"Jesus, woman. I'm gonna come."

"Tonight…"

The hard suction on his shoulder took him by surprise,

a sharp edge scraping along his skin. His wolf roared in response. *She's claiming me.* The thought spun in his head as he struggled not to orgasm.

"You're mine," she whispered. "My king."

"Ah…Jesus…oh Goddess," Hunter cried out loud, the sharp sting of her teeth piercing his skin. *What the fuck?* Without warning she'd begun the mating process, hellfire sparking in his mind's eye. A kaleidoscope of colors danced in his mind, her royal energy tearing through him.

Jesus Christ, what has she done? The Alpha's dominance rose, his wolf feral for its mate. He'd never anticipated the mating happening so soon, but he lost control.

As she released her bite, Hunter flipped her over onto her back. His mouth crushed onto hers, tasting his own blood on her lips. His tongue probed her mouth, claiming her with his kiss. There was no turning back. Devouring her mouth, he drove his cock inside her. His savage beast urged him to take her in kind, but he mastered his wolf, still delaying the pleasure.

He wrenched his lips from hers, staring into her wild eyes. Flecks of fire danced in her pupils, her chest heaving with a ragged breath.

"Willa." Hunter's lips turned upward in a devious smile. "You've been a bad girl. A very bad girl."

Chapter Ten

Willa lost herself in a sexual frenzy. A whisper in her mind told her to go slow but the roar of her wolf stoked the primal need to take her Alpha. It was all wrong, yet it was a perfect storm. As Hunter made love to her, her wolf came alive, demanding she claim her mate.

She'd never planned on initiating the mating. She only sought to mark him, to sate the carnal craving, yet as she bit down, her wolf won. Her teeth broke his skin, the sweet blood on her lips. His essence coated her tongue, his magick rushing through her entire being. Memories, lust, a myriad of emotions flashed in her mind.

What the hell did I just do? The wild look in his eyes only served to spike her arousal. *A bad girl?* Oh, Goddess it was so much worse than that. She'd freaking initiated the mating without so much as a discussion. The tic of his smile told her he'd found it amusing yet the way he dragged his tongue across his lips warned her she was in trouble.

Willa shoved up onto her elbows, her heart pounding in her chest, wondering what he'd do to her. Her eyes drifted down his muscular torso, noting every delicious ridge of his washboard abs. His enormous cock bobbed as he shifted onto his knees. Her eyes caught his and a nervous giggle escaped her lips.

"I'm sorry," was all she could manage.

"Princess, princess, princess." Hunter shook his head.

"I…" Willa arched her back; her pussy ached.

"You're in trouble."

I know. Her pulse raced as he laid his hands on her thighs.

"Bad little wolf." His thumbs teased over the crease of her leg and mound. She attempted to wiggle but his grip tightened on her hips.

"I…I…" she stammered. As he grew closer, she lost all train of thought. Her breath quickened.

"You're in so much trouble," he repeated.

Willa yelped in surprise as he rolled her over onto her stomach, laughing as he wrapped his arm around her waist, pulling her onto her knees. She shifted and he quickly corrected her, gripping her ass.

"Bad."

She sucked a breath as his palm stung her bottom. *He's spanking me?* Her head lolled forward with a laugh of disbelief.

"You're wild, aren't you? Needing some taming, princess?"

"Ah, yes," she cried as he smacked her other cheek. Her pussy flooded in arousal and she gasped, clawing at the rug.

"There's no going back." Hunter pressed the tip of his dick to her entrance.

Forever. The word rattled in her mind but quickly disappeared as his stiff cock slammed inside her tight channel.

"Up on your knees, sweetheart," he ordered.

"Hunter…I…" As his hand found her breast, she struggled to speak. Her entire body lit with desire.

"You want to play?" he growled.

"Ah…yes…um, what?" Her body flushed with pleasure, she struggled to answer. She pushed onto her palms, deliberately sliding back onto his cock. Hunter's laughter burned in her ears.

"You may have been rogue most of your life, but you're pack now, little wolf." He slowed the pace, palming her ass.

"But I…what…" As the pad of his thumb teased her back hole, she went completely still.

"We could've had this discussion earlier, but I'll admit. I'm a fan of surprises. Are you?" he asked.

"I've never…" She sighed as his finger played along the puckered skin. Her clit ached in response. "Please. I'm on fire."

"Hmm…let's see if you like surprises."

"Ah…" As his thumb probed into her ass, stretching her, her face heated in response to her arousal. "No, no, no. Ah…Goddess."

"You want me to stop?" he asked, a lilt in his voice.

"No, no…please. I can't believe." *Jesus.* She should have known she'd enjoy exploring her fantasies with Hunter, but she hadn't given a thought to ass play.

Hunter plunged his cock deep inside her pussy while he

dipped the tip of his thumb into her tight hole. "Ah, that's it. You've got a beautiful ass."

"This is…oh Goddess…I didn't mean to…" As the words left her lips, she gave a small laugh, her body threading with his energy, her orgasm mounting.

"Oh, I think you did, little wolf."

"No, no, no…don't stop." Willa shook her head. He slowed his pace, and as his hand around her waist drifted into her slick folds, her body rippled with desire.

"This." He thrust hard and deep. "Right." His fingers teased over her clit, back and forth. "Here."

She heaved for breath as he filled her over and over again, increasing the pressure on her sensitive bead.

"Harder," she demanded.

"Holy sh…"

"I'm…I'm…" she repeated, her climax teetering on the edge.

Mine. The sweet sting of his bite hurled her into orgasm, his cock filling her. She trembled in release, the energy of the Alpha slamming through her mind and body.

Willa curled onto her side as Hunter withdrew and spooned behind her. She shivered, her conflicting emotions swirling in her chest. The Alpha had been her savior, and because she'd bit him, initiating the mating, he'd forever be at risk. The royal hellfire, both a curse and blessing, was a burden that gave her immortality and now the gift to move objects. But it also put a price on her head.

Julian. Her heart squeezed as her thoughts turned to her brother. It was her fault he was gone. *He's strong*, she told herself. Yet the demons were tricksters. If they took him, she'd go back into Hell to find him herself.

"Willamina." The Alpha's low voice shook her from her contemplation, but a response failed to come to her. "What just happened…it's going to be okay."

"I'm sorry." It was all she could manage. While her beast slept content, her humanity weighed heavy in guilt. "I shouldn't have…"

"Wills…it's okay. I wasn't expecting this either but," he exhaled, pressing his lips to the top of her head, "what's done is done. I'm not sure if I expected to know the person who was my mate. I've seen it happen a million times over the years. This is the one thing in life we can't change."

"You don't know what I've done." As his fingers brushed over her arm, her heart melted.

"We had sex. You bit me. It was fucking awesome sex I might add."

"I bit you and I also drank from you. I initiated it without asking."

"I went first and marked you. Let's call it even. I could have stopped it if I wanted to."

No, you couldn't have, Willa inwardly thought, unconsciously projecting her words.

"Yes, I could. Okay…It would have been extremely hard to stop you, but I could have," he lied.

"What did you just say?" He'd heard her thoughts. *Oh no.*

Oh yes. Hunter laughed softly, his lips grazing her hair.

"You heard me?" Panic settled in her belly.

"Crystal clear. Yes, I heard you. You're not controlling it. I'm your mate. I can sense all of you. Your energy. All that hellfire. You're hotter than Hell."

"This isn't a joke. You can hear me."

"That's how we roll. We're wolves. Listen, sweetheart. It's okay. All of this. Our mating. Us talking. Not using our voice. It's natural. You need to understand that no matter how royal you are or even with your super-cool moving objects power…which I admit is pretty fucking cool," he laughed. "I'm Alpha. I already can talk to my wolves without speaking. It's more like commands going out to them. I can sense the overall vibe of the pack. Their fear. Happiness. You've gone so long without pack, it's like you don't remember."

"I just…" Willa rolled over to face him, comforted by his arm wrapping around her waist, drawing her to him. "I've helped a lot of people in my lifetime, Hunter." Her palm cupped his strong chin. Her gaze drifted from his lips to his eyes. Mesmerized, it was almost as if she saw her own hellfire dancing within them. "But this choice. Ours is not an ordinary mating. We are two very special wolves. My life was good, but I took a solo path so as to not draw attention to myself or anyone I cared about. I'm marked. Now you are too. Now we've no choice because…" her thumb edged along his bottom lip, "we're mated. But honestly…even if we weren't, I don't think I could ever let you go."

As his lips captured hers, she released her doubt and guilt. *My Alpha.* Her heart squeezed, realizing she'd meant what she'd told him. Leaving him wasn't an option. More than her wolf, her heart told her this man belonged to her. Tomorrow would come soon enough, and she'd fight to the death to keep him safe.

"Wakey, wakey lovebirds."

Willa heard Viktor's voice and ignored the pestering vampire. The Alpha wasn't quite as forgiving, jumping from the bed and shoving him up against the door.

"What the fuck are you doing in here?" Hunter released him and turned on his heels. Buck naked, he yawned and rubbed his cheeks with his palms. Willa blinked open her eyes, but Hunter blocked Viktor from her line of sight.

Viktor sniffed. "Ah, have you two been being naughty little wolves?"

Hunter glanced down to his alarm clock and sighed. "What the fuck are you doing here at three-thirty in the morning?"

"It's the witching hour, friends." Viktor smiled, wiggling his fingers in the air.

"What?"

"You know. Ilsbeth. She sent me some super-secret double handshake text. Meeting her in Pirate's Alley in the Quarter."

"What? Why there?" Hunter plowed his fingers through his hair and returned to the bed.

"I know. It's super scary, huh?" He laughed.

"Are you high?" Hunter growled.

"What's going on?" Willa asked, her voice rumbling, still partially asleep. So tired, she didn't want to get out of bed.

"Yeah, you're right. Totally cliché. Ah. Well. I suppose Ilsbeth didn't get the memo."

"We should have talked to Samantha first."

"Luca's not exactly keen on us involving his fiancée."

"Why can't Kade get involved?"

"Seems Quint old boy caused a bit of ruckus at their backyard barbeque. Few demons here and there. As I remember it, it wasn't so bad. It's not like they destroyed the house. Spilled a few drinks maybe."

"You got sent to Hell. How much worse can it get?" Hunter shot back.

"Hmm. Yes. Very true. Not my finest hour."

"Get to the fucking point."

"All I know is when Ilsbeth texts me, I think we should go," Viktor told him.

"What if it's a trap?" Willa asked.

"The shit is going to hit the fan if we go meet this bitch and don't tell Samantha." Hunter shook his head.

"All true. Still though. I do enjoy a good ghost story." Viktor rolled his eyes and shook his head. "Come on, you two. The witch is back." He clapped his hands. "The Ilsbeth I know and love does whatever the fuck she wants. Samantha or no Samantha. And honestly, what is Kade going to do about it if we meet her? You're an Alpha from another state."

"I was born here," Hunter replied.

"Willa wasn't. She wasn't even born in this country. Or

continent. And besides, Kade may be in charge down here but I'm still older and so is Quint. Kade needs to get Luca in line."

"We need information. We have to go," Willa urged. "I know wolves have rules but…"

"Packs have rules. And you're a wolf, so you better get used to it, sweetheart."

"I don't need to get used to anything. I've been around far longer than any of these other wolves," she said.

"There's an order to things. You can't be tellin' an Alpha what to do. Not Logan. Not me."

"Well perhaps the rule and order is about to change," she challenged. Her pulse raced with anger as she shoved up and swung her legs over the bed.

"Okay now." The corner of Viktor's mouth ticked upward, his eyes drifting over Willa's bared body.

"She's mine," Hunter growled at him.

"What?" Viktor asked.

"I belong to no one but myself," Willa stated, her defiant eyes locked on Hunter's. "In fact, I won't be here anymore if we don't figure out how to stop the wolves and the demons after me."

"Five minutes. We'll meet you downstairs," Hunter told Viktor.

The Alpha's stare bored a hole through her, but Willa remained firm, refusing to avert her eyes. Rules belonged to the vampires and wolves, but she was not of pack.

"Now, Viktor," the Alpha growled.

"Pity. Just as things were getting interesting." Without

another word, the vampire dematerialized.

Willa turned on her heels and headed into the bathroom.

"This discussion isn't over, doc."

For now, it is. Willa deliberately shut the door and rested her forehead against it. She sighed, emotion tightening in her chest. If she didn't find a way out of Hell, it wouldn't matter in the least. She'd be dead, and now that she'd mated with Hunter, he likely couldn't live without her.

"Are you sure she's coming?" Willa asked, her eyes drawn to the shadow of Jesus illuminated on the back of the church. She and Hunter walked in silence toward Jackson Square. Sirens blared in the distance as she nervously toed at an indentation in the cobblestone sidewalk, impatient to speak with Ilsbeth.

"She's lucky it's a Tuesday. Not many humans around," Hunter noted.

"What's lucky about that? Humans equal food. I can always use a little tasty snack." The suave vampire smacked his lips and laughed.

"How can you talk about humans like that?" Willa turned to Viktor, disgust on her face.

"Because my dear doctor, they are food. I'm a vampire. That's what I do."

"Don't you have a job?" she pressed, earning a brief smile from Hunter.

"I've earned my keep. You, doc?"

"Someday I'll show you mine. Today's not that day," she replied, giving him a closed smile. Over the years she'd donated much of the money she'd earned.

"Something about this isn't right," Hunter said, scanning the area from one end of the alley to the other.

An eerie silence blanketed the darkness. The hair stood up on the back of Willa's neck and she moved closer to the Alpha. Gooseflesh broke over her skin, black magick vibrations dancing in the air.

"Do you feel it?" she asked, her breath visible as she exhaled. "It feels like death."

"Temperature drop." Hunter reached for her hand.

"What's happening?" Willa's pulse raced as it grew colder.

"That's what's happening. Up there," Viktor told them, pointing down the alley, toward the church.

Willa's heart beat like a drum as the lamp post flickered into darkness. A bright light emerged through the white stone wall of the cathedral. An aberration of a priest appeared before them, his cloak brushing the stone walkway as he passed through the cross-adorned wrought iron gate.

Although the ghost appeared as a holy figure, Willa knew better than to trust it. She lost her breath as it turned to face them, her wolf urging her to shift. The priest lifted a bible, staring straight through its transparent pages.

What is he doing here? she asked Hunter.

He's a priest. We're at a church.

Don't be a smartass. Why is he here? I don't like it.

This is a pretty cool superpower, huh, mate? A corner of his lip turned upward.

Not funny. She slowly exhaled her fear, attempting to calm herself.

The priest's mouth opened, his lips moving in silence.

In the distance, a stranger turned the corner into the alley, slowly approaching them.

"A human?" she whispered.

"A nun." Viktor rolled his eyes. "Not food."

"Now you've got morals?" Hunter asked, his voice low.

"Well, yes." He paused, his hand on his chin. "I suppose it's more of a pecking order. Hot chicks. Hot guys. Not attached. All at the top of the list. Nuns? Not exactly available. But, also not out of the question. Will do in a pinch."

"There's something wrong with you," Willa told him, her heart pounding as the nun walked with her head to the ground, unaware of the ghostly presence.

A shift in the energy alerted her to the danger, dark magick intensifying. *What's happening?* The priest turned his attention directly to Willa and began to open his mouth. His shriveled lips distorted as claws extended from his hands. Before Willa had a chance to react, the nun began running toward it, her soft chants morphing into screams.

Hunter held Willa tight. They watched in fascination as the specter exploded, shards of red flames shooting into the sky as it disappeared.

"What the hell?" Viktor blinked in an attempt to avoid the glare.

As the nun approached, she lifted her gaze. *Ilsbeth.*

Willa's stomach rolled, aware the demon had once again come for her. Although the witch had banished it, she didn't trust that the high priestess didn't have a hand in its appearance.

"Annnnndddd….she's back!" Viktor laughed.

"Jesus Christ, what the hell is going on?" Hunter asked.

"It's too dangerous out here," Ilsbeth told them. "This way."

Ilsbeth quickly strode to an arched wooden door, its planks painted green. She brandished a silver key, stuck it into the keyhole and unlocked it.

Willa looked to Hunter and he nodded, his lips drawn tight in concern. "I'll go first. Stay between us."

Willa thought to argue but acquiesced to his order. Her caution of the witch remained intact. It was not as if Viktor could protect her from a demon. He'd been just as vulnerable as she was. But he and Hunter had known Ilsbeth far longer, and it was prudent to follow their lead.

A single dim lightbulb illuminated the passageway. As Willa stepped into the tunnel, dank air rushed into her nostrils. She covered her face with her arm and coughed. The bang of the door slamming behind them echoed loudly.

The snap of fingers sounded in the small space. Ilsbeth turned to face them, her nude figure surrounded by the glow of a purple aura.

At the sight of the High Priestess, Willa drew a slow deliberate breath, attempting to calm her heart rate. Magick swirled in the air like a toxic cloud, and she slammed up her walls, sealing out any psychic connections.

"This." Ilsbeth clapped her hands and raised them into the air. "I open this passage to only four. No creature shall follow, sealed from entering this door." Her hands parted and circled the air, creating a large white ball of energy. "We've got to get out of here before they come. I go first."

"But…" Viktor began, holding up a finger.

"No arguments, vampire," Ilsbeth interrupted. "The demons will find us. If you want answers, come through the portal."

Ilsbeth nodded at Hunter once before she turned and disappeared through the white shimmering light.

"Shit." The Alpha blew out a breath.

"She's gone." Willa steeled her nerves, knowing they'd have to follow.

"Nun to naked. Now that's a trick. She has a flair for the dramatic. I'll give her that." Viktor ran his fingers through his hair and turned to the Alpha.

"We're going," Hunter told him. "Because that thing we just saw probably has friends. Okay, I'm going first. Hold my hand."

Willa nodded, her heart racing as she watched him stride into the shimmering portal. His body disappeared and her feet followed him. She closed her eyes, praying that whatever lay on the other side wouldn't kill her.

The scent of fresh cut grass and cinnamon incense swirled around her, the sounds of a sensual drumbeat in her ears. She blinked open her eyes, releasing an audible breath. Nearly twenty naked men and women danced in a circle upon the lawn.

Tantric chanting filled the warm night air, the ceremony illuminated by pillar candles placed in a huge circle. A pentagon created out of white rose petals rested under their feet.

Willa's eyes were drawn to a grand mansion. A limestone driveway and massive walkway led up to seven enormous Doric columns at the front of the home. Candlelight flickered upon the dew-kissed blades of grass.

Ilsbeth nodded in reverence toward the witches and waved her hand at Hunter and Willa. They followed her in silence toward the great home.

Willa glanced upward, noting the clear sky, millions of stars twinkling from above. The song of crickets replaced the din of the ceremony. Wherever they were was far beyond the city, but the Spanish Moss drifting from the limbs of the Southern Oak trees caused Willa to suspect they were still in Louisiana.

Ilsbeth swung open the elaborately decorated brass doors. A butler dressed in a formal white uniform presented the High Priestess with a red satin robe, which she accepted with a silent nod.

"Let's have a talk, shall we?" Ilsbeth never made contact as she strode through the home.

Willa's eyes widened as she took in the sight of the enormous foyer. The ultra-modern white stone architecture was complemented by a chic red décor. She glanced up to a domed ceiling which had been painted with an elaborate illustration of the galaxy. As they walked through a sitting area, she noted the pentacles of various sizes woven into the decorations.

Ilsbeth placed her palm upon a rectangular etched glass wall, mumbling an incantation. The hum of the enormous wall disappearing, sliding inside itself revealed a secret room. The scent of frankincense drifted in the air, and as Willa stepped inside, she instantly registered the magick all around her.

"Take a seat," Ilsbeth commanded.

"Goddess, I love the drama." Viktor smiled and put his hands up, slowly spinning. "Look at this room."

Willa's eyes widened at the two-story beveled glass curio cabinet that embodied an entire wall. Candles shone bright upon an elaborate granite altar in the corner.

Ilsbeth turned on her heels and locked her gaze on the Alpha. "I'm forever in your debt." She flipped a strand of her long blonde locks and they spilled over her shoulders. An ethereal presence, the witch seemingly floated toward them. She turned her sights on Willa and gracefully extended her hand. "I believe a formal introduction is due. I am Ilsbeth, High Priestess of Louisiana."

"I…I…thank you," Willa managed but hesitated to shake her hand. As she stared into the witch's violet eyes, she swore she detected the same hellfire that flowed inside her own veins.

"You're welcome, darling. Sometimes we have to fix each other's crowns." Ilsbeth smiled and turned her attention to the Alpha. "So, let's talk demons, shall we?"

Hunter nodded. As he gestured to Willa to sit on the blood-red velvet sofa, the entrance to the room sealed shut. Although Willa feigned indifference, the powerful magick hadn't gone unnoticed. It had existed as long as time, but rarely in her lifetime had she experienced the dark energy of an ancient witch.

"Ilsbeth," Hunter began. He wore a cautious smile, as if amused by her theatrics. "I'm glad...well, I think I'm glad you appear to be okay. I have to say, you seem completely unaffected by your trip to Hell."

"It's the latest spa treatment. Haven't you heard? Sweat it out. Your skin looks like a baby's bottom," Viktor quipped.

Ilsbeth smiled broadly and gently sat down in an intricately carved red leather chair. She delicately perched her feet upon an ottoman.

"I'm not exactly sure where to start." Hunter gave a closed smile, concealing his emotions. 'Look, we might as well not ignore the elephant in the room."

"I do enjoy a circus," Viktor mused.

"You left the coven. The only friend you're going to have left in this town might be Kade, but you know Luca's not going to have it." Hunter's brows narrowed. "And High Priestess of Louisiana? Really? Is that some new title you have? I take it Samantha's not abdicating the New Orleans throne to you."

"Coven politics is not that simple, Alpha." Her smile disappeared. "As you know, I've been missing the past year or so. Samantha is an extraordinary witch. Elemental. It was only right she led the witches. But you see," Ilsbeth paused, her gaze drifting to a life-sized painting depicting Adam and Eve, "I grew weak to temptation and accepted the fruit."

"Dimitri. Logan will never forgive you. He's going to

have my ass if I don't tell him where you are." Hunter blew out a breath. "I know you saved Viktor. Willa."

"Yes, your mate," Ilsbeth noted. "Very interesting. The coupling of a royal with a Livingston."

Willa unconsciously fingered her shoulder where he'd bitten her. Although her mating mark wasn't visible, the witch must have detected a change in their scent.

"He doesn't even know I'm here right now," Hunter continued, ignoring her statement. "You obviously got in a little over your head."

"I was…not myself," she commented, her voice soft but firm.

"Zella? She got nothin' on you. Boring. And that hair? Pluh-leeze. Personally, I'm glad you're back. You're always a little scary. That vibe works for you." Viktor gave a cool smile, his tone flippant.

"I am over a thousand years old. There is much you don't know about me. Perhaps will never know. Dimitri." She sighed reflectively. "He was a temptation. One I should have resisted. I suppose I didn't fully contemplate the ramifications."

"You could have killed him," Hunter accused. "Not only that, whatever demon you summoned, I'm guessing it's the one that stirred all that shit up in New York, that could have leaked out, if it didn't already. Jake saved your ass but only because you weren't you. Now what the hell is this?" He gestured toward the altar. "We aren't even in New Orleans. Where the fuck are we?"

"Easy," Viktor warned.

"No, no, it's true." She lowered her eyes and spoke softly. "I've had many lovers in my lifetime. But Dimitri." Ilsbeth raised her gaze. "He's quite charming. I'm not sure how it happened. It wasn't supposed to. I just fell for him." She sighed. "I knew better than to fall for a wolf. Wolves have mates. No matter how many years go by, they will eventually mate and leave you in the cold. You never know where you will find that mate. Even in Hell. It's proof that the Goddess always provides us with our destiny. And so." Her lips tightened, a sad expression crossed her face. "I knew better. It's true. Alpha, I know you may find it hard to believe but I loved him. I know he never loved me back. But it didn't matter. I just loved him."

"What happened with the demon?" Hunter asked, his eyes transfixed on hers. Although his tone carried a lilt of understanding, his face remained deadpan.

"Magick is drawn from the Goddess yet the dark forces call to us when we need assistance. It's our job as witches to only give the demon enough, a favor, a wish, that causes no direct harm to the soul. In the end, the demons use those favors to lure souls, torture them in some cases. The favor may lie in wait for years, but it is always owed."

"Did you stop to think why it's not okay to torture or lure another soul?" Hunter asked.

"It's not my place to ask when I'm seeking dark magick. All things have balance. Light to dark. Sweet to sour. Good to evil. Demons punish the innocent as well, not just the guilty. I'm not saying they are benevolent because clearly that is not the case nor is it their purpose."

"Purpose? Evil has no purpose," Willa challenged.

"It's not as clear cut as everyone would like to make it seem. Even within the wolves, beast and humanity war with each other. Ironically neither is all good or bad. Wolves. They hunt. They kill. They establish dominance. Humans do far worse. Through free will they choose good or evil. For witches, it's in our nature to use the magick we are given. It's as natural as breathing. While I could argue what I did was for good, that perhaps he'd been meant for me, I admit I was lost in a fantasy."

"What happened?" Viktor asked, running his fingers through his now tousled hair.

"I needed strong magick. It was a simple favor. I chose a lesser level demon. He said he had the power, could give me the kind of magick I needed. You see, not all can leave the underworld. Many can't. But this demon…he misrepresented himself. It draws its power from its master. It does what it wants."

"The time Jake found you in the woods in New York…" Hunter began but she interrupted.

"I'd fulfilled my debt. I'd escaped with a mere loss of my magick, but my sense of self, my soul had been damaged. Zella was merely a shell, an alternative reality in itself. But its master found me in the coven and took me back. The screams of an ancient witch was the debt to be paid. And as you know…" her focus drifted to Viktor, "scream I did."

"It's one thing we have in common," the vampire told her. "I tried not to hurt you, but I wasn't the only one."

"You didn't hurt me. And because of that," Ilsbeth

turned to Willa, "I was able to save the wolf."

"You don't even know me," Willa said in disbelief.

"I certainly know of the royal family."

"But…"

"Princess Aline Ermenjarta Lobo. Brother Julian. Or should I say Prince Joao Pedro Lobo."

"How do you…" Willa sucked a deep breath as though she'd been punched in the stomach. "Who told you? The demons?"

"I'm nearly as old as time itself. I know many things. I won't allow Hell to destroy a legacy. I may be many things, but I will not stand by while they deliberately try to erase the history of a species."

"You foretold your escape from Hell?" Hunter raised a suspicious eyebrow at her.

"If I did, it's neither here nor there."

"You knew I was coming for her?" The Alpha inquired.

"I suspected someone would come for the vampire. Quintus would never stand by and let him rot forever." Ilsbeth shrugged in indifference. "It doesn't matter where the truth lies. Either way, I chose to save her."

Hunter leaned back onto the sofa. Willa sensed his frustration but grew increasingly intrigued by the witch.

"Wolves took me," Willa stated, her voice steady. "I think there were six of them."

"Six born on the sixth day in the sixth month in a year of the sixth. They are the other."

"What?" Willa asked, an impending sense of doom settling in her stomach.

"Six. Six. Six. The number of the beast. For not all wolves were created to roam in the sun, to do good, to run and celebrate the full moon. They sought to bring you, a legacy of the royal family, as a prize. And they were paid for their deeds. Perhaps money. Possibly drugs. And so, you see," Ilsbeth paused, looking to Hunter then back to Willa, "a due is owed. Something must be given, or the wolves will die and be dragged back to Hell. And even if it kills the wolves who took you, the debt is not fully paid."

"So what? I just wait for them to come get me? Or this demon…whatever it is, comes for me?"

"My intuition tells me that if it truly wanted you dead, you would have suffered an eternal death. These wolves. They will come for you. Together. They seek to give you back before they are each killed."

"Can't I just hide out until they are all dead?"

"I don't believe it works that way. Hell has already had a taste of torturing you. It will seek an offering no matter what their outcome."

"An offering? An offering of what?" Hunter asked.

"Or who?" Viktor added.

"I have a suggestion," she said. "It's a bit of both."

"We can't sacrifice anyone. I won't do it," Willa protested.

"This isn't my first, what I'd like to call misunderstanding with a demon." Ilsbeth stood and walked to the corner of the room. She retrieved a bottle of cognac off a shelf and carefully set four snifters onto the granite bar. She unwrapped the foil off its top, continuing to speak as she poured it. "My nerves. I'm not quite myself yet, I'm afraid. They did unspeakable things. I…" She sighed. "Perhaps it was penance for what happened with Dimitri. And although I now walk the earth, the wolves, others, they judge my actions. They all know I'm too powerful to kill. And this place I'm in now," Ilsbeth lifted a glass, her hands trembling as she brought the rim to her lips, sipping at the golden-brown liquor, "we're in Louisiana. I cannot go into New Orleans for quite a long while. I'm safer than I'd be in the city but not truly safe. You had no permission to take me from Hell. I had no permission to leave. So, I, too, would like to make an offering."

Hunter pinched the bridge of his nose with his fingers. "What kind of offering would possibly suffice?"

"I'd like to make a proposal." Ilsbeth crossed the room and handed them each a snifter. "And before you ask, it's just cognac. No spells. No poison."

Willa cupped the snifter, warming the glass with her hands. She kept her eyes on Ilsbeth as she once again sat down to join them.

"I have an impressive library. Research on creatures. Data collection dating back a couple of thousand years. I believe there is an artifact, that in this particular instance, will sate the demon. The wolves though…they must be killed."

"Consider it done," Hunter assured her.

"The reason you are no longer with your parents. The battle that led to your exile. There was a King and Queen. At first when they mated, they were in love. The Queen, while a wolf, practiced the craft, exploring the hellfire in her veins."

Willa said nothing, recalling her new power she'd used to move the brush with her mind.

"The King. He enjoyed the temptations of the flesh."

"As men should," Viktor quipped.

"Outside of the approval of his mate. She was unhappy. Unloved. But the bonds of the mate are strong. Too strong to break with witchcraft alone. She called on the Alpha of the wolves of six to kill the King using demon magick. They killed him. Then they skinned him and with the very skin of the King, the Queen created a book."

"A skin book?" Willa's nose crinkled in disgust.

"He dipped his pen in the ink of too many wells and got himself turned into a damn book? That seems a bit drastic," Viktor laughed.

"While humans date the practice to the sixteenth century, it's actually much older. Unusual but what better way to capture the essence of a human or creature?" Ilsbeth answered directly.

"What's in it for you? Because I know there's always something in it for you." The Alpha placed his palm on the arm of the sofa, shaking his head.

"I see this as a way to appease the demons."

"What else?" Hunter pressed.

"Spells. The Queen. Supposedly an ancient. She wrote spells. I'm a collector. If I can touch the book, I can absorb them. But the book must be delivered to the demon."

"What's the catch?" Hunter asked.

"There is no catch. But that doesn't mean it's going to be easy to get it. It's hidden. If you can find the book, and that's if, we will have to summon the demon and then banish it back to Hell."

"We can't just kill it?" Viktor asked.

"No. It's a higher-level demon. Destroying it, at least at this point, while I'm weak, it's simply not an option. I believe if we offer the book ourselves, he's likely to go back to Hell. If this is to be done, we shall do it together. But we must kill the wolves. We can't allow them to get it."

"I killed one of them on my territory already. Five to go. They'll either be looking for her in Guatemala, where they found her, or here in New Orleans."

"New Orleans?" Ilsbeth asked, a lilt in her voice.

"Kellen. The fae. He's the one who helped them find her in the first place. He came snoopin' round my territory and I kicked his ass back into the fire. My guess is that he's not going to be hangin' out in that bar on Frenchman anytime soon."

"Kellen's a slippery one but I haven't met a fae I can't handle. If you get me the book, I'll capture the fae. He owes me several debts and it's not in his nature to settle."

"You wouldn't happen to know where we can find this book?" Viktor asked.

"So, you agree to go get it?" Ilsbeth pressed.

"I'll do it," Willa blurted without hesitation. There was no other choice.

The High Priestess smiled, pleased with her enthusiasm. "And this is why royal blood is important. An Alpha to match an Alpha."

"Please don't tell me it's in Hell or someplace shitty." Hunter plowed his fingers through his hair.

"It's in a cave," Ilsbeth told him. "It's in another country."

"What the hell. I need a vacation. Maybe I'll hit Hawaii on the way back," Viktor joked.

"In Central America," she clarified.

"Please don't say the jungle," Hunter replied.

"Hey, I'm with him. We were just there and let's just say it was a shit show and leave it at that. You see Julian here? Yeah, no. Ya don't," Viktor said.

"We'll discuss him in a minute," Ilsbeth replied.

"Do you know where Julian is?" Willa asked, her pulse racing at the sound of his name.

"In a minute." Ilsbeth's tone was firm, her lips drawn in a tight line. "First, the skin book. And no. Not a jungle. A cave."

"Awesome. A cave. Nothing could possibly go wrong in there." Hunter gave a cold laugh, shaking his head.

"I didn't say it would be easy. The Karst caves. They're made of limestone. It attracts the paranormal, the otherworldly. Channels the energy. It is believed the wolves who killed the King brought the skin from Brazil to Belize, safeguarding it somewhere within the cave system. I understand human researchers may have found it during the 1970s but were mysteriously killed. It's theorized it's hidden within the cave system but to date, no one has claimed its discovery."

"The wolves that attacked me. Why don't they know where it's at?" Willa asked.

"Because they killed the Alpha, never knowing its location. I've heard the folklore for years, but I've never needed the artifact for this purpose. Of course, I'd love to gain its magick but as I've said, it's not going to be easy to locate it. It's my suspicion that your shared hellfire might lead you to it. You must concentrate as you search, sensing it, without seeing."

"Cave systems are extensive. We're going to need at least a target of where to start searching," Hunter insisted.

"It could be dangerous. Demons. Wolves. They will sense Willa as soon as she leaves my property. They could follow you. You must get it and then come back as soon as possible. We'll summon the demon under the light of the full moon. The wolves will have to be dealt with properly."

"We'll get in and out of Belize and back here with the book. Don't worry about the wolves. They're as good as dead." The Alpha pinned her with a hard stare. "What's going on tonight, Ilsbeth? You wouldn't happen to be summoning another demon? I can't help but notice you have several witches on the property."

"Hot witches." Viktor smiled and winked at Willa. "Naked witches. The best kind."

"Focus, vampire," Hunter snapped.

"I'm not wrong." Viktor laughed with a shrug. "Just sayin'."

"These women are the outliers. The solo practitioners who have no tribe. The ones that add value will stay to help conjure the demon. The others must go. I cannot risk drawing the ire of the coven if one is killed. No. I won't risk it."

"I can't believe this is happening," Willa said, her voice trailed with anger. "I want to kill these wolves myself. This is why you don't get involved with demons."

"Sometimes one has no choice," Ilsbeth told her.

"My brother. Where is he?" Willa changed the subject back to Julian.

"You went to Guatemala. Tell me what happened in the jungle."

Guilt flooded Willa. "There's a plant I found in the jungle. It grew inside an ancient building in a hidden Mayan city. The structure was once used for healing. I was destroying the formula I'd created…burning it…I don't know how the demons knew I was there. My guess is between Julian and I they sensed our energy."

"You spilled your blood for this formula you speak of?" Ilsbeth gave a closed knowing smile.

"Yes. And before you say it, I know it wasn't a good idea. My blood alone doesn't heal humans or anyone else. But combined with this plant I found, I cured a girl. A human."

"We aren't meant to intervene," Ilsbeth said.

Viktor rubbed his forehead. "It's true we turn humans but it's rare. Like really rare."

"I know but…" Willa had grown far too attached to the humans to let one die. Yet it was the very action of saving one that had put them all in danger.

"The Goddess gifts all supernaturals. You run with the animals. Witches possess magick. Vampires? Their blood can heal humans should they choose. If the demons got into the structure, my intuition tells me the plant holds a tie to

Hell. And while I'd normally ask to have a leaf for my collection, now is not the time. They're still after me."

Although Willa knew a plant grew outside the ruins, still living within the rainforest, she deliberately kept silent. The specimen she'd attempted to take with her was destroyed as she'd left the tunnel. Her hands trembled, her heart heavy with guilt. "Julian. I can't feel him but something…I don't know why…I have to believe he's alive."

"There may be a good reason why he hasn't contacted you. Perhaps they're on his tail and he doesn't want to lead them back to you. Or the wolves are involved. Either way, now is not the time to look for your brother," Ilsbeth told her.

"We need to go get the book," Hunter began.

"Once you bring it to me, we can safely summon the demon. Make the exchange," she suggested.

Viktor stood and walked toward the windows, gazing toward the dancing witches. "You think you can help with narrowing down the exact cave?"

"I can do more than that. I have the knife that is supposedly tied to the skin book. Before you ask, it was given to me years ago by a wolf in exchange for a favor. She'd supposedly inherited it but who am I to ask? None of my business really, but I'm certain she was truthful. I had always intended to use the blade for a spell. It should lead you to the skin book, from the soul from whence it came. I will direct it and you, dear Viktor, can use it to guide them."

"I'm not sure I can handle another flash thing. The last time…" Willa blew out a breath.

"We can take a private jet. Four hours, tops. We can be back by tomorrow night." Hunter pulled out his cell phone and tapped at the glass.

"Are you sure this is going to work? This skin book?" Willa stared at the witch, doubting her intentions.

"I sense your hesitation." Ilsbeth brought the rim of the glass to her lips and took a small sip, her gaze settling on Willa. "There are no rules when it comes to demons."

"The plane will be ready to roll this afternoon. We can get down there before sunset. We'll be back tomorrow night, but it could be late," Hunter warned.

"The witching hour. It's almost daybreak as we speak. May I suggest you stay here until you leave? The demons…they search for you. My home is protected."

"No offense, Priestess, but that would be a hard no from me. I'm good." Viktor turned to face her, a smirk turning upward on his lips.

"Yeah. No. We'll go back to my place and take our chances with my wards," Hunter agreed.

Panic curled inside of Willa's chest. "We have to be realistic. They could come after us anywhere. And Julian's still missing."

"Willa, look at me," the witch demanded.

As she gazed into Ilsbeth's violet eyes, everything around her faded, a silver glow surrounding the otherworldly witch.

"The skin book is *the* only way I can think of to sate the demon. I cannot guarantee it will work. I can't even say that finding the book will be easy. Or safe. I swear to you on the Goddess that I will help you, but a wolf, *a royal wolf* in particular, is the only one who can take the book from the caves. It will not release itself to any others. I suspect the researchers who claimed to have found it were killed by a curse, although I can't be certain." Ilsbeth drew a deep breath and released it, her eyes transfixed on Willa's. "I know the Alpha does not trust me. Nor the vampire. And perhaps with good reason. I want the spells. But I assure you that I have no other motivation at this point beyond my own salvation and redemption. I will not go back to Hell. And neither will you."

Tears welled in Willa's eyes, her thoughts drifting back to Julian.

"We will find your brother. I can scry for him now. Come." She extended her hand.

Without hesitation, Willa reached for Ilsbeth, her heart pounding like a drum, their combined magick sizzling through her. This woman had saved her. *Powerful. Ancient. Dangerous.* Their connection, for good or for bad, was sealed into her soul.

Willa followed her to the far-right corner of the room to her altar. Wax dripped from candles, a myriad of colors melted onto its dark wooden surface. Surrounded by red rose petals and cinnamon sticks, a white skull-shaped candle burned brightly. Although Willa's curiosity spiked, she resisted the urge to ask.

Ilsbeth released Willa's hand and reached for a glass bowl and pitcher. "This has been blessed by the Goddess in many rituals over the years. I don't often do favors without return but I will search for him."

Willa's pulse raced as Ilsbeth poured water into the bowl and set the pitcher upon the altar. She released a deep breath as Hunter approached, the warmth and comfort of her mate behind her.

"While blood is the usual sacrifice for such a spell, I can do it with your hair. Minimal pain but causes discomfort, nonetheless. Do you agree to this?" Ilsbeth asked, her tone indifferent.

"Yes."

"Not so fast, witch," Hunter challenged her.

Willa spun to face the Alpha. "I want to know where my brother is. If she can help me, I have to know if he is alive."

"No. If you give her any part of you, she'll have it forever."

"One hair. That's all she needs." Willa turned to Ilsbeth. "Right? That's all. No extra ones for later."

The high priestess nodded and held the bowl with her hands, waiting.

"I swear to the Goddess, witch, if you harm Willamina in any way, if she so much as gets a papercut, you're a dead witch. No more resurrections. I will kill you myself with my bare hands."

"Hunter," Willa admonished. "She's trying to help me."

"I have no interest in hurting your mate. You have my word." Ilsbeth nodded to the bowl. "Put it in here."

"I really don't get a good feeling about this," Viktor interjected.

"Please Willa. We'll find him without her," Hunter pleaded.

"I'm sorry, but if I'm going to concentrate on finding

this book, on us, I have to know now." Willa fingered her hair and tugged, wincing at the sharp pain on her scalp. She held the single strand over the bowl and stared into Ilsbeth's eyes. "If you try to hurt me or anyone I love with this, my mate won't kill you. I will."

Willa released the hair into the water. Her eyes widened as it disappeared, and the fluid morphed into a swirling sea of colors. "What is happening…"

"Silence!" Ilsbeth turned toward the altar, humming softly, mesmerized by the swirling concoction. "He comes. Do you feel it? No. Shh."

Willa closed her eyes and prayed to the Goddess. In her third eye, her wolf ran through a dark forest. An owl flew from a branch into the night sky. A rabbit froze in the distance. Her wolf crouched down low to the ground, deliberately stalking her prey. The dew-soaked leaves succumbed underneath her paws and the scent of the earth faded as she approached the creature. She lunged at it but missed, rolling into the wet grass. Willa's heart pounded, hearing the familiar growl. She recognized him instantly, long before his amber eyes met hers. *Julian.*

You're alive. Meu irmão. Elation rushed through her.

You know all you need to know. Now you see me, now you don't. It's time to go. They're coming. I will see you again one day, minha irmã.

Julian bared his teeth, his head snapping toward the far darkness of the woods. His eyes flashed to red glowing orbs of light. An impending sense of doom twisted inside her, overtaking her psyche.

Run Aline, run. Don't ever look back. RUN!

She cowered at the sound of his deafening howl. Helpless to resist the overwhelming power of his Alpha nature, she submitted, turning and running. *Run harder, run faster.* Julian's childhood voice played in her head. Twigs and tree limbs snapped behind her, sulfur filtered through the air.

"Willa!" her Alpha's voice commanded. She sucked a breath, her eyes flashing open.

"What did you do to her?" Hunter demanded.

"I'm okay," Willa managed, losing control of her balance. Her legs wobbled as if they were made of jelly. She fell into Hunter's arms, relieved she'd woken from the trance. "Julian. He's running. I was running."

"We're getting out of here," Hunter said. "Vik, grab the knife."

"Be quick, Alpha. Demons are on the chase. The wolves seek the Princess," Ilsbeth warned. "Use the knife to release the book. You'd best be resourceful."

"Can you walk?" Hunter asked Willa.

"Yes, I'm better." She held tight to the Alpha as he set her onto her feet.

As she took several steps toward the door, she glanced back at Ilsbeth. Willa's mind spun with thoughts of her brother. He was but a dream but as real as the wolf who held her. Leaving the witch, she prayed the trade, a book for their lives, would sate the demon.

Chapter Eleven

Hunter cursed as the limo pulled away from the mansion. The minute they'd arrived at Ilsbeth's house, he'd used his GPS, and texted the coordinates to a personal driver. Willa slept soundly next to him, her heart beating in rhythm with his.

Mate. He still couldn't believe this woman was his. Feisty and brave, Willa both played and fought. His heart squeezed as he traced his finger over her cheek, brushing a hair from her eyes.

He'd spent hundreds of years without love, watching others find their mates. His brother Tristan. His sister Katrina. Yet living remotely in Wyoming, he'd never given consideration that he'd actually find a she-wolf who matched his beast.

Willa. So delightfully unexpected. A serendipitous encounter. Meeting his mate in Hell did make for a good bar story, but it wasn't exactly romantic. He glanced down at his beautiful mate, her hand resting on his thigh. Willa should have loving memories of her mating, not simply a chance relationship born of Hell. When this nightmare ended, he planned to court her like she deserved…*fitting for his princess.*

"She's special, yeah?" Viktor commented, sitting across from him in the limo.

"Our mating shouldn't have happened like this."

"You can't control it. You know that. The Goddess does what she wants."

"But it should have been different. She deserves flowers and dancing, not death and demons. We should have had time to get to know each other."

"Says who? You? The universe does what it wants. And besides, you're one lucky son-of-a-bitch."

A corner of his lip turned upward, his heart warmed at the sight of her snuggled in his lap. "I am."

"She's a princess."

"I'm a king." Hunter laughed.

"Don't get too crazy. Don't let all the royalty bs go to your head."

"Definitely the king."

"You'll have time when we get done with all this demon shit. Time to woo. Have a life. Not everyone gets that." Viktor's expression flattened. "You've got a few hours until the plane leaves."

"That we do." Hunter smiled.

"Maybe I can help you out with a little romance. I've got friends in high places. Don't get me wrong." Viktor laughed. "Plenty of friends in low places too. Wouldn't want you to get the wrong impression of me."

"I don't want to do anything to attract the wolves or the demons before we leave."

"Are you sure you're going to be safe at your house for a few hours? I know you're not in town much."

"As safe as anywhere. It's daybreak and unless we go outside and start to deliberately provoke 'em, we should be okay. Wards are up but it's never one hundred percent. We should probably eat before we leave for Belize, but it's not like we can go out, so I guess I'll have to make something."

"That's where I come in. I'll flash in and flash out. Bring you what you need. I'm like a regular fucking fairy Godmother." Viktor raised his hands in the air, wiggling his fingers, a mischievous smile growing on his face.

Hunter laughed. "I don't know. Don't take this the wrong way, Vik, but you don't strike me as a party coordinator."

"I've got this."

"I don't know if that's a good idea. Willa's got to sleep. I can just make us eggs or something. Soup and sandwiches maybe. Got some French bread back at the house. I'll scrounge somethin' up."

"Ten hours until the jet's ready. Besides, you can sleep when you're dead."

"Easy on the d word." Hunter's eyes widened as he shot the vampire an annoyed look.

"I've got this." Viktor lit up in amusement.

"There is something wrong with you, you know that?"

"You'll thank me later."

Hunter considered the vampire's suggestion. He glanced

to Willa. She'd been through so much, tortured, lost her brother, and now believed she'd had a vision with him alive. She'd sworn she'd connected with Julian, that he was running from wolves to keep her safe.

Hunter used to think that being immortal was a given pleasure of life. But his taste of Hell reminded him that immortal meant 'you live until someone kills you.' Searching for the skin book was rife with danger, he was certain. He didn't trust Ilsbeth, unconvinced the artifact would sate the demon.

No, Willa deserved so much more than the shitty cards she'd been dealt. His clever doctor. His princess. His mate.

"Promise not to get crazy," Hunter told Viktor, uneasy with his decision to let the vampire plan his date. "Keep it simple. We don't have a lot of time." A corner of Hunter's mouth turned upward, a sinking feeling churning in his stomach. What could this vampire possibly know about romance, besides sex?

"Scout's honor." Viktor held up two fingers.

"I'm in." The words passed through his lips before he could stop himself, but he wanted to do something nice for his mate.

"Delightful. Well, then. I guess it's best if I get going. Chop chop. Things to do. People to buy off." Viktor edged toward the front of his seat.

"Be careful."

"Ah yes, well you too then." He raised his hand into the air. "Alpha. One more thing."

"What?"

Viktor grinned from ear to ear. "I was never a boy scout."

Hunter shook his head as the vampire disappeared, praying to the Goddess Viktor didn't draw attention to them.

Willa moaned, and he protectively laid his arm over her.

"Shh…. it's all right, sweetheart. Get some sleep. Your Alpha's not goin' to let anything happen to you."

What the ever-loving fuck? Hunter sat on the sofa, stunned at the sheer number of candles illuminating the room. It was official. He didn't need to worry about the demons or the rogue wolves trying to kill them. Viktor was going to burn down his whole damn house. *Fucking vampire.*

The Alpha glanced up at the two-story-high ceiling. Over a hundred black and silver balloons danced in the air. His dining room table had been formally set; a silver candelabra sat centerpiece accented by exotic flower arrangements. In the foyer, a string quartet played Bach while flames lit up the fireplace. While it wasn't his jam, the quiet smooth strokes of the violin calmed his nerves.

It was as if he'd hired a bad wedding planner. Except there was no wedding. And they had exactly five hours until the jet was ready to go. Skin book. Demons. No fucking wedding.

Hunter sucked in a deep cleansing breath, wishing he'd paid more attention at the hot yoga class his sister, Katrina, had made him attend. There wasn't enough meditation that could keep him calm when it came to Viktor. Don't draw attention. Keep it simple. Yeah, no. He should have known Viktor wasn't capable.

Damn vampire had insisted he dress up and had sent him downstairs so he could attend to Willa. *Why did I listen to him?* he inwardly asked himself, exhaling a deep sigh.

Hunter closed his eyes and listened. *Footsteps.* He reached for Viktor but didn't sense him. The distinctive sound of a woman's heels tapping down the staircase sent him to his feet.

His eyes flashed open, his heart pounding in his chest as Willa descended. As he took in the sight of his gorgeous mate, blood rushed to his dick. The skin-tight, virgin-white, satin dress hugged every inch of her sexy-as-sin body. *Goddamn vampire planned a wedding.*

"Willa," he managed. "You're…you're stunning."

"Thank you," she whispered. "What is happening here?"

"I wanted to do something special. I know we've just met but you're my mate, and I just thought…Viktor offered to help but clearly he's gone overboard with some kind of human-themed romantic shindig…I'm going to take you on a proper date when this is all done but I…" Hunter lost his words as she drew closer. Her hair had been swept up, revealing the beautiful contours of her face, her red lips parted. *Stop stammering like a fucking teenager and get it together, boy.* "It's just…I wanted to do something special for you. Is it inappropriate? We can stop all this."

Willa smiled and reached for him, gently placing her finger across his lips. "No. It's perfect."

Hunter's heart squeezed. "You sure?"

"No one has ever done something like this for me." She closed the distance between them, tilting her head.

"I can't take all the credit. Viktor." Hunter glanced to the balloons and back to Willa. He wrapped his arm around her waist, her energy sizzling through him as her body brushed against his.

"But you agreed to this? For me?" She smiled broadly.

"Yes." Hunter studied her face, the swell of her bottom lip, aching to devour her. Hints of her floral perfume complemented the distinctive scent of his mate. He smiled at her and began a slow dance.

"This is special," Willa told him, her eyes swimming with happiness.

"It's almost like we're real people."

"Exceedingly, wonderfully real."

"If we were human, it's almost like we really did get married."

"If we were human, I'd marry you in a second, but I much prefer you as wolf." Hunter dipped his head toward Willa, his lips edging close to hers. "You're absolutely stunning."

"Kiss me," she whispered.

"I thought you'd never ask." Hunter's lips crashed onto hers, his tongue sweeping into her mouth. Passion threaded through him as she kissed him back and his wolf growled, seeking his mate. His cock stood at attention as she rubbed her body against his. *Jesus, she's fucking incredible. No, no, no. Not yet. Dinner. Feed her. Get through dinner. Stop acting like an animal.*

Willa laughed into their kiss, and as he slowly pulled his lips from hers, their foreheads touched.

"Dinner?" she smiled.

"Do you see what you do to me? I've lost my head."

"Don't do that now. I need both." She winked. "Hmm…what is that smell?"

"What? Oh yeah…that. Food. Real food."

"I'm starving. I think we should eat quickly because I don't think we're going to get through dinner."

"I'm not sure where Viktor…"

"You called?" the vampire materialized before them, holding a massive-sized golden giftbag in the air. He glanced up at the balloons. "Awesome, aren't they? I missed my calling."

"What are you doing here?" Hunter asked. "Can't you see we're on our date?"

He laughed. "Well yes. But it's not a party without me. They do say the best things in life are free."

"They do," Willa agreed with a small laugh. "Thank you for all of this. It's quite lovely."

"You're welcome, princess." Viktor held the bag up into the air. "Congratulations on your…mating. Weddings always make me cry."

Willa accepted the gift as he handed it to her.

"Weddings are for humans," Hunter told him.

"Who's to say they get all the fun? I was married once and I…" Viktor's words trailed into silence, and he took off toward the kitchen.

"What was that about?" Willa asked Hunter.

"I don't know. He spends all this time denying his humanity. Perhaps he misses it more than he lets on."

"I feel his sadness." Willa wrapped her arms around herself.

Hunter gave a closed smile, his gut tightening at her statement. He'd drank her blood. No matter his denial, he'd created a small bond with Willa.

"Whoever he married, he must have loved her," she guessed. "The sadness. He hides it. I'm worried about him."

"He's going to be okay. Let's just focus on us tonight. He did this for us. For you. We deserve a little celebration." Hunter smiled.

Two servers came scurrying out of the kitchen, placing steaming dishes of food onto the table. A loud pop sounded, and they began pouring champagne.

"Bon appétit," Viktor cheerfully declared as he entered the dining room, wearing a white chef's hat. Both Hunter and Willa stared up at him wearing a look of surprise. "What?"

"What's with the…" Hunter gestured to his head, "get up?"

"Oh this. The hat? What, does it clash with my red suit? I thought so." Viktor snatched it off his head and tossed it across the room. "Ah well, I must be going. I have to get these people back to where they came from. The musicians are wolves. These guys," he nodded toward the servers, "they're vampires. But don't worry. They have no idea where they are. They've all been sworn to secrecy. Trust me when I say they won't talk. Or they'll die. No choice really."

"We weren't worried about any of that…" Willa began but was interrupted by Viktor.

"Hurry now. The food is getting cold. Open the gift before I leave and then I'll be off."

"Um. Okay. Do you want to do the honors?" Hunter shrugged and smiled at Willa, nervous about Viktor's gift. He didn't trust him after the one hundred and one balloons floating above their heads.

Willa reached inside the gift bag, laughing as she retrieved a black leather paddle and handed it to Hunter. "It's, it's…it's lovely. Really. I was expecting something Tiffany's perhaps, but this is a surprise."

"What the hell, vampire? Seriously?" Hunter shook his head. Not that he opposed giving her a good spanking, but Viktor had no business giving his mate sex toys.

"I knew you'd like it. Trust me when I say you will love the feel and the sound of it." Viktor clapped his hands together, his eyes lit with delight. "It's my favorite."

"Well…my…now this…gee, I don't know. I already have one but it's in pink." Willa laughed as she handed Hunter a two-foot-long silicone penis. "What do you think, dear? Will it go with the curtains?"

"I thought you'd like it. Don't worry. I didn't forget the lube. Blueberry flavored. You're going to love it. Goes well with dessert."

"Time to go, Viktor," Hunter told him, his voice firm. "We're done now."

"What? She said it goes with her curtains."

"We'll meet you at the jet in three hours. Now off with

the cooks and the musicians."

"You'll thank me later. Give me a minute." Viktor strode into the kitchen pressing through the swinging doors and returned within seconds. "Musicians are next." As he began to walk toward the foyer, he paused, turning his head toward them. "You're blessed, you know. Not everyone finds someone…gets to have a lifetime with their person."

Hunter sensed Willa's sadness as Viktor disappeared with the musicians. Her empathetic smile touched his heart. "He's going to be all right. He doesn't think he's going to find anyone again but he's wrong."

"How do you know?" she pressed.

"Because if I can find a princess in Hell, our vampire…our friend…the Goddess has someone for him too. Even if he doesn't know it, I have faith."

"Yes." She nodded.

"Come…let's eat." Hunter took her hand as she set the bag onto the ground.

"This is beautiful," she admired the incredible spread on the table, lobster and fresh vegetables, candles and flowers.

Hunter drank in the sight of his magnificent mate, and his cock twitched. He was never going to get through dinner.

"That was amazing." Willa brought the glass of champagne to her lips. "I've never had someone treat me so…like…just so nice…like a princess."

"I love that you're independent, that all this time you've survived, but you've got me now. I'm not saying it will be easy. But we're going to get through this, Wills. And when it's all over, we'll have dates. Lots of them. Maybe we'll go horseback riding."

"Skydiving," she suggested.

"Horseback riding," he repeated, giving a low chuckle.

"Skydiving then horseback riding." She smiled, batting her eyelids at him.

"Wolves are hard to kill, but not impossible."

"It'll be fun."

"I can think of some other things that would be even more fun." He winked.

"Perhaps we should open the rest of our gifts?" she suggested, a flirtatious lilt in her voice. "You stay there."

Hunter watched in anticipation as his delicious mate stood and glided across the floor. With her back to him, she stopped in front of the bag, pausing to look over her shoulder, a sultry smile forming on her lips. Her hand found the back of her dress and she teased down the zipper. Hunter sucked a breath as the entire gown pooled around her feet.

Wearing nothing but heels and a thong, she bent over, ever so slowly reaching for the bag and turning toward him. A sexy smile crossed her face as she held it into the air. "Do you want to go first or shall I?"

Hunter laughed, his cock hard as concrete. Little wolf wanted to play.

Candlelight and the shadows of the balloons reflected off

her olive skin. Her devilish smile told him she'd try to test him.

"Maybe…" Willa pulled out the paddle and held it up in the air, shifting her hips back and forth. "A spanking?"

Hunter laughed, without revealing what he'd planned on doing to her. If she only knew. He'd love nothing more than to see her beautiful ass a nice shade of pink.

"No?" She tossed it onto the sofa and dug her hand back into the bag. "Ooh kinky." Willa wore a broad smile as she retrieved a shiny bulbous toy. "Look. It has a pink crystal on the end. Ah…there's a note attached." She fingered the white paper that had been tied with a white silk ribbon. "*For the princess who has everything. Your friendly neighborhood vampire.*' He included lube. How thoughtful." She winked and tossed it along with the paddle. "It's a keeper."

Hunter adjusted his painful erection that strained against his zipper. Jesus, this woman was going to fucking kill him.

She held up the two-foot-long dildo and dropped it onto the floor with a shrug. "Hmm…that would be a nope. Maybe we can regift it. You never know when someone's going to have a secret Santa at the office."

"We can give it back to Viktor. Something tells me he'd find a use for it."

"Ah, now this…" She held up the penis-shaped sleeve. "Is this some sort of an extension?" Willa shook her head and threw it clear across the room. "Definitely don't need this." She shot him a sexy look and licked her bottom lip.

"The vampire is dead to me."

"Nipple clamps? No thanks. The only thing I want on my nipples is your mouth." She laughed, tossing them. "But wait. There's more." Willa dangled a pair of red leather handcuffs from her finger.

"Now those I could use." Hunter stalked toward her, enjoying her nervous laughter.

Hunter's smile broadened. *Thank you, Vik.* The Alpha resisted taking his mate, simply reaching for the handcuffs. His eyes drifted to her lips and to her pert breasts, her taut nipples standing at attention. Her thong, fashioned from fine white lace, barely covered her mound.

"Is red your favorite color?" The smell of the fine leather teased his nostrils, his dick hardened as she presented her arms to him.

"Yes, yes tonight it definitely is." Her voice trembled.

Hunter reached for her, trailing his fingers down her inner wrists, and turned her palms upward. He made quick work of securing the cuffs and tugged on the chain that connected them.

She smiled as he pulled her toward the sofa. He glanced to the toys and his gaze met hers, fascinated by her sinful smile. His little wolf wanted to play? Play they would.

"These here…all keepers?" He glanced to the silver butt plug she'd thrown on the sofa.

She laughed, her cheeks blooming pink.

"You." Hunter pulled her toward him and glided his hand down her stomach. His fingers slipped underneath the delicate fabric, delving into her slick pussy. "You're wet."

"Always for you." Willa moaned, her head lolling forward.

His fingers played over her clit lightly, never offering enough to sate her. She released an audible sigh as he withdrew and his hand trailed up her stomach, between her breasts.

Hunter's dick lengthened as he wrapped his fingers around her neck, his fingertips teasing behind her ear. She lifted her heavy lids, her hungry gaze settling on his.

Just a taste, his wolf urged. With restraint, he pressed his lips to hers and she melted into him. Tasting his mate sent desire surging through every cell of his body.

He reluctantly tore his lips from hers. "Hands above your head," he ordered, his mouth dipping to her chest. "Don't move."

"Yes," she replied, her voice breathy. Gooseflesh broke over her skin as his lips brushed her nipple.

He gently rolled her taut rosy peak between his fingertips, gently pinching as she arched her back, thrusting her breasts toward him. Sucking her nipple into his mouth, he flicked his tongue over it.

"Hunter. I…I…" she breathed.

He groaned, his dick throbbing to be released. The second her fingers speared into his hair, he laughed softly. "You don't listen well, do you?"

"I do but…" She giggled as he turned her around, bending her over the sofa, resting her arms on its cushions. He smiled as he slipped his fingers under the edges of her panties, slowly tugging them off and tossing them aside. His fingers trailed over her bared bottom, her feral energy sizzling his fingertips. "I've been waiting so long to do this but who knew my naughty little princess enjoyed a little kink."

"You never asked," she replied, her coy smile hidden by her long mane that feathered around her face onto the sofa.

"Ah, well, we have a lifetime to explore, don't we? But this," he paused, palming her ass. "Oh yeah. This. This is nice."

She wiggled her bottom at him and laughed, her forehead lolling forward onto her arms. "Hmm…you can't leave me like this."

"Don't you worry. I've got plans for my bride." Hunter unzipped his pants, making quick work of shucking his clothing.

"The longer you leave me like this…" She squirmed, widening her legs, deliberately revealing her glistening pussy. "I'm suffering."

Fuck. Hunter blew out a breath, ready to come just at the sight of her. His devilish mate enjoyed teasing him. A fresh rush of blood surged to his cock. He took his shaft into his palm, giving it a firm stroke, and glanced to the silver bulb. "You know, you've got a beautiful ass."

"Lonely ass. So lonely," she whined. "I'm dying."

Hunter smiled at his sassy she-wolf. Reaching for her hips, he pulled her towards him, the broad crown of his dick brushing over her bottom. He tapped his shaft up and through her slick folds. She moaned as the tip teased her clit.

"I can't wait…" Hunter eased his cock inside her wet pussy, slowly plunging inside her as she adjusted to his size. "Ah."

"Alpha…yes. More," she begged, her wrists bound.

Hunter shivered and sucked a breath. Her quivering pussy contracted around his cock, milking him as he slid in and out of her.

"Oh fuck, you feel so good. I could just," he paused and gave a sharp thrust, plunging himself to the hilt, deep inside her, "fuck you all night long. Ah yeah. But. Toys."

"No, don't stop," Willa panted. As Hunter fucked her harder, her limp body dangled over the sofa, her fingers still curled onto the edge of a cushion.

"This." He reached for the toy and a small bottle. Willa pushed back on him, sending a fresh rush of arousal to his dick. He resisted the urge to come. "No, no, no movin', sweetheart. I've got somethin' special here for you."

"I need…" she breathed.

With his cock still inside her, Hunter dripped the cool gel over her ass and glided the smooth metal plug down her cleft, stopping as it reached her back hole. He gently circled its tip over her puckered skin.

"Easy now." He sucked a breath, as he pressed it inside her bottom. "There you go…fuck, it's so tight."

"Oh Goddess. It's so…so…" Willa panted, losing her words.

"Almost…there. That's it. What a pretty ass you have, princess." Hunter smiled as the pink crystal plug lodged firmly in her ass, her pussy tightening around his cock.

As he slowly withdrew his shaft and slid back inside her, he leaned over Willa, pressing his lips to her shoulders, gently making love to his mate. With every hard thrust, his energy spiraled, arousal building, his orgasm on the edge.

He wrapped his arm around her chest, his palm finding her breast. As he lifted her upward and brought her toward him, his fingers dipped into her slick pussy, teasing her clit.

"Oh, Goddess…" Willa arched her back into him as he drove himself deep inside her. "Fuck me. Hard."

At his Queen's demand, he slammed hard inside her core, his orgasm hurling into him. As Willa fell into ecstasy, her pussy contracted, fisting his cock, milking every last tendril of his climax. His wolf growled, in awe of his mate, and Hunter lost himself in feral pleasure, wondering how he'd gone his whole life without her.

Chapter Twelve

Willa curled into her Alpha's embrace, her heart tight with emotion. She'd never been so vulnerable with anyone in all her years, allowing a man to restrain her, dominate her, bringing her to new heights of pleasure. Despite the tendrils of passion still flittering in her body, doubts about their future bloomed in her mind. As his mate, she'd be expected to move to Wyoming, to rule the pack with her Alpha. But would Teton Wolves ever accept her into the pack? Her skin glowed with hellfire, forever singed by the flames of Hades. Would she bear the Alpha's children, or would his legacy be lost to a prophesy of her infertility?

Her mind drifted to the witch. Although Ilsbeth had perpetrated the ultimate betrayal of wolves, attempting to steal Dimitri's ability to shift, she'd saved Willa's life by offering herself to Viktor. Instinct told her they had to trust the witch, yet she knew her Alpha never could. With cautious optimism, no other choice but to go in search of the skin book, she resigned herself to the task.

In the morning, she told herself. In the morning, fears

would become bravery. They'd do what they needed to do. She refused to give up…to Hell, to wolves, to the devil himself. Her wolf stirred in her mind, anticipating the fight. *Sleep now. In the morning.*

"If this doesn't remind you of Hell, I don't know what will." Hunter shined a flashlight into the cavernous room.

"What is this?" Willa's clothes dripped as they emerged from the waist-high water. Deep in the belly of the caves, they made their way onto higher, dryer ground.

"Ancient civilizations," Viktor commented, glancing at the ceramic pots along the walls.

"These limestone caves do more than house a few trinkets." Hunter set his palm onto the cool stone wall.

"I think it's safe to say we're not alone." Viktor walked deeper into the cave.

"There aren't many places where you can avoid ghosts, but yeah, limestone attracts all sorts of energies." Willa concentrated in an attempt to detect any other supernatural entities but sensed nothing. "If we get lucky, the most we will have to deal with is bat guano."

"What's all this?" Viktor pointed to a pile of bones.

"Xibalba. The Place of Fright. The Mayan Hell." Willa shone her light upon etched artwork that had been carved into the wall. A figure held up a heart. "Whatever this space was for…people died down here."

"Human sacrifice." Hunter pointed to skeletal remains,

that lay perfectly on the earth as if they'd been preserved in a museum. "This one here."

"These bones look like they belong to a woman. Look at the shape of the pelvis. It's likely she was murdered," Willa surmised. "They were often tortured before they were killed. But it was their way of life. To satisfy the Gods."

"An offering. How lovely." Viktor laughed. "And here we are. Back in the pit of Mayan Hell looking for a book to give to another Hell-bound demon. Quite fitting."

"This woman." Willa glanced at the skeleton, and her stomach clenched at the thought of her heart being cut from her chest. "She had no choice."

"Humans. They never seem to learn," Viktor added.

"I'd say that's pretty accurate." Hunter stepped toward a pile of vases. He lifted one and carefully set it aside.

"Humans possess an inner magick without ever even knowing or believing it." Willa stared at the bones. "Yes, they are fragile. But like all beings, the Goddess made them for a reason."

"I don't mean to be a killjoy but how are we ever going to find the book down here? There are several cave systems. We don't have all day." Viktor blew out an annoyed breath.

"I don't know. I mean you zapped us into here. You must have felt something." Willa smiled.

"Oh no. Don't go putting all this on me." Viktor held up his palms defensively. "I just picked up on the vibe. That knife must have done something. And this is where we landed."

"He's right though," Hunter agreed. "This has got to be

the place. Not only do we have that knife, Willa is connected to this book. Its skin is from her ancestors. It's tied to her. I can't help but think it would want her to find it."

"I'm not so sure about that." Willa's voice rose, her eyes questioning his logic. "Maybe we need to use the blade Ilsbeth gave us. If it's tied to the book…"

"I've got it, but knowing Ilsbeth we've got to do something with it. Some kind of a blood spell."

"She didn't give us a spell. She only gave us the knife. It must be something else." Willa shivered, a cool breeze blowing over her skin.

"Something's coming for us. I can feel it," Hunter said.

"Come on then, Alpha. Whip it out," Viktor said with a smirk.

"You're sick," Hunter replied.

"He's not wrong though." Willa smiled and shrugged.

"In the middle of some Mayan sacrificial death pit and you two are making bathroom jokes? Okay, yeah."

"It's all well and good until someone summons the God of Hell." Viktor picked up a ceramic bead and inspected it.

Hunter shook his head and removed his backpack, retrieving the weapon, then slung the sack back onto his shoulders.

"I do love a good knife," Viktor said.

"Okay, now what?" The Alpha inspected the blade. "Ilsbeth said it would help us get to the location, but she didn't mention where to actually find this book. There's got to be miles of caves here."

"She is a tricky witch," Viktor noted.

"Last time I was in the catacombs with Quint, they did some kind of blood magick."

"My brother has all sorts of tricks up his sleeve, doesn't he?"

"It was Gabriella. She's a witch. *Was* a witch," Hunter corrected. "Lost her magick. Whatever. It doesn't matter. They did this thing. Mixed their blood. Put it on this symbol and bam. Just like that, it worked. First bone found."

"Bone." Viktor laughed. "I could use one of those."

"You're like a fucking teenager."

Willa laughed in response and quickly recovered. "There are too many symbols carved on these walls. We'd be here all day. If Ilsbeth says that knife helped create the book, maybe it does something else. Something special."

"I think you should hold it. It's tied to the origin of the wolves. Like it or not someone took the skin of a royal and made this book. You're the key, Willa."

"I'll try. But for the record, I'm setting the bar low because I'm no witch. Believe me, I'd cut open my own hand and spill blood to find it, but I don't think it's going to work." Willa stretched out her palm, breathing deeply as Hunter placed the knife into her hand. Her fingers wrapped around its hilt; a slow foreign energy danced over her skin but quickly dissipated. "I don't know. I thought I felt a little something, but it's gone now."

"I've seen one before," Viktor said casually.

"Seen what?" Hunter replied.

"A skin book. It was a phase in the sixteen hundreds, you

know. Miss ole Ma? Wrap her up in a book and keep her forever."

"Ew." Willa shook her head, gooseflesh erupting over her skin at the thought of it. "I heard humans did that but just no. I don't care if it was in fashion. Not cool. Just sayin'."

"I'm with Wills on this one."

"Some had good intentions. Doctors bound them too. Perhaps a thankful send off into Heaven."

"Or Hell," Hunter added.

Willa nodded. "It doesn't surprise me. Humans. As much as I care for them, they are capable of so much destruction. Evil."

"One hundred percent," Viktor agreed. "And we're the monsters? Hardly. Vampires are simply hungry. Not all of us kill. We give you the best orgasm you'll ever get. You wash my back…I'll wash your whole body."

"Hunter's right. There's something wrong with you." Willa rolled her eyes.

"War. Genocide. Torture. Even remote civilizations engaged in cannibalism. Makes skin books look like fairy dust." Hunter sighed and glanced to the knife. "Maybe you need to concentrate on it."

"Flaying was a common punishment. The skin displayed for all to see."

"Got it Vik. I think we're good on the history lesson," Hunter told him.

Willa rooted her feet to the rocky earth. "Whoever decided to hide the skin book here may or may not have known I'd come looking for it. Ilsbeth said researchers found it in the 1970s. Something about a curse. But maybe they weren't researchers. Could've been pirates looking to steal artifacts. Happens all the time."

"It's possible," Hunter agreed.

Viktor sniffed into the air. "There's no other scent but humans since we arrived. There's you two, of course, but your scent is fresh. Unique to me."

"I don't want to know," Hunter responded.

"He means that…" Willa attempted to explain.

"Nope. I'm good. Pretty sure what he means."

"Humans. Their scent. Their blood. It's distinctive. The scent of wolves is…earthy. Yes, I do believe earthy is the correct word."

"We're not a couple of crunchy hippies."

"Nothing wrong with earthy. The blood is so…organic."

"Sometimes I think, 'why did I save the vampire?' Could have just left him in Hell. Quint would've got you out eventually."

"Because you love me." Viktor winked at Hunter and laughed.

"I think he loves you back." Willa smiled.

"Focus, people." Hunter plowed his fingers into his hair and sighed. "Not that I don't enjoy a nice stalactite every now and then. But I'd like to get the fuck out of here."

"Stalagmite," Viktor challenged.

"Stalactite, asshole. That one right there." He pointed to a rock formation delicately hanging from above. "C for ceiling.

"It's spectacular." Willa's focus was drawn to the ceiling, searching for clues.

"Vik…" Hunter held up a hand, silencing him. "We've got to get this book and get out of here."

"If you were a pirate, where would you hide your treasure?" Willa asked.

"Somewhere scary. People would be less likely to look for it," Hunter replied.

"I'm old school," Viktor declared.

"Would have never noticed." Hunter laughed.

"Pirates bury their treasure." Viktor inspected a crevice in the cave wall, careful not to trip on the pottery.

"Some do. Most don't." The Alpha studied the carvings on the far side of the cave.

"This ground is fairly hard. I'm not saying they couldn't dig a hole, but it seems more likely they'd hide it somewhere else."

"Where else would they put it?" Willa asked, frustrated.

"This place is wet." Hunter looked upward. "Bats. Humidity. Seriously. No matter what the outside of the book is made of, its pages are paper. There's no way it could survive in here. It would be destroyed within months if not weeks."

"It's magick so it's possible the book was fine for many years. But if humans took it, they'd assume differently. They'd probably keep it up high. Out of the way of any water." Willa slid her hand up the wall. The dampness dissipated as she glided her fingers further up the jagged stone.

"Maybe they'd put it in something airtight." Viktor stopped in his tracks, studying the rock formations.

"All that water in the entrance? It probably floods during a good rain. It would wash it away," Willa said.

"You're right." Hunter approached a massive cascading slab of limestone. The rippling rock appeared as if it were a waterfall.

"It has to be here." Willa gripped the knife, willing it to direct her, but still she sensed no energy. Frustrated she spun around toward the back of the cavern. A single beam of sunlight streamed in through a thin crack, glistening like sparkling crystal on a far wall. Logic told her the book had to be further inside the cave, protected from the elements, but the flickering captured her attention. "What's that you're always saying about humans, Viktor?"

"That I'm hungry. Food."

"No, not that. They're not like us." She smiled.

The vampire sighed. "They're fragile."

"Exactly. So, if a human did this, researchers or just someone looking to pick off an artifact, they'd know it was valuable. Maybe they'd put in some kind of acid-free preservation bag. But because they're human…"

"They'd be extra careful in a dangerous cave," Hunter surmised.

"They wouldn't risk going so far into it at night. They'd work to hide it in plain sight. Somewhere where they could work in the light." She pointed to the beam of light and walked toward it.

Hunter followed behind her. "They'd still put it up high.

Higher than a human could reach. Up there."

"Out of sight but within the light." Willa pointed to a stalactite. "To the left of that one. There's a pattern in the rock. It's been smoothed over, but the stone isn't the same as the rest of the wall. Do you see it?"

"I see but…"

"Can you get me up there?" she asked Viktor.

"Now she wants me to flash her," he commented to Hunter.

"I'll go," Hunter volunteered. "You stay down here. What if something happens?"

"The ledge isn't big enough for all three of us. It has to be me. It's from my family."

"Vik, if you drop her or let her fall, it's going to be your head," Hunter threatened.

"Just get over here, vampire." Willa nervously pumped her fingers. *You can do this, you can do this.* "Do that flashy thing you do. Get me up to the ledge but don't let go."

"Bossy…like a queen," Viktor noted, sidling up next to her.

"Don't hurt her," Hunter warned again.

"Let's do this shit." She nodded.

"As you wish, Your Majesty…careful with that knife now."

"Don't call me that." Willa's stomach flipped as she disappeared.

"Easy now." Viktor held an arm around her waist as they precariously materialized onto the one-foot-wide ledge of slippery limestone.

Willa clutched her fingers around a jutting rock, her pulse racing. "I'm not sure this was such a good idea."

"I think you should get down. We'll find another way," Hunter insisted.

"No. No. It's okay, really." Willa inhaled deeply, focusing on a smooth anomaly in the stone.

"Wolves don't fly, Wills. This is a bad idea."

Viktor rapped his knuckles along the rock. "This." He knocked over the smooth section. "None of this is hollow."

Willa pressed the hilt of the knife to the stone. She shuddered as the foreign energy sizzled through her. Viktor tightened his grip around her waist.

"Something. It's here. I feel it."

"There's nothing. It's solid," Viktor said.

"I don't care. Just because we can't see it…"

"I'm sorry, but this rock is solid."

"No…"

"She's right," Hunter shouted up toward them. He pointed toward the left. "The sunlight. It's hitting the crevice just over there. It's a sliver. I don't know. The knife…"

Willa shuffled her feet toward it, her heart pounding as she glanced down to Hunter. *Wolves don't fly.* "Right."

"What?" Hunter asked.

"Nothing," she murmured under her breath. "I've got this." The pads of her fingers grazed over the rough edges of the crystalized rock. The energy intensified as she probed the crevice. "This has got to be it."

"How the hell would a human get up there?" Hunter asked.

"Ladder? Airplane?" Viktor smiled down at him.

"Drone," Willa guessed. "Yeah, that's a stretch. I don't know. This opening. It's doesn't feel like anyone made it, but I don't think there's anything in here."

"Viktor. Can't you help her?"

"Maybe this knife. Fucking Ilsbeth." Willa stabbed it into the crevice.

"Fucking Ilsbeth is right. She gets us into this shit every single…." Hunter began.

"Wait…I hit something." Willa tugged at the hilt. "It's stuck."

"Jesus, Vik. Would you help her? This is ridiculous."

Willa yanked at the knife and it loosened. "No. Wait. I've got it. Just a little bit more…it's coming."

"At least someone is." Viktor rolled his eyes.

"Get her down now. I don't like this."

Willa ignored them, her pulse racing as she slowly pulled the package toward her. The sound of the bag scraping against the rock spiked her anticipation. A beam of light shone onto the clear plastic, and she caught sight of the thick brown book, the edges of the cream-colored pages coming into view.

"It's here! I've got it!" she yelled.

"See. Crisis averted." Viktor laughed. "Here we go!"

Oh Goddess. Willa felt it before she saw it. It tickled over her forefinger, its skinny brown legs poking out of the darkness. Her chest seized in terror. She yanked the knife, tugging the book straight out of the crack, and her adrenaline surged.

"Spider!!!!" *No, no. no.* The insect launched off her hand onto her face. "Get it off of me! Get it off me!"

Willa screamed at the top of her lungs as it scampered over her cheek. Her heart caught in her throat, her grip inadvertently loosened around the hilt. As her heels tilted backwards, the book, with the blade still lodged inside it, slipped out of her hands toward the water.

"Help!" Willa's stomach lurched as she sailed backwards.

"I've got Willa. You get the book," Hunter called out to the vampire with his arms poised to catch her.

"Fuck me." Giving a quick nod to Hunter, Viktor flashed away.

"I've got you!" Hunter yelled.

"Oh Goddess!" All the breath rushed out of her lungs as she landed safely within his arms. Her heart pumped a million miles per minute, her eyes fluttering open to meet his.

"You're okay," he told her, clutching her tight.

The sound of splashing across the cavern drew their attention.

"No, not the book," she cried.

Sunlight flickered upon a fist as it punched through the dark water, holding the book. Viktor emerged, drenched. "Got it!"

"Oh, thank the Goddess." Willa exhaled in relief.

"Jesus, Vik."

"I know, I know. Don't say it. I know. I'm amazing. A real God. Now can we get the fuck out of this hell hole? I'm over the bugs. And the heat. The fucking water." He sniffed. "And I smell."

"You got enough juice to get us back? Please tell me yes because I don't think any of us wants to track back through all this water." Hunter gently set Willa onto her feet.

"Yeah, sure. But you owe me. I nearly drowned getting this book. Get a good look. Superhero here."

"I know we took the jet, but I'm thinking we should just flash back to my place," the Alpha ignored his hyperbole. "It'll be faster. I don't want to waste time."

"But Ilsbeth…" Willa's eyes lit up, anxiety gripping her chest.

"I want to see this book first before we go back to her house."

Doubt weaved itself into her thoughts. "She wants it, but you're right. Something about this whole thing doesn't feel right. She's manipulating us. This book belongs to my family. I think she wanted me to get it because she knows I was the only one who could release it."

"Of course, we aren't giving it to her. Not right away anyway. She can't be trusted. Not for one witchy minute." Viktor violently shook his head, sending water droplets flying into the air.

"I had a spider crawl up my face! *My face*!" Willa visibly shuddered. "Get me out of here."

"Let's go." Hunter reached for Willa's hand and set his palm on Viktor's shoulder.

Willa's mind swam as she drifted, billions of atoms reconnecting all at once. Her bottom landed on the hard wood with a thud. A rush of sea air filled her lungs and she blinked toward the blinding sun. She shoved to her feet, but the floor seemingly moved beneath her and she tumbled back onto the smooth wooden planks.

"Where are we?" she managed.

"Viktor." Rage blazed in Hunter's voice.

"Are we…." Turquoise waves rolled into view as she steadied herself on the rocking surface.

"What are we doing on a boat?" The Alpha knelt down and extended his hand to Willa. "You okay?"

As her eyes caught his, butterflies danced in her stomach. *How could I forget that I almost died after having my face eaten by a spider? My sexy Alpha. Yeah, that's why.* She smiled.

"Willa? You good?" he asked gently, a corner of his lip tugging upward.

"Yes, sorry. I'm okay." Willa reached for his hand, grunting as Hunter pulled her onto her feet. Thankful to be alive, she wrapped her arms around him, holding tight. "Just hold me."

"Hey, now." Hunter kissed the top of her head, his eyes meeting Viktor's.

Overwhelmed, she fought to regain control of her emotions. "I'm good."

"It's okay, sweetheart." Hunter glanced at Viktor who smiled at him.

"Welcome aboard the Bloody Mary." The vampire held the book up in the air, the knife still protruding from its cover. "Ahoy matey. Or in your case, just mates."

"Fuck me." Hunter sighed as he scanned the horizon,

noting there was no land in sight. "What the hell, Vik?"

"As much as I'd love to chat, I smell like pig's ass. And you two." He sniffed. "Dog's ass."

"We've got to get to Ilsbeth." Willa wrenched herself out of Hunter's arms, glaring at Viktor.

"We do. But not right now. We're about to go fight a demon. This isn't a backyard boil party we're going to. You both need to rest after that little adventure."

"I hate to admit it, but the vampire's right. Whatever battle awaits us isn't going to be a day in the park."

"But…" she protested.

"We're safe out in the open water. My boat has wards, but it's well known that demons have a harder time materializing in water."

"Viktor," Hunter began.

"Not another word. Come. It's time to get clean. We'll talk after."

Although Willa's first instinct was to argue, she considered their predicament. Within hours they'd go to Ilsbeth's, and hand a book to the demon responsible for her torture. The possibility of death or eternal damnation loomed over their heads. They had to be at the top of their game. Strategy over impulsivity; she resigned herself to accept the needed respite. *Food. Sleep. Then fight like hell.*

"The Bloody Mary?" Hunter brought the glass of whiskey to his lips. "Clever, Vik."

"Makes the humans at the yacht club more comfortable. I fit right in."

"Yeah. I doubt it."

Willa smiled at the vampire, who had donned baby blue pajamas. "Nice pjs."

"Versace. Never underestimate the comfort of silk." Viktor smoothed his hand over the lapel.

"Where are we?" she asked.

"Mary's home dock is Coconut Grove. I have a charity event in Naples next week, so we're catching a ride in the Gulf of Mexico."

A formal butler dressed in all white approached. Viktor tapped on the edge of his empty champagne glass.

"What are you drink…" Willa lost her words as the thick sanguine fluid flowed from the bottle.

"Ah, thank you, Brann." No words were spoken as the server left in silence. "He's not much of a talker. I'm afraid the medieval times were a bit difficult for him. Blasphemers."

"Their tongues," she whispered.

"I saved him from certain death. But there was nothing I could do to repair the damage. He enjoys the sea, though." Viktor sipped from the glass and grimaced.

"What's wrong?" Willa rested her hand on his forearm.

"This is bottled. I really need the fresh stuff. I used quite a bit of energy flashing. I'm afraid I might have to leave."

"You can't leave us on a boat staffed by vampires," Willa blurted out without thinking. "I mean…not that there's anything wrong with…it's just that…it's…"

"Dangerous. No fucking way, Vik. You flash us all the

way out here and…" Hunter went silent as several servants placed dinner plates in front of them and proceeded to pile them with crab legs and grouper. "Thank you."

"This looks amazing. Thank you, Viktor. But where…" Willa watched with curiosity as the servants retreated to the galley.

"Just because I don't eat human food doesn't mean I don't keep it in stock for guests. Look around. We're in the Gulf of Mexico. It's plentiful."

"All this. We could have just gone back to my house." Hunter picked up his fork and flaked off a chunk of fish.

"We're a team." The vampire took another sip.

"We are, aren't we?" Willa laughed, intrigued by their unlikely friendship.

"The grouper's delicious," Hunter commented. "Tell me. All the crew on this ship are vampires, yeah?"

Viktor nodded. "Of course."

"How do vampires know how to cook like this if they don't eat?" Willa asked with a moan. "Hmm…so good."

"It's delicious," Hunter agreed.

"We need blood to survive. To be strong. But," he held the glass up to the moonlight, "some choose to still eat. Like Quint. My chef too. I had to make the break."

"The break?" the Alpha asked, continuing to eat.

"Yes. The break. Quintus prefers to remember his humanity, but I cannot allow myself to go there." He stared off into the darkness, the lights of the boat flickering on the waves. "My life. I can barely remember it now. Life before Baxter. In Scandinavia. I had a wife, children. And then in one day in a battle…well, needless to say it didn't go well. I never saw my family or my homeland again." He looked to Willa and Hunter, giving a wistful smile. "So, you see. The day I awoke from being nearly dead to being newly turned, I broke. I broke from human ways. The pain of living was far worse than dying. Trust me on that."

"I'm sorry, Viktor," Willa told him, her voice soft with empathy.

"Ah, no worries. Life evolves and so did I." He set his glass down onto the table. "Let's discuss the skin book, shall we?"

"After our meal, we can take a look at it, but I doubt that it's going to tell us anything. Right now, we just have to trust like hell that the witch isn't lying about the demon wanting it."

"I think it's safe to assume she's lying about something," Viktor countered. "It's Ilsbeth."

"She could double cross us. She seemed sincere but…" *Julian.* "I have to find my brother."

"Wherever he is, he's trying to keep you safe. Divert the wolves. Which it seems he's done a pretty damn good job of so far." Hunter cracked open a crab leg and slid the delicious meat into his mouth.

"We'll find him," Viktor assured them. "He's powerful. Can hold his own."

"I know he's trying to protect me, but I don't like the thought of him on the run by himself. If anything happens, we can't help."

"We're on the run too," Hunter said.

Viktor stood and walked into the living room, returning with the book in one hand and the knife in another. He placed the items onto the table and sat. "While you both were cleaning up, I took a look at this diabolical thing and guess what? Surprise, surprise. It has some kind of a self-locking mechanism in place."

"Honestly I could care less what's inside of it. I just want to trade it," Hunter told him. "Freedom for the book. Done."

"But she said there were spells…" Willa said.

"I could break it, but the witch…I suspect she'll know how to open it." Viktor shrugged.

"Normally I'd say, yeah let's bust into it but I can't see what we have to gain," Hunter said.

"I agree with Hunter. If it's made from who she said it was, he may have had royal blood, but that doesn't mean he was a good person." Willa reached across the table and brushed her hand over its cover. The tanned supple skin tingled beneath her fingertips. "This book still has energy. I can feel it."

She quickly withdrew her hand and shivered. "No. If the demons want this, there's something bad inside. Something dark. Something that doesn't belong here. We shouldn't open it. None of us practices the dark arts."

Viktor raised his eyebrows and smiled. "Speak for yourself, princess."

"Something you want to tell us, vampire?" Hunter asked, setting down his fork.

"You don't think I've lived all these years off my good looks, do you?" He tilted his head. "I dated a witch a long time ago. And no, it wasn't Ilsbeth. Whatever. It doesn't matter. Your point is taken. This book." He glanced at it then focused back on Willa. "It's bad mojo. Maybe you're right. Nothing good is going to come from opening it. I know Ilsbeth says she wants the spells, but I think we hold on to it. Let her summon the demon and we'll get rid of it."

"I'm with you. Ilsbeth wants the spells but I doubt she forgets her latest tour of Hell. It's not worth it." Hunter lifted his glass and took a drink of his whiskey.

"I don't trust her," Willa said.

"Something else we all agree on." Hunter reached for her hand. "This is going to be all over soon."

"All I know is I have exactly zero plans on going back. As far as I'm concerned, they owe me one. I was dragged there trying to do something good." Viktor stood and lifted his glass into the air. "I do love a warm gulf breeze."

"Nice boat, Vik."

"Thank you. All two hundred feet of it. I enjoy being here perhaps more than anywhere else. When I'm not partying on a penthouse deck in Miami. Or New York. Love New York. Of course, there's WeHo. Malibu. Ibiza. Ah…and Paris. Thailand. Forgot Thailand. The Mediterranean. Ah…I did love Mary."

"Did?" Willa asked.

Viktor smiled. "A girl from Croatia. Austrian duchess. Long story but I'm afraid not enough time."

Willa exchanged a confused look with Hunter.

"I'm going to have to flash to go get a donor. I won't be gone long," he promised.

"No, please." Willa refused to be stuck in the middle of the Gulf of Mexico with a crew full of vampires.

"I'm sorry but if I don't feed, I may not be strong enough for what we are about to do. I can't risk not being one hundred percent when we go summoning demons from the depths of Hell. I think I just mentioned it but I'm not going back. I'll die before that happens."

"If any of these…" Hunter glanced up to the bridge, "vampires…well, you know. I know you'll say you trust them, but I don't. The only reason we're safe is because you are here. You're going to have to take us with you, take us back to New Orleans or…"

"Not an option. It's not safe in New Orleans. Out in the middle of the sea makes it harder for them to find us."

"Then drink whatever bagged blood you have on board to get you by until we get back. You can drink from a witch at Ilsbeth's."

"No that's not going to work. It'll take too much time. It's too risky."

"We'll take our chances."

"No, I won't risk your life or mine. I…"

"Take my blood," Willa whispered. As the words left her lips, Hunter's anger rushed over her. Her heart pounded in her chest as her eyes met Viktor's.

"What did you just say?" His eyes widened in disbelief.

"I…" Willa glanced to Hunter whose lips were drawn tight. "I said you should take my blood."

"Willa…" The Alpha began but she interrupted him before he had a chance to finish.

"No, listen to me." She squeezed Hunter's hand, focusing on her mate. "He needs to feed. We can't make any mistakes. Not one. Leaving us here with the vampires isn't an option. We can't trust that they're all loyal. Someone or something could have gotten to one of them. A demon might detect Viktor leaving us. Seriously, we're only safe for a few hours until all Hell literally breaks loose back in Baton Rouge or New Orleans or wherever we're making this shit happen with a witch none of us trust. All of us have to be at the top of our game. There cannot be any weakness. He must be as strong as you and me. We are a team."

"But Willa…you know the implications, right?" The corner of his mouth ticked upward. "It's just not that easy at this point. You saved his life in Hell. He saved yours. You're lucky you haven't created a bond already."

"Viktor senses me. He probably could find me anywhere. I'm certain of it. But the only bond I'll ever truly have is with you…my mate. Maybe there's a way…" Willa plowed her fingers through her unruly mane. Her thoughts spun with possibilities. "He could bite you too. Spread it out. We won't be weakened but he'll have both royal blood and Alpha blood. You know that would make him stronger than any old human blood."

Hunter blew out a breath and looked at Viktor. "Maybe…I don't know about this."

"It will work," she insisted.

"You both understand the ramifications, yes? Because I'd never ask you to do this. You're newly mated and Willa… you've already helped me."

"You've helped us too. You stayed with me and Hunter for far longer than you should have."

"That's what friends do. We don't leave each other when the going gets bad. And as unlikely as I would have thought it, I care about both of you."

"We *are* friends and that's exactly why we're agreeing to it," Hunter told him. He smiled at Willa.

"The twenty roaming vampires had something to do with it," Viktor replied.

"True, but this is your boat. And we're safe because of you," Hunter said.

"The effects of my bite. You know how this works. There's only two ways." Viktor shook his head and looked off into the distance. "I refuse to hurt her. Or you."

"You won't. We know what we're signing up for. I can't promise my reaction or what's going to happen but…" Willa reached for Hunter's hand and nodded.

"Do not attempt to form a bond with her, vampire. I just fucking mated with her. This is a one-time deal. Get that straight. Whatever goes down, you'd better damn well take note." Hunter blew out a breath and looked to Willa. "Are you sure about this? Like really sure? Whether you know it or not, you're probably traumatized from what happened to you in Hell. This could trigger something."

"It could but my wolf…my heart…you're here. As long as I'm with you I know I'll be safe." Willa took a deep breath. *Viktor won't hurt me.* "I can't explain it. If there was any time he could have killed me, it would have been in Hell. But he saved me."

"Ah good then. Because if I don't eat soon, I won't be dematerializing us anywhere." Viktor raised his glass with a chuckle.

"Where's our room?" Hunter grumbled.

"The Alpha doesn't waste time, I'll give him that." The vampire set his drink on the table and clapped his hands together. "All right then."

"I'm well aware of the effects from your bite," Willa told him. "I want to be comfortable. As much as I love this warm breeze, I won't feel safe out in the open. Our guard will be down."

"Exactly. We both need rest too," Hunter said.

"No time like the present. Shall we?" Viktor gestured to the galley.

Willa's stomach fluttered as she rose from her chair and headed into the yacht. She smiled, admiring its lush interior. The vampire didn't do anything small. Opulent white leather furniture in the living room matched a grand piano that sat next to a marble fireplace. A life-sized black and white portrait of a gorgeous nude woman stared back at her as they made their way to a staircase, and Willa couldn't help but wonder who she was.

Her heart raced as her palm slid over the cool chrome railing descending to the guest quarters. A series of overhead crystal lights illuminated the sleek hallway. They passed several rooms before coming to an intricately designed golden door. Viktor inserted his palm into a scanner and glanced back to them with a smile.

"Biometric devices. Not sure what we ever did without

them." A lock clicked open and Viktor opened the door, ushering them inside the master bedroom. "Safe. From humans. Witches. Vampires. Other underworldly creatures we dare not speak of."

The lock clicked as the door shut behind her, and as she took in the sight of the room, her eyes widened. Located in the bow of the boat, two arched metallic shutter walls lowered to reveal windows. The ship's lights reflected onto the blue gulf water. The enormous bed sat against a rich mahogany wall, a large sitting room with leather sofas to the right.

"I'll leave you to sleep in here after we're done. It's the one place I can absolutely ensure your safety. Don't worry about the windows. We can see out, but no one can see in. I'll put the shutters back up if it makes you more comfortable."

Willa approached the window and placed her palm onto the glass, taking in the sight of lights twinkling on the water.

"I've instructed the Captain. No anchor tonight. I don't want any ties to the earth. Whatever seeks us from below will not find us," Viktor assured them. He turned and looked to the sofa. "I've got the sofa or the bed. I'm not sure…well, where you'd like to begin."

Willa smiled, hearing a tremor in his voice. Was the usually overly confident vampire actually nervous?

"The bed?" Willa took a deep breath and looked to Hunter.

"You sure?"

"I just want to lie down. It's pleasurable, right?" she asked.

"Of course. I swear on my life I won't hurt either of you," Viktor promised.

Willa climbed onto the mattress. Like a cat she stretched out onto the soft black satin comforter. She closed her eyes and moaned. "Nice bed, vampire."

Hunter laughed. "I don't ever want to hear those words again."

She smiled. Her eyes fluttered open, excitement swirling inside her belly as he crawled onto the bed towards her on his hands and knees.

"You look pretty comfortable."

"That's because I am. I really, really miss my bed."

"I'm going to get us a new bed. Our bed."

"Hmm…in Wyoming? I suppose I'm leaving Guatemala?"

"You can hire someone. I need my own personal physician."

"But wolves don't get sick."

Hunter lay on his side, draping his arm over her waist. "You've got me tied up in knots, woman."

Out of her peripheral vision, she caught the flicker of candlelight, Viktor blowing out a match. "Hmm…you're definitely hot. So hot." She laughed, rolling toward him. "You do know what you're doing to me?"

"Help me, doctor." He brushed his lips to hers.

Willa's heart raced as his mouth captured hers, passion burning between them. She ached to be in his arms, to have Hunter deep inside her once again. Vampires. Demons. Danger. Nothing mattered in that moment but her Alpha.

Hunter tore his lips from hers, leaving her panting for

breath. Her hands drifted underneath his robe, exploring his muscular chest. The throbbing between her legs intensified as she stared deep into his eyes.

"You know what's going to happen here? You don't have to do this," Hunter told her.

"He's right."

Willa heard Viktor's voice but couldn't see him. She turned toward the window and caught sight of him watching them from a distance.

"Unless you've got really long fangs, you're not going to get much blood from over there." Willa released a nervous laugh. She couldn't have imagined in what lifetime she'd willingly let a vampire feed from her, but she couldn't deny the connection with Viktor.

"Are you sure?" he asked, his tone serious. "Are you both sure? Once this is done, it cannot be undone."

"You can't leave us on this boat alone, Vik." Hunter told him. "This is our choice."

"I swear it. Nothing will happen to you." Viktor unbuttoned his shirt.

Willa's pulse raced at the sight of the vampire's bared chest. Well-built and muscular, like a Nordic God, he approached, his usually coiffed blond hair casually tousled as if he'd been in the wind.

"Willa. It's just you and me," Hunter whispered.

"No." Willa smiled. "We're a team. You, me and the vampire. We started this in Hell, and we will escape this nightmare together."

"Did I tell you how beautiful you are today?" Hunter

cupped her cheek, love stirring in his gaze.

"You can tell me for the rest of my life, and I won't ever tire of it." Willa's heart fluttered as he brought his lips toward hers. She meant every word. This Alpha owned her, and for the first time in her life, she accepted she'd no longer be alone.

His lips crushed upon hers, his tongue sweeping into her mouth. Her body ignited with passion, her hands gliding over the hard planes of his chest. Her fingers trailed down toward his stomach, and she shoved open his robe.

"Willa," he whispered into her lips.

"Goddess, I love this." *I love you.* Her pussy ached with arousal. She wrapped her hand around his thick cock and glided her thumb over his wet slit.

"Ah fuck," Hunter hissed, thrusting into her fist.

Willa reluctantly broke their kiss, her chest heaving with emotion. *Viktor.* She sensed him before he ever touched her hand.

"My dearest pet, you're exquisite." He smiled. "Don't let me interrupt."

"Hmm…it's okay." Willa rolled onto her back to face him. "You've taken care of us here. We're clean. Warm. Fed. And now," she glanced to Hunter then back to the vampire, "we feed you."

Viktor lifted her wrist and brought it within inches of his lips. Gooseflesh broke over her as he spoke, his warm breath teasing her skin. "Are you sure?"

"Yes," she whispered, transfixed on his ice blue eyes that swirled with lust.

"Absolutely sure?"

She nodded but startled as his fangs dropped. A kiss on her neck from her mate calmed her beast. "Yes."

As he teased his tongue over her wrist, her nipples tightened with desire. So lethal yet so gentle. Sensual.

"Alpha?" He sought his permission.

"Look, Vik. I appreciate you being all PC but I'm kind of…ah…" Hunter lost his words as Willa palmed his dick in her hand. "We're ready."

"Very ready." Willa laughed softly.

Viktor smiled and nodded at Willa. "Such a brave princess."

Captivated by his fangs, she stilled in anticipation. His tongue darted over her wrist, and her entire body went on alert. "I promise this will be the best bite you've ever had."

Like a cobra, he struck, his teeth slicing into her skin. Her body seized in pleasure. She sucked a breath as Hunter's fingers grazed down her stomach, his fingers playing over her clitoris.

"Oh Goddess." She released a euphoric breath, her robe falling open to reveal her bared body. "More…"

"Easy," Hunter told her, fingering her wet pussy.

Viktor's energy sizzled through her. He withdrew her lifeblood, imbuing her with his own force, strong and sexual.

Hunter's mouth crushed down upon hers, and she kissed him with a mad fervor, unable to get enough of him. She raked her fingernails down his shoulder as he moved his lips to her breast.

"Fuck me. Fuck me now," she demanded. *What the ever-loving hell is happening?* As Viktor sealed her wounds shut with his tongue, she cupped his cheek. "No, no, no. Don't stop."

"Willa," Hunter breathed.

"I…I…" She lost her words as Viktor gently released her arm. The connection lost, a sense of emptiness touched her mind.

"Viktor." The Alpha lifted his gaze, pinning him with a hard stare.

"I didn't hurt her. I…don't need to bite you if you don't…"

"Get over here." Hunter rolled onto his back and stretched out his arm.

Willa shifted onto her mate, trailing kisses over Hunter's chest. She nipped at his skin, the taste of him wakening her wolf. With her eyes trained on Viktor, she watched with fascination as he rounded the bed and sat on the mattress, taking the Alpha's arm into his hands.

Her heart pounded against her ribs as the vampire's fangs sliced into Hunter's wrist. She broke eye contact with Viktor, her gaze flashing to her mate. Her lips brushed over his hip as her hand tightened around his cock.

"Ah…fuck," Hunter moaned, throwing his head backwards. As the vampire sucked harder, he arched his back. "Goddess…yes."

Willa gave a slight smile as her lips hovered over the broad head of his dick.

"Please…Willa." He bit his lip and lifted his head so he

could see her. "Suck my cock."

"I got ya baby," she purred, her tongue darting over the slit. The salty taste of his essence registered, and she moaned in response.

"Shit. This is not right. But fuck, Viktor. Why does that have to feel so…oh Goddess," Hunter groaned as Willa plunged his cock into her warm mouth without warning.

The taste of her mate urged her wolf to surface. She howled in exaltation, celebrating her power, her mate.

He pressed his hips upward driving his shaft deep into her mouth. She caught Viktor's hazy state of arousal as he lapped over Hunter's wounds.

Her excitement spiked as her Alpha took control, clamping his hand around Viktor's wrist. "You're not leaving. You started this and you're going to finish it."

"Stay, Viktor," Willa whispered, her lips brushing the broad crown.

She smiled as the vampire relaxed back onto the bed. Willa had never considered herself an exhibitionist but the desire in Viktor's eyes amped her arousal. As if having an astral power over both the Alpha and the vampire, she held their complete attention as she swallowed Hunter's cock down her throat. The masculine scent of her mate urged her wolf to rise.

Hunter shoved up onto his elbows, watching his gorgeous princess suck his dick. He groaned as she wrapped her hand around the base, pumping her mouth up and down his shaft.

Willa released him with a loud pop and lapped her

tongue over his head. With her free hand, she cupped his ass, her fingers trailing down toward his back hole.

"What are you..." He lost his words as she explored.

"You're not the only one who likes to play, Alpha." Willa smiled, plunging his cock between her lips, her finger circling his puckered skin.

"Fuck..." Hunter threw his head back as she probed him, her finger sliding deep in his ass and teasing his pleasure point. "Jesus, you're going to make me come."

Hearing his pleading delighted her, driving a rush of heat between her legs. Willa tilted her hips, seeking relief on the bed but couldn't get friction. She glanced to Viktor, who adjusted his visible erection but made no effort to remove his pants.

Viktor, she heard the Alpha's voice in her head. With the vampire's energy still flowing through her, she'd considered the possibility.

"Willa's beautiful, huh, Vik?" Hunter managed.

"Gorgeous," Viktor agreed.

"I'm allowing this once. Understand. And only I make love to my mate."

Willa slowly released his cock, still stroking it in her hand while circling his anus with the pad of her finger.

"Come here, Willa," Hunter ordered, his tone sensual and firm.

Like a tiger she stalked her prey, shedding her robe. She straddled Hunter, her pussy sliding over the length of his hardness. As she stared down at him, her heart tightened in emotion. She'd only met this incredible man days ago, but it felt as if she'd known him her entire life. So perfect, both dominant and loving, she'd follow him anywhere.

"Closer," he instructed.

Hunter reached for her, cupping her face. Her lips brushed his, the searing kiss evidence as to whom she belonged. As they broke contact, she sucked in a deep breath, her entire body willing to submit to his desires.

"You want this?" He stroked his cock through her wet folds.

"Oh Goddess," she breathed.

"Up on your knees, Princess."

Willa's skin tingled with desire at his demand. She complied, her heart racing as she did so. Hunter slid out from under her, coming to her side. Her head lolled forward as his palm caressed her back, finally reaching her bottom.

"Open your legs. Let us see you."

Willa did as she was told, careful to keep her balance on the mattress. With a heated gaze, the vampire watched intently as the Alpha commanded his mate, revealing her bared flesh.

"This woman is everything to me," Hunter told him.

Willa sighed as his fingers trailed down her bottom, teasing her core.

"Touch your breasts," the Alpha ordered.

Willa's nipples ached as she complied, bringing her hands to her chest. The throbbing between her legs intensified and she moaned. With nothing to sate her but the cool air that brushed over her wet clit, her body ached with arousal.

"Now, Viktor."

"Ah…" she cried as her mate slid his finger inside her.

"I want to see her come. You like to eat my mate? Lick her pussy," Hunter ordered.

Viktor stood and made quick work of removing his pants. His cock sprung forward and Willa sucked a breath as Hunter fucked her with his fingers.

"Please," she heard herself beg, her body on fire.

"But of course, Princess." Viktor settled in front of her.

"Ah Goddess," she breathed as the vampire's mouth found her mound, his thumb gliding over her clit. "Please…I need you inside me."

"Soon…but first." Hunter continued to fuck her with his hand as he came up behind her. His lips found her shoulder, peppering her with kisses as he watched Viktor delve his head between her legs, his tongue darting over her sensitive bead.

Surrounded by the Alpha and the vampire, Willa submitted to the unrelenting pleasure. Lost within the sensation, she accepted their love.

As Hunter bit down onto her shoulder, he added another finger inside her tight channel. "Please, please, please…" she begged.

As Viktor's tongue slid through her wet folds, Willa's body heaved forward.

"Easy, there. Let him taste you."

"I…." Willa panted for breath as she edged toward her orgasm.

"I'm going to fuck you so hard after but now…this."

Viktor sucked her clit between his lips, relentlessly lapping at the sensitive nub.

As Hunter kissed the back of her neck, her entire body hurled into release. "Oh Goddess, oh Goddess, oh Goddess…" Willa shuddered as Viktor lapped at her pussy, giving no quarter as she attempted to recover from her orgasm.

"That's a girl. That's it. So beautiful." He guided her cheek toward him so that he could capture her lips. "I have to be inside you now. Viktor, lay down. Easy…"

The Alpha guided Willa over Viktor as the vampire adjusted himself onto his back. Willa remained on her knees, supporting herself with her hands. She panted for breath, her hair spilling onto Viktor's thighs. Hunter's fingers were soon replaced by the broad head of his dick probing her core.

Willa reached for Viktor's dick, settling onto her forearms with her bottom presented for her mate. She smiled up at the vampire and stroked his cock, gliding her thumb over its crown. His eyes lit with delight, enjoying her slow tease.

"Isn't my mate delightful?" Hunter asked, tapping his cock on her ass before gliding it through her slick folds.

"Hmm…" She moaned, lapping the tip of her tongue over Viktor's shaft. "Please…fuck me…"

As Hunter slammed inside her, stretching her open, Willa parted her lips, sliding Viktor's cock into her mouth. Her body ignited in desire, her Alpha dominating her body, thrusting in and out of her tight channel.

The sting of his palm on her bottom sent a shiver through her. The vampire threw his head back with a groan, as she gently teased his sensitive skin with her teeth and lapped over his shaft with her tongue.

The sound of flesh slapping flesh echoed as Hunter pounded into her from behind, the scent of sex lingering in the air. Tightening her grip on his shaft, she sucked Viktor hard, her head bobbing in rhythm as her Alpha fucked her.

Hunter wrapped his arm around her waist, his fingers delving into her wetness. Willa sucked a breath as his thumb strummed her clit. A thousand synapses fired, her core contracting around his cock.

The supernatural connection intensified. Like a trifecta of power, the Alpha, royal princess and ancient vampire became one, their energies intertwining, electrifying the air with passion.

"Fuck yes. Willa. I'm coming." Hunter gently pinched her clit, thrusting hard and long into her pussy.

"Yes, yes, yes," she repeated, gasping for breath. Willa came undone, a wave of ecstasy crashing over her. Her core tightened around Hunter's cock as she pressed back onto him, every hard inch of him stroking inside her.

"Holy…oh yeah." Viktor tilted his hips as Willa fisted the root of his cock with her hand and swallowed his shaft down her throat. He grunted, spilling his seed as she sucked him hard, milking every last shiver of his climax.

"Fuck yes, Willa," Hunter grunted, giving a final thrust. He wrapped both his arms around her waist and rolled them onto their sides.

Willa's body melted into his, tendrils of her orgasm still threading through every cell of her body, her skin tingling. His warmth surrounded her, and she succumbed to the dreamy afterglow. Emotion for the Alpha churned in her chest. Too much to process, she simply accepted the love of the incredible man that had ignited her soul. *Her Alpha.*

Chapter Thirteen

The vampire stood solemn as Hunter approached him from behind. Although he remained silent, the Alpha knew his mind raced with the possibility of going back to Hell.

"I'm not going to let them take you."

Viktor silently gazed upon the turquoise waters, not responding.

"The thing about Hell is that it's like going into the fun house. It's all smoke and mirrors. Ain't nothin' gonna get you." It was a lie, he knew. Nothing truly could describe the pure terror of Hades.

"It wasn't your first time." Viktor turned to face the Alpha.

Hunter sighed, contemplating what to tell the vampire. In 1695, he'd left New Orleans. He'd always been a wanderer. While exploring the great west, he'd fallen for the daughter of a Spanish explorer. *Maria Lopez.* Gorgeous and flirtatious, her vivacious energy attracted every man who had the fortune of being in her presence. Hunter had fallen hard and fast for the lovely human. He shouldn't have indulged, aware that he could only mate with another wolf. After a summer romance, she'd professed her love.

Maria. The only human to whom he'd ever revealed his wolf, explaining he'd never be able to marry her. Although she'd kept his secret, she'd been devastated. After paying a witch to summon a demon, she'd traded her soul in an attempt to become wolf. But the divine magick of wolves was gifted by the Goddess. There was no way to become a shifter without being born into pack. Before Hunter could help her, Maria spiraled into madness and the demon condemned her to Hell.

"There was a human. A woman," Hunter began.

Viktor gave a closed smile. "There always is."

"Maria."

"A lovely name."

"I cared about her. I really did." Hunter shrugged. "I don't know…perhaps I loved her in some way. It was a different time."

"Ah, but wolves don't mate with humans."

"I know. I was prepared to watch her grow old…to make some sort of a commitment. But I knew that my mate could come. It was stupid of me. I was young."

"And your pack? Your father? I can't imagine they'd take kindly to you shacking up with a human."

"They didn't know." Hunter smiled, recalling how his dad had reamed him out after rescuing his ass from Hell. "Well, not at first anyway. Pa was down in New Orleans. I'd gone west. San Antonio, Texas."

"No cell phones back then I suppose?"

"I was a young buck." Hunter released a reflective sigh. "It was a shit show. Pa was fucking pissed."

"Meet human girl. End up in Hell?"

"Girl gets dragged to Hell. I go after her. But she was too far gone. Evil does that to you. You can't make deals with demons and not expect to get burned."

"True."

"It was the first and last time I ever got involved with a human. But Hell?" The Alpha closed his eyes, refusing to allow the painful memories to rise to the surface. The torture had nearly killed him, but his father had found a way in and out of Hell to save him. "I can't go back either, Vik. I won't. The last time I got lucky. We all got lucky. No. What's gonna happen is that we're going to go back to the witch, get her to summon up the demon owed, shove this book up his ass and go on our merry fucking way. If I have to order up an exorcism from the Pope himself, I will. It's time to put this shit to rest."

"Sounds like a generic plan. A million things could go wrong. Good on the shoving something up its ass, though. Yeah, that'll work." The vampire laughed. "I like it. I'm down."

"Trust me when I say I plan to deal with the Priestess. If that bitch as much as waves her little finger the wrong way, she's losing her head. She fucked Dimitri and she's not going to fuck me. *Us.*"

"There is something you need to know." Viktor's smile fell flat.

Hunter's gut tightened, his intuition warning him that whatever the vampire had to say, it wasn't going to be good.

He clenched his fist and stretched his fingers, easing the tension that thrummed through his body. "I'm afraid to fucking ask. What is it?"

"Ilsbeth. She cannot go without consequence for her actions. She needs to be brought to justice."

"What exactly does that mean?" Hunter paused and shook his head. "It's not that I don't know what she did to Dimitri. She's no friend of the pack right now…Acadian or mine. But in Hell…"

"She's been dealing with demons."

"All witches aren't white. They dabble in dark magick."

"Demons have been brought into this world. Summoned by the witch. She cannot contain them. Dimitri. The incident in New York. They are after your mate."

"Who seeks this justice besides us? You know what? It doesn't matter. I'm sorry, Vik, but if you've got some plans to go after her, you're on your own. I can't risk any more time away from my pack. My beta's fucking AWOL. He attacked Willa. I've gotta deal with him and the rogues still. But taking down the High Priestess? No. I'm out. Logan can deal with her and get her back. Jax fucking Chandler. Get his ass back down to Louisiana. He can do it. She's not my problem. Once Willa gets whatever dispensation from Hell she's gonna get, we're outta here."

"I hear you, brother. But it's Samantha who calls on my assistance. I can't say no."

"It's always the quiet ones that are the toughest."

"She is engaged to Luca." Viktor raised an amused eyebrow at him. "We both saw her that day at their house."

"How do you know? You flashed in and out."

"I was slightly incapacitated but still. Red wields some of her own tough love."

"I don't know her that well, but clearly she's a High Priestess and she can deal with it. I get she's probably not happy that the bitch is back."

"This is a favor to Kade. He's not my child or even within my line but Quintus'." Viktor shrugged. "I feel as though we owe Kade for keeping the peace that day. Luca isn't the easiest to get along with."

"Not at all charming like you?" The corner of the Alpha's lips tugged upward.

"Easy now." Viktor gave a closed smile, his hands to his chest. "I'm the consummate gentleman."

"Except for when you rip someone's throat out." Hunter smiled. "Hey, I'm sure they always deserve it. No offense."

"But of course, they always do," Viktor answered, his tone light but serious.

"So, what's Kade's big plan?"

"Not my issue. My only responsibility is to escort the lovely Ilsbeth to the coven."

"For the record, Vik. I'm telling you this is a bad idea right now. I know you want to make things right with Kade. That day at Luca's was a shit show," he said, recalling how he and Quintus had visited Samantha at their home. A demon-witch had materialized out of nowhere and almost killed their young daughter. "If Sam wants to go at her, then more power to her. I'm just saying that it's best for you not to mess with Ilsbeth."

"It's a calculated risk with low reward so of course I'm all in." Viktor laughed.

"I'm serious, man. If she gets a whiff of this before we strike a deal with the demon, she's likely to fly off on her broom. But before she goes, she's gonna fuck some shit up. That's how she rolls."

"I've known Ilsbeth for a long time. While I agree with your assessment, it's my responsibility to bring her to the coven. Nothing more. I'll get her to go willingly. If I can anyway. If not, all I need is a small touch. She won't be happy to be flashed against her will, but she'll get over it."

"Yeah, because Ilsbeth is the understanding type." Hunter rolled his eyes. "Hey, if we get through the demon shit, then it's all good. You can marry her for all I care."

"Bite your tongue, wolf."

"That's what you humans do. You said so yourself."

"I'm a vampire. There's very little human left in my soul. I embrace my dark nature. It's why I'm irresistible." Viktor smiled and turned back toward the ocean, concealing his expression from the Alpha.

"None of us are perfect. Not supes. Not humans."

"Look, none of this matters. Back to the topic at hand. It shouldn't surprise Ilsbeth that Samantha wants her back at the coven. I'm simply doing Luca a favor for his woman and then moving on. Perhaps I'll take a vacation on the French Riviera."

"I think you should…" Hunter lost his train of thought as Willa emerged from the galley, walking out onto the deck. As if she was the only woman in the world, she captivated him. Dressed in jeans, with a black leather jacket and boots, his mate appeared tough as nails. But as the smile broke over her face, his heart melted. "Hey, beautiful."

"Hey, handsome," she responded.

As she reached for his hand, her magical energy tingled on his palm. Her smile widened and his chest tightened with emotion.

"You look sexy," Willa purred.

"What can I say? Seems the vampire has taste in clothes." Hunter glanced down to his black t-shirt and shredded slim fit jeans.

"Why he has female clothes here on his yacht I don't know, but I'm grateful he does."

"Old girlfriend," Viktor interjected. "Several girlfriends, actually. I do enjoy shopping."

"Of course you do," Hunter replied.

"Are we going to go over the game plan now? Or would you two like to stand out here on the deck for a few hours and make eyes at each other? I mean I'm willing to go another round if you are."

She laughed.

"First of all, there will be no other round. That was a one-time, limited deal." Hunter smiled at his mate, who wore a sexier-than-fuck smile, tempting him to sweep her off her feet and take her back into the cabin.

"Young love, so sweet but so bitter for me. To be denied what I once…"

"Shut it, Vik." *Love.* The Alpha slammed down his guards, ensuring neither his mate nor the vampire could read his thoughts. *Jesus, Hunter. Love? Really?* Hunter smiled at Willa, briefly brushing his lips over hers, taking care not to linger too long, so as not to reveal his feelings. *What the fuck is happening to me? This mate thing.*

"We flash onto the property. Pick a spot behind the brush or something." Hunter released Willa's hand, his voice serious. "We're adapting more to the dematerialization, but we can't risk flashing into her house and then needing a moment to recover. Not with her there."

"Further from the house, I can do. But honestly, I wish you two would get used to it," Viktor replied, a hint of annoyance in his tone.

"It's getting better," Willa told him.

Hunter nodded. "It's going to be dark when we get there which is good. Gives us time to assess the situation. If things are clear, we go to the house. We stay together at all times. Ilsbeth isn't getting the book. I'm going to hold on to it. We can't risk her skipping off to a tropical island and leaving us with a herd of demons. No way."

"Although I have to say the thought of her in a bikini is…"

"Focus! Please." Hunter shot him a glare.

"We can't let her take the book anywhere," Willa said.

"She won't. If I have to give up the book for any reason at all, it's going to one of you two. The book…it's our leverage. We give it to the demon and off we go. Willa and I can take a car back. And you can do your thing."

Willa's eyebrows furrowed in confusion, her hand on her hip. "Why isn't he going with us?"

Hunter exchanged a knowing look with the vampire.

"What?" Willa asked. "What's going on?"

Hunter took a deep breath and gave a closed smile. "He, uh, he told Kade." He paused, aware of how crazy it was for the vampire to go after the witch. "He told him he'd bring Ilsbeth back."

"Bring her back where?" Willa's voice grew louder, her gaze pinned on Viktor.

"I'll be fine," he replied, not answering her question.

"Bring her back where?" she repeated.

"To Samantha. I'm literally the messenger. Pick up package." Viktor shrugged with a laugh. "A deadly package. Witchy. Kinda hot sometimes. Whatever. You get my meaning."

"Why doesn't she get her herself?" Willa demanded.

"He'll be okay," Hunter assured her.

"No, no. He actually might not be okay. He's our friend. What we just did together…" She exhaled loudly and shook her head. "It doesn't matter. Again. He's our friend. Friends don't let friends fly off with witches. No. He's not going."

"But sweetheart…"

"I just said no. Did you hear me over there in the back? That'd be you, vampire. Not going."

"Ah dear pet, it's sweet of you to be concerned but I can handle myself. I'm hundreds of years older than even you, Princess."

"Sweet my ass." She turned to her mate. "Are you going to just let him go? Come on. You're an Alpha. I'm your mate. I'm a fucking princess. We've got to stop him."

"Wills…he has an obligation to Kade. Just like we have to the pack. I know it's not the same but it's family."

"But he didn't sire Kade. Or Luca." She cocked her head in thought. "Did he sire Luca?"

"No but his brother did. That's his family. And Logan's mine. And Dimitri. Ilsbeth laid down some bad mojo. She gets what she gives."

"I know," her voice softened, sadness in her eyes. "But he's our family too. I have a bad feeling about this. I know she saved our lives, but she was vulnerable then. She's not now. You saw her in that mansion of hers. Somehow, I don't know how but she's regained her power. What if she doesn't want to go? What if she goes and she hurts Samantha?"

"I have to trust that if Sam is asking for him to bring her back, she knows full well what she's getting into. And Viktor knows what he's doing." Hunter turned his focus to Viktor. "You do know what you're doing, right?"

"One hundred percent." He smiled broadly. "I'm going to ask her first. Nicely. Say pretty please. I'm going to get in close proximity. Hmm…"

"What?" Hunter asked.

"Perhaps I'll kiss her."

"You're fucking crazy, you know that?"

"Just a thought. As much as I'd like to plan out every little detail, I simply can't. I'll float the idea and if she says no, then I'll go for seduction."

"And if that doesn't work?" Willa asked, her lips drawn tight, not finding amusement in his answer.

"I'll simply give her a tap and then we're off. Easy peasy. I'm in. I'm out."

"He's gotta do this, sweetheart. I don't like it either but at the same time, Ilsbeth fucked some shit up back in New Orleans and New York. It's not right that she got off with no consequences. It's not our place to get in the middle of it anyway."

Willa sighed. "I know you're right. It's just I don't feel right about it." She paused and settled her gaze on Hunter. "Hey, do we still have that knife? I think we should bring it just in case."

"It's in the living room there. If any shit goes down tonight, I want you to shift to wolf and get the fuck out of there. Just run as fast as you can, okay? I'll deal with her and any demons. Got me?"

"But I can't just leave you there. No, I…"

"Listen to me, Willa. This is your Alpha talking to you now, not your mate. I'm not letting anything happen to you. You will listen to me on this. No arguments. We're walking into a volatile situation tonight and you won't survive another round of Hell. Promise me you will go."

"I'll try. But if anything happens to you, I'm not leaving."

"Ah, the first lovers' quarrel. How touching. So…" Viktor rubbed his hands together in amusement. "Shall we get this show on the road? I'm gassed up and ready to fuck with some demons, then I'd really love to get on with life."

"I'm sure you are." Willa rolled her eyes and smiled.

"I'll get the knife." Hunter turned to go retrieve it.

His mate's trepidation drifted over his mind. No matter

how brave she was, she feared the loss of the vampire. His connection to her would forever be a part of her yet their bond as mates took precedence, and the Alpha appreciated Viktor's loyalty and friendship. He shut down his feelings about the situation, aware he'd sense his concern.

Whatever had torn down the vampire's humanity hadn't destroyed his sense of family. Transporting Ilsbeth was a risk. Viktor knew it more than anyone else. Yet for Quintus, Kade, Luca, this family built on generations of sired vampires, he'd bravely taken on the High Priestess. And perhaps for Dimitri, justice would be served.

Hunter reached for the hilt of the knife and held it in the air. When it was all said and done, neither the book nor the blade would end up in Ilsbeth's hands again. Even if there was a miniscule probability that she'd double cross them, he'd block her before she ever got the chance.

As he stepped onto the deck, the salty sea breeze rushed his lungs. Both Viktor and Willa wore a solemn expression. They all knew what was about to go down.

His stomach tightened, his wolf growling in anticipation of the hunt. Tonight, they'd shut the door to Hell and send whatever demons showed up to the party back to the fiery pit from whence they came. He'd protect his mate at all costs even if it meant giving up his own life to do so.

***

The chanting grew louder, and Hunter was grateful they'd materialized several feet into the woods. Concealed within the brush, they assessed the situation.

"What's happening?" Willa whispered.

Flickering lights in the distance drew Hunter's attention. "Witches."

"You both okay?" Viktor asked them. "Best you be ready before we do anything."

"I'm good."

"What are they doing?" Willa asked. "I don't see any people moving."

"Witchy voodoo that they do. Conjuring a portal to Hell." Hunter shrugged.

"Cooking up a demon like she's making a Thanksgiving turkey. Steaming hot and fresh out of the oven," Viktor joked.

"She's determined, I'll give her that. She went through a whole hell of a lot to get those precious ingredients she keeps in her house. She took time finding a demon that would help her with Dimitri. And find him she did." Hunter glared at the mansion.

"How did she know for sure we'd show up?" Willa asked.

"I texted her, of course." Viktor gave a sly smile. "There's a place and time for magick. I've got no time for games. Hers anyway. She knows we're comin'. All this fuss? She's taking care of shit."

"Hopefully she's worked out a plan to send the demon back," Hunter said.

"She'd better." Willa reached for her mate's hand.

"I'm not going to let anything happen to you. The

rogues had no right to sell you to Hell anyway. The most you did was wake up these assholes to your royal presence by saving the kid, but Goddess knows you were only trying to save a life. No, they sold something that didn't belong to them. Hell's for shit but even the demons have their rules."

"He isn't wrong." Viktor stepped forward and peered around a large oak tree, attempting to get a better view.

"Do you have the book?" Willa asked.

"Got it," Hunter responded. "And the knife."

"But of course."

"Let me deal with Ilsbeth," Hunter told them. "I saved her ass and out of all of us, she owes me."

"As you wish." Viktor set his sights on the witches in the distance. "Ilsbeth must be inside. I feel her energy but it's not strong."

"Her blood," Hunter commented, acutely aware that he shared the same bond now with his mate.

"Yes. I'm sure the High Priestess knows I can detect her. If Ilsbeth is truly Ilsbeth, she understands the metaphysical aspects of blood exchange. I'm not saying she likes it or won't try to cast a spell to rid herself of me. She definitely will try. She's still Ilsbeth. She won't like it at all."

"I say we hit the front door first," Hunter suggested. "From a distance, it looks clear of demons. If the witches are channeling energy or whatever, they shouldn't notice us."

"I have a bad feeling," Willa whispered.

"We have no choice." Hunter lifted her hand and brushed a kiss to the back of it.

"Correct," Viktor agreed. "There is no other way. It's

best we face things head on. Time's wasting and I'm envisioning a trip to a tropical island in the South Pacific."

"Be careful," Hunter warned. "In and out. No matter how naked those witches are, no distractions."

"No worries. I've got this. See ya on the flip side homies." Viktor flashed a smile and gave a dismissive wave.

As the vampire disappeared, Hunter turned to Willa. "Stay by me, okay? I know you've got that royal vibe, sweetheart, but don't give the demons a reason to go after you. Remember what I said. If it all turns to shit, I want you to shift and take off running. I'll find you afterward."

"I can't just leave you…" she protested.

"Promise me. No arguments, Wills."

"I'll try. It's all I can say. I'm not going to run my whole life."

"You won't be running your whole life. We're going to be fine." Hunter knew his words held an empty promise. Whatever they were walking into was dangerous, yet the need to reassure her took precedence over pessimistic thoughts.

"There's a reason I started getting powers," she said. "I'm going to use them."

"Only if you need to but don't underestimate Ilsbeth or the demons. She's danced with the devil before."

"But she lost," Willa challenged.

"True but she did a helluva lot of damage in the process to a whole lot of people. I know she saved you and you two had that…" he shook his head, "moment or whatever you want to call it but I'm telling you she's dangerous. And demons are no picnic either. I'm just sayin'. We don't know what we're going to be up against. I swear to the Goddess if that bitch tries to double cross us, I'm gonna burn her at the stake myself."

"I'll be careful. I promise." Willa nodded.

"Stay behind me. I'll go first. And Willa? I…" His eyes flashed to hers and emotion stirred in his chest. He slammed down his guards as the words crossed his mind. *I love you.* Impossible he could have gone a lifetime without Willa, now in an instant he could lose her. "I'm glad you're my mate. I promise we're going to have a lifetime of happiness when this is over."

"Me too." Willa smiled in return, but her eyes remained cloaked in concern.

"Ready?" He gave a closed smile.

"Absolutely."

***

The Alpha caught sight of the candlelit pentagram spread over the grass and held tight to Willa's hand. As they quietly passed the chanting witches, they took care not to disturb the circle of salt that had been poured onto the lawn. Wearing black satin robes, the women stood circling a bonfire.

The distinctive scent of hickory burning lingered in the air. By the time they reached the stairs, Hunter detected the shift in the energy, dark magick swirling around them. No crickets sang, deafening silence filling the night.

The wooden planks creaked under their feet as they ascended the porch. The front doors swung wide open by themselves, slamming against the siding. Dragon's blood incense filtered throughout the foyer as they stepped inside the mansion. In near darkness candlelight flickered, illuminating the room.

Hunter wasted no time, calling on the High Priestess. "Ilsbeth. Show yourself."

The sound of clicking heels echoed off the wooden floors, growing louder as she drew closer. The Alpha steeled his mental shields as she approached, her dark energy washing over him.

As she stepped into the light, he took sight of the High Priestess. She wore a skintight black leather jumpsuit, a silver pentagram hung protectively around her neck. Her long platinum hair glistened in the candlelight. Hunter was not deceived by her ethereal beauty, knowing all too well the danger that lurked within her soul.

"We're here. What's next?" Hunter asked.

"Do you have it? The book?" she replied.

"We've got it." The energy shifted but for a second and Viktor materialized directly in front of Ilsbeth.

"What are you doing?" Ilsbeth snapped, her lips drawn tight. Her eyes narrowed onto the vampire.

"Just having myself a little looksee, Priestess. Don't want any surprises."

"Where's the book?" she demanded.

Hunter retrieved it from his backpack. The skin resonated with evil energy but with a swift rush of his Alpha power, he sent it back into the hard cover.

"I need the spells," Ilsbeth insisted.

"For what? Looks like you already have something cookin' outside. I can smell the dark magick. No, no, no. You don't need the spells, you *want* them. Big difference."

"I can't do this without them," she insisted.

"Just stop with the bullshit, Priestess. You conjure up the demon. I'll give up the book."

"Pfft. What do you know?" Ilsbeth's mouth tightened in discontent.

"We don't have time for this shit." Anger rolled through him. He glanced at Willa, whose brave façade reminded him exactly why she was royalty. But he had no intention of living his life constantly fearing retribution from demons.

"I'm going to have to plead my case. Demons are unpredictable. If the book is not required, I'm keeping it." Ilsbeth defiantly glared at him.

"No can do. I wanna hear the words from the demon. The book for freedom. Willa. Viktor. Julian too. But this book here." Hunter waved it in the air. "Whatever is inside here isn't good. There's a reason this thing was stuck between the rocks in that godforsaken cave. It's because no one is supposed to have it. I don't know if it should be destroyed but I know it's not supposed to be with you."

"Nonsense. I am the High Priestess. I gave you that knife."

"Not up for discussion," Hunter said, his voice firm, noting Viktor's unusual silence. "Anything else?"

"Fine, but it doesn't belong to you," Ilsbeth told him.

"If it belongs to anyone, it's me." Willa stepped forward. "This slain wolf was from my lineage. His energy." She reached for the book.

Hunter held his breath as his mate placed her palm on its cover. She closed her eyes and quickly removed her hand.

"I don't know what the spells do but the energy inside this book must not be released."

"Of course there are spells. I'm the one who told you."

"If this book belonged to you, you would have gotten it sooner. You sent us for it. Something evil is in here. Something no one is ever supposed to see. It belongs in Hell."

"Whatever is inside, if the demon wants it in exchange for Willa, he can fucking have it," Hunter told her.

"All right then." Viktor sighed. "Miami's waiting, people. No offense but this cookout is boring. I'm ready to roll."

"When I bring him forth do not bargain. Do not ask for favors. Do not engage," Ilsbeth instructed.

"Demons. Slippery little suckers," Viktor added.

"My witches can only hold it for so long. It's dangerous."

"Tell us something we don't know." Hunter stared at Ilsbeth with distrust.

"Keep your mate on a leash. We cannot have any slipups," she spat back.

"Easy, witch. You're the one who needs a leash. Playing with demons got your ass a round of hurt."

"I need to offer the book," Willa told them. "I know you don't want me to." Her focus went to Hunter. "These wolves who took me. They must be killed. But this offering. If the witch is telling the truth and Hell wants this, then it must be me to hand it over."

Willa's energy penetrated the air and danced over his soul. In spite of the danger, instinct told him she was correct. "Willa keeps the book."

"This is never going to work!" Ilsbeth yelled. "You wolves. You're always messing up everything. Just because you're an Alpha doesn't mean you know what to do."

"And we're supposed to trust you?" Hunter laughed. "You landed in Hell."

"To be fair. We all have our bad days." Viktor shrugged.

"She was in Hell," Hunter repeated. "And she's no longer the High Priestess of New Orleans."

"I will always be the High Priestess!" Ilsbeth held up her hands. Lightning flashed and thunder rumbled throughout the house. A painting to the left of Hunter shook. A pair of crystal candlesticks toppled off a bookshelf, shattering onto the floor.

"Stop it!" Willa screamed at her.

"You're nothing but a wolf!" Ilsbeth shot back. "Your royalty means nothing. You *are* nothing."

Hunter sensed his mate's rage but before he had a chance to speak, Willa extended her hand. With her newfound power, she sent a vase of flowers hurling across the room. Petals flew into the air as it smashed into a wall.

"Wills…" Hunter began.

"No," Willa protested with a sharp tone. "This witch. This bitch. She thinks this is some kind of joke. That she has power over me. Over you. She may have saved me, but she didn't do it for me. She doesn't even know me. But she knew this secret." Willa waved the book. "That a wolf had to call it. To use it. You didn't see her ass down in Belize."

"The drama." Ilsbeth rolled her eyes but didn't deny the accusation.

"I see you, witch. I don't care what your game is down here in New Orleans. I just want my freedom. Don't mess with me." Willa glanced to Hunter and Viktor. "Or my friends."

Hunter's chest swelled with pride. His mate dressing down Ilsbeth sent a rush of blood to his cock. Fuck yeah, she'd kick some ass when they got home. He tamped down the flicker of excitement.

"It's settled. You want your freedom? Willa keeps the book. Now what else?"

Ilsbeth blew out a breath and set her hands on her hips. "The knife. Someone must stab it with the knife."

"Who is going to get close enough to stab it?" Willa asked.

"I will." Viktor stepped up and extended his hand. "Here. Give it to me. I'm the only one who can get in and out fast enough. Once the deal is declared out loud, Willa is safe. There's no way anyone else can get that close."

"I'll distract it. Keep it talking," Hunter told them.

"I want the spells," Ilsbeth repeated.

"Are we ready to do this?" Hunter asked, ignoring the witch's demand. He glanced at Willa, who nodded. The Alpha reached for her hand, sending his calming energy to his mate. Within the hour, they'd be free of the demon. "Let's go."

Chapter Fourteen

Willa stood on the porch and glanced up at the enormous pentagram that loomed above their heads. The ancient pagan symbol represented protection, yet the inversion reeked of dark intentions. The irony wasn't lost on Willa. Ilsbeth had sacrificed herself, saving her from death, but she'd also summoned demon magick to alter the very nature of the universe, nearly destroying the wolf she supposedly loved. A blended aura of both wickedness and a dash of misplaced justice best described the High Priestess.

An ominous energy sizzled in the air, reminding Willa of Ilsbeth's true nature. The only way to survive the High Priestess was to avoid the lethal slice of her potent dark magick.

As they descended the stairs and reached the edge of the patio, Willa drank in a deep breath of the cool dewy air. She ran her fingers down the spine of the skinbook, tendrils of a sinister yet familiar energy seeping from its pores. Willa was convinced that whatever lay between its covers should burn for eternity, where no one could ever release the spells.

Spawned by murder, it belonged in Hell.

Willa lifted her gaze to find Ilsbeth staring at her. She shivered as a chill blanketed her shoulders, but she never broke eye contact. Willa's beast growled in response, itching to shift and demonstrate to the witch who was truly Alpha.

"Form the circle," Ilsbeth called out to her witches, who reached their palms into the air. A white neon light flickered around the pentagram. From large pits of wood, flames flared high into the sky. "I call on the elements. Air. Fire. Water. Earth. I command you, demon. You shall surface before the High Priestess."

Lightning flashed in the distance. The low rumble of thunder violently shook the wooden planks beneath their feet, and Willa reached for Hunter's hand.

It's ok, sweetheart. You're not going anywhere.
Promise?
Promise. Easy now. It's going to get a little rough.

A bolt shot down from the sky, scorching the earth in the center of the pentagram. The scent of sulfur danced in the air.

"I love a good show." Viktor smiled and waggled his eyebrows at Willa. Hunter shot him a stern look in response. "What? We've got good seats. Better than Vegas."

"I call on you, demon, within the confines of our circle. I demand you show your face," Ilsbeth continued.

"Here comes the good part," Viktor whispered, fisting the hilt of the knife in his hand.

"*Venite ad me daemonium. Et vocavi te nomine. Zaebos. Expellere non ego te meis circulus ad infernos. Et dimitte nobis debita nostra factam acceptare. Adjuro te per Zaebos. Ipsum revelare. Nunc,*" Ilsbeth screamed.

"Oh Goddess." Willa held tight to Hunter's hand as the wind whipped across her face.

The ground trembled as it cleaved open, revealing smoke and fire. The skyclad witches protectively knelt and tucked themselves into balls, avoiding the lick of the flames. Sweat beaded over their bare skin, a low chant echoing from their lips.

Willa's heart raced as the horned creature ascended from the earth, its red glowing eyes glaring at Ilsbeth. Hovering five feet above the circle, it swiped a clawed hand toward the ground, screeching with pain as the white light zapped its fingers. A stream of blood spewed from its mouth toward Ilsbeth, but she held out her palms, sending it flying into the open pit.

What the fuck? Willa's eyes darted over to her Alpha.

Deep breaths. It'll be over soon.

Ilsbeth addressed the demon. "Zaobos."

"I will break through this magick, witch. Come with me and I will spare the others." As it opened its mouth, a two-foot-long pointed tongue slithered into the air. Whipping it from side to side, it attempted to lash the witches. It thrashed its head toward Willa and pointed a clawed finger at her. "You belong in Hell too. There will be no escape, Princess. Your blood is mine. Your body is mine. You will give birth to the legacy of Hell."

"Like hell she will, fuck face. We're here to make a deal," the Alpha called out to it.

The demon roared at Hunter, its diabolical laugh shaking the earth beneath. "I'll skin you alive while I rape her a thousand times. Tear your dick from your body and shove it down your throat."

Willa felt the Alpha's anger rip through her as if it was her own. He held tight to her hand and stepped toward the creature.

"Fuck you and the hellhound you rode in on. You want this skinbook?" Hunter asked.

Willa waved it in the air, her heart pounding against her ribs. *Show no fear.*

You've got this, Princess. She heard Viktor's voice in her head.

Her eyes flashed to his, concerned that only her mate should be able to speak with her telepathically. *How are you doing that?*

Hand it the book. It can't hurt you during the trade.

What?

It can't hurt you during the trade. Just do it. I'll handle the rest, pet.

Willa took a deep breath and addressed the hideous creature. "Hey. Look. I have the book. The book of my ancestors. If you release us, you can have it."

"A trade," Hunter yelled at the beast.

"A price must be paid for the magick," it countered, eyeing the skin book.

"Ilsbeth has paid her price in Hell. Whatever remains is paid with the spells. She has not touched them," Hunter promised. "The evil perpetrated by the wolves is within this skin book. The spells."

"The spells are mine," it contended. "Mine!"

"You want it? Then declare the deal valid under the reign of the Goddess or may she strike you down. Declare the deal by the rules of Hell. Willa and Ilsbeth are released forever. Viktor and Julian too."

"The witch will come again." Zaobos dragged its tongue across its bloodied lips. "I will have her."

"Not today. She's under the realm of the Goddess. Release her or no book." Hunter stood firm, staring down the demon.

It hissed at Ilsbeth, once again spitting at her. "One day witch. One day you'll be mine. No one will be able to save you."

"We had a deal, nothing more. I promised the book and here it is. You owe me now, not the other way around."

Willa exchanged a brief but confused look with Hunter. *She made this deal a long time ago. The book is owed.*

Dimitri. Hunter's face tightened in anger.

"It's mine," Zaobos repeated.

"Ilsbeth and Willa go free. Release them. Viktor and Julian too. Say it or no book."

Zaobos roared, clawing at the white light that contained the demonic creature.

"This book contains spells, yeah? I bet ya Ilsbeth here could whip up something to destroy your ass if she tried hard enough," Hunter baited. "I felt the evil in that skin. I bet we could bring out a higher-level demon to take you out in exchange for this book. What do you think, Priestess?"

"Absolutely." Ilsbeth wore an icy smile.

"You did torture her. She's a vindictive witch. I imagine it wouldn't take too long," Viktor added.

"Make the trade. Say it now, demon," Hunter ordered. "Or go back to Hell and we'll bring back one of your bosses to take care of you."

"I release the Priestess," it growled.

"And Willa. Say their names, demon. No tricks."

"Ilsbeth, High Priestess. Princess Aline Ermenjarta Lobo. Prince Joao Pedro Lobo. Viktor Christianson. *Et nunc absolvo vos in commutatione ad librum. Sed Ilsbeth transire mihi in sempiternum: et tu dormies cum in inferno.*" Zaobos released a deafening roar.

"I bind you to your word, demon. The trade has been made." Ilsbeth closed her eyes and held her palms up toward the demon. "*His verbis promissum tuum es bound to. Adiuro vos huic. In nomine sancte et arsisse ferunt multorum deam vobis noceat, si quis hic. Sic fiat semper. His verbis promissum tuum es bound to. Adiuro vos huic. In nomine sancte et arsisse ferunt multorum deam vobis noceat, si quis hic. Sic fiat semper. His verbis promissum tuum es bound to. Adiuro vos huic. In nomine sancte et arsisse ferunt multorum deam vobis noceat, si quis hic. Sic fiat semper.*"

"It's time." Hunter glared at the creature and turned to Willa. "Together."

Viktor nodded at her, the blade of the knife reflecting the flames.

Her stomach rolled as she put one foot in front of the other, slowly approaching the demon. Zaobos flung its tongue from side to side, blood dripping from its mouth.

Closer. Closer. Willa's pulse raced as they closed the distance. The putrid stench of the demon filled her nostrils, and she coughed. She willed the nausea churning in her stomach to calm.

"Don't even think to touch her," Hunter warned.

The echoes of Ilsbeth's chanting grew louder in Willa's mind. With her eyes transfixed on the demon, she extended the book to it. Her hands shook as the creature leaned toward her and stabbed a scaly talon into its cover, sending sparks flying into the air. As she released the book, Hunter yanked her into his arms, protectively shielding her from the fire.

Willa sucked a breath as Viktor appeared, brandishing the knife. *Please, Goddess.* Smoke billowed out of the crack and the earth quaked beneath their feet. Hunter tugged her outside of the circle and they rolled onto the patio.

Willa screamed in horror as Ilsbeth lunged at the demon. "No!"

The Priestess clutched onto the edges of the book, and as Viktor stabbed the beast in the neck with the knife, Zaobos released a horrific shriek. Instantly, the crevice widened, sucking the demon inside it, but the witch refused to let go.

"No! Stop him!" Willa watched in horror as the earth swallowed both Viktor and Ilsbeth. Her stomach clenched, bile rising into her throat. "Viktor! No! No!"

Although Willa attempted to wrench free of Hunter's arms, he held tight. The earth crumbled on itself, sealing the portal to Hell. With a single bolt of lightning, the heavens opened from above, releasing a torrential downpour.

The cold rain stung her skin as she yelled for the vampire. "Viktor! Where is he? Hunter…no…please."

"We'll find him," Hunter promised.

Shock seized Willa, tears streaming down her face. As the witches dispersed, Willa wrenched away from Hunter and ran to the center of the pentagram. She fell to her knees and pounded on the earth with her fists. "Viktor! Viktor. No! No!"

As she clawed at the wet dirt, reality registered. Nothing would ever be the same. The vampire was forever lost to Hell.

Chapter Fifteen

"We'll find him," Hunter assured Willa, who lay curled on the leather sofa, despondent.

Hunter had insisted they take the private jet back to Wyoming as soon as possible. Rafe had texted him that rogue wolves had broken into a meeting, and that nearly all his wolves were held up in the pack house. Hunter made multiple attempts to call him but was unsuccessful. Anger and guilt rolled through him, aware he'd brought this evil onto his pack. They'd come for Willa, he was certain, but now they'd get the Alpha, an angel of death who would bring their swift demise.

The only good news was that with the demon sated, his mate was free from their contract. But Viktor had been sucked into Hell, and Hunter knew as well as anyone that the vampire would not survive a second round.

Fucking Ilsbeth. In an attempt to steal the skin book, to absorb its dark spells, the witch had disappeared into the fiery pit. Hunter questioned why Viktor risked his own life for Ilsbeth, instead of simply letting go of her.

The shaken voice of his mate drew him out of his contemplation, and he turned toward Willa. "Hmm what, sweetheart?"

"I don't understand how any of this happened. The demon agreed. Why did he take both of them? If he wanted Ilsbeth so bad, just take her. Why didn't Viktor just let go and let that bitch fall into Hell? And why are the rogue wolves still in Wyoming? They should've been in New Orleans after me."

"I don't know. Whatever it is, it's about pack." *Remus.*

"This is all my fault. If I hadn't stayed with you, none of it would have happened. They all probably know I'm your mate. This is so messed up."

"It's not your fault, Wills." Hunter shoved out of his seat and sat on the floor next to his mate, resting his hand on hers. "I still don't know how I could have been so wrong about him, but I think this has something to do with Remus. He's been my beta for a couple of months but it's not because we're friends."

"How did he become beta?"

"He earned it. I've had several different betas over the years. Blake. He'd been my beta for twenty years." Hunter sighed. "His mate was killed by a human. Apparently, she wanted to be with him. In a jealous fit, she shot his mate up with enough silver to take down a demon. It doesn't matter. What matters is that he couldn't cope. Went rogue. I had to take someone on. Remus had been pack for about five years, had come in from Chicago. He fit right in. No problems. From the very beginning he was a good leader.

When the wolves fought for their place, Rafe lost to Remus. At the time, it was the right thing to do. My beta is important within the pack. I can't always be here."

"That day at your house. Remus was ice cold," she recalled. "Seriously. He was like a serial killer. I'm worried about what he's done."

"I've got to get back. Fucking Rafe, man. If it weren't for the brute strength of Remus." Hunter blew out a breath. "It still doesn't make sense. He never acted like this. Not ever."

"Maybe the demons got to him. Maybe he needed something and made some kind of a trade," Willa suggested.

"Or a fae. Kellen seemed pretty fucking comfortable on my territory. Wouldn't surprise me. Whatever turned him knew how to give a good mind fuck. That's for sure."

"We're going to get your wolves out. If Viktor…" Willa's words drifted into silence.

"We're gonna get him back. I promise." Hunter brought the back of her hand to his mouth, brushing his lips against her soft skin.

"I can't believe he's gone," she whispered.

Willa's grief threaded through him. Hunter grew more determined to put a swift end to the rogues.

Hunter rested his head into her palm and closed his eyes as she stroked his hair. Soon the Alpha would fight. A seasoned warrior, he'd mete justice, sending the rogues back to Hell one by one. Like the others who'd challenged him in the past, they'd submit to his mighty beast.

"How far is it?" Willa asked.

"We'll be home soon." *Home.* Hunter smiled, glancing to his mate. "We're going to have a proper date when this is all over."

"We already had a wedding." She laughed.

"I suppose we did. I'm going to have to get someone to send our gift." Hunter kept his eyes trained on the road as he drove. "I'd love to see the mailman's face."

"I'm not sure how I'll cope in the pack," Willa stated, changing the subject out of the blue.

"You've been rogue for a long time, but you're going to fit in well. I know it."

"I always loved being in a pack. It's just…they might hate me."

"They're going to love you. You're my mate."

"Not necessarily. I've got this hellfire. And powers. There could be a challenge," she guessed.

"Possibly, but honestly Willa; I haven't seen you in your wolf many times, but I've seen you. You're not going to take any shit from anyone. You've literally been to Hell and back. You just put a damn skin book into a demon's claw. Nope. Girl, you've got this. Word gets around you've been to Hell, no one is going to look at you the wrong way. You're good."

"I've been in Guatemala for so long. I'm not sure what I'll even do in America." Willa nervously twisted a lock of her curly brown hair around her finger.

"We've got humans here who need health care. Lots of them, unfortunately. We could use another clinic." Hunter knew far too many people who died from lack of proper medical care due to no health insurance. They weren't his responsibility, but the Alpha believed in a karmic sense of justice and did what he could to help them.

"There's need for another clinic?" Willa's voice perked up at the possibility.

"Absolutely. We actually have a few doctors in the pack who work over at the city hospital so I can introduce you to some of your future colleagues." Putting thoughts of death aside, Hunter smiled, knowing that Willa would be a great resource for the pack as well as the human community.

"You know, I'm really excited to…" Willa lost her words as her attention was drawn to the side mirror. "Hunter…do you…"

"Yeah, I see them." The Alpha gunned the gas, stomping the pedal to the floor. The car lunged forward.

Hunter sensed the magick before he had a chance to warn her. A flicker of light against the silver spike strip ahead on the road was all the warning he had.

"Hold on!" he yelled as he slammed on the brakes.

A loud blast boomed as a tire exploded, the scent of burning rubber permeating the interior of the car. Hunter veered right, spinning out of control toward a herd of bison that meandered toward the edge of the road. He wrestled the steering wheel, attempting to regain control but the car flipped, skidding toward a row of lodgepole pine trees.

In the half second before the crash, Hunter glanced to Willa, her eyes locked on his. *I love you.* As the metal crumpled around them, a pinprick of light morphed into darkness and the Alpha succumbed. *Willa.*

Hunter! The word reverberated in his mind as he fought the confusion. Searing pain shot through the side of his head. He blinked away the hot trickle of blood that trailed from the gash on his temple.

Memories of the crash rippled through his mind as he attempted to process the situation. He glanced to the empty passenger seat. *Willa.* Panic ripped through the Alpha. He struggled to release the seat belt, tugging at it. With a snap, he tore it from its socket. White hot pain streaked up his back, his leg throbbed.

Hunter reached for the lip of the broken car window, the razor-sharp shards slicing his palms. With a grunt, he hoisted himself through the opening and rolled onto the grass, his face landing on the gravel at the road's edge. He spat and brushed the grit from his eyes.

"Fuck. Fuck. Fuck." Hunter grimaced at the sight of his femur protruding through his thigh. Although he'd hurt himself several times over his lifetime, it'd been a while since he'd broken a bone.

The Alpha shimmied his shirt over his head, readying to shift. Extending a talon, he sliced through his jeans, removing them. With a groan, he fell back into the grass, panting for breath, pain resonating through his entire body. Blood spurted from the massive wound in his leg. Specks of light danced in Hunter's eyes, a tunnel closing in on him

"Ah fuck. Don't pass out. Not fucking now." Anger shot through him, igniting the magick of his wolf.

The spectacular beast howled, pissed as hell. *Willa.* He reached with his mind. Her terrifying scream registered in his head. *No!!!* A surge of rage tore through the Alpha and he took off running toward the pack house. His paws clutched the earth, hurling the powerful lithe wolf through the forest. *They're all gonna die.*

Hunter crouched, hidden in the bushes. Through the branches he spied light coming from the back yard, smoke billowing up into the air. He sent tendrils of his energy to his pack, reaching for them. Their palpable fear slammed into him. *It's all right Teton. I'm here. This ends now.* Instantly the energy shifted in anticipation of his kill.

As he rounded the building an eerie silence blanketed the night. His heart pounded, fury ripping through him as he caught sight of Willa, her bared body curled into a ball on the lawn. Remus, stood naked in his human form, looming above her while two other rogue wolves watched, brandishing guns. He recognized a few of his stronger male wolves, who were writhing in pain, cloaked in a silver net. Rafe lay whimpering, his gray beast bloodied, his feet twitching. The weapon, a blood-stained baseball bat, lay in the grass next to him.

"Shift, bitch," Remus demanded.

"No," Willa gritted out.

He cracked the horse whip onto her back. She released a blood-curdling scream but held tight into a ball.

Blind with rage, Hunter sprang from the shadows, and lunged onto Remus, tearing at his forearm. In a flash, white hot pain sliced through his shoulder and he rolled onto the ground, releasing the beta.

"Move again Alpha, and the next bullet goes into the bitch."

Hunter growled, stilling as his magick threaded through his cells. The wound burned hot with silver poison, but the shot had gone clean through.

"Maybe she'll change if we torture you." Remus laughed and fired another round through his hind leg, forcing the Alpha to shift.

"No!!" Willa screamed, jolting upward. Nude and bloody, her hands were bound with barbed wire.

Although Hunter's leg bled, the bullet had burned straight through his flesh. Hunter released a loud groan and rolled onto his side, feigning serious injury. *Easy, princess.*

Let them have me. Save your pack. Tears streamed from her eyes.

Not a chance, sweetheart.

You've been shot. I'm going to shift. They can have me.

No. Hunter locked his eyes on hers, targeting his Alpha energy on Willa. It broke his heart to force her submission, but he couldn't risk her sacrificing her own life for his. *Get ready, Wills. I need you to fight. On three. Wait for it.*

"Hey, asshole. The demon's taken care of…you don't

need to do this." Hunter groaned loudly as if he was in pain, distracting Remus from his mate.

Willa reluctantly complied with her Alpha's demand. She rolled onto her side, concealing her hands. Her fingers slowly manipulated the wire, untangling it.

"Looks like we're getting somewhere. You ready to submit to me, Livingston?" A diabolical smile bloomed on Remus's face. "Tell you what? Submit to me. Right here right now, and I'll spare the bitch. Can't say I'd mate her because she's been used up. But then again, Benny could use a whore."

Hunter let his anger roll through him. With the power of the Alpha flowing through his veins, he dug his fingers into the ground, preparing to shift.

"I got a better idea, Remus." Hunter's temple ticked in anticipation of the kill. "How about you die?"

"What did you say?" Remus asked, incredulous. He turned and aimed the gun at him.

"Get ready to say hello to Hell." In a flash Hunter transformed, his powerful wolf lunging onto the beta.

Remus shifted as the Alpha shoved him to the ground. He lost control of the gun, firing off a shot and sending it flying into the air. Hunter's fangs sliced into Remus' shoulder. Iron-tanged blood coated Hunter's tongue. The beta struggled under the attack, horns protruding from his head. With demonic strength Remus rolled, attempting to shake Hunter's hold. A cry from Willa distracted him, and his attention went to her.

Willa broke free of her restraint, readying to shift. A

rogue wolf charged, and she stretched her hands forward, sending the coil of barbed wire flying at him. He yelped as the metal stabbed into his eyes but quickly shook it off and lunged at Willa.

As she shifted into her wolf, the familiar voice soothed her soul. "Late to the party again. Please forgive me."

Willa barked at Viktor, warning him as the large grey wolf flew through the air toward him.

"No worries, pet." The vampire whipped around to face the wolf and dropped his fangs. As it snapped at him, Viktor wrapped his hand around its throat, holding it high in the air. "Bad doggie."

The animal snarled, nicking his wrist. "See now, that's what I'm talking about. Someone must have missed obedience school. Time for a lesson."

Viktor hissed with a cold smile and sunk his fangs deep into its fur, piercing its skin. The rogue thrashed, but the vampire clamped down, refusing to release his prey. Viktor ripped the flesh from its body and spat a clump onto the ground. Blood dripped down the vampire's face as he laughed and turned to Hunter.

Exhilaration rushed through the Alpha at the sight of his lethal friend doing what he did best. Remus struggled underneath his jaws to escape. Out of the corner of his eye, he caught sight of Willa attacking another rogue. Although of smaller stature, she easily wrestled the wolf onto its back.

In the heat of the moment, Hunter made the decision not just to kill but to make an example for anyone who ever thought of attacking his pack again. The Alpha sunk his teeth deeper into Remus' neck, slow and deliberate, tearing off chunks of his flesh, until the beta convulsed, his blood gushing onto the dirt. Hunter released a guttural scream as he shifted, a firm hand wrapped around what was left of Remus' neck, the Alpha's grip lodged around his spine.

"Tonight, you go back to the demon who spawned you. Enjoy your time in Hell," Hunter growled. He extended his claws and gored straight through his beta's chest. The Alpha's fingers wrapped around the beta's still-beating heart. Remus' eyes bulged as the Alpha showed no mercy, extracting the organ from its cavity and tossing it onto the dirt.

"It appears your friend has a bit of heartburn." Viktor licked his lips as he held the rogue.

"Please...please..." Blood gurgled out of his mouth.

The vampire's eyes flashed to black, devoid of all emotion. "Tell the demons to go fuck themselves."

"No, no, no...." he pleaded.

"Debt's paid." Like a cobra striking, Viktor's fangs sliced into his limp body as he twisted the wolf's neck. Blood spewed from his mouth as he spat onto the ground. "Consider yourself trained."

Hunter shifted into his mighty wolf and ran to Willa who was fighting with the rogue. Instinct urged him to kill it, to rescue his mate, but Willa turned her head and snarled at him. *He's mine.*

His heart pounded in his chest as the rogue took advantage of her distraction and lodged his teeth into her neck, forcing her to her side. He growled in warning, but she protested. *No.*

Hunter shifted, trusting his instincts, suspecting his

royal mate harbored the magick of the Alpha within her. "Kill him, Willa! Now!"

Shock slammed him as his mate's white fur morphed into a glowing ball of light. She clamped down her jaw, biting deeper and deeper into the wolf's flesh. The large grey wolf yelped in agony as the light penetrated its organs. Willa's energy burst through its eye sockets, bodily fluids spraying onto the ground.

Silence blanketed the night as the light poured through the rogue, its body bloating with her powerful energy. With a loud growl, Willa snapped her head toward her Alpha, her eyes meeting his. As she tore a large section of flesh from the wolf's neck, the beast exploded. Like a flesh balloon being popped, strands of organs and blood spewed into the air.

"You don't see that every day," Viktor commented with a bloody smile.

"I..." Lost for words, Hunter's chest squeezed, amazed by his incredible mate.

As she shifted to her human form, Willa stood onto her feet, slowly straightening her spine, her gaze meeting his.

"Jesus, you're beautiful." Stunned, the Alpha watched as she stepped toward him unscathed.

"Rafe," she managed, her words soft but strong.

"It's like she just swatted a fly. More like crushed it until its guts exploded all over the dining room table."

"Enough, Vik." Hunter ran to Willa and brought her into his arms "How did you...?"

"The pack," she responded, gently pulling out of his embrace.

His majestic mate demonstrated her dynamic energy by dominating the demonic wolf. Hunter stood proud as she walked toward several wolves who cowered whining under the silver nets and began to remove them one by one.

The Alpha rushed to Rafe's side and reached for him. Hunter peeled away the metal, revealing the devastating damage. The deep wounds oozed with silver pus, poisonous shards lodged deep within his skin. They'd tortured him.

"You've got to shift, brother." Hunter's stomach clenched in anger.

"I…" Rafe coughed up blood, his body riddled with boils. He struggled to turn his head toward his Alpha. "I'm sorry."

"Nah man. You're gonna be fine. The horses. They need you." Hunter lifted his shoulders off the floor, cradling the injured wolf. "Come on, bro."

"I…I…" Rafe sucked a hard breath and coughed, blood dribbling out of his mouth. "Tell my ma…"

"Fucking tell her yourself. Jesus, Rafe."

"Too much silver. Can't shift," he whispered, his breathing labored.

"You've got to fucking shift. You will shift." Hunter closed his eyes, blasting his Alpha energy into his friend. Tears streamed down his cheeks as his spirit slipped away.

"This is the end of the road, Alpha." Rafe clasped his hand onto Hunter's forearm. "Good friends? Yeah?"

"You can't leave us." Guilt slammed into Hunter, his chest tightening. Emotion overwhelmed him at the sound of Rafe's failing heartbeat.

"Alpha, if I may." Viktor flashed to his side, kneeling beside him.

"This is shit. This is all my fault," Hunter said.

"Whatever they did to him…these wolves aren't ordinary wolves." Viktor held up the pistol that Remus had used to fire the bullets.

"Silver is silver. I can't get him to shift."

"Perhaps I can see about a favor. No promises."

"What?" Hunter sucked a breath, shaking his head.

"A favor."

"Vampire, I don't have time for this. Just let my wolves come and say goodbye in peace."

"I can do that, but Hunter," Viktor set his hand on the Alpha's shoulder, "if you let me, I might be able to save him. I don't know how long it'll take. I can't promise you it'll work."

"What are you talking about?" Grief swam with confusion as Hunter considered the offer.

"I'm ancient, so much more so than this young pup, than you, than any here in your pack. Not all secrets can be told. Just trust me. At worst he'll die. But if I can bring him back to you…look, you saved me. I owe you one."

Rafe's eyes fluttered open. "Do it."

"Where are you going?"

"I can't tell you. You're gonna have to trust me."

"Jesus, Vik." Hunter closed his eyes, his lips tight. He could have done so many things differently. Rafe would die because of his actions.

"Trust him," Willa whispered.

"Are you sure, Rafe? I can't promise what will happen to you," Hunter said.

"Fuck, man. I got no time. Just do it," he managed, blood gurgling in his throat.

"No pressure, but from the sounds of his heartbeat, he's got about two minutes. I've got to do this now," Viktor urged.

"Where are you going?" Hunter asked.

"We don't have time!" the vampire yelled.

"Stop it, Viktor!" Willa demanded.

The vampire hovered his palm above Rafe's head. "One minute. Tick tock."

"Hunter. Please. It's time." Willa brushed her palm along his cheek, a comforting hand on his shoulder. "It's okay. You can trust Viktor. He's family."

Viktor nodded, his expression somber.

"You're gonna be okay, Rafe. You can trust the vampire." Hunter spoke, although Rafe no longer responded.

"Thirty seconds."

"I love ya, bro." Hunter nodded at the vampire.

"See ya on the flip side. Fiji awaits." Viktor knelt and placed a hand on Rafe's shoulder.

Within a blink of the eye, they disappeared. Hunter stared at the blood-stained earth, grief churning inside his chest.

"He's going to be okay," Willa said.

"We may never know. But I trust Viktor." Hunter turned to his mate. "This will never happen again under my watch. Not ever."

"You killed the rogues. You saved me and the pack." Willa bowed her head in both reverence and submission for her Alpha.

Hunter heard their paws treading towards them before he ever saw their eyes. Two rogue wolves barreled out of the woods toward him. He reached for the shotguns that lay on the ground and threw one to Willa. As the wolves lunged, they fired off several rounds directly at the wolves. Smoke and dust spun in the air, the dead animals landing on the ground with a thud.

Hunter stepped toward the rogues, who'd been forced into their human forms. He stared down at the lifeless intruders and spat on them. "Enjoy Hell." With the final rounds, he unloaded silver into their foreheads.

The Alpha rose, turning to address his pack. Women and children ran outside onto the grass, exiting the pack house. Each and every one shifted before him, lowering their gaze, submitting.

"Teton Wolves. I stand before you humbled. Our brother Rafe chose to go with the vampire. Viktor. He can be trusted. Rafe is now in the hands of the Goddess." Hunter reached for Willa, her palm in his. "I want to introduce you to my mate, a true Alpha female. Princess Aline Ermenjarta. An original wolf of the Lobo. She is my mate. My queen."

Hunter smiled at Willa as she sent her light through him, their skin glowing. Awe and acceptance from his wolves registered. "Now we run."

Shifting into his mighty beast, he set off into the woods

with his mate by his side. Through tragedy, they'd grown stronger. By risking his life to go into Hell, he'd saved not only Viktor but himself, finding his mate. His pack rejoiced as Willa released her power, tendrils of her royal energy threading through the pack. Energized, they ran through Yellowstone, strong and united. *Teton Wolves.*

Chapter Sixteen

It had been a week since she'd been accepted into Teton Wolves. Willa had privately funded the construction of a new clinic and had arranged for another doctor to take her place in Guatemala.

Hunter spent the week individually visiting all his wolves, reassuring them of his protection. Kade Issacson had sent one of his employees, a vampire, Xavier, to create a new blood club and arrange for proper management.

This morning, her Alpha had left a sealed invitation on her pillow. *A date.* It had been so long, Willa couldn't remember what it was like to simply have fun. Laugh. Watch a movie. To be wonderfully boring, settled and happy. It had been a dream for so long she'd forgotten it existed. *Until Hunter.*

Exhilarated, Willa ran with her mate under the light of the full moon. Learning the trails, she followed the Alpha, playfully weaving between the trees. They'd watched from afar as a mama bear nursed her cubs. Willa gave a cheerful scream as they finally reached Old Faithful, shifting to their human forms.

"Yes!" She jumped up and down, the night air cooling her skin. "That was amazing!"

"It's why I moved here. Don't get me wrong. I love New Orleans, but the open space of the west drew me like a moth to a flame. Nothing like it."

"It's quiet but it's not. All the animals."

"You still get contact when you go into town but out here? It's nothing but animals, wildlife."

"It's incredible."

"In the winter it's brutally cold for the humans, but it's perfect for my wolves. You'll see a few of the die-hards stay wolf for days, not shifting back. You can be as wild as you want. Run wherever you want. Whenever you want."

"That's how it was in the jungle. Aside from the village, I could run wherever I wanted." Willa took a deep breath, smiling. "I can't wait until it snows."

"We'd better get going. The humans are going to see us if we stay out here long enough." Hunter laughed. "And then I'm gonna hear it from the rangers."

"Where're we headed?" she asked.

"Follow me. It's a surprise."

Before she had a chance to question further, he transformed, barking for her to follow suit. Willa laughed, filled with happiness and love. Her spectacular Alpha ran a circle around her, urging her to shift. Releasing her magick, her beast emerged, and she chased after him.

As they ran through the thick forest, the leaves crunched under their paws. In the distance the delicious scent of food grew stronger. As the enormous white tent came into view, she transformed into her human form.

"You did this?" Willa smiled at the sight of the strands of white lights strung over the trees. "How? What is this?"

Hunter laughed as he shifted. "It's a proper date, remember?"

"How did you do this?"

"Ah, it's a secret, my queen." He reached for her hand and led her towards the tent.

Willa gasped as she stepped inside and took in the sight of her surroundings. The enormous room had a king-sized bed in the corner. Steam billowed out of a wooden tub sitting across from it. Two plates covered with gold domes sat upon a romantic candlelit table. The gentle rhythm of blues played over speakers. "How did you get all this in here?"

"It's a secret." He winked and reached for a bottle wedged into an ice bucket.

"Did Viktor do this?" she asked.

"Vik has his hands full. But you're close. Quint owed me a favor." A loud pop sounded as he uncorked the champagne.

"Any word on Rafe?" Willa asked, accepting a glass.

"Vik says he's alive. But he said it's taking a while to get him better."

"It's a miracle he saved him. I can't help but wonder what he did, though."

"I can say with certainty he didn't use demon or fae magick, that's for damn sure."

"What did he do?"

"Says he used his own blood but if I'm honest, something doesn't feel right. Cagey bastard won't tell me what he did."

"Rafe…" Willa sighed, guilt twisting through her. "I've seen some pretty bad injuries before, but he was…"

"I know what you're going to say, and I hear ya. With the amount of silver they loaded him with, he should have died. The blood of an ancient can help. But it should have been quick."

"Where are they?"

"He won't say. He won't even answer my damn phone calls. Keeps sending fucking texts."

"Send nudes?" she laughed.

"Exactly. Sends me memes. Stupid shit like that. He's stalling."

"I haven't heard from my brother either." A sad smile formed on her lips. "I know he's alive. Somewhere."

"He is alive. And some day he's going to show up here in Yellowstone and I'm going to kick his ass."

"He'd better come back. Or I'm going to go look for him, you know, right?"

Hunter sighed. "Unfortunately, yes, my beautiful but stubborn queen. But if you do, you won't go alone. Because you have a mate who cares about you very much."

"We are meant for each other, aren't we?" she laughed.

"We are. Now I was thinking, a proper date. We've got

the champs." He nodded at the table. "Food."

"A hot bath, which I'm so ready to use." She smiled.

"A bed." He winked. "We're camping."

"Glamping." She laughed.

"Maybe. Just a little." Hunter closed the distance.

"It's perfect," she said. Her stomach fluttered as her sexy-as-sin Alpha took her hand in his.

"You're perfect." He held his glass in the air. "To my beautiful mate."

"To a hundred, no, a thousand dates," she countered.

"A lifetime."

With a clink of their glasses, they sipped the champagne. Willa's heart pounded in her chest as her gaze painted over his muscular body, candlelight flickering over his tanned skin. As he smiled, her focus was drawn to his strong lips and her pussy flooded in arousal, anticipating what they'd do to her.

A knowing smile crossed his face, his eyes lit in amusement. "Do you know what I love about you?"

Love. Her heart tightened at the sound of the word. It had been an emotion she'd tried so very hard to ignore, yet one she'd yearned to hear from her mate.

"I love you," she blurted out, unable to stop the words. She spun around on her heels and bit her lip. *Shit. You've only known him for a few weeks. What are you doing?*

She startled as his strong arm curled around her waist, the warmth of his firm chest along her back spiking her arousal. Her body tingled in awareness, his lips brushing her shoulder. *Oh Goddess.*

"Did you just say what I think you said?" His lips brushed over her shoulder.

"I…I…." As his hand cupped her breast, she lost her train of thought. "I don't know what I said."

"That's funny, because I think," he kissed her neck, "you said you love me."

"What? You must have heard wrong," she lied, a shiver dancing through her body.

"Really, huh? Because funny thing is that I love you."

Willa melted at his words. She spun around to face him, her hand cupping his cheek. "What?"

"I love you, Wills. I never met anyone so strong. So giving. I'm not fooling myself. I know this is the magick of our wolves. The attraction. But fuck if I'd ever give this up. That mark there on your shoulder…I want this. I want everything with you."

Willa's stomach sank. *Everything. Children.* She blinked away the moisture welling in her eyes.

"What is it, sweetheart?"

"I was supposed to be the last of a generation. We never talked about it. You want everything, but what if I can't give you everything? A family?"

"You are my family."

"Kids, Hunter. What if I can't have them? I love you. I really, really do. I thank the Goddess you found me that day, that she gave me such an amazing man…you."

"If we can't have kids, we can adopt a pup. If we want to. And if we don't…we won't. Right now, though, all I ever want is you." Hunter brushed a lock of her silken hair from her eyes. His gaze drifted to her lips, and he took her glass and set it on the table. "I love you. I want one million and one dates. I want a lifetime."

Willa nodded, her heart crushed with love for him. "A lifetime."

She moaned as his lips captured her mouth, tasting her mate, lost in his devastating kiss. He lifted her into the air, and she wrapped her legs around his waist. She tunneled her fingers into his hair as their tongues swept against each other's. Their passionate kiss was all-consuming. Skin against skin, her body lit with desire.

Willa laughed, her lips on his as he stumbled towards the bath and eased them into the tub, her toes dipping into the warm water.

Their bodies slick, she reached for his erection and stroked it. He groaned, pumping his hips toward her.

"Jesus, I'll never get enough of you," he growled.

"I'm not going anywhere," she promised.

"Willa," he murmured into her lips, deepening the kiss.

She tightened her grip and reached for his balls with her other hand, gently massaging them.

Hunter tore his lips from hers, attempting to catch his breath. "Holy fuck."

Her taut nipples brushed his chest, her pussy aching in arousal. "I want you in me."

Willa squealed as he reached for her waist and settled her onto the ledge of the wooden tub. Arousal flooded through her as she drank in the delicious sight of her masculine Alpha. Beads of water dripped down the hard-cut ridges of his abs toward the V of his pelvis.

Hunter stroked his thick cock. Gooseflesh broke over her skin as he gently spread her knees open and knelt before her.

She released a soft gasp, his fingers trailing over her nipples. Willa closed her eyes, focusing on nothing but his touch, her skin tingling with his energy. With the first lap of his tongue over her clit, she heaved a breath. Her fingernails dug into the soft wood, and she cried out as he plunged his finger inside her tight core. Willa reached for Hunter's head, tunneling her fingers into his hair.

"I love your pussy. My pussy. So good." The Alpha mercilessly flicked his tongue at her sensitive nub.

"Ah…I'm going to…" She tilted her hips upward, her body lit with desire.

"Fucking delicious." Hunter slid another digit deep inside her.

Willa panted as he licked relentlessly at her clit, his fingers driving inside her core. Her orgasm rolled through her and she clutched his head to her pussy, her hips gyrating.

"Ah…my Alpha." Her back arched, tendrils of the climax sizzling through her body.

Willa's eyes fluttered as Hunter rose above her, her heart pounding.

"Now, my queen."

She lost her words, engrossed in the presence of her mate. He reached and lifted her, and she wrapped her arms around his neck.

"I love you, Willa. Always."

"I love you too, my king."

He plunged his cock inside her pussy, and Willa cried his name out loud. The water sloshed out of the tub onto the floor as he gently rocked inside her, easing them into the bath. His mouth crashed down upon hers, kissing her breathless.

Time stopped as they made love, her body glowing, their power merging. With a slow rhythm, they became one. His hands cupped her breasts, teasing her nipples between his fingers. She gripped his shoulders, grazing her pelvis against his. Each slow stroke to her clit brought her closer to orgasm, his thick cock filling her.

"I…oh Goddess," she cried.

"That's it…just like that." Hunter thrusted hard, increasing the pace.

"Yes…yes…yes…"

"I fucking love you."

"I love you too. Hunter. Please…" Willa panted, her body on fire with ecstasy.

He tore his lips from hers, his mouth finding her shoulder. "You're everything."

As he bit down on her mark, Willa splintered apart, her orgasm slamming into her. She screamed his name, their bodies gyrating.

A rush of emotion seized her chest, so in love with this incredible man. Although royal blood ran through her veins, Hunter was her king, giving her unconditional love, a sense of acceptance, belonging, family. A love so great that she'd follow him to the ends of the Earth. *Hunter Livingston. My Alpha.*

Hunter lifted Willa from the tub, settling them into the bed. As she curled into him, his heart squeezed tight with love for his mate. He brushed his lips over her hair and wrapped them both into the warmth of a soft blanket.

He smiled as he considered the irony, how saving Viktor led to a chance encounter in Hell, a blessing from the Goddess. Even within the fiery underworld, the demons could not escape her or divine destiny. Teton Wolves was stronger than ever, a royal mate alongside her Alpha to protect and lead them.

With his queen nestled against his chest, the Alpha smiled, a rush of love threading through him. Never in his long life could he have predicted a world where he'd willingly submit to anyone. Within love and life, both equal parts of a concerto, they'd make beautiful music together for a lifetime.

Epilogue

Viktor stared down at the wolf. He should never have offered to save him. He'd only planned on feeding him his blood but when it didn't work, he took to drastic measures to destroy the demonic silver.

"It's going to be okay, wolf. You just have to get through this little stage here, and when you wake up, you'll be fine." Viktor lifted Rafe's upper lip with his thumb, examining his teeth. He slid the pad of his finger over the razor-sharp incisor. *Fuck. What the hell did I do?*

"Don't let him out of your sight." Viktor looked to the nurse who sat attentively at his bedside. "Text me when he wakes up. Keep him comfortable. He's got a fever, but it should be gone by tonight. We'll feed him again and then all should be good." *I hope.*

"Yes, sir."

Viktor nodded at her and glanced again to the sick wolf. As he turned his back and walked toward the heavy metal door, he considered the ramifications of what he'd done. If Hunter had never traveled to Hell to save him, Rafe would be alive and well. Granted, the Alpha wouldn't have his mate but nonetheless, an uneasy feeling settled in his gut.

Viktor materialized on the white sandy beach. There was nothing like fresh blood on a warm sunny day to relax a vampire.

He sighed, taking in the sight of the gorgeous woman who lay tanning on the chaise longue. From her perfectly manicured toes to her matching red bikini, she had a killer body he'd love to fuck, if only it wasn't complicated.

She lifted her floppy straw hat and removed her gold filigree cat-eye Dolce and Gabbana sunglasses. "The Alpha is going to stake you himself."

"It's merely a complication. You'll find a way to reverse this, witch." *Ilsbeth.* It had seemed like a good idea at the time. After attempting to save him with only his blood, Rafe had flatlined. So, he did the dumbest thing he'd ever done in his life…turned a wolf. Some would say it impossible, but Viktor knew all too well the secret powers of an ancient. But when things became sketchy, the wolf still ill with silver and sprouting fangs, Viktor decided to fetch the High Priestess and feed him her blood.

"I'm ready to get off this damn island you brought me to. It's in the middle of nowhere," she complained.

"It's near Fiji." Viktor waved to his private waiter, who promptly scurried to hand him a coconut filled with a frozen blood concoction. "And I own it."

"Why couldn't we stay mainland? Jesus, Viktor."

"Too many prying eyes in Miami." He fiddled with the miniature pink paper umbrella and promptly stabbed it back into his drink. "If it gets out I fucking sired a damn wolf hybrid." He released a frustrated breath. "Well let's just say I'm going to be fucked."

"I want to get out of here," she demanded, sitting up straight on her chaise.

Viktor snapped his head in her direction. "Listen here, Priestess, because I'm only going to say this once. You're lucky I saved your ass from that demon. Your greed almost cost us both our lives. So, settle down and enjoy the sun. You'll leave the island when I say you leave the island. And that will be when that wolf in there is stable and we know for certain he's going to live. Not one second sooner."

"You don't have to be nasty about it." She adjusted her hat and sniffed. "I suppose I could have been kidnapped somewhere worse."

"Exactly. So, stop complaining. You could have bigger problems."

"Like a big bad Alpha from Wyoming? He's going to kill you. I can count on one hand the number of times I've ever heard of an ancient turning a wolf. But whatever. I'm along for the ride now."

"I gave the wolf the choice. Death or rebirth. It's always the same deal. And frankly I'd let most of them die. I have only one other I've ever turned and…" His child carried the same evil as his master. Worry crept inside his mind. He couldn't guarantee what would happen to Rafe. "It doesn't matter. Once he's stabilized and learns to feed, I'll return him to Hunter."

"That's if he shifts. You don't know that he will."

"He'll shift."

"Who's to say the Alpha will accept him?" she countered.

"One more word and you'll be wearing a ball gag for the rest of this trip." Viktor smiled, delighted with the possibility of seeing her both quiet and at his mercy.

"As if." Ilsbeth straightened in the chair and set her feet into the sand. "I'm going for a swim."

"Don't get any ideas. I may need your blood again."

"I knew you'd enjoy it," she mumbled as she stood and stretched.

Viktor's cock twitched as she shifted her hips and thrust her chest forward. The manipulative little witch knew what she was doing. As much as he'd like to fuck her, he'd rather stick his dick in a bee's nest than allow her to have one strand of his hair, a single drop of his seed. Although vampires couldn't breed, he knew damn well witches were capable of bending the laws of the Goddess, becoming impregnated with child.

His emotions warring between lust and hate, he glared at Ilsbeth as she stepped into the surf, bending over to present her ass. Clever witch wore a thong that appeared more like dental floss than fabric. *Fucking hell.*

Although momentarily distracted by the seductive priestess, Viktor's attention snapped to a dark haze emerging over the horizon. Lightning flashed, thunder rumbling in the distance. The wind kicked up, sending a chair flying down the beach.

The familiar scent of sulfur rolled off the ocean, and he cursed. "What the fuck now?"

Ilsbeth turned to him, fear registering in her eyes. "Demons."

"In the water! Now!"

"What?" she screamed over the roar of the wind.

"It's the only place you'll be safe. Do it now!"

As the explosion hit the beach, the blast sent him flying towards the bending palm trees. He rolled into the brush, shielding his eyes. As a tunnel cloud whipped the sand into the air, the deafening growl of hellhounds intensified.

Viktor rose to his feet, prepared to fight them. Nothing would touch the wolf or the priestess, not on his territory.

The great funnel spat out a beast and it landed with a thump. The vampire dropped his fangs and extended his claws, prepared to kill it. With great restraint, he waited for the creature to show its face, readying his attack. Yet as it shifted before his eyes, he stopped cold. *Julian.*

"It's coming!"

Romance by Kym Grosso

The Immortals of New Orleans

Kade's Dark Embrace
(Immortals of New Orleans, Book 1)

Luca's Magic Embrace
(Immortals of New Orleans, Book 2)

Tristan's Lyceum Wolves
(Immortals of New Orleans, Book 3)

Logan's Acadian Wolves
(Immortals of New Orleans, Book 4)

Léopold's Wicked Embrace
(Immortals of New Orleans, Book 5)

Dimitri
(Immortals of New Orleans, Book 6)

Lost Embrace
(Immortals of New Orleans, Book 6.5)

Jax
(Immortals of New Orleans, Book 7)

Jake
(Immortals of New Orleans, Book 8)

Quintus
(Immortals of New Orleans, Book 9)

Hunter
(Immortals of New Orleans, Book 10)

Club Altura Romance

Solstice Burn
(A Club Altura Romance Novella, Prequel)

Carnal Risk
(A Club Altura Romance Novel, Book 1)

Wicked Rush
(A Club Altura Romance Novel, Book 2)

About the Author

Kym Grosso is the New York Times and USA Today bestselling author of the erotic paranormal series, *The Immortals of New Orleans*, and the contemporary erotic suspense series, *Club Altura*. In addition to romance novels, Kym has written and published several articles about autism, and is passionate about autism advocacy. She is also a contributing essay author in *Chicken Soup for the Soul: Raising Kids on the Spectrum*. In 2012, Kym published her first novel and today, is a full-time romance author.

• • • •

Social Media/Links:

Website: http://www.KymGrosso.com
Facebook: http://www.facebook.com/KymGrossoBooks
Instagram: https://www.instagram.com/kymgrosso/
Twitter: https://twitter.com/KymGrosso
Pinterest: http://www.pinterest.com/kymgrosso/

Sign up for Kym's Newsletter to get Updates and Information about New Releases:

https://www.subscribepage.com/kymgrossomailinglist

Printed in Great Britain
by Amazon